SHE'S HIS DRUG, HE'S HER THUG 4

# SHE'S HIS DRUG, HE'S HER THUG 4

By

Nirvana Blaque

# SHE'S HIS DRUG, HE'S HER THUG 4

If you purchased this book without a cover, you should be aware that this book is stolen property. It was reported as "unsold and destroyed" to the publisher, and neither the author nor the publisher has received any payment for this "stripped book."

This book is a work of fiction contrived by the author, and is not meant to reflect any actual or specific person, place, action, incident or event. Any resemblance to incidents, events, actions, locales or persons, living or dead, factual or fictional, is entirely coincidental.

Copyright © 2022 by Nirvana Blaque.

This book is published by Fat Boy Publishing.

All rights reserved, including the right to reproduce this book or portions thereof in any form whatsoever. For information, address Fat Boy Publishing, P.O. Box 2727, Cypress, TX 77410.

ISBN: 978-1-937666-92-7

Printed in the U.S.A.

## ACKNOWLEDGMENTS

I would like to thank the following for their help with this book: GOD, first and foremost, for always giving me strength and making a way, and my family, for all their continuous support.

# SHE'S HIS DRUG, HE'S HER THUG 4

Thank you for purchasing this book! If you enjoyed it, please feel free to leave a review on the site from which it was purchased.

Also, if you would like to be notified when I release new books, please subscribe to my mailing list via the following link: http://eepurl.com/gShzML

Finally, for those who may be interested, I have included my blog and social media info:

Blog: https://nirvanablaque.blogspot.com/

Facebook: https://www.facebook.com/nirvana.black.3597

Twitter: https://twitter.com/BlaqueNirvana

# Chapter 1

Mika had never been in a marijuana dispensary before, but she had to admit to being impressed. She'd had no idea all the shit you could make from weed: gum, coffee, lotion, cake pops... There were even weed-infused tampons!

Of course, she'd known about *some* weed products, like pot brownies. She had tasted some about a year earlier, when her friend Ubiquity had tried her hand at it, but that stupid bitch had baked up a pan of shit that was filled with stems and seeds that got stuck in your fucking teeth. The dispensary brownies, on the other hand, actually *looked* like brownies. Likewise, their pre-rolled joints seemed more like cigarettes, as opposed to some shit you might get off the street or at a party that looked like it had been rolled by a blind muthafucka with arthritis, and then licked by some nigga with black lung disease.

All in all, compared to niggas hustling on street corners selling shit weed in plastic bags, the dispensary came across as a high-end establishment. That fact was also reflected in the clientele. The people in this place – mostly White – didn't exude the same criminal demeanor you found with niggas in the hood.

"Excuse me, miss," said a feminine voice, interrupting Mika's reverie.

Turning to the speaker she saw a perky blonde about her own age, with a beatific smile on her face.

"We're closing in five minutes," the blonde continued, "so whenever you're ready I can check you out."

"Oh, so you're one of the salespeople here, uh…" Mika trailed off for a moment as she look at the blonde's nametag. "…Gwen?"

Gwen gave a quick nod. "Actually, we're called 'budtenders'."

"Budtenders?" Mika repeated. "That's cute. Like 'bartender' for a bar."

"Exactly."

"Somebody here come up with that?"

"No," Gwen informed her. "It's a common term for salespeople in dispensaries."

"Good to know," stated Mika. "Anyway, I'm not here to buy *product*. I here to buy this *place*."

"Excuse me?" muttered Gwen frowning. Then her eyes went wide. "Oh my… I mean, you're, uh… you're the, um…" She took a second to compose herself, then said. "Just wait here."

Gwen went scurrying off without giving Mika a chance to reply. While continuing to peruse but also watching out the corner of her eye, Mika saw Gwen speak to someone behind the dispensary counter – a middle-aged White guy with a long ponytail. They both stared at Mika for a moment, then the guy with the ponytail went through a door that seemingly led to the back.

Mika went back to faux browsing then, while Gwen and another budtender – this one a twenty-something brutha with curly brown hair and green eyes – quickly served the last few patrons and then locked the place up. The brutha then asked Mika to follow him, at which point he led her through the same door the guy with the ponytail had gone through.

At that juncture, they were in a narrow hallway, with doors to various rooms on either side. Glancing into a few open doorways, Mika saw that most of them looked like storage rooms of some sort – full of boxes that probably contained supplies to restock the items they sold in the dispensary.

Ultimately, she was escorted into what appeared to be a meeting room, with a mid-sized conference table in the center. On one side was the guy with the ponytail, along with Gwen, a dumpy-looking White lady in her forties, and a dark-haired guy with a scraggly beard who came across as a wannabe-biker. They were joined by the brutha who had escorted Mika, and as she walked in, a big nigga covered in prison tats closed and locked the door behind her. Mika simply looked him up and down for a second in a dismissive manner.

The forty-something lady then approached her, saying, "Do you mind?" At the same time, she lifted her arms in a suggestive manner.

Mika, understanding what was being requested, lifted her arms and allowed the woman to pat her down. She had been expecting something like this, so she wasn't surprised. As the woman checked her for weapons, Mika noted that the muhfucka with the ponytail (whose nametag said "Jude") had a gun tucked into the front of his pants. Not to be outdone, the biker had something like a rifle slung over his shoulder

After satisfying herself that Mika wasn't packing, the woman nodded at Jude before rejoining him and the others on the opposite side of the table. The nigga by the door then rolled a wheeled chair over and then glared at Mika, as if trying to force her to sit by the weight of his stare.

Mika ignored his ass. She wasn't about to sit and have all these muhfuckas looming over her, making her crane her neck to talk to them. So she just stood there, staring at each of them in turn.

"Well," she said after a few seconds, "we gone get this shit started, or wait 'til y'all can get some mo' backup and guns?"

Her words had the desired effect, and she saw both Gwen and the young brutha looking a little embarrassed.

"So you're one of Bush's people?" Jude asked.

"Why the fuck else would I be here?" Mika demanded. "Ain't this the date and time set for negotiations?"

"We were told it would be a *guy*," argued the lady who had patted her down.

"Well, maybe I'm fuckin' gender fluid," Mika shot back. That got her a snicker from Gwen, who quickly hushed, however, when all her compatriots turned to stare at her.

"Anyway," Jude continued as he turned back to Mika, "you can tell your people I ain't selling. I spent years building up this business – not just growing shit, finding suppliers, getting licenses and all that, but also fighting off dope dealers, gangs, and all kinds of motherfuckers. I didn't go through all that shit just to hand over the keys to this place to some asshole who thinks he rules the universe. So tell your boss thanks, but no thanks."

Mika appeared to mull that over for a second, then simply said, "Okay."

She then turned and headed for the door, but found the big nigga with the tattoos standing in front of it with his arms crossed.

"Yo ass gonna turn into vapor or some shit?" she grumbled at him. "Or just get the fuck out the way?"

Before the nigga blocking her way could respond, she heard Jude say, "So that's it?"

Mika turned back to him. "I'm sorry...is *what* it?"

"That's all you got to say – 'Okay?'" he asked. "No threats that I'll be sorry, or that some goons will come around to make me change my mind? That I might want to be careful, that I ought to think about my family, or if I won't sell, my widow will?"

"You got the wrong idea 'bout us," Mika admonished, shaking her head. "Bush ain't gotta stoop to doin' shit like that to get what he want."

"I ain't wrong about shit," Jude countered. "I know about motherfuckers like Bush, and he's the type who'll do all kinds of despicable crap to get his way. He wants to own the world, but he can't own what's *mine*."

"Ha!" Mika laughed, clapping her hands. "You mean this shop? Bush *already* own this muhfucka. You just don't know it yet."

Jude frowned. "What the hell does that mean?"

Mika gave him a sly smile. "You rent this place, right?"

"Yeah," Jude answered with a nod. "Got a ninety-nine year lease."

"You recall gettin' a lil' notice recently, sayin' that the property been sold? Well, guess who yo new landlord is?"

Jude looked at her for a moment, then let out a deep breath. "Bush."

"Bingo," Mika declared, still grinning.

"So what's he gonna do – try to jack up the rent? Start making me have problems with the plumbing or electricity?"

"There you go again, misjudgin' us," Mika told him. "Bush ain't gotta do nuthin' like that. He own this whole fuckin' block. Yo shop's in the middle, so he'll just put a damn dispensary on each corner. Muhfuckas from either direction will have to walk past a weed shop with better product and lower prices just to get to yo place. Yo foot traffic and sales gone get cut in half."

"Now when that happen, you might think you can compete by lowerin' yo prices," Mika added, "but how long can you keep the doors on this bitch open sellin' shit at fifty-percent off? Maybe a couple of months? Bush got enough resources to do that shit forever."

"We had shitheel competitors pull crap like that before," said the forty-something woman. "It never works out for them, even when we *don't* lower prices."

"That's right, babe," Jude chimed in, then looked at Mika. "See, regardless of what you assholes think about us or our product, we got customers who are loyal and will buy – even if we don't discount our prices."

"That may be true," Mika countered, "but it's gonna be hard as fuck to compete without product to sell in the first place."

That got her a bunch of confused looks, but before anyone could ask any questions she continued. "Oh? Didn't I mention? Bush is also buyin' yo supplier."

"What?" muttered the lady who had patted Mika down, looking stunned.

"It's bullshit, Janine," Jude declared. "She's lying."

"No, it's *not* bullshit, Janine," Mika argued. "See, Bush is a businessman, and when it comes to any enterprise he's engaged in, he likes ownin' the entire supply line from cradle to grave – or in the case of weed, from seed to sale. That means ownin' the land where dope seeds are planted, the shops where weed is sold, and everythang in between – which in this case includes yo supplier."

"So," Jude droned, "assuming that's true, I guess you're going to cancel all our orders."

Mika shook her head in disdain. "You still don't get it. All this grimy shit you keep imaginin' is stuff we ain't gotta do. Any orders you got in the pipeline gonna get fulfilled. But any new purchase orders prolly gone get denied."

"No big deal," Jude insisted. "I got land that I've been growing cannabis on for twenty years. It was easier for me to buy some stuff from a supplier, but I can always go back to personally growing everything I need."

"Muthafucka, who you thank you foolin'?" Mika demanded. "You got a coupla acres of cracked, dry-ass ground, and the only thing it's capable of producin' besides *tumble*weeds is some shitty reefer that even crackheads will only smoke at gunpoint." Jude raised an eyebrow at this, at which Mika commented, "Oh yeah – we done our due diligence. We know everythang 'bout yo ass."

Jude seemed to contemplate. "So your boss wants to keep his hands clean, while still pressuring us into selling. Basically, he ain't going to do anything illegal, but he's still playing hardball. Well, we can play it, too."

"Hardball?" Mika repeated incredulously. "You thank any of the shit I mentioned is hardball for Bush? It ain't. What I've described is basically Bush lobbin' a slow-ass underhand pitch with his hand in a fuckin' cast. Trust me, you don't wanna see his version of hardball."

Janine and Jude exchanged a glance, which made Mika feel she was gaining ground.

"Look, this shit ain't gotta be contentious," she said, pulling a folded piece of paper from her pocket. "Here's our offer."

She held out the piece of paper, which Janine took.

"Now before you do some dumb shit like tear it up as a symbolic fuckin' gesture," Mika went on, "at least look it over. It's a generous offer."

As if on cue, Janine unfolded the paper, with everyone except the big nigga by the door looking over her shoulder. From the expressions on their faces, Mika knew they were impressed – especially when Jude and Janine once again shared a knowing glance.

"Just to be clear, that's for sixty percent ownership," Mika announced, directing her attention to Jude. "We recognize the amount of work you put into buildin' the business, and that you deserve a piece of it going forward. Plus, you'd stay on as manager."

"But your boss would be majority owner," Jude surmised. "I'd be working for *him*."

"You'd still own forty percent, so you'd be workin' for yo'self, too," Mika corrected. "And think about all the headaches that'll be gone: rent, accountin', utilities… Bush's people will take care of all that, and other shit, too. Got some special product or flower you want in the shop? We'll get it for you. Need your license renewed? We'll complete the paperwork and fast-track that shit. Plus, you'll de-risk the business."

"Are you serious?" Jude inquired. "How the fuck is getting into bed with a motherfucker like Bush going to lower my risk?"

"For starters, it'll let you take some cash off the table. Right now, pretty much everything you got is tied up in the business. Again, you done well so far, but you got all yo eggs in one basket."

Jude frowned, but looking at Janine, Mika got the sense that the woman was pretty much open to what she was hearing. That gave Mika an idea.

"This yo lady, right?" she asked, gesturing towards Janine.

"Yeah, why?" Jude asked suspiciously.

"How long y'all been together?"

Jude didn't answer right away, suggesting either he didn't know exactly or didn't like where the conversation was going.

"I been with him over twenty years," Janine chimed in.

"Yeah," Jude agreed, nodding. "It's been a good ride."

"So lemme asked you sommin'," Mika remarked. "When's the last time you took her on a vacation? And I don't mean some backwoods cabin with no indoor plumbin' that's owned by your hillbilly cousin, or goin' to Great-Aunt Tilly's funeral in Tennessee and then stayin' an extra day to go to Dollywood. I'm talkin' 'bout a *real* vacation."

"See," she continued. "my man just took me to Hawaii a few weeks back. We ain't even been together that long, to be honest – definitely not twenty years – but he said he wanted to treat me the way he felt I deserved. It was my first time goin' and I ain't gone lie: that trip was off the fuckin' hook. I had a fantastic fuckin' time. Nobody ever did anythang like that for me befoe', but you know what? They should have, because I really did deserve it."

"Now Janine's been by yo side for two decades," Mika went on. "Through thick and thin, ups and downs, and everythang else. Ain't it about time you started givin' her all that shit I know you promised her when you were younger? That nice house with the white picket fence. That trip to Europe. That shoppin' spree on Rodeo Drive. You got a chance now to do right by that woman who's always done right by you. Don't pass it up."

By that time, Mika could see the longing in Janine's eyes and knew that she'd hit a nerve. Like most men, Jude had probably promised her the moon and she was still waiting on him to deliver. More importantly, Mika had watched Jude turn towards Janine while she was in the middle of her little narrative, and stare at her like he hadn't seen her in years.

"Alright," Jude finally said after a few seconds. "Tell Bush we'll think it over."

"Sounds great," Mika said. "But just to be clear: I don't tell Bush shit. I ain't never even seen him, or know anybody who has. That's how far above me he is on the food chain. This lil' business deal we discussin'? That shit ain't even on his radar. Word just came down from the mountaintop that Bush wants to own some weed shops, so here we are. Everything that's happened so far – like becomin' yo landlord and buyin' yo supplier – was done by people on Bush's payroll to make sure he gets what he wants. So at the end of the day, if we do this deal, don't thank you and Bush gone be drankin' a toast together. You'll prolly never set eyes on his ass, 'cause just like me, you on the part of the totem pole that's buried in the ground."

Jude simply nodded, taking that in stride. "Still, we'll think it over."

"Fair enough," Mika remarked.

# SHE'S HIS DRUG, HE'S HER THUG 4

## Chapter 2

Kane was waiting out front in a black SUV when Mika left the dispensary. Stepping quickly to the car, she opened the front passenger-side door and slid inside.

"How'd it go?" Kane asked.

"Fine," she told him as she shut the door. "They gone sell."

"Really?" Kane said skeptically as he started to drive away. "They agreed to that?"

"Not yet, but they will. Trust me."

Kane frowned in response but didn't say anything. Nevertheless, Mika understood what he was thinking. There was a lot riding on this deal. Not monetarily – Jude's little weed shop wouldn't even be a blip on the fiscal radar. The important thing was Mika's ability to get shit done.

Basically, the two of them were new to Bush's organization, and technically, Mika wasn't even on the payroll. Kane had been adamant that the two of them were a team, but Regis – the guy who had brought Kane into Bush's group – wasn't having it.

"*You* got a skill set we can use," Regis had told Kane. "But yo girl? I don't even know if that bitch can piss on snow."

In essence, Regis wasn't considering Mika as an official part of anything until she proved herself. The situation with Jude's shop had been her litmus test. Initially, it was supposed to be Kane talking to them, but it made sense to let Mika handle it and show what she could do.

Oddly enough, she'd been nervous leading up to the meeting. She had never really done anything like that before. She had been in car chases, gotten into shootouts, fought off niggas in an alley with a switchblade... All that shit had practically been second-nature to her, but for some reason, doing something as banal as offering to buy someone's business had given her butterflies.

Fortunately, Kane was able to read her mood and knew she was getting anxious. He also knew that the last thing she needed to do was go into a meeting with Jude and his people all high-strung, so about fifteen minutes before she was supposed to head to the dispensary, Kane drove them to a nearby underground garage and parked in an empty corner on a deserted floor. He had then dragged her into the back seat of the SUV and eaten her out.

Mika had cum with earth-shattering intensity – twice. She had wanted him to fuck her, but it would have been really unprofessional to roll up into the meeting afterwards reeking of sex. So she'd had to settle for the cunnilingus. Thankfully, it was enough; when she finally stepped into Jude's dispensary, she had been completely relaxed. (Two orgasms in quick succession will do that to a bitch.)

"So," Kane droned, interrupting her thoughts, "they gone call or sommin'?"

"Yeah," Mika replied. "I gave 'em my number befoe' I left."

"We s'pose to call Regis...let 'im know how it went."

"So call his Black ass," Mika said, crossing her arms.

Kane gave her a hard look, as if trying to figure out if she was joking, then pulled a cell phone out of the pocket of the jacket he was wearing. It wasn't a burner, but it was supposed to be untraceable all the same. It had been given to him by Regis with some pretty basic instructions –

namely, it was only to be used for communication between the two of them, and whenever it rang, Kane had better pick up.

Kane pressed a few buttons on the phone and a second later it started dialing. To a certain extent, he hoped that Regis – a forty-something guy with dreadlocks and a goatee – wouldn't pick up. No such luck; it was answered on the second ring.

"Talk," ordered a masculine voice – Regis – on the other end of the line.

"It's me," Kane announced, turning on the speaker-phone.

"So how'd it go?" Regis asked.

"No problem," Kane told him. "They gone sell."

"So we can send some niggas over with the paperwork?"

Kane hesitated for a moment, glancing at Mika before stating, "Not just yet."

There was a silence for a moment, then Regis blurted out, "Da fuck that mean? You told me yo bitch could handle it, but that ain't what I'm hearin'."

"First of all," Kane countered, "she ain't a bitch. Second, she *did* handle it."

"Damn. You comin' to her defense mighty fuckin' quick," Regis noted. "That mean she right there next to you, and you got me on speaker."

Kane frowned, mentally noting that this was the type of astute observation Regis was known for. Almost nothing got past that muhfucka.

However, before Kane could comment, Regis spoke in a casual and congenial tone that was obviously directed at Mika. "Hey sweetheart – how you doin'?"

"I'm a bitch, if you haven't heard," she shot back.

Regis chuckled. At that point, most niggas would have been trying to walk back that "bitch" comment – saying it was "just a figure of speech" or "no offense meant." Not Regis; he simply acted like he'd just told her how pretty she looked today. Moreover, if he was concerned about Kane having him on speaker-phone, it didn't show.

"So riddle me this," Regis said, getting back to business. "How is it that the shit got handled, but I can't send the paperwork for this muhfucka to sign and make it official?"

"Look, he gone get on board," Mika insisted. "But I'm in there talkin' to him in front of all his crew *and* his lady. Yeah, between ownin' the buildin', his supplier, and everythang else, we could squeeze his ass like a grape, but you gotta leave the man his pride. It still need to look like it's *his* decision – like he can tell us to fuck off if he want to. That way, when he say 'Yes,' it's a choice *he* made and he's happy about it. But if we strong-arm his ass, he gone fuckin' hate us and undermine us at every damn opportunity."

Regis didn't immediately respond. Kane imagined the nigga leaning back, drumming his fingers on his desk while he considered what Mika had said.

"A'ight," Regis finally droned. "You make a decent argument. You ain't convinced me of shit, but it's good enough to buy you some time." The phone went silent for a minute as he considered. "Twenty-fo' hours. At the end of that time, you bettah be tellin' me this muhfucka ready to sign on the dotted line."

An audible click followed, indicating that Regis had hung up. Kane eyed Mika skeptically as he put the phone away.

"What?" she uttered defiantly. "Don't be givin' me no crazy-ass look, like I don't know what I'm talkin' 'bout."

"I ain't even say shit," Kane stressed.

"You ain't have to. You lookin' at me like you thank Regis is right. That I fucked this up."

"Naw, that ain't what I thank. It's just that this was yo audition, and we needed this shit to go smooth."

"It'll be fine," Mika predicted.

"I hope you right," Kane told her.

"Why?" she asked. "What Regis gone do if this Jude guy don't sell?"

Kane shrugged. "Fuck if I know. I only been workin' for these niggas for a minute. But I'm assumin' he just gone say yo ass is benched – permanently."

Mika considered for a moment, then said, "You prolly right, but it won't come to that. This weed shop muhfucka gonna get with the program."

Kane simply nodded at that, although he wasn't as confident as Mika. Thirty minutes later, though, she was proved right when Jude called saying he'd take the deal.

## Chapter 3

After giving Regis the good news, they decided to go out and celebrate. They had been headed to a fast-food place when the call came in, but immediately altered their plans. Ultimately, they ended up going to a chic new eatery called "A Cut Above" that was popular among the *nouveau riche*.

Of course, Mika and Kane didn't fall into the category of "rich." They'd previously had a nice pile of cash, but a huge chunk of it had been spent getting a bounty off their heads. It had cost them over a mill, but as far as Mika was concerned it had been money well spent. Plus, they'd still had a more-than-decent stack of bills left when it was all over.

This all flitted through her mind as, after valeting the SUV, they went inside. It was immediately obvious that the place was upscale, as evidenced by the hardwood floors, crystal lighting and a decadent bar.

There was a cozy waiting area filled with about a dozen people expecting to be seated soon. Mika flopped down in a nearby chair while Kane went to speak to the maître d' – an elegantly dressed man with a neatly trimmed mustache who stood at a podium near the restaurant entrance. A few moments later, Kane came back and sat beside her.

"Shouldn't be long," he told her.

His statement was more prophetic than he knew, because he'd barely been seated a minute before the maître d' gestured towards them. They quickly walked to the podium, at which point the maître d' told them their table was ready and escorted them through the restaurant.

The place was full of diners, but didn't feel overcrowded. Once at their table, the maître d' pulled out Mika's chair for her; then, after they were seated, he placed their napkins in their laps.

"Your waitress will be with you shortly," he assured them, then returned to his post at the restaurant entrance.

There were two menus on the table, which Kane and Mika picked up and began looking through. One look at the prices, and Mika knew without a doubt that they were in a ritzy place.

Setting the menu down for a second, she asked, Kane, "So how much this set you back?"

"Huh?" he muttered, closing his own menu for a second.

"This place is expensive as a muthafucka," she explained, "and we walked up in here without a reservation and practically got seated right away."

"A'ight," Kane chuckled. "You right – it did cost a lil' sommin'."

"How much?"

"A Benjy."

Mika appeared to ruminate on that for a second. "A hundred bucks to skip the line? Is that a lot here?"

Kane shrugged. "Don't know. I just knew I didn't want to be waitin' forever to be seated, so I slipped homeboy at the podium the cash when I asked for a table."

"So that's all dinner with me is worth?" she teased. "A hundred?"

"Naw, baby a hundred ain't even close," Kane insisted, shaking his head. "But I told 'im to keep the change."

"Fuck you," she said, giggling.

Kane winked. "Maybe later."

That caused them both to snicker

"Anyway," Mika said after a few seconds, "I feel sorry for that guy at the podium. The people waitin' prolly pissed that he seated us first, and he gotta deal with that."

"I doubt it's an issue. It's a lot easier to seat just two people, and everybody knows that. Plus, I thank all those people were together, so it's not like he screwed somebody out of a six-top in order to give us a table."

Mika was about to comment on that when their waitress, a cute redhead, came over.

"Hi," she greeted them with a bubbly voice as she filled their water glasses. "I'm Madison, I'll be your waitress. What can I get you to drink?"

"I'll have a sex-on-the-beach," Mika said, giving Kane a lascivious look.

"I'll take a mojito," Kane stated.

"Okay, I'll be right back with those," the waitress informed them before walking away.

"Well, you got a one-track mind," Kane declared.

"Whachu mean?" Mika asked.

"Sex on the beach," he said, raising an eyebrow.

Mika laughed. "You know that's my drink now. Ever since…"

She trailed off, grinning, but Kane finished her thought. "Ever since we had sex on the beach."

Mika smiled at the memory. She hadn't been lying when she told Janine about going to Hawaii. It had been a little respite for her and Kane, after all the shit they'd been through with a bounty on their heads and niggas trying to kill them at every turn. But everything about that trip – from the weather, to sightseeing, to the food – was straight fire.

# SHE'S HIS DRUG, HE'S HER THUG 4

And the sex? That shit had been fucking divine. She and Kane already had an amazing connection when it came to slamming bodies, but there's always something extra exciting about getting your fuck on in a new place. Thus she had thoroughly enjoyed screwing Kane every day in their hotel room's king-sized bed, and had even given him a blowjob on the balcony.

But the *crème de la crème* had been their last night on the island. They were driving back from a late-night luau (which itself had been off the chain) when Kane pulled their rental car over to a deserted stretch of beach. They had then taken a stroll on the sand, holding hands, until they came to a secluded cove. That's when Kane unexpectedly pulled her down to the sand, removed the bottom portion of the bikini she was wearing, and then fucked her so good that she came three times and had drool running down the side of her face when they were done.

Since then, she always asked for sex-on-the-beach whenever they went out for drinks. It typically wasn't all she drank, but it was generally the first cocktail she ordered.

"So whachu like on here?" Kane asked, bringing her back to herself.

"I don't know," she replied as she opened her menu again. "Everythang looks good, so it's hard to decide." Suddenly, she got an idea and closed her menu. "Hey, why don't you do that alpha male thang and just order for both of us, like niggas do in the movies."

"I can do that," Kane stated with a nod as the waitress came back with their cocktails.

After placing their drinks on the table, Madison asked, "Are you ready to order, or would like more time to look at the menu?"

"We ready," Kane declared, at which point the waitress produced a small pad and pen. "The lady will start with the Creole crab cakes, and I'll have the Wagyu sliders. We'd also like to try the lobster rolls."

"Excellent choices," Madison noted. "And for your entrée?"

"I see there's a forty-ounce porterhouse on the menu," Kane said. "How many people actually finish that?"

"Actually, it's intended to be shared," Madison informed him.

"Great," Kane uttered. "We'll take that – well done – and have the *au gratin* potatoes on the side."

"Awesome," their waitress said. "I'll get this to the kitchen asap." She then turned and walked away.

"That was good," Mika told Kane. "You got this alpha male shit down."

Kane grinned. "If you thank I'm in alpha mode now, just wait 'til I get yo ass in bed tonight."

"I'll drink to that," Mika retorted, taking a sip from her cocktail.

*****************************************

The meal was fantastic. The crab cakes were mouthwatering, and Mika traded some for one of Kane's sliders, which were also delicious. She hadn't had Wagyu before – it was typically out of her price range – but after one bite she understood why it was one of the most expensive cuts of beef. Likewise, when they got the porterhouse, it was so perfectly seasoned that she didn't even need steak sauce.

Outside of commenting about the food, the ambience, and a few double entendres, most of their conversation had been small talk up until that point. However, as they dove into their entrée, Kane gave her a somewhat somber look.

"So," he droned, "You good here?"

Mika frowned. "You mean the restaurant? I told you, it's nice – not too stuffy, not too hood-ish."

"Naw, I mean the *town*."

"Oh," she muttered, now understanding.

Kane's question alluded to the fact that, after coming back from Hawaii, they hadn't gone home. Even without a bounty on their heads, there had been too much heat on them in their hometown so they had needed to relocate. Apparently there was a need in Bush's organization for someone on the West Coast, which is where they now found themselves.

"It's fine," Mika assured him. "In case you forgot, I spent months movin' from town to town. Gettin' used to a new place takes me, like, five minutes now."

Her statement was a reminder of the fact that – not too far in the past – Mika had been a girl on the run, thinking that someone was after her. Ironically, the person she had assumed was on her tail back then was Kane. Reflecting on all that, it seemed odd that they would end up a couple, yet here they were.

"Just thought I'd check," Kane said.

"What about you?" Mika inquired.

Kane shrugged. "A town's a town to me. I'm not one of those stupid niggas who think a place is shit if they don't have a certain fast food joint, ain't got a red light district, or don't have cockfights in the alley. Long as I can get a meal and got a place to lay my head, I'm good."

"What about the job? I mean, you cool not bein' the boss?"

Kane took a moment to consider. Back in their hometown, he and a partner had run their own crew and had quickly moved up in the game. In short, they had been their own bosses, so he really hadn't taken orders from anybody in a while. That said, he had known what he was getting into when he agreed to work for Bush; joining the team was the cost of getting Bush's help in dealing with the bounty situation, and considering the alternative – having muhfuckas constantly trying to collect the reward that had been on him and Mika – it was a reasonable price to pay.

"I'm cool," he finally said. "When I was bossin' a crew, I still had to stay on my connect's good side, had to pay cops what they wanted to look the other way, and so on. Basically, I couldn't just do whatever the fuck I wanted."

"So even when you was a boss you had people you had to answer to," Mika concluded.

"Everybody answer to *some*body…'cept maybe Bush."

Mika didn't argue with that. Like she had told Jude, Bush ranked way above anybody she had contact with. In fact, from what she'd heard, Bush was on par with heads of state. But it did bring up an interesting question.

"So where do we rank?" she asked.

"Huh?" Kane muttered, his confusion obvious.

"Where do we rank in Bush's organization?" she clarified. "Are we at the bottom, near the top, what?"

"Hell if I know," Kane declared with a shrug. "It's not like they showed me a friggin' org chart. I just know that wherever we are, there's fuckin' geological layers between us and Bush."

"What about Regis? Where's he at on the corporate ladder?"

"Somewhere in the middle."

"Nigga, I *know* that," Mika shot back. "But is he closer to the top rung or the bottom?"

Kane reflected on that for a moment. Regis had described himself as a "king" in Bush's organization, and – given the strings he'd been known to pull – Kane didn't doubt it. However, Regis had made it very clear that if he himself could be construed as a king, then Bush was a fucking deity.

Bearing all that in mind, Kane said, "If I had to guess, I'd put Regis closer to the penthouse than the basement."

"So that's good," Mika noted. "If we workin' for him, it means we ain't startin' at the bottom."

"I guess," Kane muttered noncommittally in response.

In all honesty, he had essentially argued his way into the job by convincing Regis that he had a unique talent that he could bring to the organization: "non-linear thinking." Of course, Regis hadn't just taken his word for it. Instead, Kane had been forced to prove he had that particular skill set by talking his way out of a situation that should have been certain death. He'd managed to avoid getting killed (which had impressed the fuck out of Regis) and now he was on the team.

"Anyway," he droned, "Why you all worried 'bout where we fit in the corporate hierarchy? You one of those women who focused on her man gettin' to the top?"

"Nigga," she retorted, "the only thing I'm wantin' you to get on top of, is *me*."

Kane laughed so hard at that, he almost choked on the potatoes he had just put in his mouth.

# SHE'S HIS DRUG, HE'S HER THUG 4

## Chapter 4

They finished eating shortly thereafter, deciding to skip desert. When the check came, Kane reached for it, but Mika beat him to it.

"My treat," she said. "Since we celebratin' me landin' a nine-to-five."

"Fine by me," Kane assured her with a grin. "I enjoy bein' a kept man."

Their exchange was a little bit of a joke. Basically, all of the money Mika possessed had actually come from Kane. She had come into the relationship essentially broke, while Kane had initially possessed cash on top of cash. After using a chunk of it to get rid of the bounty on their heads, Kane had split the remaining cash between them.

"I can't have you holdin' yo hand out every time you want a pack of chewin' gum," he had told her. "Plus, you earned a slice of the pie."

Mika fully agreed with him on that last point. She had been flat out ride-or-die since they hooked up, and Kane recognized that fact without argument.

That said, it hadn't been an even split – not by a longshot. Kane had kept the bulk of the cash for himself, but in Mika's mind that was fair. After all, he was the one who had earned it.

More to the point, what he had given her amounted to a healthy sum. Ergo, if he kicked her ass to the curb the next day, she could go for a long time without hurting for money. In addition, Kane still generally paid for everything when they were out, so Mika rarely ever had to reach for her purse. Tonight, however, was an exception.

She spent a moment contemplating how to pay the bill, which – including a tip – would come to a couple of

Benjamins. She had banked most of the money Kane had dropped on her (and still got a thrill every time she looked at her bank account), but still had a few hundred on her. However, she had plans for that cash, so she ultimately decided to settle up with a prepaid credit card.

As the waitress took her card and the bill, Mika found Kane giving her an odd look with a sly grin on his face. She was on the verge of asking him what he was smiling about when he spoke.

"Well, you definitely gettin' used to a change in circumstance," he said.

Mika frowned. "Whachu mean?"

"A coupla weeks ago, you was bitchin' 'bout the mark-up in convenience stores. Now you droppin' at least three hundred on a meal and ain't batted an eye."

Mika thought about that for a moment. "You remember when we went to Hawaii?"

"It was just a few weeks ago – how the hell could I forget? Plus, that trip was fuckin' amazin'."

"Yeah, but how much that set us back, money-wise?"

"At least ten large, but it was worth it."

"True dat. But one of the thangs you said befoe' we even got on the plane was not to thank about the cost, 'cause thankin' 'bout the money would ruin the whole damn trip. And you was right."

"I see where you goin'," Kane said with a nod. "You ain't thankin' 'bout the cash that might get spent tonight 'cause it'll fuck up the celebration."

Mika smiled "Now you get it."

At that moment, the waitress came back. Mika put her credit card away and then signed off on the bill.

"We good?" Kane asked, to which Mika responded with a nod. They both then came to their feet and began walking towards the exit, with Kane leading the way.

When he reached the podium, Kane stopped to thank the maître d', as well as slip him another hundred. He and Mika probably wouldn't be eating here on the regular, but if they did he wanted the staff to remember them for the right reasons. It was at that point that he realized that Mika wasn't with him.

Curious, he looked around and saw her still standing near their table, talking to their waitress. He was about to go ask if there was a problem when Mika seemed to wrap up her conversation and started walking towards him.

Kane gave her an inquisitive look when she got close. "Problem?"

Mika shook her head. "Naw. Just pickin' her brains."

"About what?" Kane inquired as they headed towards the exit and stepped outside.

"What club we should go to now."

Kane gave the valet the ticket for his car and then glanced at his watch. "It's a lil' early to start clubbin'."

"Not for what I have in mind," Mika uttered in a salacious tone.

*******************************************

"What's this place?" Kane asked, looking up at a large neon sign that spelled out "Busybodies," with the flashing outline of a nude woman next to it. It sat in the parking lot of a nondescript, windowless building that had a sign on the door which read, "Nude Girls!"

"It's a strip club," Mika informed him as they got out of the SUV.

"I can see that. I mean, what we doin' here?"

"It's Bingo Night," she quipped sarcastically as they walked towards the entrance. "Da fuck you thank we doin' here? We 'bout to see some naked hoes."

"Hmmm," Kane droned, giving her an odd look.

"What?" she asked, sensing something odd in his tone.

"Nuthin'," he replied. "I guess I didn't know you rolled like that."

"Look," she muttered, coming to a halt. "Just be honest for a sec. If you was out celebratin' wicha boys, ain't this the kinda place you'd be hittin' up?"

"Yeah," he conceded, "but I ain't never thought 'bout brangin' my girl up in one these fuckin' places."

"Well, I don't want tonight to be some half-ass celebration just 'cause you with *me*. I wanchu to have as much fun as you would if you was out with yo crew."

"So you *not* a part-time lez?"

"Actually, after bein' with yo limp-dick ass for a while, I'm 'bout to go *full*-time dyke," she quipped.

"Oh, so you got jokes now," Kane noted.

"Nigga, just brang yo ass on," Mika told him with a grin as she resumed walking towards the door.

Kane followed, although he wasn't sure what to expect. Surprisingly, he ended up having a blast.

First of all, Mika got them bottle service – champagne, in fact – which included seats right at the center of the stage. A couple of bouncers made the muhfuckas who had been sitting there clear out; they didn't look happy at losing a prime spot, but there wasn't really shit they could do about it.

Next, Mika cheered as loud for the strippers as the rest of the horny muhfuckas in there. She was constantly shouting shit like, "Show my man yo titties!" and "Shake that shit, girl!" to the dancers on stage, which Kane found hilarious. And to make sure the strippers didn't wander too far from where they were sitting, she kept running to the bar for singles and tossing them on stage directly in front of them. (She also tucked them into the strippers' g-strings occasionally, which would net her a kiss on the cheek.)

In addition, she kept asking Kane which of the girls he thought looked best. To Kane, it felt like a trap – one that had he had walked into several times before with women in the past. (Basically, they ask you if you think some other bitch is fine, and if you say anything other than "No" then it's like you stepped on a relationship landmine.)

However, Mika didn't seem to be baiting him; she seemed sincerely interested in finding out which of the strippers he found appealing. More to the point, as Kane continued drinking champagne, he mellowed and finally gave in, pointing out to her which of the women struck his fancy. And that's when Mika pulled her trump card.

Not long after he told her who he thought was the baddest stripper in the place – a fine-ass shawty called Starlight who had tits and ass for days – Mika pulled him up from their spot at the stage. Taking him by the hand, she led him to a sectioned-off area of the club that he recognized as a VIP lounge. They continued in that direction, ultimately ending up in a private room, where Starlight was waiting for them.

"This him?" Starlight asked.

"Yep," Mika answered, at which point Starlight practically shoved Kane down onto a nearby couch and began dancing to the music that was playing. Within thirty seconds, she had stripped down to practically nothing. Technically, she was still wearing a g-string, but it was thinner than fucking gauze and only nominally met the definition of the word. The next thing he knew, Starlight had straddled him, and then began giving him the lapdance of his life.

It didn't take a lot of effort to figure out how this arrangement had come about. After Kane pointed out Starlight as being the best-looking bitch on stage, Mika had apparently used one of the occasions when she was getting singles to set up a private dance.

All of this went through Kane's mind as Starlight started grinding on him. He was already hard from watching strippers on stage, but suddenly his dick was straining forcefully against his pants, begging to be released. At the same time, she pressed her body close to his, and he could feel her rock-hard nipples pressing against him through his clothes. An image suddenly came to mind – unbidden – of him throwing Starlight onto the couch and fucking the shit out of her.

However, Kane knew better than to give in to any primal urges. First and foremost, the room they were in didn't really have a door – just a full-length curtain over the entry. More importantly, a couple of big-ass bouncers roaming the hallway outside regularly peeked in to make sure shit wasn't getting out of hand (which primarily consisted on niggas putting their hands on the strippers). On top of that, Mika was in there with him, so – even though she had paid for the lap dance – he didn't want it to even look like he was tempted. (Basically, if a nigga was willing to play grab-ass with some chick while his girl was in the room with him, what the fuck was he up to when his lady wasn't around?) Bearing all that in mind, Kane kept his hands firmly planted on the seat cushions on either side of him.

"It's okay," Starlight whispered unexpectedly as she shimmied her tits in his face. "Yo girl paid extra for you to be able to touch me."

Rather than reply, Kane glanced towards the doorway.

Starlight followed his gaze for a moment, then turned back to him, saying, "You worried 'bout them niggas in the hallway? Don't be – they cool, long as I don't call'em."

Kane wasn't convinced. He had seen strippers encouraging muhfuckas to touch them before, saying it was okay. Occasionally some gullible sucker would do it – and next thing you know a bouncer's got that nigga in a chokehold, screaming in his ear about how it's against the rules to touch the girls before body-slamming his ass on the concrete outside. Reflecting on that, Kane gave Starlight an unsure look.

"Come on – touch my titties," she pleaded. "You know you want to."

As she spoke, she tugged on Kane's right arm, lifting his hand from the couch. She then began slowly guiding it to her tits. However, just before he made contact, he noticed Mika on the couch just a few feet from him, grinning broadly. Suddenly self-conscious, Kane snatched his hand away from Starlight, which made Mika roar with laughter.

"I'm good," Kane insisted, placing his hand back on the couch.

"Well, you know what to do if you change yo mind," Starlight said with a wink.

# SHE'S HIS DRUG, HE'S HER THUG 4

She then stood and turned around, showing him her well-sculpted ass. She shook it for a moment in front of him – putting all kinds of thoughts in his head – then dropped her ass onto his crotch and began gyrating her hips. Next, she leaned back onto him, pressing her cheek to his while letting her ass slide up and down on his groin, continuing to tease his dick as she began to moan like he was actually fucking her. Now getting into it, Kane closed his eyes and began to let his imagination run wild.

All of a sudden, he felt something warm but firm beneath his fingertips. Opening his eyes, he suddenly realized with a shock that his hand was on the stripper's inner thigh. Almost as a reflex, he swiftly yanked his hand away. Starlight continued moaning and grinding her ass against his crotch like nothing had happened.

Raucous laughter drew his attention, and he turned to find Mika sitting right next to him.

"Come on," she muttered with a snicker as she took his hand. "Don't act like you didn't like it."

She then began guiding his hand back towards the stripper, and that's when he realized what had occurred. He had assumed that he'd instinctively put his hand on the stripper's thigh, but it hadn't been him at all; it had been Mika who had done it. And now she was trying to do it again.

Kane attempted to extract his hand from hers, but Mika held on tight, grinning. Suddenly, he found himself in a tug-of-war as she began struggling to move his hand to the stripper's chest.

Straining with effort but smirking all the while, Mika grunted, "Nigga…touch…that…damn…titty."

A second later she gave up, letting Kane's hand go as she burst into laughter again.

After taking a few moments to regain her composure, she said with a grin, "Nigga, why you bein' difficult? I paid good money for you to be able to paw this chick."

"And I don't come cheap," Starlight added as she turned to straddle Kane again.

"Well, I appreciate that," Kane declared. "But I ain't tryin' to give those muhfuckas in the hallway any excuse to come in here and fuck me up with a coupla blackjacks."

"But I told you, it's cool," Starlight insisted.

"Yeah," Mika added with a grin. "S'all good, so loosen the fuck up."

"Easy for you to say," Kane shot back. "You not the one those muhfuckas in the hallway gone pounce on, and I left my piece in the car."

Mika sighed. "You bein' a pussy."

Kane shrugged. "You are what you eat."

That netted a giggle from Mika.

"Fine," she said. "Just finish gettin' yo lap dance and we'll get outta here."

Kane simply nodded, then went back to enjoying Starlight's dance. It was admittedly a little awkward, though, with Mika sitting right next to him, watching everything. Of course, she found his discomfort hilarious, but in the end, he found a way to turn the tables.

Basically, when his lap dance ended, Mika stood like they were getting ready to leave while Starlight gave Kane a kiss on the cheek. At that point, Kane whispered something in her ear. In response, Starlight stared at him for a moment, then gave a curt nod before standing up. She then stepped towards Mika in a sultry fashion.

Mika looked at Starlight in surprise. "I paid you upfront, remember?"

"You did," Starlight confirmed as she eyed Mika suggestively.

There was silence for a moment as the two women faced each other, but before things got awkward Mika said, "Well, I guess you earned an extra tip." As she spoke, she began reaching into her pocket.

"I don't want yo money," Starlight informed her, putting her hands on Mika's shoulders and gently guiding her back.

With the couch behind her, Mika basically flopped down onto the cushions, and the next thing she knew, Starlight was straddling her. Seconds later, the stripper was grinding on her, muttering that it was okay for Mika to touch her tits.

Needless to say, Mika was confused. She'd had women come on to her before, but Starlight had caught her flatfooted. Somewhat dumbfounded, she looked towards Kane – and saw him laughing.

At that juncture, understanding dawned on her. This lap dance from Starlight was Kane's doing – a spur of the moment, tit-for-tat endeavor on his part. Presumably, he was thinking that with the shoe on the other foot, he'd get some laughs at her expense like she had done to him.

*We'll see about that*, Mika thought. Turning to Starlight, she said, "Oh yeah, girl – show me them titties. That nigga with me might be too much of a pussy to touch'em, but *I'm* not."

As she spoke, she began touching – no, *manhandling* – Starlight's tits: squeezing them like they were balloons she was trying to pop, tweaking her nipples like they were radio dials, and so on. On her part, Starlight moaned erotically, like she was getting completely turned on.

As to Kane, he simply stood there, trying to keep his mouth from falling open, which Mika found funny as hell. Feeling bold, she smacked Starlight on the ass hard enough to make the stripper yelp slightly. Unfortunately, that was the precise moment that one of the bouncers chose to peek inside.

For a second Kane worried that all hell was about to break loose. After all, ninety percent of what bouncers did in places like this was stomp patrons for touching the girls, and Mika's hands were roaming all over the fucking place. That being the case, Kane was already sizing up the nigga in the doorway, assessing how he'd go after the muhfucka, if necessary.

Thankfully, however, the bouncer seemed to recognize the fact that Starlight's current client was a woman. Plainly speaking, females in that situation tended to get a lot more leeway from club security than men. Hell, a woman could practically finger-fuck a stripper on stage and barely have the bouncers bat an eye; but if a nigga laid so much as a finger on those bitches, it was lights out.

Mika noticed the bouncer, too, but continued fondling the stripper's tits like her life depended on it. In her opinion, the nigga lingered in the doorway a little longer than necessary, but maybe he was just trying to make sure Starlight was okay.

*Or maybe he was gettin' off a lil' on this lez shit*, she thought as the bouncer finally moved on, because she knew that girl-on-girl shit got most men excited. She didn't know if Kane fell into that category, but he had obviously been surprised by her response to the lap dance. The expression on his face had been priceless, and even looking at him now – as he watched her with the stripper – made her giggle.

Eventually, the lap dance came to an end. Starlight kissed Mika on the cheek and then gave her a suggestive wink. As Mika came to her feet, she saw the stripper turn to Kane, who pulled a small wad of cash from his pocket. Peeling off a couple of hundreds, he gave them to Starlight, who thanked him by rubbing her ass against his groin one last time before grabbing her shit and leaving.

Kane and Mika left almost right on her heels, except they exited the club rather than return to their seats. Once outside, Kane unexpectedly grabbed Mika, pulling her in close and giving her a heated, passionate kiss that she returned with equal fervor. It was so fierce and intense that when they finally separated a few seconds later, Miak was damn near breathless.

"Hmmm," she muttered softly as Kane nuzzled her neck, "Guess that lesbian shit really turned you on."

Kane harrumphed dismissively. "I don't need outside motivation to make me want to fuck you."

Mika laughed. "Hold on there, cowboy. We ain't done celebratin' yet. You tryin' to skip the entrée and go straight to dessert."

"Fine," he muttered, taking a step back. "So what else is on the menu?"

"Well, since you got to gawk at some naked hoes, I figured next we go see sommin' *I'm* interested in."

"Like what?"

"There's this male revue I been meanin' to check out," she told him.

"Male revue?" Kane repeated, frowning. "You mean a show with a bunch of muhfuckas strippin' for a crowd of fugly bitches and lonely housewives?"

"Yeah," she confirmed, "but they also strip for fine-ass bitches who got it goin' on."

As she finished speaking, she put a hand on one hip and thrust it out provocatively.

"Fuck *that*," Kane declared, causing Mika to laugh.

"It'll be fun," she insisted. "Plus, I wanna see the look on you face after some nigga gives you a lap dance."

## Chapter 5

Much to Kane's relief, they didn't go to a male revue (although Mika kept teasing that they should). Instead they ended up at a nightclub – a place that Mika selected based on a suggestion from their waitress at the restaurant, Madison. Bearing in mind who the recommendation had come from, Kane was initially skeptical that it would be the kind of place where they'd have a good time. He needn't have worried.

His first indication that the club was a solid choice came when they drove by and he saw a long line of brothers and sisters (along with a few White people) waiting to get up in that bitch. It was obviously a popular spot, which is seldom a bad thing.

After they found a parking spot, he got a second sign that the club would meet expectations. Basically, as they were walking towards the entrance, he could hear the music long before they got close. He recognized the song – a recent hit that was constantly getting airplay everywhere: office buildings, restaurants, elevators...

"Fuck," Kane muttered, getting a good look at the line as they approached. "It's gone take us an hour to get in this muhfucka."

"You don't thank you can bribe the bouncers to let us in?" Mika asked, tilting her head towards two thuggish bruisers standing at the door.

Kane shook his head. "From what I can see, they not lettin' *any*body in. They mean this bitch is probably at capacity. Nobody can go *in* unless somebody come *out*."

"Well, let's try anyway," Mika suggested. A few moments later, they were at the entrance.

Mika looked over the two bouncers. One was a White guy with a crew cut, maybe six-four in height. From his stance and demeanor, she immediately pegged him as an off-duty cop.

The other bouncer was even taller – at least six-foot-eight – and Black. Not just *racially* Black, though; he had a complexion that practically mimicked coal in terms of color. Plainly speaking, the nigga was so dark that he was damn-near purple.

"You Grape?" Mika asked him, which made Kane draw in a sharp breath, as it seemed to be an obvious – and derisive – comment on the man's appearance.

However, rather than get angry, the bouncer simply looked Mika up and down for a second. "Who's askin'?"

Mika stepped towards and motioned for the bouncer to bend down. When he did, she whispered in his ear, "Madison sent me."

"Name?" the bouncer asked without missing a beat.

"Mika," she replied.

The bouncer nodded as he straightened back up, then told his partner, "These two are good."

He then motioned for Mika and Kane to follow him inside.

# SHE'S HIS DRUG, HE'S HER THUG 4

## Chapter 6

The interior of the club was as they expected: noisy and packed, with the smell of cigarette smoke and weed intermingled throughout. It was also hot as fuck, making Kane glad he'd left his jacket in the SUV.

They spent a moment getting scanned with a handheld metal detector. The guy who scanned them – some overweight muhfucka currently chomping on a burger – barely waved the wand in their direction before letting them through. Afterwards, Grape led them over to a counter where a girl in a skimpy outfit manned a cash register and credit card reader.

"They want a lounge," Grape told the girl. Almost as an afterthought, he turned to Kane and Mika. "You *do* want a lounge, donchu?"

His tone and expression made it clear that, although phrased as a question, he wasn't offering options. Mika and Kane could either get a lounge or they could get the fuck out.

"Yeah," Kane responded after a few seconds. "We lookin' to get a lounge."

"Great," said the girl behind the counter, "because there's no mo' room on the club level."

Her comment seemed to jibe with Kane's earlier assessment that the place was at capacity. Or almost at capacity, if the "lounge" area was still open. But the fact that there was a line around the block when a part of the club was still available told him one important thing: this was not going to be cheap.

"So how much is a lounge?" he asked.

"Fifteen hundred," the girl told him. "But you get a complimentary bottle of Cristal."

"Sounds good," Kane noted with a nod. "You take Visa?"

*********************************************

Grape took off as soon as Kane paid, presumably returning to his post outside the door. After taking payment, the girl behind the counter placed wristbands on Kane and Mika.

"Keep those on," she told them. "They'll get you back up into the VIP area if decide to come down for something, and also in and out the club."

At that point, another chick had come along – a beautiful, twenty-something girl with caramel skin, green eyes, and long, braided hair.

"I'm Kat," she told them. "I'll be your personal server tonight."

With that, she led them into the club proper. However, they swiftly passed through the club level, heading for a set of carpeted stairs guarded by a two-man security team. The duo checked Mika and Kane's wristbands, then allowed them to follow Kat up the stairs.

On the second floor, they found themselves in a broad hallway that appeared to travel in a circle. As they walked through it, they began to pass open doorways that led into private rooms facing the interior of the club. These, then, were the lounges, as evidenced by the fact that – next to the doorway of each – was a gold plaque with elegant black lettering that identified the various rooms as the "Playboy Lounge," "Passion Lounge," and so on.

Eventually, they came to the spot reserved for their use: a room designated as the "O.G. Lounge." Stepping inside behind Kat, Kane noticed that it was about ten-by-fifteen feet in size. It was populated by a couple of oversized easy chairs, a sofa, and a loveseat, all encased in expensive leather. There was also an elegantly-designed coffee table and a couple of matching end tables. Finally, the area facing the club's interior consisted of a waist-high glass railing. In fact, the loveseat was pushed up against the glass. All in all, the place had the feel of an owner's box at a pro sports arena.

"Will this do?" Kat asked. "It's one of our best VIP rooms."

"Yeah," Mika stated with a nod as she glanced around. "It's nice."

"Great," Kat said. "I'll be right back with your complimentary bottle."

As she turned and left, Kane flopped down onto the loveseat. However, he sat down sideways – a position that allowed him to glance down at those on the club level, as well as look around to see who else had booked a VIP slot. (In this instance, most of the other lounges were empty.) Mika took a seat in the same sideways manner, facing him.

"It's not as loud up here," she noted. "Down on the club level, we'd have to scream in order to hear each other."

Kane nodded. "Yeah, the acoustics are dampened up here. Whoever designed this place was a fuckin' genius."

"So you like it?"

"It's cool. To be honest, though, it didn't seem like the kind of place our snowflake waitress would know about."

"Shows what you know," Mika said with a grin. "From what she told me, this is *exactly* her kinda place. She like that dark meat."

"Huh?" Kane muttered with a frown.

"That bouncer who let us in – Grape? That's her boyfriend."

"Ohhh," Kane droned. "I see how this work now."

Mika gave him a curious look. "Whachu mean?"

"Think about it," he told her. "Madison works in a fancy restaurant, where dinner cost as much as a car note. It's the kinda place with customers that can afford to splurge. So she feels 'em out, and if it seems like they're lookin' to go out and have a good time, she directs 'em here, where her boyfriend is workin' the door."

"At which point that gorilla sets you up with a VIP lounge," Mika concluded.

"Pretty much," Kane agreed.

Mika thought for a moment. "So how much you thank gets kicked back to her?"

"Who, Madison?" Kane asked. "I don't know. Probably at least a third of the lounge price. Maybe more if they have trouble gettin' VIPs in this bitch."

"Not a bad way to earn some extra cash."

"Yeah. Our lil' waitress got more game than I thought."

"You pissed about it?"

"What – that she gettin' sommin' outta sendin' us here?" Kane inquired. "Naw. I mean, she ain't swindle nobody. The girl's just hustlin'."

Mika felt the same and was about to comment to that effect when Kat came back in pushing a wheeled cart in front of her. Looking the cart over, Mika noticed a wine bucket on top that was full off ice and a bottle of champagne. She also saw a tray of food.

"Here's your Cristal," Kat announced as she set the wine bucket on the coffee table, along with a pair of champagne glasses. "It's supposed to chill for thirty minutes before you drink it. In the meantime, I brought you a couple of beers and some hors d'oeuvres – all on the house.

"Thanks," said Mika as Kat placed the beers on the coffee table.

"No problem," Kat assured her before setting down a platter containing chicken tenders, celery sticks, cheese squares, and various dips. Finally, she placed some serving saucers and napkins on the table.

By that time, Kane had reached into his pocket and pulled out a couple of bills. He then leaned over and handed the cash to Kat.

"Thanks," she said with a smile as she took the money. "I'll be back to check on you in a bit." A moment later, she was wheeling the cart out.

Watching her, Kane said, "Madison's not the only one hustlin' tonight."

Mika laughed. "She prolly get paid in tips. Throwin' a couple of freebies like chicken fingers at VIPs will most likely get her a bigger gratuity at the end of the night."

"Gratuity?" Kane repeated. "Look who gettin' a vocabulary."

"I was a waitress, shithead," Mika shot back in mock anger. "It's a common term in restaurants, and tips were sometimes more than yo salary. That bein' the case, you'd bring a nigga an extra pack of sugar for his coffee, an extra piece of bacon, or whatever if it would make the difference between a two-dollah and a foe'-dollah tip."

"With a spread like this," Kane noted, gesturing towards the food, "I'd say Kat's lookin' for mo' than foe' dollahs."

"Prolly," Mika agreed, sliding towards the coffee table. "You want any of this?"

"Naw," Kane answered. "I got enough at dinner."

"Yeah, but you didn't eat a balanced meal."

"Huh?" Kane muttered with a frown.

"You ate meat, bread and potatoes," she reminded him as she picked up a celery stick and swirled it in a bowl of dip. "No veggies."

"Oh, so you watchin' my diet now?"

Rather than respond, Mika merely turned towards him, saying, "Try this," as she lifted the celery stick towards his mouth.

"No thanks," Kane told her, gently pushing her hand away. "I'm not really a veggie type of guy."

Mika merely stared at him for a moment. Then, deciding on a new approach, she placed one end of the celery stick in her mouth, holding it firmly with her teeth. She then leaned forward towards Kane, bringing the end of the celery stick with the dip towards his mouth.

For a second, he looked as though he didn't know what was expected of him. A moment later, however, he opened his mouth and bit down on the celery.

There was an audible crunch as he bit into the veggie stick, matched in volume by a similar sound coming from Mika. The dip was unexpectedly tangy – sharp and full of flavor. Enjoying it, he took another bite; Mika did the same, and their parallel action brought them closer. Smiling now, Mika ate more of the celery stick, her eyes never leaving Kane's. There was an intensity in the gaze between them, an energy that charged the air as they eyed one another.

When they took their next bite, their lips met. At that point, Kane was smiling as well, and they both closed their eyes as they suddenly found themselves caught up in a deep and fulfilling kiss. For Mika, it was one of those blissful moments that the two of them occasionally shared, when it felt like the world just melted away, leaving them the only two things in existence. Kane didn't talk about his feelings a lot, but he had made it clear that he felt the same way.

"Oh shit! I'm sorry!" a feminine voice suddenly blurted out.

Breaking off the kiss, Mika found that she had somehow moved onto Kane's lap. Looking around, she saw Kat, who had apparently just come into the room.

"I was just coming to check on you," Kat explained. "I didn't mean to—"

"It's fine," Mika told her, sliding back onto the couch. "We was 'bout to go down to the dance flo' anyway."

"We were?" Kane asked in surprise.

"Yeah, nigga," Mika told him as she stood up. "This my song."

As Mika grabbed his hand and pulled him up, Kane turned an ear to the music. The song that had just started was a nightclub staple – a popular tune that would usually have people packing the dance floor. Glancing down at the club level, he saw that exact thing happening: people were taking to the dance floor in droves.

"Come on," Mika said, beginning to drag him to the doorway.

"Hang on," he said as they passed Kat, causing Mika to cease pulling on him for a second. Looking at their server, he asked, "Is it cool to leave the room unoccupied like this?"

Kat nodded. "Yeah. Servers like me are always around watching the rooms, so people can leave their purses, coats, whatever."

"Good to know," Kane said, not bothering to mention that Mika's purse – like his jacket – had been left in the SUV, tucked under the front passenger seat.

However, he had no more time to reflect on Kat's comment as Mika started dragging him out again, obviously wanting to get to the club level before the song ended. Moments later, they were on the dance floor.

# SHE'S HIS DRUG, HE'S HER THUG 4

## Chapter 7

Being on the club level with Mika reminded Kane of all the shit he disliked about getting on the dance floor: being hot, sweaty, and cheek-to-jowl with a bunch of muhfuckas who were constantly bumping into you (and occasionally acting like it was your fault and wanting to fight about it). On the flip side, though, he actually liked dancing, and grooving with Mika was a hell of a lot of fun. It also boosted his ego to know that – given the way she was twerking, doing hip rolls, and grinding on him – he was the envy of every nigga in there.

After a couple of jamming dance records, the DJ put on a slow song. That was the cue for most muhfuckas to abandon the dance floor like there was a cop out there looking to serve them with a warrant. Kane was on the verge of walking off as well, but Mika grabbed his arm, indicating that she wasn't ready to leave yet. Moments later, they were slow-dancing to a romantic R&B ballad.

As with their earlier dancing, this wasn't an activity that Kane engaged in often. Again though, he was good at it and actually liked it. Of course, it also helped that he was with a woman whose company he sincerely enjoyed, not some random hoe he just wanted to stick it to.

This time when the song ended, Kane was almost reluctant to leave the dance floor. There had been something magical about being out there with Mika pressed against him, just swaying to the music. However, they had been in the sweltering heat of the club level long enough, and both were relieved to get back to the second floor, where cool air was circulating abundantly. In fact, having worked up a sweat, they were chatting about how great it would be to crack open the Cristal, but when they reached their lounge they got a surprise: someone was in there.

To be specific, there were actually five people inside – three niggas, and two skanky hoes – all of whom appeared to be in their late teens or early twenties. One of those niggas was sitting on the loveseat with one of the girls, while another was on the couch with the second bitch. The last muhfucka was sitting in one of the easy chairs.

Caught somewhat off-guard, Kane took a moment to double-check the plaque by the doorway. It said "O.G. Lounge," confirming that this was the right room. Wondering what the fuck was going on, Kane marched inside, followed by Mika.

The nigga on the loveseat noticed him first. He had been laughing with his boys, but looked up as Kane and Mika stepped in. He stopped smirking and merely stared at Kane, as did his friends.

For a moment, no one said anything, causing an uneasy tension to form and grow. After about thirty seconds, the guy on the loveseat – apparently the leader – muttered, "Can I help you with sommin'?"

Kane's initial thought was to tell that nigga and his crew to get the fuck out – especially after he saw that they had been eating his and Mika's food. But before he could say anything Kat came rushing in.

"Oh, I'm so sorry!" she blurted out to Kane and Mika. "I placed you in the wrong lounge."

Looking at her in confusion, Kane simply said, "Huh?"

"She sayin' she put y'all in the wrong room," the nigga on the loveseat chimed in. "See, this *our* spot – the

O.G. Lounge. It's the room we get every time we come here."

Kane merely stared at the nigga for a moment, digesting what he'd heard.

"If you'll come with me," Kat uttered anxiously, getting Kane's attention, "I'll get you in the right room."

Still not saying anything, Kane just looked at her. Kat's eyes darted back and forth between him and the muhfucka on the loveseat. She was obviously nervous, and Kane's silence wasn't making things any better. That said, he got the sense that she hadn't made a mistake at all in terms of placing him and Mika in the O.G. Lounge; she was just trying to keep the situation from escalating.

"Come on," Mika said, drawing Kane's eyes to her. "Let's just go to the other room."

Unlike Kat, Mika wasn't nervous. But looking in her eyes, Kane saw what she hadn't said in words – namely, that they were supposed to be celebrating, so they shouldn't let some ignorant assholes ruin their night.

"A'ight," Kane said with a sigh. "Let's go check out this other spot."

Seemingly relieved, Kat began walking towards the door, as did Mika. Kane, however, reached towards the coffee table and picked up the wine bucket, which still held the unopened bottle of Cristal.

"Hold up, nigga," said the muhfucka on the loveseat. "Whachu thank you doin'?" As he finished speaking, the two niggas on the couch and easy chair came to their feet and walked over, flanking Kane.

Unfazed, Kane simply hoisted the wine bucket, saying, "I paid for this."

The dude on the loveseat shook his head. "Naw, homey – that stay with the room."

Kane's head tilted slightly, and he stared at the muhfucka who had spoken like he didn't believe what he'd just heard, or that he must have heard it wrong. But before he could comment, Kat interjected.

"It's okay," she told Kane anxiously. "I'll get you another bottle."

Kane glanced at her as she spoke, then at Mika. On her part, Mika could sense the tension in Kane and knew that he was a hair's breadth away from going apeshit – even with two muhfuckas flanking him and inside his personal space. Fortunately, looking at Mika appeared to calm him, and a moment later he seemed to relax.

"S'all good," Kane suddenly declared to no one in particular.

"Damn straight it is," stated the nigga on the loveseat, as Kane bent down to place the wine bucket back on the coffee table. "You just lucky I'm in a good mood."

Following this comment, the muhfucka who had just spoken started chuckling, and a second later he was joined by his friends and the two stank hoes with them. Kane was still bent over at the time, with his hand on the wine bucket. Nobody but Mika noticed that he had suddenly gone rigid – or understood what it meant.

Faster than seemed possible, Kane grabbed the bottle of Cristal by the neck and whacked it fiercely against the kneecap of the guy on his right. That nigga doubled over, howling and grasping his wounded knee.

Straightening up, Kane then swung the bottle at the guy on his left, who was still laughing. It connected solidly with that fool's jaw, snapping his head viciously to the side and spinning him around before he fell face-forward onto the floor, unconscious. By that time, Kane had turned back to the muhfucka on his right, who was still bent over. Kane brought the bottle down heavily on the back of that nigga's head.

At that point, the bottle apparently decided it was tired of the abuse it was receiving and shattered, leaving Kane holding only the broken, jagged bottleneck. The dude that Kane had just hit dropped bonelessly to the floor and lay still. It was then that a couple of things seemed to happen at once.

First, the chick on the couch came to her feet like she wanted to do something. At the same time, the nigga on the loveseat jumped up and tried to rush Kane.

The bitch from the couch came at Kane with one hand raised overhead, holding what looked like a beer bottle. Mika, however, was already in motion.

Catching the hoe's raised forearm, Mika wrenched it backwards, hard – almost making the bitch's elbow point straight up in the air. The girl screamed in pain, as it probably felt like her shoulder was being yanked out of its socket. Moreover, the pressure being applied to her arm made her bend backwards at the waist, like she was trying to win a limbo contest. A moment later, as Mika released her forearm, the chick hit the floor, landing on her back as the beer bottle hit the floor and broke.

Whimpering, the girl merely stared at Mika for a moment. The bitch had obviously been totally focused on Kane, and had either forgotten about Mika or dismissed her as a non-threat. That had been a costly mistake, but just in case she got some stupid idea about rectifying it, Mika kicked her in the mouth. The girl cried out and rolled to the side, blubbering loudly, and with all of the fight clearly knocked out of her.

On his part, Kane had to deal with the nigga rushing him from the loveseat. The muhfucka presumably didn't realize that Kane held a weapon: the broken bottleneck, which he slashed in an arc in front of him. That made the nigga charging at Kane not only check his advance, but also contort his body in an attempt not to get sliced. The effort threw him a little off balance, and he went stumbling backwards until the back of his legs struck the loveseat, causing him to flop down onto the seat cushions. But before he could recover Kane was on him, gripping his jaw with one hand while holding the broken bottle to his neck with the other.

The second girl, who had never moved from the loveseat, suddenly looked like she wanted to be elsewhere. She was breathing hard – damn near hyperventilating – and clearly scared shitless. Staring at Kane with a deer-in-the-headlights expression, she swiftly slid off the loveseat. Keeping her hands in view, she stepped over to the other hoe, who was still on the floor. Once there, she switched her attention from Kane to Mika, keeping her eyes on the latter as she slowly bent down towards her friend.

"Come on, Sadie," said the bitch from the loveseat. "Get up. We gotta go."

As she spoke, she grabbed her the arm of her friend – Sadie – and started pulling her to her feet. Sadie was still whimpering and Mika noticed that she had a bloody lip, but she did as suggested and came to her feet. Seconds later, the two women were headed out the door, with Sadie leaning on her friend for support.

"Get off me, muhfucka!" the dude on the loveseat suddenly growled, bringing everyone's attention back to him.

"Ha!" Kane sneered, tightening his hold on the man's jaw. "Nigga, you seriously need to learn how to read the room. Yo ass ain't in no position to be makin' demands. You might wanna get familiar with a concept called 'leverage'."

"Leverage?" the nigga hissed. "Im'ma show yo ass some leverage."

"You gone do it in the next two minutes?" Kane asked. "Cause that's how fast you gone bleed out after I slice yo throat open."

"You ain't gone do shit," the guy uttered defiantly. "Do you know who the fuck I am?"

"Yeah," Kane shot back. "You that muhfucka they gone be referrin' to as 'the body' and 'the victim' on the six o'clock news. 'Course, that's only 'til they can identify yo remains and then notify next of kin."

As Kane finished speaking, the nigga on the loveseat audibly gulped. He suddenly seemed very cognizant of the situation he was in.

"Anyway," Kane went on, "I can see that you thank you a big deal, and that you got some kind of name or rep that niggas s'posed to recognize. So go ahead and tell me: who do I have the fuckin' honor of addressin'?"

Surprisingly, the nigga stayed quiet.

"Come on, muhfucka," Kane said after a few seconds. "Don't keep me in suspense." When the dude still didn't say anything, Kane pushed the broken bottle a little harder against his neck, drawing blood and making the guy wince. "I ain't gone ask you again."

"Sway," the man suddenly blurted out. "I go by Sway."

"Naw, nigga," Kane told him. "I want yo *real* name."

Sway swallowed and then stated, "Robbie Williams."

"Like the singer?" Kane asked with a frown.

Sway gave him a confused look. "Who?"

"Nevermind, dumbass," Kane told him. "Just show me yo driver's license."

Slowly, Sway reached into his back pocket. A moment later he pulled out his wallet and flipped it open.

Kane noted that the wallet was a trifold model, with storage pockets that seemed to contain debit and credit cards. It also had an ID holder with a transparent cover, and it was there that he saw Sway's license.

"I'll be damned," Kane muttered upon seeing that Sway's name really *was* Robbie Williams. He also noticed something else: Sway had a decent amount of bank in the billfold section of the wallet. He probably had a stack in his pockets as well.

Still eyeing the cash, Kane stated, "Seeing as how you fucked up my evenin' and cost me a bottle of Cristal, I *should* make you reimburse me. But if I take it right now, it's gone look like I robbed yo ass, and a punk bitch like you is just the type to run to the cops."

Sway seemed to bristle at Kane's comment, but wisely held his tongue.

"But I gotta get satisfaction some kinda way," Kane continued. "So…"

As he trailed off, Kane swiftly drew back the hand that had been gripping Sway's face and then sent it rocketing forward, clocking the nigga on the jaw. Sway's head jerked to the side, and for a moment he looked dazed – then he slumped over, unconscious.

Kane stepped back, then let the broken bottle fall from his hand. Walking towards Kat, he pulled some cash from his pocket and peeled off two hundred dollars.

"Sorry for the mess," he apologized as he held the money out to Kat, who looked stunned by everything that had happened. However, a moment later, she seemed to recover and took the cash. Turning to Mika, Kane simply said, "Let's get the fuck outta here."

## Chapter 8

Mika and Kane went straight home after leaving the club. At present, they were living in a nice two-bed, two-bath apartment that they rented on a month-to-month lease.

They had barely stepped inside and shut the door before they were all over each other, at the same time practically ripping their clothes off. But that's how it was with the two of them. They typically had the hots for each other twenty-four-seven, but occasionally something happened to increase their ardor. In this instance, it was the incident at the club with Sway and his crew.

Basically, hostile confrontations would sometimes give the two lovebirds a head-spinning adrenaline rush. (Mika, for instance, would find herself incredibly excited, anxious, and restless.) Generally, when that happened, the only way to get back to normal involved naked bodies coming together (and *cumming* together). Ergo, when they got home, instinct and desire essentially took control, overriding conscious thought.

They were going at each other so aggressively that Kane almost forgot to deactivate the alarm system, which had begun beeping when they entered. Fortunately, despite Mika smothering him with kisses and running her hands all over his body, he managed to turn it off before the thirty-second timer triggered the actual alarm and notified law enforcement.

By that time, Mika had already kicked off her shoes and stripped out of her pants. Somehow, her top was off as well, but she didn't have a firm recollection of removing it. Still kissing Kane, she reached behind her, preparing to unsnap her bra, but he never gave her a chance. Plainly impatient, Kane simply grabbed her bra straps and yanked them down, exposing her girls but leaving the bra encircling her stomach. A moment later, he was squeezing one of her tits with his hand while putting the other in his mouth, gently biting the nipple in a way that drove Mika crazy.

On her part, she reached down towards his groin. His pants were still on, but already unbuttoned and unzipped, so she had easy access to his dick. She spent a second stroking it through his underwear, feeling it throb eagerly in response to her touch. Then she slipped a hand inside his underwear and let her fingers caress the shaft, noting how hard and heavy his dick felt, then slid her hand down farther and cupped his balls. That elicited a moan from Kane, which made Mika smile.

While the foreplay was going on, Mika devoted some effort to easing them towards their bedroom. However, her efforts were thwarted by Kane, who guided them to the kitchen instead.

The apartment was designed with an open concept, so there was no wall separating the kitchen from the living room. The line of demarcation between the two spaces was denoted by a large island with a marble countertop that also served as a breakfast bar. It was here that Kane guided her, with the lights in the kitchen – tied to a sensor that detected movement – coming on automatically.

Still sucking on her titties, Kane backed her up to the island. Thinking he wanted to fuck her on it (something that had happened before) she was about to shimmy up onto the countertop when Kane unexpectedly raised up. Placing his hands on her shoulders, he spun her around so that she was facing the island. She then felt his hand push against the small of her back — not roughly, but firmly enough to make her bend over.

The countertop was cold against her tits, but Mika barely noticed; she was too excited about what she knew was coming next, and she braced herself in anticipation.

She heard Kane hurriedly getting out of his clothes and then shuddered slightly with excitement as he grabbed her panties and yanked them down around her ankles. Not wanting to be restricted, she slipped one foot out of her underwear and then flicked her other leg to the side, sending the panties flying into the living room somewhere.

Mika suddenly found herself breathing hard as she sensed Kane getting into position behind her. A moment later, the head of his dick was rubbing up against her pussy, teasing her with the promise of things to come. Mika was dripping wet even before her panties had come off, so just rubbing up against her snatch had probably soaked his cock completely. She heard an odd keening sound, then realized that it was her, almost squealing in anticipation. It was an overt indication of just how badly she wanted the dick — how desperately she *needed* it. And just when the wait was starting to become unbearable, Kane's dick slipped smoothly into her pussy.

Mika moaned loudly in satisfaction as he slowly slid inside her, inch by glorious inch. Feeling his dick penetrate, going both wide and deep, was absolute bliss. Likewise, when he began pulling back, the sensation was pure pleasure. When he thrust forward again, it was slightly faster, as expected, but no less enjoyable.

From there the tempo increased exponentially so that less than a minute later, Kane — with his hands gripping her hips — was pounding that shit like a maniac. In fact, he was hitting it so hard and so fast that when their bodies came together, with her ass smacking up against him every time he went balls deep, it sounded like someone was in the room clapping their hands in applause.

Her moans and gasps were a dead giveaway, but Mika flat-out loved being railed like this by Kane. In fact, she enjoyed having his dick inside her in any position, from any angle, at any time. Likewise, Kane's groans were a textbook indicator of how much he relished fucking Mika. For him, her pussy was a magic circle – a place of eternal ecstasy that was as close as you could get to heaven without actually dying.

In a similar fashion, Mika considered Kane's dick to be the Eighth Wonder of the World – a rare marvel to be praised and admired. Arching her back, she bent her head so that she could see down the length of her body. The space between her torso and the island was narrow and it wasn't a great angle, but she was able to get an eyeful of what she wanted to see: Kane's dick – engorged and wet – slamming and in and out of her pussy at a rapid-fire pace.

She had thought it would take her a little longer to orgasm, but the sight of Kane's rod in action – repeatedly and relentlessly pounding her snatch – was too much. Seeing it immediately gave her goosebumps and pushed her over the edge. A moment later she climaxed unexpectedly, cumming explosively and screaming so loudly that she was sure the neighbors would call the police saying some bitch was in there being murdered.

# SHE'S HIS DRUG, HE'S HER THUG 4

## Chapter 9

Out of breath, Mika collapsed onto the island. Having cum as well, Kane flopped down on top of her, completely spent. Making an effort not to put his full weight on her, he took a moment to gently nibble on Mika's earlobe before wearily straightening up and taking a step back. As his dick slid out of her pussy, it left a euphoric tingling sensation in its wake that almost had Mika moaning again.

Once he was out of her, Kane moved a little to the side, plainly giving Mika room to come to her feet. But when she tried she found that she couldn't stand; her legs had basically turned to Jell-O.

*This nigga's dick done paralyzed me from the waist down*, she joked to herself. She then took a moment to rest on the island again, closing her eyes for a few seconds while she gathered her strength.

However, she must have dozed off, because the next thing she knew, Kane was carrying her to the bedroom. Once there, he somehow managed to pull back the covers while still holding her. He then lay Mika down gently before also getting into bed and spooning her. Feeling marvelously content, Mika snuggled up next to him. Moments later, she was fast asleep.

*******************************************

Mika woke up alone in bed the next morning. Checking an alarm clock on her nightstand, she saw that it wasn't late, but she had slept in to a certain degree. Almost reluctantly, she got out of bed and then spent a moment stretching before wandering into the bathroom freshen up.

Fifteen minutes later she emerged wearing a plush terry cloth robe, feeling fresh and clean after having a shower and going through her morning routine.

Leaving the bedroom, she headed to the kitchen. There she found Kane, sitting at the island/breakfast bar and drinking a glass of orange juice while looking at a computer tablet.

Like Mika, he was wearing a robe. In fact, theirs was a matching set. There was a time when Mika would have thought that type of thing was cheesy, but now she kind of enjoyed it. Basically, it was an overt symbol and acknowledgement of the fact that they were a couple. More to the point, it had been Kane's idea to get the robes, so to Mika they represented something special.

However, that wasn't to say that no one had ever done anything like that for her before. In fact, an old boyfriend had bought her a robe one time, but it had been rough, scratchy, and had given her a rash – much like the nigga who had gifted it to her. (To be specific, she had picked up poison ivy from that muhfucka.)

Quite like the difference between that earlier piece-of-shit robe and the one she currently wore, the distinction between Kane and her prior boyfriends was stark and pronounced. Therefore, when he did things like buy matching bathrobes, she found it cute instead of hokey.

Kane looked up as she came into the room, watching as she approached him.

"Mornin'," she said, giving him a quick kiss. "Breakfast?"

"Microwave," he said in response, pointing.

Giving his cheek a momentary caress, Mika sauntered over to the microwave. Opening it, she saw a plate containing sausages and French toast. She reached inside and touched the plate. It was cold – and so, presumably, was the food. Closing the microwave door, she set the timer for one minute and then turned back to Kane, who had returned to perusing his tablet.

Mika knew without asking that Kane was probably reading the news. He read more than almost anyone she knew, which she had initially found surprising considering the fact that he had been a drug dealer. Those two things just didn't seem to go together, but – as she had discovered – Kane was atypical in quite a number of ways.

She smiled as she watched him, thinking about how nice it was that he had made breakfast for her. It was the kind of thing that she loved about him and another way in which he didn't conform to expectations. In essence, Kane didn't view those kinds of actions as somehow undermining his masculinity or relinquishing power in the relationship. More importantly, the fact that he was willing to do stuff like that made Mika feel *valued* – like she wasn't just a sweet piece of ass that he was tapping until the next bitch came along.

However, he hadn't just stopped at making breakfast; he had also cleaned up after himself – washing the items he had cooked with and putting them on a nearby drain board. He had also picked up the clothes they had stripped out of the night before. In fact, her cell phone, keys, and other personables were on the end of the breakfast bar, and if she knew Kane, the clothes themselves were already in the washer.

The washer in question was a high-end, front-load model that – along with the dryer – had come with the apartment. In fact, the entire place had come fully furnished. Truth be told, two bedrooms was probably more than they needed, but Kane had stressed that he'd feel cramped in anything smaller. Regis had actually offered to put them up in a place owned by Bush, but Kane had nixed the idea.

"Don't know who all gone have a key to that muhfucka," Kane had stated. "At least if we payin' rent somewhere, there's the expectation that access is limited to the landlord."

The logic of that was sound, and Mika had found herself agreeing with him. Ergo, they had shopped around until they located their current digs, which she enjoyed more than any other place that she had lived.

The sound of the microwave going off brought Mika back to herself. Taking the food out, she grabbed a fork from a nearby drawer and then took a seat next to Kane.

"Anythang interestin' goin' on?" she asked, pointing to the tablet with her chin.

"Just the same ole shit," Kane replied. "Political parties wranglin' over shit that don't matter, like sayin' the pledge of allegiance in school. And as usual, dumbass criminals doin' dumbass shit."

"Like what?"

"Well, one nigga decides to break into this mansion on the ritzy side of town while the owners are out. He gets a bunch of jewelry and fancy watches – shit that's easy to fence – but on his way out decides to take a dip in this hot tub they have out back. Musta felt good, 'cause the muhfucka fell asleep, and that's where the owners find 'im when they come home. Next thang he know, cops are haulin' his ass out the water like a fuckin' big-mouth bass."

Mika snickered. "That *was* kinda stupid on his part."

"But niggas do stupid shit like that all the time. They thank all you need to pull off a lick is a gun and balls. What you really need, though, is *brains*. Basically, if you gone be a criminal – a successful one, meaning you don't get killed, locked up or some other shit like that – then you always gotta be the smartest guy in the room."

Mika nodded, understanding that this was part of the reason why Kane read so much.

"But you not a criminal anymoe', babe," she reminded him.

"Don't mean I'm ready for a lobotomy," Kane shot back. "Plus, it don't hurt to stay informed. Take this nigga I knew back home called Scooter, for instance. Now Scooter's specialty was knockin' off convenience stores. But not just any convenience store. He only robbed those that were out by the city limits."

Mika frowned. "What's the purpose of that?"

"Because a cop's jurisdiction is limited to the place where he's the law. He can't just go into another city or county and arrest somebody. But if he's like chasin' yo ass and you cross the county line or sommin', then he can stay on yo ass until he catches you."

"I know about that," Mika noted with a nod. "It's called 'hot pursuit' of a suspect."

"Technically, it's 'fresh pursuit,'" Kane corrected, "but people use 'em interchangeably. Anyway, Scooter would rob a convenience store that was maybe one or two miles from the city limits, county line or whatever the fuck it was. Then he'd jump in the getaway car and zip over to the other jurisdiction, where he'd swap cars asap. As long as there wasn't a cop followin' 'im after he left the robbery, he was basically home free because the law couldn't just randomly go outside their district lookin' for 'im."

"Yeah, but wouldn't they just radio the cops in the other area and tell 'em to keep an eye out for some nigga who just robbed a store?"

"Yeah, they could issue a BOLO," Kane agreed, "but that was the whole point of switchin' cars. They might say, 'Be on the lookout' for a muhfucka pushin' a white caddy, but by that time Scooter would be rollin' around in a station wagon."

"Damn," Mika uttered in admiration. "That's pretty smart."

"Well, befoe' you go givin' Scooter too much credit, you should know that robbery scheme wasn't anythang that he personally came up with. It was the brainchild of this other dude Scooter used to hang with."

Giving Kane a sly look, Mika asked, "And who might that have been, I wonder?"

"Just some cool-ass mofo with brains," Kane said with a grin. "Scooter, on the other hand, had the IQ of a potted plant. Still, he had paid enough attention to mimic what he'd learned from this other nigga, and so he had a lil' success for a while as a stick-up man. Then one day, he robs this place, but when he tries to cross the county line, the road's blocked. Not only that, but there was cops all over the place."

"So they were expectin' 'im?"

"Not exactly. A fuckin' train had derailed, so damn near every protective service you could think of was out there: cops, fire trucks, ambulances... Anyway, Scooter – not knowin' what the fuck is goin' on – completely panics. He slams on the gas tryin' to get outta there, drawin' all kinds of attention when nobody was even lookin' for his ass. But even then he might have got away, but he was so busy checkin' his rearview mirror to see if he was bein' followed that he ran into a fuckin' lightpole."

"And I'm guessin' that's how they got his ass."

Kane nodded. "Yeah. By then the report was 'cross the radio about the robbery, so they had a description of him, the car, everythang. But you know what's funny? That train derailment had been on the news all fuckin' morning. If Scooter had just turned on the news or opened the mornin' paper, he wudda known about it. Hell, if he had just scouted his escape route first he would have seen what was up."

"So basically," Mika concluded, "all he had to do was make an effort to stay informed."

"Exactly, but Scooter was a dumb fuck," Kane stressed. "And speakin' of dumb fucks, I been thankin' 'bout what happened last night at the club."

"You mean those fuckin' wannabe gangstas?" Mika grumbled. "What about 'em?"

"They was up in the lounge area, but from what I could see, none of 'em had on wristbands."

"So what – you thank they snuck up there?"

"I guess they *could* have, but I didn't get that impression. Plus, I thank it would be hard gettin' past those mufuckas guardin' the stairs. Lastly, that nigga whose throat I almost slit was talkin' like he was some kinda bigshot."

"Niggas always talk like they bigshots, even when they broke, unemployed, and livin' with they momma."

"Yeah, but considerin' everythang from last night…"

He trailed off, but Mika knew what he had been on the cusp of saying. "You thank he's connected."

"Maybe," Kane stated with a shrug. "If we was back home I wouldn't give a fuck, but since we new here, I'd like to start off by not makin' enemies if we don't have to."

"So whachu wanna do?"

"Try to get a handle on it," Kane declared. "So I guess I'll call Buggy."

# SHE'S HIS DRUG, HE'S HER THUG 4

## Chapter 10

When they had first arrived in their new town, Kane had asked Regis for two points of contact. The first was for someone that he could count on as reliable muscle, should the situation ever require it. Regis had referred him to a guy called Mikey – a dour nigga who always looked like someone had just pissed in his coffee.

Mikey wasn't huge – he was maybe five-eight in height, with a solid (but not bulky) frame. However, he had an incredibly intimidating presence, and could cower niggas who stood a head taller than him. More importantly, he had a fierce and well-earned reputation; as a result, nobody fucked with him.

The other request that Kane had made was for a liaison. Basically, since he and Mika were fresh off the boat, it would take time for them to establish a network – to become familiar with and trusted by people in certain circles. However, they could short-circuit that process if they were introduced by someone with the proper connections. To that end, Regis had pointed them towards Buggy, who had ultimately been the right man for the job.

Although wheelchair-bound, Buggy was a garrulous and spirited muhfucka with a bright outlook on life. He also seemed to have an extensive network, so that within two weeks of meeting him, Kane and Mika had gotten a personal intro to almost everybody worth knowing. As a result, if they needed anything from nose candy to an untraceable piece, they knew exactly who to call.

Kane reflected on all this as he got his cell phone and dialed Buggy's number. It was answered on the third ring.

"Yo, Kane," said an enthusiastic voice. "Whaddup, my nigga? I knew you was about to call me, 'cause my asshole started itchin'."

"Nigga, you paralyzed from the waist down," Kane retorted. "The only time you can feel yo asshole is when you wipin' it."

"Not even then," Buggy shot back, "'cause I keep a girl around to do shit like that *for* me." They both chuckled at that for a moment, then Buggy continued, saying, "Well, I'm sure this ain't a social call, so whachu need, homey?"

Kane sighed. "Me and my girl had a run-in with some muhfuckas at a club last night."

Suddenly somber, Buggy asked, "Y'all okay? Was it serious?"

"Serious enough, be we all good. Can't say the same 'bout those other niggas, though."

"So what's the problem?"

"One of 'em seemed to imply that he was connected. Don't know if it's true or not, but I'd rather see if it's some shit that needs to get resolved, rather than worry 'bout whether some muhfucka's out there gunnin' for me."

"I can check it out. You got a name?"

"Just the leader – some shithead named Robbie Williams."

Buggy paused for a moment. "Like the comedian?"

"No, that's *Robin* Williams," Kane explained. "This muhfucka was named *Robbie* Williams, like the singer."

"Who?" uttered Buggy, sounding perplexed.

Kane shook his head in disdain, then said, "I thank he said he go by 'Sway.'"

"Okay, I thank I know who you talkin' 'bout," Buggy stated.

"Anybody we need to be worried about?"

"Not really. If it's the nigga I'm thinkin' of, he's fuckin' super flyweight at best. But now that I thank about it, he does have a brother whose in a heavier weight class. It's prolly worth havin' a conversation."

"A'ight – set it up," Kane said.

"Will do," Buggy assured him. "I'll hit you back in a bit." With that, he hung up the phone.

Kane, who was still in the kitchen with Mika, set his cell phone down on the breakfast bar.

"Well?" Mika asked, subtly reminding Kane that his conversation with Buggy hadn't been on the speakerphone.

"He thank he knows the muhfuckas we bumped heads with last night," Kane told her. "The one whose throat I almost opened up – Sway – has a brother we probably need to powwow with."

Mika considered that for a moment. "You think we should call Mikey?"

"If we need Mikey," Kane answered, "the shit's way too serious for a conversation."

Mika simply nodded at that. "So when's this chat supposed to happen?"

"Who da fuck knows?" Kane muttered with a shrug. "Today, tomorrow, next week… Buggy's gonna call back and let me know."

"So what do we do – just hang out 'til we hear back from him?"

"You can if you want," Kane told her, "but I'm gone hit the gym."

## Chapter 11

Kane actually worked out regularly, which explained his fine-ass bod. However, it was something Mika hadn't realized initially – mostly because they were on the run those first few weeks together and were too busy trying to stay alive. It wasn't until they went to Hawaii, where Kane started going to the hotel gym on a daily basis, that she realized he had a regular exercise routine.

"You can't expect good genes to do all the work," he had told her when she asked about it. "You gotta put some effort into it."

Mika had been one of those who fell into the "good genes" category. Simply put, she had inherited a face and physique that had been turning heads since middle school. Her body had always been tight and toned, and she had spent almost zero time exercising in order to get it that way; it was pretty much all genetics.

Bearing all that in mind, she had originally been fine with hanging back while Kane went to work out. (Frankly speaking, their sex life was active and vigorous enough to work up as much of a sweat as any session at the gym.) More importantly, Kane didn't seem to care whether she had an exercise routine or not. In short, it was okay that she didn't view hitting the gym with the same level of importance that he did.

Since moving to their current digs, Kane had tried to work out every day. In fact, Mika suspected that one of the reasons why Kane had favored this place over several others they had considered was because the apartment complex had an excellent gym.

At first, she had been content to let him go by himself, but around the fifth day at the new apartment, some flat-ass, flat-chested blonde snowflake had greeted Kane by name in the hallway. Kane had spoken to the woman in return, calling her "Heidi." When Mika asked later how they knew each other, Kane mentioned that they had met in the gym. Since then, Mika had made it a point to join Kane for his workouts. If Kane had any suspicions about her sudden change of heart regarding exercise, he kept them to himself.

Now that she had started doing it regularly, Mika found that she enjoyed working out. She only did some moderate weight lifting and spent most of her time on the exercise bike, but it left her with a feeling of accomplishment. Also, she got a certain level of satisfaction from knowing that almost every guy in the place was eyeing her – if only surreptitiously because of Kane being nearby.

On this particular occasion, however, Mika claimed that she was still exhausted from their fuck session the night before and told Kane to go ahead with her. That admittedly played a little to his ego, but kept him from getting suspicious. After he left for the gym, she hurried to the living room, where her own computer tablet was sitting on the coffee table.

Much like the robes, the tablets were another instance in which Kane had operated in couple mode, picking up one for Mika when he bought his own. Of course, Kane's tablet had been a gift to himself because he had grown weary of constantly having to read on a "tiny-ass cell screen," as he put it. Mika, on the other hand mostly used hers for games. However, she had another used for it at moment.

Opening up an internet window, she quickly navigated to an online auction site and logged in. Next, she went to the list of items she had bid on. There was only one: an authentic men's Rolex watch.

The timepiece in question normally went for about ten grand, but the bidding on this one had started at fifty bucks. Apparently, the seller was the forty-something ex-wife of a corporate CEO who walked in on her husband fucking the pool boy. As part of the divorce settlement, she got his luxury watch collection and was auctioning them at firesale prices just to piss off her ex. Moreover, she was selling them on a second-rate auction site – a place for budget-minded consumers – presumably because letting them go for cheap would really twist the knife in her ex-husband's gut.

Mika had stumbled upon the site by sheer luck, and upon seeing the watch, she had thought it would make a great gift for Kane – not for any particular occasion, but just too show what he meant to her. Therefore, she had put in a lowball offer initially; the bidding, however, had quickly shot up to a thousand dollars. Mika had been part of that bidding war, but had decided to drop out rather than help continue driving the price up. Instead, she had changed tactics. Now her goal was just to swoop in at the end of the auction and – depending on price – make the winning bid.

Checking her watch, she saw that there were ten minutes left before the auction came to a close, and the top offer was fifteen hundred – a price she could easily beat. In an ideal world, she would have waited until the last minute, literally, to make her bid. However, as time ticked buy, she found herself worrying about all the shit that could go wrong: the auction site going down, internet service going out, and so on. Ergo, she decided to go ahead and get her bid in.

Mika's gut reaction was to go a hundred above the current high bid. However, she didn't want to fuck around with a bunch of back-and-forth with others who might be trying to use the same strategy she was employing. That being the case, she decided to just go for the kill, putting in a bid for two thousand.

It was a hefty jump in price, and she thought it might take the heart out of any other potential buyers. Thus when she was shocked when she immediately saw a competing bid come in for two-thousand-and-one dollars.

*What the fuck?* Mika thought, then bumped the price up to twenty-one hundred. After a few seconds, the bid went up again by a dollar.

Starting to feel frustrated, Mika raised her bid another hundred. When about thirty seconds went by with no other action, she smiled to herself, thinking she'd won. But her grin swiftly faded when the bid rose again by a single dollar.

*Alright, bitch*, Mika mentally told her unknown adversary as she gritted her teeth. *This shit is on…*

# SHE'S HIS DRUG, HE'S HER THUG 4

## Chapter 12

Mika was sitting on the sofa playing solitaire on her tablet when Kane came in.

Looking up, she asked in a cheerful voice, "How was your workout?"

"Good," he replied. "What are you so chipper about?"

"Oh, nothing," she told him, although mentally she was still high-fiving herself on winning the auction. It had cost her three grand, but she couldn't wait to see Kane's face when she gave him the Rolex. "You 'bout to take a shower?"

Kane nodded. "Yeah."

Mika gave him a lascivious look. "Want some company?"

"Normally, I'd love it, but we don't have time."

"Oh?" Mika said, suddenly curious.

"Buggy called while I was at the gym," kane explained. "He set up the meet."

"When?"

"About an hour. We need to roll out in about thirty."

Mika nodded. "I'll be ready when you come out."

*******************************************

Mika was as good as her word. When Kane emerged from their bedroom twenty minutes later, Mika was sitting on the living room couch dressed in a pair of jeans, a black top, and matching black boots. But she wasn't alone. Sitting in an easy chair diagonal to her was Mikey.

Kane frowned slightly but never broke stride as he headed towards Mikey, who rose from the chair.

"Whaddup, my nigga?" Kane said, giving Mikey some dap.

"S'all 'bout you," Mikey replied, looking surly as always.

Kane didn't have to ask what Mikey was doing there. Apparently Mika had called him while Kane had been in the shower. Hell, for all he knew, she had called Mikey and told him to be on standby while Kane was working out. Regardless, she had obviously felt that they needed backup for this meeting Buggy had set up.

"So, we doin' this?" Mikey inquired, interrupting Kane's thoughts.

"Yeah," Kane declared with a nod. "Let's roll."

# SHE'S HIS DRUG, HE'S HER THUG 4

## Chapter 13

They rode to the meet in their SUV, with Kane driving while Mika sat in the front passenger seat, and Mikey sat in back. Mikey could have driven his own car, but – since he was there as muscle and backup – it made sense for him to be on hand.

Normally, having a sour-faced nigga who was packing sitting directly behind him would have made Kane wary. However, despite only having a couple of interactions, he felt comfortable with Mikey. Simply put, he got the impression that he could trust Mikey – that he was the type of nigga who would keep his word when given, no matter what.

Mika also seemed to trust Mikey. In fact, she had made it her mission to get him to smile at least once. To that end, she had brought her tablet along, and kept turning around to show Mikey various cat videos that were allegedly funny. Much to her chagrin, Mikey barely even raised an eyebrow.

"You definitely gone laugh at this one," Mika said, showing him a video of a feline with its head stuck in a tissue box.

"Hilarious," Mikey deadpanned in an emotionless tone after watching the screen for a few seconds.

Mika sighed in exasperation. "You know, you got the wrong fuckin' name. 'Mikey' is what you call somebody you can laugh and joke with. That ain't you. You mo' like a fuckin' 'Ebenezer' or 'Drac' or some shit like that. But you ain't no damn 'Mikey.' How you even get that name anyway?"

"Mika, chill with that shit," Kane blurted out. "Force-feedin' the man kitty-cat home movies is one thang, but you don't get to go after his name."

"It's cool," Mikey assured him, then turned to Mika. "Long time ago, there used to be these commercials 'bout this kid name Mikey, who hated everythang. My momma said I was the same way as a kid – I didn't like shit. Not the food they fed me, not the clothes I wore, not the toys they gave me. I liked nothing and nobody, so she called me Mikey after the kid in the commercials."

"Damn," Mika muttered. "Maybe it's the right name after all."

# SHE'S HIS DRUG, HE'S HER THUG 4

## Chapter 14

The meet took place on the back lot of a shuttered grocery store. When Kane, Mika and Mikey pulled up, everyone else was seemingly already there. In fact, Kane was surprised at the number of vehicles present.

There were two sport utility vehicles and a sedan, all with tinted windows. Those were in addition to the late-model minivan that Buggy always rode in. It wasn't the most stylish vehicle on the road, but the sliding side doors – in addition to a custom-made ramp that had been installed – made it easier for Buggy to get in and out. In fact, having apparently seen them approaching, Buggy was already rolling out in his wheelchair when Kane brought the SUV to a halt. Following Buggy's lead, the doors on the other three vehicles opened, and Kane counted four niggas getting out of each.

"Shit," Kane muttered. They were vastly outnumbered, making this seem like much more than just a chat to clear the air. All of sudden, he was glad that Mika had shown the foresight to call Mikey.

Needless to say, Kane's group was packing, and he suspected that everyone else at this meet was as well. That meant this place could quickly become a war zone if shit went sideways.

Turning to Mika, Kane said, "Wait here."

"Fuck that," Mika said, performing a press check on her gun and then tucking it into the back waistband of her jeans.

Kane just smiled at her. He hated the thought of Mika getting hurt, but he loved how she was always willing to back him, no matter the odds. This was just another instance of her proving that she was unashamedly ride-or-die.

"Alright, showtime," Kane declared, then all three of them exited and walked to the front of the SUV.

Buggy was in the midst of giving some dap to a guy who had exited one of the sport utility vehicles. The dude in question had a coffee-colored complexion and appeared to be in his late twenties. He was tall – maybe six-three – and just a tad on the heavy side, but not enough to really be called fat. He sported a Van Dyke beard and had his hair faded on the sides, while the top consisted of long braids currently tied up in a bun. Given the fact that Buggy didn't appear to address anyone else, Kane assumed that the nigga he was talking to was the leader – Sway's brother.

After a few seconds of general chitchat, Buggy began wheeling himself towards Kane. Had he been able to stand, Buggy probably would have been about six feet tall. Most people assumed that he was in a wheelchair because of a drive-by or some shit like that. As a result, he generally got treated with the respect due to an O.G. or someone who had paid their dues on the streets. The truth, however, was far more pedestrian.

Buggy wasn't in a wheelchair because a bullet to the spine, or something like that, had fucked up his legs. He was in a wheelchair with fucked up legs because he was born that way.

Basically, he had some kind of degenerative bone disease in his lower extremities that had robbed him of the ability to walk. (Rumor had it that his legs were disgusting to look it, which may have been why Buggy always kept them covered with a blanket that sat in his lap and went down to his feet.) However, he compensated for the weakness in his legs by working out his upper body like a maniac. As a result, from the waist up, he was built like a fucking gorilla.

Buggy came to a stop a few feet from Kane. He had been followed over by Sway's brother and the rest of his crew, including Sway himself. One side of Sway's face was puffy (presumably from when Kane had hit him), and there was a Band-Aid on his neck where the broken bottle had drawn blood. Kane also noted another nigga limping pretty badly; he wasn't sure, but thought it was the muhfucka he had kneecapped with the bottle the night before.

Kane didn't recognize anyone else in the other group, and – other than Sway and the nigga limping – he doubted that he looked familiar to any of them. However, they seemed to know who Mikey was, as a number of those muhfuckas started whispering amongst themselves and glancing in Mikey's direction.

"Whaddup?" Buggy asked, drawing Kane's attention. At the same time, he reached out with a fist, which Kane bumped with his own. "Kane, Mako," Buggy continued, tilting his head toward Sway's brother. "Mako, Kane."

Kane gave Mako a what's-up nod, then said, "Mako – like the shark?"

"Yeah," Mako confirmed. "Caught one when I was a kid – part of a fishin' program that was s'posed to keep lil' niggas like me off the street. Didn't do shit on that front, but to this day, I do love fishin'." He chuckled as he finished speaking, joined by the rest of his crew (even though they'd probably heard him make that comment a million damn times).

"Anyway," Buggy droned, "we here to clarify a few thangs and address any issues that might need to be resolved. But before we start, in the spirit of harmony, I thank it's always a good idea to break bread."

As he finished speaking, Buggy gestured towards the minivan, and Mika saw a woman come traipsing down the wheelchair ramp. She was about twenty years old, with shoulder-length hair done in butterfly locs that framed an angelic face. She sported black spandex pants that showcased her finely-toned legs and ass, and also wore a crisscross halter top that showed more of her bosom than it concealed. Simply put, the bitch was fine as hell and fucking gorgeous to boot, and Mika was comfortable enough with her own appearance to admit it without feeling jealous. Needless to say, she turned the heads of just about every nigga present.

The girl carried a couple of large white paper bags that appeared to have some kind of symbol on them. A moment later the girl gave one of the bags to Mako, then handed the other to Kane. She then went sashaying back to the van, spurred on by a smack on the ass from a smiling Buggy. It was an overt reminder that Buggy only had an issue with his legs. His dick worked just fine.

Glancing at the bag, Kane saw that the symbol was a cartoon hen with a prurient look in her eye, and a phrase below her that read, "Pluck me, Big Boy." Based on the aroma coming from the bag, Kane assumed it contained fried chicken.

That assumption was proven to be fact when Mako opened his bag, saying, "Hot damn, Buggy! You got King Pluck?"

"Nothing but the best for my constituents," Buggy declared as Mako pulled a chicken leg from his bag and took a bite. Turning to Kane, Buggy asked, "You ever had it?"

Kane shook his head. "Naw."

"You gotta try it," Buggy told him. "It's the best damn chicken on the planet."

"Maybe later," Kane stated. He still didn't know how this situation was going to play out, and the last thing he needed was to suddenly be reaching for his piece with chicken grease all over his fucking fingers.

With that in mind, he handed the bag to Mika. She, in turn, gave it to Mikey, who put it on the hood of their SUV.

Still eating, Mako handed his own bag of chicken to one of his boys and then looked at Kane, saying, "I see you brought the big guns." As he finished speaking, he pointed with his chin towards Mikey, then added, "Where the rest of 'em at?"

Kane frowned in confusion. "The rest of who?"

"Yo crew," Mako explained as he finished the chicken he was eating and dropped the bone on the ground.

Still trying to figure out what Mako was talking about, Kane asked, "What crew?"

Mako didn't immediately answer. Holding his greasy fingers out in front of him, he glanced around for a moment as if looking for something. Thankfully, Buggy produced a paper napkin from somewhere and handed it to him.

"The crew you had wichu last night," Mako finally stated as he used the napkin to wipe his hands. "The ones that jumped my brutha and his boys."

Kane shook his head, perplexed. "I don't know whachu talkin' 'bout. I ain't have no crew. I mean, I had my girl with me" – he gestured towards Mika – "but that was it."

Mako just stared at Kane for a second with his mouth open. He then turned to Sway, who was next to him.

"Are you shittin' me?!" Mako shouted angrily at his brother. "You told me y'all got jumped by half a dozen niggas."

"Naw, um..." Sway began. "See, uh, what I said was—"

"Shut the fuck up," Mako ordered. "You got me out here lookin' like a complete asshole, brangin' a fuckin' army to a sit-down with one nigga."

"Yeah, but—" Sway began explaining.

"Didn't I tell you to shut the fuck up?" Mako ordered. "Go wait in the fuckin' car." Then, looking around at the rest of his crew, he added, "Matter of fact, *all* you muhfuckas go wait in the car."

Looking chastised, Sway began to head to one of the sport utility vehicles. Likewise, the rest of Mako's group went back to their respective rides. A minute later, Mako was the only one of his crew still outside.

"Look," Kane began, "my girl and I are fresh faces 'round here, and we ain't lookin' to make enemies. That bein' the case, we thought it made sense to bury the hatchet over the shit that happened in the O.G. Lounge. Now, I don't know whacho' brutha told you, but—"

"Hold up," Mako interjected. "This went down in the O.G. Lounge?"

"Yeah," Kane confirmed with a nod.

"Say no moe'," Mako told him. "I already know what happened."

Kane raised an eyebrow. "You do?"

"Yeah," Mako declared, nodding. "My lil' brutha got an affinity for that spot – like bein' in a room called the

'O.G Lounge' actually make you a fuckin' gangsta. He always tryin' to get that room when he go to the club, and if somebody in there he try to intimidate they ass into leavin'. I told 'im that shit would catch up to 'im, and I guess he know now that karma is a bitch."

There was silence for a moment, prompting Buggy to suggest, "So it sound like maybe we all cool here."

Kane didn't say anything. Instead, he merely looked at Mako, who appeared to contemplate for a moment then declared, "Yeah, we cool."

"Works for us," Kane stated.

At that point Mako stepped forward, extending a hand. Kane reached out and shook it.

"Hang tight for a sec," Mako said, then turned and walked towards one of the sport utility vehicles. Opening the rear door, he leaned inside for a moment.

Both Kane and Mika went tense, not knowing what the fuck was going on. Mikey's expression didn't change, but suddenly there was an automatic in his hand, held loosely at his side.

Now thinking that this might actually be some kind of set-up, Kane gave Buggy an intense look. On his part, Buggy shrugged in a *fuck-if-I-know* manner, making it clear that he didn't know what was going on either.

After a few seconds, Mako turned and began walking back. Thankfully, he kept his hands in full view, holding them in front of him. Mika saw that he was holding something in his right hand. It looked rectangular, but before she could make out what it was, Mako tossed it to Kane saying, "Here ya go."

Reaching out, Kane caught the object in one hand. It turned out to be a sheaf of bills – Benjamins – bound with a plain white currency band made of paper. Handwritten on the band was the amount "$5000."

"For ya trouble," Mako explained.

Kane simply nodded, understanding that Mako was going beyond just simple words and making an actual peace offering. Still wary, though, Kane handed the money to Mika. The cash could just be a distraction, and he didn't want to be staring at a stack of bills if Mako suddenly pulled out a gun.

But Mako just gave him a nod, told Buggy he'd catch him later, and then headed for his vehicle. A few moments later, he and his crew were on the move.

"And that's that," Buggy summed up as Mako's group drove away.

"Yeah – 'preciate ya help," Kane told him sincerely. At the same time, he reached into his pocket and pulled out a small wad of rolled-up money bound with a rubber band.

"Happy to help," Buggy said as Kane tossed him the cash.

Buggy then pulled the blanket down slightly from his waist, and Kane saw that he was wearing a waist pouch. (He also saw what looked like the handle of a gun under there.)

"Never figured you as the type to wear a fanny pack," Kane noted with a grin as Buggy unzipped the pouch and placed the cash inside.

"Fuck you," Buggy shot back as he zipped the pouch up. "It's a belt bag, you ignorant muhfucka."

Kane laughed as Buggy readjusted his blanket to cover the pouch.

Grinning as well, Buggy said, "A'ight, I'm outta here. Stay safe, my brutha."

"You, too," Kane told him.

With that, they parted ways, and a minute later the lot was empty, with no sign that they'd been there except a gnawed chicken bone and a greasy napkin getting buffeted by the wind.

# SHE'S HIS DRUG, HE'S HER THUG 4

## Chapter 15

The drive back to their apartment complex was uneventful. Once they arrived, Mikey was about to exit and head to his own vehicle when Kane stopped him.

"Hold on," Kane said just as Mikey was opening the rear door. Turning to Mika, he said, "Gimme that stack we just picked up."

Mika handed him the cash they had gotten from Mako, and Kane started flipping through the bills, counting.

Apparently understanding what Kane was about to do, Mikey suddenly said, "Don't worry 'bout it."

Kane turned around and gave him a curious look. "You sure?"

"Yeah," Mikey confirmed with a nod. "Yo girl already took care of me."

With that, he got out of the car. Kane watched him walk away for a moment, then turned to Mika.

"So what'd you give 'im?" Kane asked.

"A massive blowjob," Mika retorted, then burst out laughing at Kane's expression.

*******************************************

Once back in their apartment, Kane headed to their bedroom. Mika, who was carrying the bag of chicken Buggy had bought, tossed it onto the breakfast bar and followed him. Once there, she went to the bed and stretched out, while Kane walked to their closet. A moment later he pulled out a rolling duffel bag that they had used on their trip to Hawaii. He opened the bag and shifted some clothes around, ultimately revealing what he

# SHE'S HIS DRUG, HE'S HER THUG 4

was after: a small box safe that was both waterproof and fire resistant.

Kane took the safe out of the bag and set it on the floor. It was roughly one square foot in size and maybe six inches high. Pulling out his keys, Kane spent a moment searching for the right one and then inserted it into a keyhole on the safe.

Mika looked on as Kane opened the safe, although she already knew what was inside: a couple of pieces of jewelry and some important documents like their passports, but for the most part it contained wads of cash. Some of it was cylindrically rolled like the money Kane had given Buggy, while other stacks were folded over, and still more were just bills laid out flat. All, however, were bound with rubber bands. Moreover, the way they were bound was an indication of how much money each contained: the cylindrical rolls contained one thousand dollars, the folded stacks contained fifteen hundred, and the flat bills held two thousand.

This, of course, was their stash – a healthy chunk of cash that they kept on hand for emergencies. They had another lockbox that they kept under the bed, but it was a piece of shit made of thin metal, with a lock you could pop with a screwdriver.

In essence, the second box was a head fake; if anyone broke in, it was in a spot – under the bed – where it would easily be found. More to the point, if a would-be-thief opened it up, they'd see that it was full of cash. However, it was almost entirely loose singles with a couple of hundreds and twenties tossed on top to give the impression that it contained a lot of money. Basically, if a burglar came across it, they were likely to think they hit the motherlode and take off without ever finding the *real* stash, which was exactly what Mika and Kane wanted.

"You need any of this?" Kane asked, bringing Mika back to herself.

Understanding that he was talking about the cash, Mika shook her head. "Naw. I needed to pay Mikey, so I got some out earlier. And since you asked befoe', I gave 'im a thousand."

Kane simply nodded at that as he tossed the stack they had gotten from Mako into the safe. Of course, Mika had gotten out more than just the cash to pay Mikey, and Kane surely realized that.

Technically, the money in the safe was Kane's – part of what he kept when he split the cash they had between them. That said, he had given Mika her own key, showing how much he trusted her. In return, Mika tried not to take advantage of the situation, typically only getting enough bills to have an adequate amount of green on her person, and to pay for occasional expenses like Mikey.

Now with cash outlays on her mind, Mika asked, "You gave Buggy a thousand, too, right?"

"Yeah," Kane answered as he closed the safe and put in back in its hiding place.

"Did y'all agree to that befoe'-hand? I mean, he didn't even count it."

"I though you knew, but Buggy don't operate like that," Kane told her as he took the duffel bag back to the closet. "You pay him based on how you value his services. If it ain't enough, he won't say anythang. But the next time you need his ass for sommin' he won't be available."

"So you thank a thousand was enough?"

"To make a few calls, travel to and from a meet, and buy some fried bird? It fuckin' better be."

"Well, it *is* the best chicken on the planet," Mika noted with a snicker as Kane came back and stretched out on the bed beside her. "You want me to get you some?"

"I'm not really hungry for bird right now," he answered as he nuzzled her neck. "I think I'd rather eat *cat.*"

"Cat?" Mika mused, closing her eyes as Kane gently bit her neck.

"Yeah," he answered as he began kissing his way down her body. "*Pussy* cat."

# SHE'S HIS DRUG, HE'S HER THUG 4

## Chapter 16

The meeting with Mako marked the end of a somewhat leisurely period for Kane and Mika. Over the next two weeks, they stayed busy closing deals for Regis. It was mostly dispensaries, but a few growers as well, and their work caused them to occasionally interact with other people who worked for Bush.

Surprisingly, Mika appeared to have an intuitive knack for getting deals done. Whereas it might take Kane hours to convince someone to sell to Bush's organization, Mika could get an agreement in thirty minutes. Even muhfuckas who previously swore they'd never sell had a change of heart after talking to her. She was so good at it that eventually she took over negotiations.

On his part, Kane became more of a liaison and troubleshooter. For instance, one dispensary that they picked up had actually been paying protection to a local gang. Kane had paid the gang leader a visit, hoping to resolve the situation with diplomacy. However, when diplomatic relations broke down, Kane ended up breaking the nigga's arm (and by extension broke up his protection racket). It wasn't the ideal solution, but the end result was what mattered.

All in all, though, things were going smoothly. Regis wasn't the kind of nigga to hand out compliments, but he made it clear that Kane and Mika were doing good work. And since no good deed goes unpunished, that meant an increase in responsibility, which Regis bestowed on them one night via a message left on the untraceable cell Kane carried.

"I got sommin' new I need you to handle," Regis' message said. "I'll give you moe' details later, but for now just be on the lookout for a package that's headed yo way."

After listening to the message with Kane, Mika checked her watch and noted that it was a little after ten o'clock at night. The fact that they had missed the call was something she would have expected Regis to be pissed about, but he hadn't sounded upset.

Truth be told, she and Kane had been in the midst of an intense bout of fucking when the phone started to ring. Kane was on top of her at the time, making her practically scream in ecstasy with every stroke of his dick. Remembering the rule from Regis about always answering his call, he had initially started to get off her when Mika suddenly dug her nails in his back, making him yelp.

"Da fuck you thank *you* goin'?" she had demanded.

"The phone," Kane had replied. "It's Regis."

"I don't give a fuck if it's yo mama on her deathbed," Mika had declared, staring at him fiercely. "You don't pull outta *me*. Not *now*. Not *ever*."

She had continued staring into Kane's eyes, giving him a look that was almost frightening in its intensity until he gave a slight nod to show that he understood.

Only then had she seemed to relax, then said, "Now, finish fuckin' yo woman."

Mika smiled now reflecting back on it (especially the way Kane had complied with her last statement). She could be aggressive in the bedroom, but she'd never said anything quite like that before – to Kane or any other man – and it had been a little bit of a turn-on for them both. Thankfully, it wasn't looking like they'd have to deal with any fallout from Regis because of it.

"So, whachu thank this package is he sendin'?" Mika asked.

"Don't know," Kane said. "Right now, I'm just tryin' to figure out if it's comin' tonight or tomorrow."

"The message *was* a lil' vague," Mika noted.

"Prolly did that shit intentionally – keepin' details fuzzy 'cause we missed his call."

"Maybe, but I'm sure we'll find out soon enough," Mika stated.

**********************************************

Her statement turned out to be almost prophetic when, about ten minutes later, a knock sounded on their door. Gun in hand, Kane went to the door and put his eye to the peephole. He relaxed when he recognized the person outside – a nigga called Sledge who was on Bush's payroll. Kane swiftly unlocked the door and opened it.

Dismissing with any pleasantries, Sledge held out a black travel bag to Kane, saying, "Here ya go."

Kane took the bag, but before he could ask any questions Sledge began walking away. Kane watched him for a moment, then closed the door and locked it. When he turned around, he saw Mika standing just a few feet away with her piece in her hand, plainly ready to back him up if it had been necessary.

Kane carried the bag to the kitchen and set it on the breakfast bar, along with his gun. Next, with Mika looking over his shoulder, he unzipped it and took a look inside.

The bag filled to the brim with stacks of cash.

# SHE'S HIS DRUG, HE'S HER THUG 4

## Chapter 17

Seconds after seeing what the bag contained, Kane was calling Regis, who answered almost immediately.

"What the fuck's with this bag I just got?" Kane demanded without preamble, practically yelling into the cell, which had the speakerphone on. "What is this shit?"

"You fuckin' blind?" queried Regis on the other end of the line. "It's greenbacks, nigga."

"I can see that, but I told you I didn't wanna do any gangsta shit."

"Oh, you mean like breakin' a gang leader's arm? *That* kinda gangsta shit?"

Mika's eyebrows went up in surprise. She didn't think Regis had heard about that, but she should have known better. The nigga had eyes and ears everywhere. However, if Kane was surprised at how well-informed Regis was, it didn't show.

"Naw, muhfucka," Kane stated. "I'm talkin' about drugs. Part of the agreement when I came to work for you was that I work on the legit side of the house. That means I ain't in the illegal drug trade."

"And ain't nobody askin' you to do a damn thang with illegal drugs."

"Bullshit," Kane declared. "The only time you see this kind of money is when it's a fuckin' drug deal."

"Okay, nigga," Regis said. "I can see now that I need to educate yo ignorant ass. You been doin' shady drug deals for so long that the full range of *legitimate* transactions is outside yo field of view, so let me enlighten you."

"Unlike a few years ago," Regis continued, "cannabis is now legal in most states. The problem is that it's still illegal at the federal level."

"I know that," Kane stated. "But luckily the feds don't waste a lot of time tryin' to convict people on weed charges."

"True, but them fuckers still make it hard to do business – bankin', for instance. Banks can do business with cannabis companies, but there's so many regulatory hurdles to jump through that most of 'em just say 'Fuck it.' Even banks that will give you an account are still likely to pull some bullshit, like sayin' you can't do cannabis transactions on they network. So if you got a dispensary, you bettah not be using yo credit or debit card to pay yo supplier or any shit like that, cause they'll shut you down."

"I get it," Kane said. "Despite being legal, marijuana is still pretty much an all-cash business."

"Now you unnastand. And because of that, we sometimes gotta pay in cash when we make a big buy from somebody – like the guy you gone be takin' the cash to."

"What's *his* story?"

"Name's Augustus, and he's a major supplier of marijuana bud, concentrates and other cannabis shit. He tried the bankin' thang once, but the bank all-of-a-sudden decided they didn't want to deal with the regulations and told him he needed to move his cash 'cause they were closin' his account. Problem was, he had deposited millions, but the bank didn't have that much in any one branch, so he couldn't just go and withdraw it."

Kane nodded in understanding. "Most money is digital these days. Just about every dollah that people earn and use to buy shit with is on computer. Less than ten percent of the world's money is actually physical."

"That's right," Regis agreed, his tone making it clear that he was impressed with Kane's knowledge on the subject. "The bank expected Augustus to just transfer the cash electronically, but he had trouble findin' another financial institution that would take it. They had the same fuckin' attitude as the first bank about cannabis transactions. Eventually he was able to get his money, but after all that shit he was done with fuckin' banks, so any transactions with Augustus have to be in cash."

Kane pondered that for a second. "So if he ain't dealin' with banks, where he keepin' his money?"

"Damn, man, I should know that," Regis uttered acerbically, "'cause he regularly post on social media where he keeps millions of dollars in cash."

Kane rolled his eyes at the sarcasm in Regis' tone, then said, "Okay, so we just takin' cash to this Augustus muhfucka, and that's it?"

"Yeah," Regis confirmed, "except for a couple of minor details."

"Like what?"

"For starters, the buy is tomorrow."

"Not a whole lotta notice," Kane remarked.

"I guess that mean you gotta cancel yo mani-pedi."

Ignoring the jibe, Kane asked, "Anythang else?"

"Yeah – you also need to pick up this dude named Castor and take 'im wichu."

"Is he like backup or sommin'? Extra muscle in case shit hits the fan?"

"Fuck naw. Castor wouldn't know which end of a gun to point at a target, and prolly ain't got the stomach to pull a triggah."

"Then why the fuck is he taggin' along?" Kane asked irritably.

"Muhfucka, do *you* have a lot experience with premium weed? Know how to tell primo flower from absolute shit? Can look at bud and know if we gettin' it at a good price?"

Kane didn't respond. His prior experience was mostly with hard drugs – cocaine in particular – and Regis knew that.

Ergo, it came as no surprise when, after a few seconds of silence, Regis declared, "That's what I fuckin' thought."

"Fine," Kane growled. "So this muhfucka Castor is like the damn Einstein of cannabis. He there to make sure you gettin' the quality of shit you payin' for, and we just there to escort him and the cash, and make sure shit don't go off the rails."

"Pretty much," Regis agreed. "But to be clear, Augustus is a friendly. He been doin' business with Bush a long time and everybody trust each other, so I don't expect shit to pop off. And lastly, this ain't some shady deal for a couple of keys in a dark alley at two in the mornin'. This is a completely legit purchase of product."

"I still don't like it," Kane told him. "It's a lot of cash, and that attracts attention – even for legitimate businesses. Why the fuck you thank banks and armored trucks get robbed?"

Regis sighed. "You know, I figured you'd bitch 'bout this assignment, so I got a special gag to shut you the fuck up."

"Huh?" Kane muttered in confusion.

"There's a side pocket on the bag of cash," Regis told him. "Check it."

Kane looked at Mika, motioning for her to do as Regis said. She quickly unzipped the side pocket and reached inside. A second later, she withdrew a plain white envelope. Noting that it was unsealed, she peeked inside.

Then, looking at Kane with an astonished expression, she showed him the contents of the envelope: A thick bundle of hundred dollar bills.

"You got it?" Regis asked.

"Yeah," Kane told him.

"Cool," said Regis. "Now, that's a 'bitch bonus' – basically, a payoff so I don't have to listen to you bitch 'bout doin' yo fuckin' job. And now that you got it, I'm just gonna assume we all good. So have a good fuckin' night, and look for my text with the other details."

With that, Regis hung up.

## Chapter 18

After the phone call with Regis, Mika took the envelope of cash and put it in the safe in the closet. She then tried to drag Kane to bed, but he insisted on staying up in order to see the expected text from Regis as soon as it arrived.

"Don't wanna wake up in the mornin' and find a long-ass, complicated list of instructions," he'd told her. "You go on. I'll be in soon."

Thus, she had reluctantly gone to bed alone. Normally they slept in the nude, but without Kane next to her, the bed felt cold. That being the case, she slipped on a T-shirt and got under the covers. Kane's absence left a void – an emptiness that was almost tangible – but eventually she managed to fall asleep.

Kane came to bed maybe thirty minutes later. Mika woke up briefly as he slid under the sheets and snuggled up next to her. Drowsily, she turned on her side so he could spoon her, her mouth curving into a smile as he put his arm around her and drew her close. Still sleepy, she took his hand and slipped it under her T-shirt, guiding it up to her bosom. She didn't know exactly when it happened, but at some point she had grown accustomed to Kane cupping her tits at night. Then, with his hand comfortably in place, she drifted back off to sleep.

\*\*\*\*\*\*\*\*\*\*\*\*\*\*\*\*\*\*\*\*\*\*\*\*\*\*\*\*\*\*\*\*\*\*\*\*\*\*\*\*\*\*

Mika woke early, an hour or two before dawn, feeling a bit parched. That wasn't completely uncommon. If she and Kane worked up a serious sweat (like the night before), she'd sometimes get thirsty in the wee hours.

Lightly slipping out of bed so as not to wake Kane, she swiftly made her way to the kitchen. Once there, the automatic lights switched on. She grabbed a glass from the cabinet and got a quick drink of water. Then, her thirst slaked, she quickly went back to the bedroom.

She got back into bed, but didn't immediately get under the covers. Instead, she tuned towards a lamp that was on her nightstand. The lamp's brightness could be adjusted, so – after setting the illumination to "low" – she switched it on and then turned her attention to Kane.

He was still asleep, lying on his back but no longer under the covers. Under the soft glow of the lamp he looked incredibly serene, and for a moment Mika just stared at him. Simply put, she loved seeing him like this; just looking at his handsome face gave her an inexplicable peace of mind. However, as he was only wearing boxers, it wasn't long before her eyes wandered over the rest of his body: muscular arms, sculpted pecs, washboard abs…

Her gaze came to rest on his boxers. Through them, she could see that Kane had an erection; in fact, it pulsed as she watched, straining against his underwear. This wasn't unusual; Kane regularly got morning wood while sleeping – several times during the night, in fact.

Almost before she knew what she was doing, Mika reached down and began rubbing Kane's dick through his boxers. He moaned slightly, but didn't wake up. Emboldened, Mika reached into the boxers, gripping his dick directly. It was like holding a lead pipe, and she stroked it gently, careful not to disturb Kane's slumber.

Leaning close to Kane's ear, she whispered, "You want yo dick sucked? You know you do. You know you want me to deep-throat yo shit. Just say the word and I'll do it."

## SHE'S HIS DRUG, HE'S HER THUG 4

Once again, Kane moaned but didn't wake up. Taking that as her cue, Mika delicately pulled down his boxers while at the same time switching positions so that her head was at his groin. A moment later, his dick was in her mouth.

As always, she sucked and licked his cock dotingly. She loved giving oral, and got off on how much pleasure it gave her man. Only this time, although it was nice, it wasn't quite as enjoyable because Kane wasn't awake for her to see his reaction – to watch him shudder when she ran her tongue around the head; to feel him tremble when her mouth worked the shaft; to hear him gasp when she licked his balls. As a result, it turned out to be a rather short blowjob, but Mika wasn't done. Sucking Kane's dick had gotten her juices flowing, and she wasn't about to go back to sleep unfulfilled.

Swiftly, but gingerly, she straddled him, still taking care not to wake him up. Grabbing his dick with one hand, she waggled the head back and forth against her already-wet pussy, closing her eyes in delight at the sensation.

Leaning forward, she again put her mouth to his ear and declared in a silky whisper, "I'm gonna fuck you now."

She then dropped her hips, her pussy greedily swallowing his dick. The feeling as he penetrated her was damn near magical – a rapturous enchantment that seemed to pull Mika out of her body and send her soaring into the clouds. And as impossible as it seemed, the sensation grew more intense as she began methodically lifting and lowering her hips, sliding up and down Kane's pole. From there, her pace swiftly increased, and a short time later she was bouncing up and down on his dick like a basketball being dribbled at high speed.

Oddly enough, Kane didn't wake up, but Mika really didn't expect him to. This wasn't her first time mounting him in the middle of the night, and Kane seldom woke up – even with Mika riding his dick like a rodeo star. (That nigga was definitely a sound sleeper.)

Truth be told, she kind of liked the fact that he stayed conked out, because it allowed her to use that nigga like a human dildo. Basically, at times like this, Kane was nothing more than a sexual object to her – a fuck-toy. She didn't have to worry about pleasing *him*; the only reason he existed was to get her off. She could do whatever the fuck she wanted, and that was a complete turn-on for Mika.

So if she wanted to fuck hard and fast, with her pussy flying up and down his cock like a jackhammer, she could. If she wanted to go nice and slow, savoring how every rock-hard inch of dick felt as it went in and out of her snatch, that was cool. If she wanted to pull off a reverse cowgirl and ride that nigga into the sunset, no problem. It was all good.

In fact, it was so good at the present moment that Mika quickly found herself on the brink of a powerful orgasm. A moment later, she climaxed ferociously, cumming so hard that she had to bite down on her hand to keep from crying out.

## Chapter 19

Kane awakened early the next day, but Mika was already up. From what he could hear, she seemed to be banging around in the kitchen. He hurriedly showered and got dressed, then checked his text messages. There was nothing new, but he double-checked the message he had received from Regis before coming to bed. After confirming that he hadn't misread or misinterpreted anything the night before, he went to the kitchen, where he found Mika. Dressed in a low-cut shirt and jeans, she was humming to herself as she took a plate of pancakes out of the microwave.

"Those for me?" he asked, taking a seat at the breakfast bar.

Mika nodded as she placed the pancakes in front of him. "You might need to warm them up again. I tried to time it when I heard you in the shower, but you took a lil' longer than I expected."

"I was lookin' over the instructions from Regis again," he stated as Mika handed him a knife and fork, then placed a bottle of syrup in front of him.

"He say anythang special?"

"Not really," Kane answered as he poured syrup on his pancakes and began to eat. "We got a lil' bit of a road trip, though, so we'll need to leave soon."

"When?"

"Maybe ten minutes."

"Cool," Mika uttered with a nod. Turning her attention to Kane's food, she asked, "Pancakes okay?"

"Yeah," he told her. "And you were right: this frozen brand is just as good as made-from-scratch."

"Told you," she noted with a grin.

"Well, instead of gloatin', you might wanna eat so you don't get hungry on the road."

"I got sommin' earlier."

"I bet you *did*," Kane said in an impish tone.

Giving him an odd look, Mika blurted out, "What's *that* supposed to mean?"

Kane simply stared at her for a moment, then said, "You fucked me last night."

"And *you* fucked *me*," she shot back, giving him a wink. "So I guess we fucked each other."

"I'm not talkin' about when we were goin' at it like animals right before Regis called. I'm talkin' about in the middle of the night. You stole a fuck while I was sleepin'."

"Stole a fuck?" she repeated incredulously. "Nigga, you sound crazy. I don't even know what the hell that mean."

"It means you broke yourself off a piece while I was knocked out."

"What makes you say that?" she asked.

"'Cause of the way you actin'," Kane explained. "Some muhfuckas wake up, and they cranky 'til they get they mornin' coffee. You kinda the same – you can be a grouch if you don't get yo mornin' *dick*. But today, you walkin' round the kitchen practically whistlin'."

Mika snickered. "Okay, maybe I did get a lil' taste while you was sleep."

"If I was sleep then I couldn't give consent. That mean you assaulted me."

"Assault, my ass!" Mika growled. "We talked about this shit. I said it was okay for you to get yo fuck on even if I wasn't awake, and you told me I could do anythang I wanted to you when you was sleep."

"Not *any*thang," Kane countered. "I don't wanna wake up with a fuckin' gerbil shoved up my ass."

"Whatever," Mika said dismissively. "I didn't do anything that you wasn't okay with – unless you hate havin' yo dicked sucked, or gettin' yo brains fucked out."

"The point is, you got to cum and I didn't."

"Ohhhh," Mika droned. "Now I get it. This is some petty, tit-for-tat shit."

"You wouldn't callin' it petty if *you* was the one who didn't cum."

Mika appeared to ponder that for a moment, then said, "Okay, how 'bout I make it up to you later?"

"What's wrong with right now?"

"We ain't got time," Mika argued. "You just said we gotta get on the road in a few minutes."

Kane didn't respond. Instead, he just gave her a sad, puppy-dog look while sticking out his lower lip as if deeply disappointed.

"Fine," Mika muttered with a giggle as she pulled off her top. "You got two minutes to pound out a quickie."

# SHE'S HIS DRUG, HE'S HER THUG 4

## Chapter 20

It took a bit longer than two minutes, but that was mostly because of Mika. As Kane pounded her pussy like a piston working overtime, she swiftly got into it, ultimately begging him to make it last so she could get off as well. Kane complied, but later complained after they were finished that Mika was still "one up" on him. In the end, she had to sign a handwritten IOU stating that she owed him "one mind-blowing orgasm."

Afterwards, they took a quick shower, got dressed, and prepared to hit the road. With Kane carrying the bag of cash, they headed to a parking garage that adjoined their apartment complex. Each apartment resident had a designated parking spot, and Mika was headed for theirs when Kane stopped her.

"We not takin' our car," he told her.

"Oh?" she muttered in surprise. "So how we s'pose to get to this buy...walk there?"

"Not exactly," Kane answered.

He then began guiding her towards an area with parking spots for visiting guests. Once there, he pulled a key fob out of his pocket and pressed a button. Almost immediately, the front and rear lights flashed on an SUV that was parked in one of the visitor slots.

It as a late-model, high-end vehicle with darkly tinted windows. It also had shiny new tires, and a sleek, eye-catching design. Finally, the SUV not only sported an exquisitely detailed paint job, but the body was immaculate – not a scratch or dent in sight. All in all, it looked like it had just rolled off the factory floor.

"Nice," Mika noted in admiration as she headed to the front passenger side of the vehicle. "I'm guessin' this came courtesy of Regis?"

"Yeah," Kane replied as he went to the rear driver-side door. "Part of the instructions he sent mentioned takin' this as our ride. The key was in another pocket on the bag."

As he spoke, Kane slipped on a pair of thin driving gloves. Not that he didn't trust Regis, but he didn't like the notion of putting his prints all over some strange vehicle. At his direction, Mika did the same, donning some form-fitting gloves Kane had purchased for her. At that juncture, Kane opened the rear door and tossed the cash onto the back seat.

"Not that I'm complainin'," Mika noted as she got in, "but any particular reason why he want us in this?"

"I got a few suspicions," Kane told her as he briefly examined the rear door.

After a few seconds, he closed it and opened the driver's door. Once again, however, he spent a few moments eyeing the door panel and window. Mika, on the other hand, was ogling the inside of the vehicle, which had – among other things – a leather interior, captain seats, and a chic instrument panel with a natty touchscreen in the center.

"Damn, this is nice," she commented.

"Hmmm," Kane droned, still giving the door a once-over.

"Sommin' wrong?" Mika asked in concern.

Kane shook his head. "Naw, but do me a favor – ride in the back seat. We gotta go pick up this Castor guy now, and I'm a lil' worried about some muhfucka I don't know sittin' behind me next to a mill plus in cash. Nigga might start gettin' ideas."

"No problem," Mika assured him.

A moment later, she was in the back seat while Kane was in the front behind the wheel. As she watched, he pressed a button near the steering column twice. Almost immediately, she heard the engine softly come to life – so softly, in fact, that she could barely hear it.

"Oh shit," she muttered, plainly impressed. "How'd you do that?"

"It's a keyless ignition," Kane explained. "You just press *this* twice and it cranks up."

As he spoke, he pointed to the button he had pressed earlier. It was now lit up, and Mika saw that it had words written on it that spelled "Engine Start/Stop."

"When you ready to get out, you just put it again and the engine turns off," Kane continued.

"So it do everything without a key," Mika concluded.

"Well, you still need the key fob to unlock doors and set the alarm," Kane stated as he began pulling out of the visitor parking spot. "But as far as drivin' goes, no key necessary."

"Seems like that'll make it easy for niggas to steal this bitch."

Kane laughed as he started driving towards the garage exit. "The key fob need to be within, like, a hundred feet for it to work, so any dumbass who thank he can just press the button and drive off won't get far."

"Well, there go my plan to knock you upside the head and take off with the cash," Mika joked.

"Sorry, babe, but you stuck with me," Kane uttered with a grin as they left the garage and pulled into traffic.

"Or I could just take the key fob, drive off with the money, and leave yo ass sprawled in the dirt."

Kane appeared to contemplate that for a moment, then simply remarked, "Good point."

"Speaking of cash, though," Mika said, glancing at the bag on the seat next to her, "how much you thank in here?"

"It's about one-and-a-half mill," Kane stated.

"You counted it?"

"Not really," Kane responded. "I glanced through it and noticed that they all seemed like hundreds. Now, a million in Benjamins weigh roughly twenty-two pounds, and that bag is about twenty-five, thirty pounds."

"And that work out to about a million-and-a-half," Mika calculated. Then, after pondering for a few seconds, she asked, "So how you know how much a mill weigh?"

"'Cause I read," Kane declared matter-of-factly. "See, most people don't realize just how much money is in the drug game. You talkin' billions of dollars every year. Actually, *hundreds* of billion. Cartels make so much cash, they can't even count it – they gotta weight that shit to figure out how much money they got comin' in. So for a nigga like me, knowin' how much a mill weigh was basic info – like Drug-Dealin' one-oh-one."

"Interesting," Mika noted. "So what's Drug-Dealin' one-oh-two?"

"Don't trust sneaky bitches who fuck you while you sleepin'," he noted with a grin, "'cause all they care about is gettin' *theirs*."

## Chapter 21

The rest of the drive was primarily small talk, with Mika and Kane mostly discussing their new city's tourist attractions and the scenic spots they had yet to visit. (There was also a brief chat about the new watch Mika had given Kane as a surprise.) However, as they drew closer to their rendezvous with Castor, their demeanor grew more somber. In fact, noting that their destination seemed to be in a shopping district, Mika started to get concerned that they weren't in the right location.

"You sure this where we s'posed to pick him up?" Mika asked, looking around at various shops and the high volume of foot traffic. "This ain't a residential part of town."

"Regis didn't say we was pickin' 'im up at his house," Kane reminded her. "He just gave me an address, and the GPS say it's about a block ahead."

"Well, how we s'posed to know what this guy look like?"

As if in anticipation of the question, Kane already had his cell phone out and was pulling up photos.

"Here," he said, holding the phone up over his shoulder towards Mika. She took it, then looked at the pic Kane had pulled up.

The image was a headshot of a handsome White male, early to mid-forties in age. He had medium-length, wavy brown hair and a beard that was a little scruffy but well-maintained. His eyes were gray with a youthful twinkle, and he had what Mika would describe as a warm smile. All in all, his pic had a sort of vibrancy that made him seem open and congenial.

"He's actually kinda cute," Mika stated candidly. "Despite being old enough to be my daddy."

"He can always be yo *sugar* daddy," Kane joked.

"Already got one of those," Mika declared with a smile, then turned back to Castor's pic. "Hmmm. He kinda reminds me of those older male models you sometimes see on commercials for razors, or those dick pills they always hawkin'. I can just see him wearin' some name brand suit and a power tie."

"Well," Kane droned, "my guess is he's more likely to be sportin' a blue-and-gray plaid fedora with a scarf and a black peacoat."

"That obviously a lil' different than what I was thankin'," Mika said, looking at the pic again. "What makes you see 'im that way?"

"'Cause that's how I see 'im," Kane announced flatly. At the same time, he pointed to an area up ahead of them.

Looking where Kane indicated, Mika saw a White man in a blue-and-gray plaid fedora with a scarf and black peacoat standing near the curb. More importantly, he had a hand up, like he was trying to flag down a taxi; however, he was looking directly at the SUV Kane and Mika were in, plainly trying to get their attention.

Needless to say, it was Castor, easily identifiable because of his photo. Mika had thought that the hair or beard might be different – longer or shorter, depending on when the pic was taken – but Castor looked just like the image on the phone. The only difference was that he was currently smoking what looked like a joint, although it was practically gone.

Castor dropped his hand as Kane came to a halt right next to him. There was an audible click as Kane hit the "unlock" button, and a moment later the front passenger door opened.

Sticking his head inside, Castor scanned the interior for a moment, swiftly eyeing both Kane and Mika before turning his full attention to the former.

"Kane?" he inquired.

Nodding in response, Kane asked, "You Castor?"

"That's me," Castor told him. He then tossed the remainder of the joint he was smoking onto the sidewalk, then ground it under his foot before getting inside and closing the door.

"Nice to meetcha," Castor said, extending a hand towards Kane.

"Same," Kane stated, shaking the proffered hand.

Castor then turned towards the back seat, saying, "You must be Mika."

As he spoke, he offered his hand, which Mika shook. He then turned back towards the front and began putting on his seatbelt.

"Sorry we late," Kane apologized as he continued driving. "We got held up."

"Don't worry about it, man," Castor told him. "I ain't never been on time for shit in my life. If you'd actually arrived on the dot, I wouldn't have been out here."

"Oh?" muttered Kane curiously.

Castor nodded. "Yeah. That place you picked me up in front of was a dispensary, and I was in there buyin' some shit up until about a minute before you showed up."

"How you know who we was?" Mika asked.

"Got a text yesterday showin' a pic of the ride and the license plate," Castor said, "Also got your names."

Suddenly Mika felt foolish. Just like they'd gotten a pic of Castor and instructions, it made sense that he'd have been given info on them.

"Anyway," Castor continued, "I'm happy you were late. Otherwise, y'all would have been like, 'Ain't this a bitch. The Black people punctual, and the fuckin' Honkey on Cee-Pee time.'"

Castor had spoken the last sentence in a deep, gruff voice, and for a second Mika and Kane just looked at him – then they both burst out laughing.

"I'm glad y'all laughed," Castor said, "That joke don't always go over well – which sometimes leaves me in a fucked-up situation."

"Well, it did the job of breakin' the ice," Kane assured him, still grinning.

"Cool," Castor remarked. "And now that we all friends…" As he trailed off, he reached into the interior pocket of his jacket.

Suddenly, both Mika and Kane became somber and tense. Castor, apparently sensing the change in their demeanor, withdrew his hand slowly, revealing what he had been retrieving from his pocket: a black, cylindrical object about six inches long that vaguely resembled a colored marker.

Mika stared at it for a moment, thinking it looked familiar, then realized that it was a vape pen. She had seen enough of them while negotiating with dispensaries over the past few weeks that she should have recognized it immediately.

"You mind?" Castor asked as he waggled the vape pen, plainly inquiring whether it was okay to light up.

Kane shook his head. "Knock yourself out."

"Thanks," Castor told him, then turned towards the door panel on his side. He seemed to scan it for a moment, then growled, "Shit. I forgot what kind of car we're in."

"Huh?" muttered Mika. "Whatchu mean?"

"These windows don't roll down," Castor answered. "If I vape in here now, I'll fill this bad boy with smoke."

Frowning in confusion, Mika looked at the rear passenger doors and noticed that Castor seemed to be right. There were controls for the locks, but nothing for the windows.

Before she could ask what the fuck was going on with the SUV, Kane spoke.

"This thing's armored," he explained, "with bulletproof windows."

Mika took a moment to digest that, then said, "So the windows really don't roll down?"

"Having a window that rolls down kinda defeats the purpose of makin' 'em bulletproof," Kane replied. "But they do make some that will come down, for tossin' change into tollbooths and shit like that."

As Kane spoke, Mika found herself reflecting on his inspection of the SUV when they had first gotten in. She now had a good idea of what had drawn Kane's attention, but it also brought a question to mind.

Looking at Castor, she asked, "Are we expectin' trouble?"

He shook his head. "Naw. Believe it or not, bulletproof vehicles are standard in the weed industry – like armored trucks for banks – because it's mostly a cash business."

Glancing at the bag of money beside her, Castor's statement suddenly made a lot of sense to Mika. They might not be expecting trouble, but considering the amount of green they were hauling around, it didn't hurt to take precautions.

"Anyway," Castor continued, "since I can't vape, we're going with Plan B."

As he spoke, he place his vape pen back into the interior pocket of his peacoat. He then reached into one of the coat's side pockets and pulled out what looked like a small bag of candy.

"Cannabis-infused gummies," he explained as he opened the bag. He poured a few into his hand and then popped them into his mouth. "Want some?"

His question was directed at Kane as well as Mika, but Kane took the liberty of answering for them both.

"Not while we on the clock," he stated.

"Good," Castor remarked solemnly. "But don't get me wrong – I don't mind sharing. I just feel a lot better about us going to make a buy if I'm the only one that's stoned. I thought it would be rude, though, if I didn't even make the offer."

"Thanks," Kane told him sincerely. "We appreciate it, but we need to stay sharp."

"Understood," Castor commented. "And like I just said, I prefer it that way."

"So those candies really get you high?" Mika asked.

Castor nodded. "Yeah, but they don't operate the same as a joint. If you're *smoking* weed, you get high right away because it's immediately absorbed in the bloodstream. Cannabis concentrates are pretty fast, too. But with edibles like this" – he held up one of the gummies

— "they have to be digested first, so the high will hit you later, maybe forty-five minutes down the road."

"Damn," Mika muttered. "Sound like you really *are* the Einstein of weed."

Castor chuckled. "Is that what they call me?"

"That was *my* term for you," Kane answered.

"Well, I *do* know my shit," Castor confessed, "but I'm not credentialed or anything like that — unless you count a fucking minor in Plant Biology."

Mika found her curiosity piqued. "What was your *major*?"

"I got a bachelor's in Computer Science," Castor replied, "which I really ain't done shit with."

"So how come you know so much about dope?" Mika asked.

"You pick up a lot from just smoking, which I been doing since my teens," Castor said. "But most of what I know comes from my old man."

Mika had trouble hiding her surprise. "Your dad taught you about weed? Was he a dealer or sommin'?"

Castor laughed. "Not exactly. He's a researcher. He's got like a zillion pee-aitch-dees in shit like botany, horticulture, and so on."

"So *he's* the one in the family with the credentials," Kane noted.

"Yeah," Castor agreed. "To be honest, he's one of the top cannabis experts in the world, so we basically grew up with dope in the house. My dad didn't mind us using — actually showed us how — but he always stressed that, like everything else, you had to do it in moderation."

"Moderation?" Kane repeated. "So what that mean — only smokin' weed like once a day?"

"Fuck that," Castor shot back. "I'm high all day, every day – from sunup to sundown, and dusk 'til dawn. But it's not that manic, zonked-out-your-mind high like motherfuckers on coke. It's a nice mellow high that don't fuck up my thinking, or have me believing I'm bulletproof or can fly. It just keeps me in a good mood, and prevents aggravating shit from getting on my nerves."

"So it don't keep you from functionin' normally," Kane summed up. "It just help you stay relaxed and upbeat."

"Exactly," Castor agreed, "and that's what he meant by moderation. It's not necessarily about the *amount* that you take, but the *effect*."

"So if you can still function while high," Mika surmised, "that mean we can count of you if shit hit the fan?"

"Negatory," Castor stated, shaking his head. "I ain't even strapped. Plus, I'm the last motherfucker you want in a gunfight – my aim is for shit. I'm just as likely to shoot one of you as one of the bad guys."

"I think I heard sommin' along those lines," Kane chimed in.

"Well, whatever you heard, it was true," Castor stressed. "But look, like I said before, we shouldn't have any trouble. Augustus and his people are cool; they wouldn't fuck up a long-term arrangement with Bush by trying to rip him off."

"So I guess that mean they wouldn't try to sell him piss-poor weed," Kane stated.

"Nope," Castor confirmed. "Only the good stuff."

"So why are *you* here?" Kane asked.

"Good question, so let me explain," Castor said. "See, normally we already have purchase orders with

Augustus, so we just dump off the cash and then his people make delivery. But lately he been claiming he got some new strain of cannabis that's so good, it'll make you cum in your pants. And to whet our appetite, he's offering a taste at what he insists is a bargain price."

"So you here to inspect the new product and make sure he not bullshittin'," Mika concluded.

"It's not so much that he might be bullshitting," Castor countered. "We just might have a difference of opinion on how good it is or what it's worth."

That seemed to make sense to Mika. "Guess we'll see when we get there."

"Speaking of which," Castor droned, turning his attention to Kane. "You know where you going?"

"I think so," Kane answered. "I put the address in the GPS, and I scoped it out on a map app before we left home."

"Shit, man," Castor uttered. "You thorough as a motherfucker."

Kane shrugged. "I try to be."

"Good," Castor remarked. "Anyway, since you mapped it earlier you probably already know this, but we heading to a lil' rustic area maybe an hour outside the city. Augustus has one of his farms and a warehouse there."

"Farm?" Mika echoed. "You mean with horses, and cows and shit?"

"It's only for growing weed, so no barnyard animals," Castor said. "And actually, it's more of a plantation, so when we get out, I need y'all to start singing 'Swing Low, Sweet Chariot.'"

Mika and Kane simply stared at him for a moment, then all three began roaring in laughter.

# SHE'S HIS DRUG, HE'S HER THUG 4

## Chapter 22

The drive to the farm passed fairly quickly, mostly because of Castor. He had a lot of funny stories (many of which revolved around him getting high), and was a good conversationalist. Mika and Kane found that they both liked him a lot. He was witty, down-to-earth, and didn't take himself too seriously. More importantly, when they talked to him, it didn't feel like two Black people talking to a White guy. It just felt like three people discussing shit.

As Castor had stated, their destination was a rural area, which they reached by first taking a highway out of town and eventually exiting at a lonely country road. Initially they passed a few farms, but the farther they travelled, the fewer houses they saw.

Ultimately, they reached a point where the surrounding terrain became hilly. In fact, the road began to rise up a slope ahead of them in a zigzag pattern. It was at that point that Castor stated that they were getting close.

The ascent uphill was slightly steep, and the turns in the road were fairly sharp. That being the case, Kane drove at a leisurely pace. That gave Mika an opportunity to get a good look at their environs.

Plainly speaking, after a lifetime of cityscapes full of factories and high-rises, she had recently developed an appreciation for natural beauty. It had started with their trip to Hawaii, where she had found views of the mountains and ocean to be breathtaking. In a similar vein, the current vista, filled with rolling green hills, was picturesque in a way that was almost beyond words.

Just in case the ride with Castor had turned out to be boring, Mika had brought her computer tablet. Conversation during the drive had been lively enough that she hadn't needed it to entertain herself, but now she swiftly grabbed it and activated the video camera app. A moment later, she was filming the pastoral landscape around them through the passenger window on her side. It didn't turnout as nice as it would have if the window had been capable of being lowered, but she thought it captured the beauty of the countryside well enough.

Eventually, the road crested the top of the hill, at which point it resumed a straight course. It was then that, maybe a mile ahead of them, Kane and Mika noticed what looked like a large farmhouse and several other structures sitting on a couple of acres.

"There's our destination," Castor stated.

"That's a dope farm?" Mika inquired as they drove closer. "Don't look that big."

"This ain't where they grow the weed," Castor explained. "They've got a lot more acreage that they farm up in the hills. This is just where they conduct business and keep a lot of the farming and cultivating equipment, like bud trimmers, seed separators and so on. One of those buildings is also a refrigerated warehouse that's used for storage."

At that point, the road terminated in an expansive courtyard that was centrally located between the buildings they'd spotted earlier. It primarily appeared to serve as a parking lot, as there were about a dozen cars parked there.

Unsure of where to go, Kane drove to the center of the courtyard, facing the farmhouse (which was about a hundred feet away and much larger than he had anticipated – almost a mansion). Although he put the SUV in "Park," he didn't turn the engine off. Looking around, he saw maybe half a dozen people spread out ahead of them, positioned near the front of the farmhouse and a couple of other buildings. He also saw an eighteen-wheeler parked near what he assumed was the warehouse Castor had mentioned.

"That's interestin'," he remarked to no one in particular. "I wudda thought the road to get up here had too many sharp turns for a big rig."

"Huh?" muttered Castor, who had been looking out the windshield. "Oh, that was just the main road we came in on. There's other backroads behind some of the buildings that you can use to get here."

With that, he went back to staring ahead, frowning slightly. At the same time, the folks Kane had seen near the farm buildings began meandering towards them

"Alright, let's get this shit over with," Kane said, then turned to Mika. "Had me that bag, babe."

"Hold on," Castor urged unexpectedly. "Let's leave the cash for now."

Suddenly wary, Kane asked, "Sommin' wrong?"

"Not sure," Castor stated bluntly as the people from the farm continued walking towards them. "Usually I see at least one familiar face, but I don't know *any* of these motherfuckers."

"Is that a problem?" Mika inquired, watching as the farmhands stopped maybe twenty yards away, forming a spaced-out semi-circle ahead of the SUV. She also noted that a couple of them openly carried firearms, including a rifle and a shotgun.

"Maybe, maybe not," Castor admitted in response to her question. "But usually…" He trailed off for a moment, then said, "Okay, I see *one* face I recognize."

Following his gaze, Mika and Kane saw a woman coming from the farmhouse. She appeared to be in her mid-thirties, with jet-black hair that was currently tied into a long ponytail. She was accompanied by a man with a buzz-cut, who was maybe six-two in height and muscular.

"So we good?" asked Kane.

Castor rubbed his chin in thought. "I don't know. Her body language seems weird."

"Well, we ain't got time to figure it out," Kane told him. "So we either need to turn around and peel rubber, or get the fuck out and do this deal. But we can't keep sittin' here, 'cause it look suspicious as fuck, even if we *ain't* plannin' anythang dastardly."

Castor looked at him, then mentally seemed to flip a coin. "Well, we drove all the way out here. Might as well see it through."

Kane nodded, then spoke over his shoulder to Mika, saying, "Stay in the car. After we get out, slip into the front seat. But stay low and be ready to go."

Mika nodded. "Got it."

Looking at Castor, Kane said, "Let's do this."

# SHE'S HIS DRUG, HE'S HER THUG 4

## Chapter 23

Stepping out of the SUV, Kane and Castor walked towards the woman and man who had come from the farmhouse. Like the other farmhands, they had halted about twenty yards in front of the SUV and stood waiting as the two men approached.

As they drew near, Kane got a better look at the folks around them, starting with the woman. She was attractive, with beautiful features and flawless skin. She also had a classic hourglass figure, with an ample – but not oversized – bosom, and a nice round ass that you typically didn't find on White women. In her hand she held some greenery that he recognized as cannabis bud.

The man who had escorted her from the farmhouse stood next to her. He carried some type of carbine slung on his back and had an intense look on his face. He wore a light jacket that covered his shoulders and arms, but Kane noticed prison tats on his wrists and the back of his hands. He also noted a tattoo of a bright yellow bird on the dude's neck. You didn't have to be a genius to know that this muhfucka had been inside.

Likewise, each of the other farmhands around them – all male – gave Kane a similar impression. He didn't think they were all ex-cons, but he was convinced that none of them would have a problem skirting the law.

When they were a few feet from the woman, Castor greeted her, saying, "Raven – great to see you."

"Likewise," uttered Raven.

Castor started to spread his arms as if he intended to continue forward and hug her, but stopped short as she tossed something in his direction.

"There you go," she said as Castor snagged the object out the air. It was, of course, the cannabis she had been holding.

"I believe that's why you're here," she continued.

If Castor was bothered by the fact that she had short-circuited his attempt at an embrace, it didn't show. Instead, he just lifted the bud he had just caught and held it up, examining it from all angles.

"Not that you aren't a cutie," he stated as he looked over the cannabis, "but I thought I was supposed to be meeting with Shannon."

"She called in sick," Raven replied. "That time of the month, I guess."

"Too bad," Castor offered in sympathy. "I was going to ask her out."

"Maybe next time," Raven suggested as Castor put the bud up to his nose and in haled deeply a few times. Finally, he rolled it back and forth between his hands, and also felt it with his fingertips.

"Alright," Castor finally said. "The product's good. We'll take an initial shipment – same quantity as our regular load."

"Sounds good," Raven said, catching the bud as Castor tossed it back.

At that point, the guy next to her leaned over and whispered something in Raven's ear.

Frowning, Raven announced, "I got some stuff to take care of inside. Remo here" – she nodded towards the dude next to her – "will finish up with you."

Without waiting for a reply, Raven turned and began stalking back towards the farmhouse. Remo looked at one of the nearby farmhands – a gangly kid who appeared to be around twenty or so – and gestured towards

Raven. The kid went loping after her, plainly intent on escorting her inside.

"So what's going on with the big rig?" Castor asked, hooking a thumb towards the eighteen wheeler.

Looking in that direction, Kane saw a couple of workers loading crates into the back of the semi-trailer. Considering where they were, he assumed the crates contained cannabis.

"We just loadin' up to make some deliveries," Remo stated.

"Including ours?" quizzed Castor.

"That depends," Remo told him. "You got the money?"

"Of course not," Castor immediately shot back, almost like he'd been expecting the question. Kane, caught a little by surprise, struggled to keep his face expressionless.

"Huh?" muttered Remo in a gruff tone, clearly not liking the answer he'd received.

"Didn't they tell you how this worked?" Castor inquired. "We don't carry the cash with us; that would be stupid. We come in first and make sure the deal's aboveboard. If everything's kosher, we text the dudes with the money – who are waiting nearby – and give them a code phrase that let's them know it's cool to bring the money."

"So, are we cool?" Remo practically demanded.

"Yeah, we good," Castor assured.

"Then tell your people to bring the cash," Remo insisted.

"No problem," Castor assured him. Turning to Kane, he then tilted his head in the direction of their SUV, saying, "Come on."

"Whoa, whoa, whoa," uttered Remo, suddenly seeming suspicious. "Where you going?"

"To send the text," Castor replied matter-of-factly. "You expect us to type in a secret code right in front of you?"

Remo seemed to consider that for a moment, then send, "Okay, but why it take two of you to send a text?"

Castor gave him a hard stare. "Maybe you weren't listening, or maybe I didn't explain myself very well, but I said that *we* have to send a text. The operative word there is 'we.' Both of us have our own separate code that we need to text. It's like that fucking two-factor authentication you see on the internet these days. The motherfuckers with the cash need to hear from both of us, or they don't do shit."

Remo didn't seem to like that answer, but he reluctantly gave a curt nod, at which point Kane and Castor resumed walking back towards their SUV. Staying together, they headed towards the rear of the vehicle, walking on the passenger side. As they approached, Kane scanned the interior of their ride, happily noting that he couldn't see Mika. Assuming she had done as directed and gotten into the front seat, she was doing a good job of staying out of sight.

When they reached the back of the SUV, Castor pulled a cell phone from his pocket.

"We're in trouble," he said softly as he began tapping on his cell.

"Yeah," Kane agreed with a nod. "I figured that when you lied about us not havin' the money."

"It's a fucking setup. I'm texting Regis to let him know this shit's gone off the rails."

Suddenly remembering that he was supposed to be texting as well, Kane took out his own cell. He quickly tapped out a message to Mika:

*Setup. Be ready.*

Kane pretended to continue typing while surreptitiously glancing around. Remo had stayed in the same position, but his people had fanned out a little more, plainly in effort to keep Castor and Kane in sight. However, they could only go so far without it looking suspicious, for which Kane was grateful. Things would probably be different if they knew they'd already tipped their hand.

"So what's the plan?" asked Castor, who had continued faux typing as well.

"Now we get the hell outta here," Kane stated flatly. "Follow my lead."

Castor gave a short nod, and a moment later they began walking back towards Remo. However when they reached the passenger doors, Kane shouted, "Now!"

Kane, who had been walking slightly ahead, yanked open the front passenger door, while Castor opened the rear.

Almost immediately, Remo whipped the gun off his shoulder and opened fire, along with the rest of his people. Kane ducked as sharp metallic pings suddenly echoed all around him – the sound of bullets hitting their armored SUV. At the same time, he heard a number of crisp cracking noises as slugs hit the vehicle's windows.

He practically leaped inside as Mika, suddenly sitting up straight, put the SUV in 'drive' and slammed on the gas. The vehicle's engine operated so softly that Remo and his people had seemingly never realized that it had been running the entire time. Thus, they were caught a bit by surprise when it surged into motion – especially when they hadn't thought anyone was behind the wheel.

As they pulled away, Kane heard a distinct "Ooof" over the sound of gunfire. Glancing around, he realized that Castor wasn't in the car. As Mika cut the wheel, going into a sharp turn as she prepared to get them out of there, he saw Castor on the ground.

"Castor's down!" Kane yelled.

"Shit!" Mika shouted, but immediately slammed on the brakes, at the same time turning the steering wheel so abruptly that they practically spun around. She then hit the gas again, whipping them forward for a few seconds before bring the SUV to a hard stop next to Castor.

Kane leaped out, gun in hand and firing. Mika had positioned the SUV with the driver's side facing most of Remo's people (and therefore taking most of the gunfire). There were only two shooters with a good line of sight to the passenger side, and that's who Kane shot at as he exited the vehicle. He thought he hit one of them, while the other ducked for cover.

Knowing he only had a few seconds, Kane bent down towards Castor, who was huddled in a ball, covering his head with his arms.

"Move your ass!" Kane shouted, practically hauling Castor to his feet with one hand. It was then that he realized something was wrong: Castor had been shot.

Kane couldn't tell how badly he was injured, but there was no time to do a thorough inspection as the gunfire on their side of the vehicle started to pick up again. Continuing to return fire, he dragged Castor to the rear passenger door of the SUV and flung it open. He then practically threw Castor inside before diving in himself and slamming the door shut.

Mika didn't need any instructions after that. Once again, she slammed on the gas, peeling rubber as she headed out of the courtyard.

One of Remo's guys, holding some sort of assault rifle, dashed into the road in front of them, firing. However, he either underestimated the SUV's armor over overestimated the capabilities of his weapon, because the gunfire didn't have the intended effect. Or maybe he saw that there was a woman behind the wheel and assumed she'd be too squeamish to engage in violence. By the time he realized the error of his ways, it was too late. Mika ran him down at full speed, with the only indication of what happened being a slight bump as the wheels rolled over his body.

Moments later, they were speeding away, with the farm growing smaller in their rearview. Kane took a moment to buckle Castor in, who was starting to look pale. At a guess, Castor had taken at least one plug in the side and in his left leg. On the whole, though, he was lucky it wasn't worse, because when the SUV initially pulled away and left him, he'd been a sitting duck. The only thing that probably saved him was the fact that all the shooters had been focused on the vehicle and probably hadn't even noticed that he was down.

Buckling his own seat belt, Kane noted that they were coming to the point where the road sloped down. Knowing that the road curved sharply going forward, Mika slowed down as they began descending. However, seconds later she slammed on the brakes.

"Fuck!" she barked, at which point Kane look out the windshield and saw the problem: coming up the road, directly in their path, were a couple of pickup trucks. More to the point, the back of the trucks appeared to be overflowing with muhfuckas carrying guns – a few of whom suddenly leaped to the ground.

"Hang on," Mika ordered, turning the wheel and hitting the gas. A second later they were off the road, flying straight downhill at breakneck speed.

# SHE'S HIS DRUG, HE'S HER THUG 4

## Chapter 24

Later, Kane would say that the trip down the slope was a lot like riding an out-of-control rollercoaster.

Unlike a paved road, the terrain was completely uneven, causing the SUV to bounce up and down animatedly, like a paranoid kangaroo on crack. In fact, the rear of the car bounced so high on a few occasions that he thought they were going to flip over. (Truth be told, he found that scarier than when they went airborne, which actually happened a couple of times.)

As a result, Kane found himself flopping around wildly for the most part. However, he made a point of grabbing the bag of cash, shoving it on the floor, and pressing his feet down on top of it. Bearing in mind the way the SUV was moving, there was no way he could keep it completely grounded, but he could keep it from flying around the interior and perhaps injuring somebody.

He had to give Mika credit though; she fought like a muhfucka to keep the SUV as much under control as possible, and did an admirable job of it. That said, they still ended up sideswiping a tree by the rear passenger door at one point, and almost rammed a boulder a little later. However, they were definitely making good time. More importantly, it was highly unlikely that anyone would attempt to follow them using the same route.

While struggling to keep his elbows from getting cracked on the window or door panel, Kane spared a glance at Castor every now and then. Like Kane and Mika, he was getting tossed by the motion of the SUV. (The only time they weren't getting thrown around like rag dolls were the brief seconds when they occasionally crossed the road as it zigzagged uphill.) It wasn't clear that he was fully conscious, but Castor moaned painfully the entire time.

It seemed to take forever for them to get to the bottom of hill, but it was actually no more than a few minutes. Knowing that they'd be on the highway shortly, Kane felt relief washing over him – especially when Mika seemed to get more control over the vehicle and began slowing them down.

A moment later, however, they plowed into a tree.

## Chapter 25

When asked about it later, Mika would say that the SUV's front wheel hit a rock or something at a sharp angle. As a result, the steering wheel was jerked out of her hands. More significantly, the vehicle's direction changed, slanting towards a tree. (Ironically, the tree in question was only about five feet from the road.)

The sudden stop while having his seatbelt on caused Kane to be painfully jerked forward. He was already going to be black-and-blue just from the ride down the slope, but now the seatbelt was definitely going to leave a mark.

Checking the other passengers, he saw that Castor was still semi-conscious and moaning, with his clothes even more blood-soaked than before. However, he experienced a quick moment of panic when he saw Mika slumped over the steering while.

Throwing caution to the wind. Kane took his seatbelt off and threw the door open. Racing to the other side of the car, he flung open the driver's door and then carefully pushed Mika's shoulder's back until she was sitting up straight. She didn't have any obvious injuries, but – unlike the front passenger side – it looked like her fucking airbag hadn't deployed. As a result, she had seemingly hit her forehead on the steering wheel and been knocked out cold.

"Mika," Kane blurted out. "Mika."

He gently shook her shoulders as he called her name, but she didn't respond.

"Shit," Kane muttered.

Looking around, he didn't see any other cars in the vicinity, but he didn't know how long that would last.

Those muhfuckas in the trucks could already be on their way down the hill.

Bending down, Kane scooped Mika up in his arms. Dashing around to the passenger side of the vehicle, he opened the door and placed her inside, shoving the deployed airbag out of the way. Then, after buckling her seatbelt, he went back around to the driver's side and got in.

From what Kane had seen when he was outside, the tree they'd hit was midsized, not some full-grown forest giant. Ergo, although the SUV had uprooted it to a small extent, the vehicle itself hadn't suffered much in the way of damage aside from being slightly dented in the front. That, presumably, was a result of it being armored. However, mild damage didn't mean it wasn't fucked up in some way. In fact, just as he was getting in the driver's seat, he'd seen a stream of liquid start to run from under the engine compartment.

Thankfully, the SUV had never stopped running. Throwing it into reverse, Kane backed up; he then put the car into "drive," going around the tree and getting onto the road.

Minutes later, they were on the highway. At that point, Kane found himself facing the dilemma of what to do next. For starters, he had two people with him who were injured — one of them seriously — which meant medical care was a top priority. Next, although the SUV was currently running, it was making a lot of fucked-up sounds that were completely abnormal. Finally, the Regis phone was ringing. In fact, it had been ringing non-stop almost since the moment they'd gone bouncing down the hill. Kane had decided to forego answering it then, because if he had tried to talk at that juncture, with the way the SUV was bumping around, he probably would have bitten his tongue off.

Making a command decision, Kane ignored the Regis phone. Instead, he reached for his own phone and called Mr. Fix.

# SHE'S HIS DRUG, HE'S HER THUG 4

## Chapter 26

Back in their hometown, Kane had occasionally used the services of an old combat medic called Doc. It was a relationship that Kane had found enormously beneficial, because Doc had saved his life on more than one occasion. Ultimately, it had taught him the value of having someone on call who could deal with shit like gunshot trauma and knife wounds, without feeling the need to ask a bunch of questions (or call the cops).

It was with that in mind that he had previously asked Buggy to recommend someone in their current town with a similar skill set. Buggy had then introduced him to Mr. Fix.

Fix, of course, wasn't his real name. It was just the moniker he went by, because – as he put it – "Whatever medical problem you got, I can fix it." As to his story, Fix had apparently been a talented surgeon at one time, but at some point he got addicted to nose candy.

"I had a love affair with coke – no different than a lot of doctors," Fix had previously explained. "Except mine became a problem that spiraled out of control."

Eventually, he had lost his license to practice medicine. However, rather than hit rock bottom and stay there, Fix had gotten his shit together, managing to stay clean and sober for the past few years. The hope was to someday get his license back and return to practicing conventional medicine. In the meantime, he'd found a lucrative niche providing treatment for people who – for various reasons – couldn't go to a hospital.

All of that ran through Kane's mind as he dialed Fix's number. It was answered on the second ring.

"Hello," Fix said.

# SHE'S HIS DRUG, HE'S HER THUG 4

"Mr. Fix," Kane began, "You may not remember me, but my name's Kane. A mutual friend introduced us about—"

"I remember," Fix interjected. "You got an issue?"

"Yeah, and it's kind of an emergency."

"It usually is when people call me. Where are you?"

"I'm a lil' outside the city," Kane said, then gave his general location.

"Fuck," Fix muttered in exasperation. "It'll take me an hour to get to you."

Glancing at Castor through the rearview mirror, Kane stated, "I don't think I got an hour."

"Shit... You're not making this easy," Fix complained. "Alright, I got a colleague not too far from you. I can send you to them. They're not an em-dee, but they can take care of you until I get there."

"Wait a minute," Kane said. "They not a doctor?"

"No, but neither am I according to the state medical board," Fix responded. "So it's either them or nothing."

Kane sighed in exasperation. "Gimme the address."

# SHE'S HIS DRUG, HE'S HER THUG 4

## Chapter 27

Fix's colleague turned out to be a veterinarian named Annabelle Moreau. She was a bucktoothed blonde in her late thirties, who was a little on the short side in terms of height and also a little dumpy. According to a sign on the road that led to her clinic, she specialized in equines. That wasn't surprising, considering that her animal practice was located on some acreage that also doubled as a horse farm. However, as far as Kane was concerned, it didn't inspire confidence in her ability to treat *people*. The only benefit he could initially perceive came from the fact that she actually *was* close by. As a result, he was able to get to her practice within fifteen minutes of his call to Fix.

Fortunately, Annabelle was waiting at the door when they arrived, along with a twenty-something dude named Gavin that she introduced as her assistant. It was Gavin who took Castor from the SUV, throwing him over his shoulder and hustling him into the clinic while Kane carried Mika in.

Castor was obviously the more serious concern, but Kane had to give Annabelle credit for at least taking a moment to look Mika over.

"Mild concussion," she concluded after examining Mika's forehead (where a small bump had arisen) and checking her eyes.

She had then directed Kane to put Mika in a bed in a nearby room while she started working on Castor. After tucking Mika in, he hustled to what Annabelle had called the operating room. Castor was lying on a table with most of his bloody clothes off and tossed into a waste bin.

Annabelle, wearing a surgical mask and gloves, was in the process of withdrawing fluid from a vial into a syringe, while Gavin – also masked and gloved – appeared to be wiping away blood from Castor's body with some type of damp cloth. Annabelle momentarily glanced in Kane's direction before turning her attention back to the syringe.

"Do I need to leave?" Kane asked.

"Only if you can't stand the sight of blood and guts," she replied. "I gotta dig a couple of slugs out of your friend, and it's always a distraction when people start puking."

Kane smiled. "I think I'll be alright on that front."

Annabelle gave him an appraising glance, then nodded. "Yeah, I think you will."

"But to be clear, I was askin' more about the fact that I'm not wearing a mask or anythang."

"It should be alright," Annabelle assured him, "as long as you don't touch anything we use for surgery."

"Cool," Kane said. Then, motioning towards the syringe, he asked, "So what *is* that?"

"Anesthetic," Annabelle told him. "Your friend might have some complaints if I operate on him without it, although I typically only use this for pets. By the way, I don't think I got anyone's name."

"I'm Kane, that's Castor, and the girl is Mika."

"Well, nice to meet you Kane."

"You, too," he said sincerely as Annabelle put down the vial and stepped towards Castor. She then lifted one of his arms and inserted the syringe in a vein at his elbow.

"Not to tell you yo business," Kane remarked, "but I thought you couldn't give animal anesthesia to human beings."

"In some instances you can't," she confirmed. "But a lot of animal anesthetics are the same ones that are used for people, and I just gave him one of those."

As she finished speaking, she withdrew the syringe and placed it on a nearby counter. At that point, Gavin wheeled a tray over to her containing several scalpels, forceps, and a bunch of other surgical instruments.

"Okay, I'll give the anesthetic a minute to kick in," Annabelle stated, "then we'll start getting these bullets out. And for the record, digging a bullet out of a person isn't that different than getting it out of an animal."

"So noted," Kane replied.

"Now, I need to be honest about what might happen here," she told him. "Castor's lost a lot of blood, and he's in shock. Gavin's hooking him up for a transfusion, but I only got two units of O-negative blood here." She paused for a moment. "Do you understand about blood types?"

Kane nodded. "Yeah. People typically can only get transfusions from somebody with the same blood type. So if your type is A-positive, you need blood from somebody who's A-positive. But O-negative is a universal blood type. You can give it to anybody."

"Damn, that's pretty good," Annabelle noted. "Bet you got an 'A' in Biology."

"Actually, I got a 'C,'" Kane admitted. "But I been shot before and needed a transfusion, so I guess I learned some thangs from that."

As he spoke, he thought about Doc, who had treated his gunshot wounds before and essentially force-fed him knowledge about blood types.

"Anyway," Annabelle droned, "my point was that I only keep O-neg around for emergencies – like when somebody gets seriously hurt by an animal I'm treating, or something like that. Two units ain't a lot, so his odds ain't good from that point of view."

"Understood," Kane told her. "Just do your best."

"I always do," Annabelle informed him.

Kane didn't doubt it, and was about to comment to that effect when the Regis phone started ringing.

"Excuse me for a minute," he said, then left the operating room. Walking swiftly towards the clinic exit, he answered the phone with a solemn, "Hello."

"Da fuck you been?!" Regis demanded. "I been tryin' to reach yo monkey ass forever."

"I guess you could say I was gettin' shot at, tumblin' down a mountainside in an SUV, and slammin' into a tree," Kane replied as he stepped outside. "You know – just the usual fuckin' around."

Regis was silent for a moment, then asked, "Anybody hurt?"

"Looks like Mika might have a concussion. Castor caught some slugs."

"He gone make it?"

"Who the fuck knows? The vet's working on him now."

"Vet? You got a fuckin' veterinarian operatin' on 'im?"

"Well, the fuckin' Surgeon General wouldn't return my calls," Kane quipped. "So it was either a vet or me."

"Fine," Regis grumbled. "I guess beggars can't be choosers."

"Damn straight. But if it makes you feel any better, I got a medic on the way."

There was silence for a moment as Regis digested that before saying, "I didn't even ask, but *you* okay?"

"Fuck naw, I'm not okay. That asshole you called a 'friendly,' Augustus, set us up."

"Naw, it wasn't Augustus," Regis argued. "This was some other gang, showed up and caught his people with they pants down."

Kane mulled that over for a second. "So what was they plan – to make off with the cash from the buy?"

"That and a couple of million in weed," Regis replied. "Speaking of the cash, though, you still got it, right?"

"Yeah, it's in the SUV," Kane informed him. "By the way, you gone need a new one."

"A new *what?*" Regis demanded.

"Vehicle."

Regis didn't immediately respond, then he blurted out, "You wrecked the SUV?!"

"What da fuck, nigga?" Kane growled. "Were you not listenin' when I told you that bitch went tumblin' down a mountain? Plus there's blood all over the back seat where Castor was sittin'. So yeah, you need a new fuckin' ride. Correction: *we* need a new fuckin' ride, 'cause that one ain't quite road-worthy anymoe', which mean we stranded."

Regis seemed to ponder that for a moment before saying, "A'ight, here's what gone happen. I'm gone send a couple of guys to pick up the cash and get you a new ride. They'll be there in fifteen."

"Works for me," Kane said, although he'd barely gotten the words out before Regis hung up.

# SHE'S HIS DRUG, HE'S HER THUG 4

## Chapter 28

The guys Regis sent showed up right on time. Aside from a quick trip to check on Mika, Kane had waited inside by the window, watching for them as well as keeping an eye on the cash in the car. Surprisingly, he had practically forgotten about the money while Mika and Castor were being brought into the clinic. It wasn't until the conversation with Regis that he remembered just how much cash they'd been hauling around.

After speaking with Regis, he'd been tempted to bring the money into the clinic for safekeeping. However, even though Annabelle and Gavin were busy working on Castor, he didn't need them wandering out, seeing the bag, and suddenly getting curious about it. Thus, he had left it in the SUV and satisfied himself with keeping an eye on it. A short time later, he saw two vehicles coming down the road to the clinic.

As he suspected, one of the cars — a sedan — was driven by Sledge. The other was a black minivan with tinted windows, driven by a nigga he'd never seen before.

Heading out to the SUV, Kane opened the rear passenger door and took out the bag of cash. By that time, Sledge and the other nigga had exited their respective vehicles.

"This is Nugget," Sledge said, introducing the other guy as they both walked towards Kane.

Kane gave Nugget a what's-up nod, which he returned. Kane then handed the bag to Sledge, saying, "Careful — I think it's got blood on it."

Sledge just gave a short nod in understanding.

"Hey," said Nugget, getting Kane's attention. "Swap you."

Before Kane could ask what he meant, Nugget tossed something in his direction. Kane instinctively caught it, and upon looking at it realized that he was holding a key fob – presumably to the minivan. Knowing what was expected, he fished the fob for the SUV out of his pocket and pitched it to Nugget.

"Don't know if it still run," Kane told him.

"Let's find out," Nugget said in response, then headed to the driver's side of the SUV. He quickly got inside, and a moment the engine came to life, although not as softly as it had when Kane had started it that morning.

"Hang on a second," Kane said abruptly, heading to the SUV.

Going to the passenger side of the vehicle, he opened the front door and did a quick search, then did the same thing in the back. Surprisingly, his impromptu inspection yielded some dividends: he found Mika's gun on the floor on the front passenger side, and her computer tablet in between the seat and the center console.

"That's it," Kane said as he shut the door. A minute later, Sledge and Nugget were driving away from the clinic, with the SUV – driven by the latter – sounding even worse than it had when Kane and his companions had arrived.

## Chapter 29

Kane felt a little odd with two guns tucked into his waistband, so he placed Mika's piece in the glove compartment of the minivan (which, he happily noted, was also armored like the SUV). Afterwards he went into the clinic and wandered around for a minute until he found a bathroom. He then spent a few minutes looking himself over.

He'd known niggas who had gotten shot and not immediately realized it because their adrenaline levels were so high. But they felt it later, when their hormone levels returned to normal and the injury started hurting like a muhfucka. He didn't think he fell into that category; things had slowed down enough that he was sure he would have been feeling a gunshot wound by now.

A quick inspection proved that theory to be correct; he hadn't caught any slugs. However, he did have assorted bumps and bruises from the ride downhill, although none of them were debilitating. The most obvious ones were welts from the seatbelt – one that went from his shoulder to the opposite hip, and another across his waist. They weren't particularly painful at the moment, but he knew from experience that they would be ugly and discolored in a day or two.

The only other thing that drew his attention was some dried blood on his gloves. He hadn't noticed it before, but presumably it was from Castor. Fortunately, there didn't seem to be any on his clothes (or if there was, it wasn't particularly noticeable). After washing the blood off his gloves, he spent a few minutes thoroughly washing his hands, then went to check on Mika again.

# SHE'S HIS DRUG, HE'S HER THUG 4

She was still knocked out, but presumably that was a good thing. Annabelle hadn't stressed anything about keeping her awake, so Kane assumed it was okay to let her sleep. He still had her tablet with him, so he set it on a nearby nightstand and then flopped down in a chair next to the bed.

Mika looked so peaceful with her eyes closed that it was hard to imagine that she was indeed injured – especially since the bump on her forehead wasn't particularly noticeable. Kane gently took her hand and just held it.

By most measures they hadn't been together very long, but the relationship was incredibly deep and intense – probably because they had been through some serious shit together. Up until now, however, Kane had been the only one of the two ever injured. This time it was Mika, and even though her injuries weren't severe, it made Kane painfully aware of just how much she meant to him. It was difficult to believe that, just a few hours earlier, they had been fooling around at the crib. Clearly, their world had gone to hell in a handbasket in record time.

Unexpectedly, the Regis phone began ringing. Kane quickly exited the room so as not to disturb Mika, and then stepped outside the clinic.

"Yeah?" he said upon answering.

"Where you at?" asked Regis forcefully.

"Still at the vet's. What's up?"

"We just got hit."

"What?!" Kane exclaimed. "Where? By who?"

"Sledge and Nugget – not long after they picked up the cash from you. Needless to say, they got the money."

"Shit," Kane muttered. "We musta been followed."

"Maybe," Regis stated in a dubious tone.

## SHE'S HIS DRUG, HE'S HER THUG 4

"Well, what other explanation is there?" Kane asked.

"That this shit was an inside job."

Kane blinked as Regis' meaning sank in, then blurted out, "Da fuck you tryin' to say?"

"Let's thank about it," Regis said. "You there at the farm when shit goes haywire and some muhfuckas try to rip us off, and a lil' while later – right after I send some niggas to get the cash you holdin' – *they* get ripped off. The optics on that shit don't look good for you."

"That don't make any fuckin' sense. I just got the instructions 'bout this damn buy from you last night. When the hell I have time to engineer not just one, but two licks?"

"That's what some muhfuckas in the organization wanna discuss wichu, 'cept they don't wanna do it over the phone. They wanna do it in a basement, assisted by some hammers, pliers, and other shit you only see in horror movies."

"That's a muhfuckin' joke, right? They seriously think I had time to set all this shit up?"

"An enterprisin' muhfucka could figure sommin' out, and let's be honest: you smarter than most."

Kane closed his eyes and shook his head in disbelief. "Un-fuckin'-believable…"

"Hey, if it's worth anythang, I'm on yo side and–"

"That ain't worth shit," Kane angrily interjected.

"Well, if I could finish," Regis uttered testily. "I was gonna say that I'm on yo side and I'll do what I can, but the end result gonna be the same unless you find the muhfuckas behind this shit."

"Unless *I* find 'em?" Kane muttered, perplexed.

"Yeah, nigga. Didn't I make it clear? This *yo* fuckin' problem, so you gotta find the solution, which in this case means figurin' out who masterminded this shit."

"And how I'm s'posed to do that?"

"Non-linear thinkin', muhfucka. Isn't that what you told me yo specialty was? That you can solve problems other niggas can't?"

Kane was silent for a moment, then asked, "How much time can you get me?"

"I can buy you about a day."

"That ain't shit," Kane shot back in exasperation. "Right now, I ain't even got a startin' point."

"Check with Augustus and his people at the farm. They got a lead, and they already expectin' you."

There was silence for a moment, as if Regis was going to say something else, but then he simply hung up. However, Kane already knew what it was that Regis was on the verge of saying before he got off the phone: *Don't fuck this up.*

# SHE'S HIS DRUG, HE'S HER THUG 4

## Chapter 30

Kane left the clinic almost immediately. He only stuck around long enough to kiss Mika on the forehead, and to let Annabelle know he had to run an errand. Annabelle, who was busy working on Castor at the time, merely grunted something in response that Kane didn't really catch.

It didn't take him long to reach the farm, even though he made one stop along the way – pulling into a service station, where he bought a new pair of gloves. The old pair was still damp from when he cleaned the blood from them and felt clammy on his hands. Ergo, he tossed them under the driver's seat and put the new ones on.

When he finally arrived at the farm, the place was bustling with activity. However, there were a few changes in effect that were in stark contrast to his earlier visit. For starters, there were now horse barriers – as well as a couple of guys with guns – blocking the winding road up the hill. Thankfully, Kane was expected and didn't encounter any issues.

When he reached the courtyard, however, he saw something that surprised him: the two trucks they had noticed when fleeing the farm. It hit him then that the trucks hadn't been full of more bad guys; it was Augustus' people, presumably on their way to the farm because they somehow knew something was wrong.

At the moment, however, there was no one in the back of the trucks. However, the farm was a hive of activity, with swarms of people swiftly rushing back and forth (which was unsurprising given what had happened earlier).

A few people eyed Kane warily as he parked and got out, but he'd barely shut the door before he was approached by some dude who obviously fancied himself a *vaquero* because his attire included a Stetson hat, cowboy boots, and a belt buckle the size of a tire rim.

"You Bush's man?" he asked, to which Kane simply nodded. "They're waiting for you inside."

As he finished speaking, the cowboy pointed with his chin towards the farmhouse. Kane thanked him and headed in that direction.

The door was open when Kane reached it – in fact, someone was just coming out. He quietly slipped in and closed the door behind him.

Looking around, he noted that he was in a foyer that opened up into an expansive living room. Similar to outside, the farmhouse was full of people. However, the folks inside were moving with purpose – following the orders being barked out by a tall, wiry man in the center of the room.

To Kane, he appeared to be in his sixties, with a full white beard and wavy, gray locks of hair that hung almost to his shoulders. That said, he had a voice that was full of strength and vigor, and he projected a rugged masculinity that put Kane in mind of a nineteenth century explorer or mountain man. In short, anyone who took the color of his hair and beard as an indicator of feebleness would soon find out they were greatly mistaken. This, Kane assumed, was Augustus.

"And get on the horn to Maxwell," Augustus was saying to someone, "and tell him…" He trailed off as his gaze suddenly fell on Kane.

"Who the fuck are you?" Augustus demanded.

In reply, Kane simply said, "Kane."

Still staring at him, Augustus shook his head while simultaneously spreading his arms out, a composite gesture that seemed to ask *Am-I-supposed-to-recognize-that?* as well as declare *That-name-don't-mean-shit-to-me.*

Before Kane could expound, a feminine voice said, "This is Bush's guy."

Looking towards the speaker, Kane saw that it was Raven – the dark-haired beauty Castor had spoken with earlier.

"It's about fuckin' time," Augustus said. "I lost three of my people today, and had a dozen more get shot up. I don't appreciate having to wait before I deal with the shitbirds that did it."

"Got here as fast as I could," Kane countered. "But it sounds like you got a lead."

"We think we know who did it," Raven chimed in. "That guy Remo who was with me this morning was one of the assholes who tried to jack us. You might have missed it, but he had a tattoo on his neck."

"I saw it," Kane told her. "A yellow bird."

"A canary," Raven clarified. "It's the symbol of a biker gang we sometimes deal with."

"So that's who did this?" Kane inquired.

"Yeah, that's who it was," proclaimed an unfamiliar voice. "So let's go get these assholes."

Kane looked at the speaker, who turned out to be a kid maybe sixteen years old with a bronze complexion, fierce blue eyes, and a mop of curly, reddish-brown hair. Looking angry, he had one leg wrapped in gauze and was holding himself up with a pair of crutches.

Augustus let out a sigh. "Otto, what are you doing up?"

"I'm fine, Gus," argued the kid, Otto.

"No, you're not," Gus insisted. "You got shot."

"Only in the leg," Otto countered

Augustus looked as though he had more to say, then simply shook his head in exasperation, saying, "Fine. Just sit down somewhere and keep that leg elevated."

Otto capitulated with a nod, at which point Augustus turned back to Kane.

"Where were we?" he asked.

"You guys were tellin' me about some biker gang," Kane reminded him.

"Right – the Canaries," Augustus said. "We do business with them sometimes. They're thieving assholes, but this isn't the type of shit they normally pull. Not with *us*, anyway."

"Got it," Kane remarked. "But it's still prolly worth payin' 'em a visit."

"Agreed," noted Augustus. "We been chomping at the bit to go chat with these motherfuckers, but your boss wanted you included, so we waited."

"Well, I'm ready," said Kane. "Just point out which guys you want comin' with me, and we can roll."

"Fuck that," Augustus blurted out. "Take Raven."

"Raven?" Kane repeated, not bothering to hide his surprise.

"Yeah," Augustus confirmed. "That way I can be sure that there won't be any fuck-ups."

## Chapter 31

They didn't leave immediately. Instead, after slipping on a mid-length, hooded jacket, Raven led Kane to a locked room at the back of the farmhouse. Digging a keyring out of her pocket, she unlocked the door and went inside. Kane followed, and found himself surprised by what he saw when Raven turned the light on: the room was lined almost wall-to-wall with nothing but gun cabinets, all of which were filled with guns.

Most of the cabinets were wooden with glass doors or windows, through which Kane could see the weapons. Just glancing around, he saw rifles in one cabinet, shotguns in another. There were also semi-automatic handguns, revolvers, sub-machine guns and more. Frankly speaking, Kane wasn't sure he'd ever seen that many firearms in one place outside a gun shop, let alone the variety.

In addition to the wooden cabinets, there were also a few all-metal gun safes in the room. Raven went to one that was about six feet tall and three feet wide, then used one of the keys she carried to open it. It had twin doors on the front which she swung open, revealing a treasure trove of weaponry.

The interior of the left door had modular panels that had been configured to hold an assortment of handguns, as well as gun magazines that were full of ammo. The panels on the right door held what looked like an assortment of riot gear, including a bulletproof vest, goggles, and helmet. The back of the safe consisted of gun racks that held about a dozen long guns, including rifles and shotguns. Finally, there was a compartment below the long guns that held half-a-dozen military ammo boxes.

Noticing Kane's attention, Raven simply gestured towards the gun safe saying, "My personal armory."

Following this, Raven began going through the process of thoroughly arming herself, starting with an automatic that she took from the left door. After inserting a full magazine into it, she tucked the weapon into the waistband of the cargo pants she wore, at the small of her back. Next, she strapped on an ankle holster down by her foot, then grabbed another gun; after loading a magazine into it, she inserted it into the holster and strapped it down. After rolling the leg of her pants down over it, you couldn't really tell anything was there. Finally, she retrieved a diminutive automatic that was so tiny that – under other circumstances – Kane would have mistaken it for a toy.

"Is that thang real?" he asked.

Raven smiled. "You bet your sweet ass it's real."

As she spoke, she held it out to him. Kane took the weapon and looked it over. It was unloaded, but a cursory inspection revealed it to be a fully functional firearm, despite the fact that the barrel was only about five inches long.

"This some kind of pocket pistol?" he asked.

Raven nodded. "Yeah. It's the kind they call a mouse gun. Some people laugh at them because they think they lack stopping power, but they'll get the job done. Plus, you can pretty much carry it around in a pocket without anyone really noticing."

As she finished speaking, Kane – who at present was not wearing his gloves – used his shirt to wipe the gun down before gingerly handing it back to Raven. As she took the weapon she gave him a lingering look, plainly impressed that he'd had the presence of mind to clean off any evidence that he'd touched it. For Kane, however, that was a basic precaution, because the last thing he needed was his prints on some strange firearm.

"Well, don't be shy," Raven told him as she slid a magazine into the mouse gun before putting it into a side pocket of her cargo pants. "Help yourself to whatever you need."

"I'm good," Kane assured her.

Raven seemed to consider that for a moment, then inquired, "So what are you packing?"

Rather than respond verbally, Kane reached behind him and pulled out his piece, which he then offered to Raven.

"Nice," she declared approvingly as she gave it a once-over. Putting her nose to the barrel, she sniffed and then said, "Recently fired."

"I had a lil' trouble earlier today," Kane told her sardonically.

"How many rounds you get off?"

Kane shrugged. "Six or seven."

"Then you're low," she surmised before wiping the gun off and handing it back. She then reached for a couple of full magazines from the gun safe and handed them to him, saying "Here."

Kane didn't protest, taking the magazines and slipping them into his jacket pocket. He had rarely needed more than one magazine in the past, so he generally didn't carry extra ones on him. That said, he wasn't about to look a gift horse in the mouth.

Next, he watched as Raven took a gun range bag from her armory, unzipped the center compartment, and placed it on the floor. Into it she placed a couple of short-barreled rifles and a sawed-off shotgun, swiftly checking each weapon before stowing it in the bag.

"This gang gonna be that much trouble?" Kane asked as Raven placed an ammo belt full of shotgun shells into the bag and closed the center compartment.

"Don't know," Raven confessed as she unzipped a side compartment that ran the length of the bag, revealing a half-dozen magazine slots. "But if we end up in the shit, ain't nobody going to let us call a timeout and do a gun substitution. Better to be prepared."

She continued packing as she talked, placing full magazines into the slots and then closing the bag up. Seemingly satisfied, she grabbed the bag and slung it over her shoulder.

"Okay," she said as she closed and locked the gun safe. "Let's roll."

# SHE'S HIS DRUG, HE'S HER THUG 4

## Chapter 32

They left in the minivan, with Kane driving in accordance to directions from Raven. There was still quite a bit of hustle and bustle going on as they left, and Kane commented on it.

'Well, it's not like this shit happens every day," Raven told him. "Plus, we still have to carry on with business as usual."

"If you don't mind me askin'," Kane said, "how'd they get the drop on you? I mean, based on that gun room, you guys seem pretty well-armed."

"We were shorthanded today. Normally we'd have barriers up and a couple of folks stationed on the road to control access, but we had a lot of deliveries so we pulled some guys for that."

"Is that common?"

"It's not *un*common. And it was only going to be for a few hours."

"So what happened?"

"Well, with no barriers or guards to stop them, they just drove straight up to the farmhouse. Nobody there was suspicious because we actually were expecting people."

"Us," Kane realized.

"Yeah," Raven said with a nod. "Long story short, they caught the folks in the farmhouse a little flatfooted. They just thought it was you guys showing up a bit early. If I had been there I would have realized something was off, because Castor is never on time for shit, but I was out in the fields at the time."

"But there's a room full of guns in that place. Even caught with their pants down, seems like they shudda been able to mount some sorta defense."

"That room generally stays locked, but as you can tell from what happened today, you need firearms in this business. So we issue guns to our people from there when they start work and they turn them in when they leave, but the room's not just sitting open all the time."

"Don't trust your people?" Kane queried.

"In general, we do," Raven replied. "But there's a small fortune in firearms in there, and sooner or later, shit would undoubtedly start disappearing."

Kane nodded. "I get it. It's like when muhfuckas start working in an office buildin'. They generally trustworthy, but three months later if you go by they house, you'll find pens, staplers, sticky notes, and a bunch of other shit from the workplace."

"Exactly," Raven concurred. "Anyway, we use walkies to communicate on the farm, with the farmhouse serving as Comm Central. This morning started out as just a normal fucking day, then suddenly everybody out in the field gets a message saying there's a fire at the warehouse."

"Let me guess: that's an 'all hands' situation."

"Abso-fucking-lutely. Losing our product in a fire would be like burning millions in cash. We all came racing back."

"And that's when the thieves managed to get the rest of you."

"Yes and no," Raven said. "I can't speak for anybody else, but by the time I got back to the farm, I could tell something wasn't right."

"How's that?"

"For one thing, a fire in the warehouse meant I should have been able to smell weed burning from a mile away. I couldn't smell shit. On top of that, there wasn't nearly as much smoke as there should have been. I mean, there was a small plume of it, but turns out that was just from a barrel that the motherfucking thieves had lit."

"So what did you do?"

"I was trying to come up with a plan when that shithead Remo got on the comm and announced it was a stick-up – said that the rest of us who'd been in the fields had two minutes to give up or they'd start killing to people. And to show he wasn't bluffing, he shot one of the folks from the farmhouse."

"But if he was on the comm, how you know he actually did it?"

"Because he put Otto on and made him tell us what he'd done."

"Otto?" Kane repeated. "The kid?"

"Yeah," Raven confirmed, her eyes narrowing in anger. "And he said Otto was next."

"So you surrendered."

"Yeah…didn't have much choice."

"Okay, I get that, but couldn't you have called for help on a cell or something before you surrendered?"

"We don't allow cell phones. I mean, I've got one on me now, but they're not allowed when you're working the farm."

Kane gave her an incredulous look. "Seriously?"

"Dead serious," she told him. "It's a firing offense."

Damn," Kane muttered. "Seems a lil' heavy-handed."

"Look, we hiring these motherfuckers to do a job. In some cases, we're charging two, three thousand bucks a pound for our product. With that kind of money on the line, you want your staff out there paying attention to the crops, making sure everything is running like clockwork. A cell phone is a fucking distraction."

"It's like when they started putting computers in the workplace," she continued. "It was supposed to make workers more efficient, but they just used it for recreation – started spending all their fucking time playing solitaire and surfing the internet. A cell phone is fucking worse, because it's mobile, so if a motherfucker has one, he's always itching to use it…constantly checking social media to see who commented on his last post, or streaming music, or watching toothless drunks fight. And in the meantime, fucking boll weevils have destroyed a season worth of crops."

"Uh, boll weevils eat cotton," Kane offered.

"Fuck you, Poindexter," Raven muttered, making Kane laugh. "*I'm* telling this. But if it'll make you feel better, let's say it's aphids instead of boll weevils."

"My mistake," Kane said, still grinning. "Please continue."

"Anyway, that's the explanation as to why we have walkies and not cell phones out in the fields. Technically though, they're two-way radios, so the channel is private and communications are encrypted. And as to the rest of the story, there's not a whole lot more to tell. They kept a couple of us in the farmhouse – they needed us in case Augustus or somebody tried to reach the farm – and the rest they held hostage in the warehouse."

"How many of them were there?"

"Not counting Remo, there were six outside when you guys showed up, one in the farmhouse, and two in the warehouse."

Kane quickly did the math. "Ten."

# SHE'S HIS DRUG, HE'S HER THUG 4

"Yeah," Raven affirmed. "But after they had control of the farm it was just a matter of waiting for you guys to show up, and you pretty much know the rest."

"I know the rest from *our* side," Kane corrected. "Don't know much about things from *yo* point of view."

"That's easy enough," Raven said. "You probably remember that Remo pretty much dismissed me – sent me back to farmhouse with some gawky kid who was probably fresh out of puberty. Well, he seemed pliable, so I baited him."

"How?"

"I offered to fuck him," she said flatly. "He had 'virgin' written all over him, so as we walked back I told him he could have a taste if he promised to let me live."

Kane raised an eyebrow. "And he bought that?"

"Like I said, he was an obvious virgin," Raven stated. "Pimply-faced, socially awkward and all that shit. That meant he probably thought about pussy all the time. And then I told him how jealous his friends would be when he told them he banged some country girl against the wall of a farmhouse. At that point, he was hooked."

"So then what happened?"

"I led him around to the back of the farmhouse, lifted my shirt, and let him see my tits. His eyes damn popped out his skull. Then I started playing with my girls – squeezing them, pinching my nipples. I even took off my belt and smacked myself on the ass with a few times, gasping all seductively and shit. The kid was so fascinated, he seemed to forget that he was back there to get some pussy. Of course, all of that was just me playing for time, waiting for the gunfire to start."

"Gunfire?" Kane echoed, frowning.

"Yeah," Raven told him. "See Remo and his fellow assholes didn't wear any masks or try to hide their faces. They didn't seem to care about people being able to identify them later, which only meant one thing."

"They planned to kill everybody," Kane concluded.

"Bingo," Raven declared. "And 'everybody' included you and Castor, so after I got escorted away from you two, I knew that gunplay was going to break out soon."

"Meaning you knew they was gonna try to shoot us."

Raven nodded. "And when it started I was ready."

"What did you do?"

"The sound of gunshots seemed to break the spell my tits had cast on the kid watching me. He jerked his head in the direction of the noise, and that was my opening. I stabbed him in the jugular with my belt prong."

Kane simply stared at her a moment, looking astonished.

"What?" Raven queried. "Too cold-blooded?"

"No," Kane admitted, turning his eyes back to the road. "Just pretty fuckin' calculated, usin' an ambush on me and Castor as part of your escape plan."

"Well, I dropped you motherfuckers a hint," she argued. "Remember when Castor asked about Shannon and I said she was on her period?" Kane nodded, at which point Raven continued, saying, "Well, Shannon's actually a man, so Castor should have known something was up."

"Well, he picked on the fact that it was a setup, but I thought it had sommin' to do with the big rig."

Raven frowned. "The eighteen-wheeler? What about it?"

"It looked like some folks were loadin' weed on it. Castor asked if the dope was for us, and Remo said it was. Right after that is when Castor told me it was a setup."

"Yeah, that would have been a tipoff," Raven stated.

"In what way?"

"Cannabis is legal in most states, but still criminal at the federal level," Raven explained, reminding Kane of something Regis had previously said. "Trucks over a certain weight – something like ten thousand pounds, I think – are regulated by the Department of Transportation. Because the dee-oh-tee is a federal organization, it applies federal laws to trucking. So those federal laws that criminalize cannabis make it illegal to transport weed in a big rig. Castor knows that."

"So how you transport it, then?"

"Believe it or not, mostly in vans like this," Raven replied, making a gesture to encompass the vehicle they were in. "Usually armored the same way this one is, but below the dee-oh-tee weight threshold."

"Damn," Kane muttered. "There's a lot more to this weed business than I thought."

"So you're new to this," Raven noted. "What were you doing before?"

Kane contemplated for a moment on how to respond. He didn't relish talking about his past – especially with someone he'd essentially just met – but he liked Raven. She seemed down-to-earth, and reminded him of Mika to a certain extent.

"I was dealing with powder," he finally confessed. "But I guess I just got tired of the game."

"Well, I hope you didn't turn in your uniform," Raven uttered. "Because in case you didn't realize it, your ass is still on the field."

"So noted," Kane acknowledged with a smile. "Anyway, it sound like Remo and his guys don't know shit 'bout the weed business either, or he wudda known 'bout the weight issue."

"True," Raven concurred. "So in thinking about it, you and Castor actually got *two* hints that shit had gone off the rails."

"Personally, I got *zero* hints, because I didn't know any of that. I just knew shit had gone sideways when Castor lied and told Remo we didn't have the money with us – that we had to text someone to brang it."

"That was good thinking, 'cause Remo and his troop of assholes would have gunned you down if he thought the cash was anywhere within reach."

"That brings up another question," Kane said. "Why didn't they kill everybody before we got there, since that seemed to be their plan?"

"Two reasons. First, they needed someone who had dealt with Bush's people before so that you and Castor wouldn't be suspicious. I wasn't eager to help those shitheads, but they threatened to start killing people again, so I stepped forward."

"And with you they got a familiar face to show Castor when we arrived," Kane concluded. "So what was the second reason they didn't mow down the rest of your people?"

"They needed us for labor," Raven explained. "See, the warehouse had millions in weed inside. Remo and his shithead crew weren't just going to walk off and leave that. Plus, I overheard them talking about using us to load up the eighteen wheeler, and having us do it would be faster than doing it themselves."

"So they were planning to make off with our cash and your weed," Kane summed up.

"And the guns," Raven added.

"Huh?" Kane muttered, perplexed.

"There's usually two people with a key to the gun room," she told him. "The other person was a lady named Rosalie, and the thieves took her key when they got control of the farm. So in addition to stealing the cash and the cannabis, they were also planning to make off with the guns."

"Damn," Kane uttered. "That would have made for a nice payday."

"Well, they wouldn't have gotten far. Our people were already on the way."

"Oh, yeah – I think we saw 'em on the road as we were leavin'. We thought it was more bad guys."

"That's understandable," Raven admitted. "They thought the same about all of you, but it was more important to secure the farm so they didn't go after you."

"How'd they even know you were in trouble?"

"Despite the way things went tits-up today, we do have security protocols."

"In other words," Kane surmised, "you had some way to tell Augustus and your other people that you was in trouble, and they came runnin'."

Raven nodded. "Yeah, but by the time they got here we almost had things in hand."

"How's that?" Kane asked, plainly surprised.

"After I stabbed the guy in the neck, I took his gun and snuck into the farmhouse through a back door. The other fuckhead in there was holding a handful of our people at gunpoint. He obviously wasn't expecting trouble, so I shot him before he even knew I was there. Then I unlocked the gun room and armed everybody in the farmhouse."

"After that," she continued, "we split in two, with some heading to take back the warehouse while the rest engaged with Remo and his crew outside. They were so focused on y'all that it took them a second to realize that they were being fired on from behind. At that point they seemed to recognize that their plan had gone to shit – especially when they saw more of our people coming up the road."

"Let me guess," Kane offered. "They aborted their plan and got the fuck out of there."

"Yep," Raven confirmed, nodding. "They jumped into their cars and went flying down the back way behind the farmhouse."

"So they got away."

"Not all of them," Raven said fiercely. "Counting one who was roadkill – I assume that was *your* handiwork – we killed three of them and caught two."

"Wait," Kane said forcefully. "You caught a couple of them?"

"Well, they were wounded," Raven explained, "but yeah, we got our hands on them. And it'll come as no surprise to you that they were actually willing to talk."

"I bet," Kane muttered. "So whachu find out?"

"Not much. They're from out-of-state – at least, that's what they claimed, although they didn't have ID on them. In fact, none of the bodies had any ID. But the two we questioned both laid out the same story, saying they got recruited by Remo someplace a couple of states east of here a few weeks back. He promised them a big score."

"Anything else?"

"No, not really."

"Shit," Kane said under his breath. "I wish I'd known about them before we left the farm. I wudda like to talk to 'em."

"Well, they're not doing much talking anymore," Raven assured him. When Kane gave her an inquisitive glance, she continued, saying, "Look, you need to understand: Augustus has been dealing weed since way before the shit was legal. So when it comes to motherfuckers trying to rip him off, he has an old-school mentality."

"In other words," Kane speculated, "he's used to dishin' out frontier justice."

"That's one way to look at it. He's not a fan of people sneaking onto his property and trying to steal his product. You do that, you pay the price."

Kane let that sink in for a moment, then frowned as a new thought occurred to him.

"What about the tractor-trailer?" he said. "Didn't your people find that suspicious?"

Raven was nonplussed. "What do you mean?"

"You said before that Remo and his peeps caught everyone in the farmhouse with they pants down," Kane noted. "But given the weight issues, shouldn't your people have been wary when those muhfuckas pulled up with a big-rig in tow?"

"I should probably explain," Raven said. "The eighteen-wheeler is ours."

"Huh?" Kane uttered in surprise. Why do you have it if you can't use it for deliveries?"

"We can't use it for *cannabis*," Raven stressed. "But we can use it for other shit. For instance, we use it to bring in fertilizer for the fields."

"Oh," Kane muttered, chagrinned. "I guess that makes sense."

"Plus," Raven went on, "the cargo space on it is air-conditioned, so we occasionally use it as extra storage when the warehouse is full."

Kane considered that for a moment, then said, "But even if the thieves didn't bring it with them, they still planned to use it to haul off millions in weed, so presumably they had someone with them who could drive an eighteen-wheeler. Doesn't that seem like a bit of a fluke?"

"Actually, a big rig isn't that hard to drive," Raven countered. "There's a steep learning curve when it comes to shit like making turns and backing up, but other than that it's not that tricky."

"I hear ya, but let's think about it for a second," Kane said. "Thieves decide to hit you on a day when you're shorthanded. When you've got a customer coming by with a bag full of cash. When you got a big rig on site that would be perfect for hauling off a shit-ton of weed."

Raven gave him a hard look. "I know where you going: that this was an inside job."

"You don't think it's possible?"

"I'd agree not all of this is probably coincidence. But I'd say it's more likely inside *information* as opposed to an inside *job*."

Kane frowned. "Da fuck's the difference?"

"An inside *job* is when someone on your team is actually working hand-in-hand with the bad guys. Inside *information* is just info about the job that somebody might inadvertently give out, but that can be used in a bad way. Like if you work in fast food and complain to some friends about how the manager make you go by the bank and drop off the cash deposits after work on Friday nights, even though it's *his* job and not yours. Then the next time you go to make a deposit, you get robbed at gunpoint by a motherfucker in a ski mask. In that instance, it's not an inside job, but the robber was operating with inside information."

"I feel you," Kane said. "All it takes is the wrong word in the right ear."

"Exactly," Raven concurred with a nod. "And the next thing you know, life's a shitshow."

## Chapter 33

For much of the remainder of their drive, Kane and Raven engaged in general chitchat. She was witty and had a no-nonsense attitude that he typically associated more with Black women, and it reinforced his opinion of her as someone he could be friends with. However, as they drew near their destination, he thought it wise to find out a little bit more about what they were walking into.

"So," he droned, "what can you tell me about these Canaries?"

"They're an outlaw biker gang," she answered, "which basically means they're a bunch of racist pricks, so you'll want to watch yourself around them. They hang out at this shithole bar called *The She-Devil's Bush*, which is where we're headed."

"What kinda business you guys do with 'em?"

"Just what you'd expect: we sell 'em weed. Some of it they smoke, but most of it they sell. Of course, they're into a lot of other shit, too – most of it illegal – but we're not involved in any of that."

"What's their rep on the street?"

"They're tough, although not as tough as they think. Like all the other biker gangs, they call themselves a motorcycle club – as if that makes a difference. They've got chapters in maybe three states and claim to be a thousand strong, but are probably closer to five hundred. The local is one of the largest chapters – maybe fifty members."

"Interestin'," Kane remarked, "although you'd think they could come up with a more menacing name than 'Canaries.'"

"That's not their official name, but a long time ago they adopted the canary as a symbol. See, back in the day when miners would go down into a tunnel to dig for coal and shit, they'd often take canary in a birdcage with them. The reason was that—"

"I know 'bout canaries in coal mines," Kane interjected. "My granddaddy spent some time as a miner. They'd have a canary with them, and if they hit a pocket of gas or sommin', it would usually kill the bird first, and that would let the miners know they needed to get the fuck outta there."

"That's right," Raven affirmed. "The bird was sacrificed so all the miners could survive. These bikers liked what that represented, so the canary became their symbol, meaning that any member of the gang is expected to sacrifice himself for the others if necessary. After a while, everybody started calling them Canaries – that's even how they refer to themselves, plus they all get the tattoo. As to the official name, I doubt if even *they* remember what it originally was."

Kane reflected on that for a moment, then said, "I prolly should have asked this befoe', but how this shit s'posed to go down when we get to this biker bar?"

Eyeing him curiously, Raven asked, "What do you mean?"

"Well, you brought enough guns to arm a battalion. I'm just tryin' to figure out if the plan is to step out this fuckin' minivan blastin'."

"No, we're going to try some diplomacy first," Raven said with a snicker. "See if they're willing to have a discussion."

"So y'all on friendly terms with these guys? They gone be cool talkin' to us?"?"

"I fucking doubt it," Raven stressed. "And it ain't going to help that you're Black."

"Well," Kane intoned, "I'll see if I can lighten my skin tone before we get there."

*******************************************

The *She-Devil's Bush* was pretty much as Raven had described it: a shithole bar just outside the city limits. It was a one-story wooden structure with a threadbare awning covering the entrance, warped siding, and peeling paint all over the exterior. In short, the place had obviously seen better days.

There were at least two dozen motorcycles parked outside on an unpaved lot. There were also four guys, obviously guards, hanging around near the entrance. They looked like stereotypical motorcycle club members: White guys with long hair, out-of-control beards, and a ton of shitty tattoos of things like naked women, skulls, and the word "Outlaw."

The four bikers didn't immediately notice when Kane drove into the lot and parked the minivan. However, it quickly drew their attention – mostly because it was obviously out-of-place – and for a moment they just stared at it in surprise.

"We should probably step out before the guards get suspicious and do something stupid," Raven advised. "You ready?"

"Yeah," Kane replied. "Let's go."

With that, they quickly exited the minivan and began walking towards the bar entrance. Suddenly coming alive, the four bikers stepped forward, essentially barring the way in and forcing Raven and Kane to come to a halt.

"This a private club," one of the guards announced, crossing his arms. "You need to turn around and leave."

"We got business with Bear," Raven declared. "We'll leave when we're done."

"Don't know no Bear," the guard stated defiantly, shaking his head.

"Well, you *will*," Raven informed him. "Because when I call him on his cell and tell him the ignorant fucks he's got guarding the door won't let me in, he's going to rip your ass to shreds."

The four guards looked confused, as if her statement had somehow thrown them off. While they silently debated what to do, Raven boldly muscled her way past them, with Kane following in her wake. A moment later, they were inside the bar.

Much like the exterior, the inside of the place had a solid claim on shithole status as well. The floor was dirty and looked as though it hadn't been swept or mopped in ages, while the walls had a couple of holes in them and were generally stained (with what, in some instances, looked like dried blood). They were also a number of wobbly tables and rickety chairs strewn throughout the place, as well as a couple of booths with cracked and worn pleather seating.

Finally, there was the bar itself, the countertop of which was decrepit and covered with beer nuts, popcorn and other assorted snack remnants. Manning the bar was a middle-aged guy wearing a shirt with a Confederate flag plastered on it. In fact, a large rendition of the rebel flag was actually pinned to the ceiling over the back of the bar.

At the time, the bar's patrons numbered about twenty-five, and they were scattered throughout the room.

They were mostly men, but also included five of women. Two of the females wore property patches declaring them to be, respectively, "Property of the Canaries" and "Property of Luthor". Kane wasn't that familiar with motorcycle club culture, but he knew that the property patches indicated that the first woman belonged to the chapter as a whole, while the second belonged to some individual biker named Luthor. As to the other three women, they may have had property patches as well, but it wasn't immediately evident.

Pretty much all conversation in the bar came to a halt as Kane and Raven walked in. Apparently realizing that he and his fellows might appear to have been derelict, one of the guards – the one who had spoken to Raven – quickstepped inside and got in front of her. Then, with Raven and Kane following, he approached a biker leaning against the bar.

Kane and Raven came to a halt a few feet away while the guard hastily began whispering something. In the meantime, Kane looked over the guy he was talking to. The first thing he realized was that the muhfucka was huge – about six-six in height and weighing at least three hundred pounds. He also had a thick, unkempt beard and long, greasy hair. Finally, as if to cement his outlaw status, he had a large revolver tucked into the front of his pants. This, presumably, was Bear.

The guard stopped whispering, at which point Bear simply nodded. Following this, the guard started walking back towards the exit, while Bear motioned for Raven to come closer.

"Raven," he began, "always nice to see you, sweetcheeks." He then looked Kane over critically before adding, "But I see you slummin' again."

"Technically, slumming is defined as *visiting* a slum or a place full of low-lifes," Raven shot back. She glanced around for a second then continued, saying, "So I guess you're right."

Bear's brow suddenly creased in anger. "I assume you want sommin'?"

"We need to talk," Raven stated.

"So talk," Bear told her.

"In private."

Bear stroked his beard for a moment, then turned his attention to the five women in the bar.

"You bitches," he called out. "Skedaddle."

The women, apparently used to obeying without question, quickly and quietly headed to the door and left.

"Now what is it you wanna say?" Bear asked Raven, who glanced around critically at the remaining bikers. Understanding her reluctance, he added, "You can speak freely in front of the club."

"You're not going to want anyone else to hear this," Raven insisted.

Bear seemed annoyed, but then remarked, "We can go in the back." As he spoke, he gestured towards a hallway that appeared to lead to a rear room. "But you have to leave your weapons."

"Not a problem," Raven said flatly

Knowing he was being watched (and getting a lot of unsavory looks), Kane slowly reached behind him and pulled out his piece. He then placed it gently on the bar top, along with the extra magazines Raven had given him.

Raven did likewise, first putting the gun from her waistband on the countertop next to Kane's. This was followed by the weapon from her ankle holster and then the mouse gun from the pocket of her cargo pants.

At that point, Bear gestured at a Canary who was standing nearby, and the guy came over. He was a few inches shorter than Bear, but looked like he weighed almost as much.

"This is Trout, our Sergeant-at-Arms," Bear said, "He gone search you."

Trout stepped to Kane, who raised his arms. However, if Kane was expecting a gentle pat down, he was in for a rude awakening; Trout's hands were hard and rough as he basically smacked and slapped Kane's torso, arms and legs as he searched for weapons. All that he found were Kane's keys and cell phones.

Finishing up, Trout patted the side of Kane's face twice, saying with a sneer, "Good boy." His compatriots rolled with laughter while Kane silently seethed.

Trout then turned to Raven, who had already taken out her own keys and cell. She then smacked her hands on her pockets, intending to show that they were empty.

"Sorry," Bear told her, "but you still gotta be searched."

"Then bring those bitches back in so *they* can do it," Raven told him.

"They already left," Bear declared. "Plus, that ain't no job for women."

"Right, Bear," Trout added. "They don't know how to do it right."

"And you do?" Raven asked dubiously.

"You bet I do, lil' lady," Trout replied, looking her over lasciviously. "Doin' it right's my middle name."

This caused the other bikers to chuckle wildly.

"You can trust Trout," Bear said, "He's always gentle the first time." That got another round of chortling from his fellow Canaries.

# SHE'S HIS DRUG, HE'S HER THUG 4

"Fuck that," Raven shot back. "I'm not going to have any of you apes pawing me."

"Is that why you brought your own monkey?" Bear inquired, looking pointedly at Kane, who still managed to keep his cool. "Anyway, that's the price of admission if you want a conversation."

"Go to hell," Raven growled. "I'll strip naked first."

Bear seemed to consider that for a moment, then uttered, "If you insist."

Raven simply stared at him for a few seconds, then blurted out, "That's a fucking joke, right?"

"Nope," Bear stressed, shaking his head. "And you better get to it, 'cause I don't have all day."

Raven stood there angrily for a moment. Kane was on the verge of telling her not to fucking do it – that they should just get the fuck out of there. But before he could speak Raven started unbuckling her belt. She then swiftly began undressing, accompanied by wolf whistles and lewd comments from the bikers around them. A minute later, she stood there wearing nothing but a sports bra and panties, her appearance confirming something Kane already knew: Raven was fine as a muhfucka.

With her clothes on a nearby barstool, Raven raised her arms and slowly turned in a circle before facing Bear and asking, "Satisfied?"

"Not in the way I'd like," he offered with a leer, "but it'll have to do. Come on."

Grabbing her clothes off the barstool, Raven prepared to follow him to the back room, with Kane right behind her.

"You can leave those," Bear told her, indicating her clothes.

"Yeah, right," Raven muttered sarcastically. "So I can come out later and find them missing? No thanks."

Bear looked like he wanted to say more on the subject, then just shrugged. "Suit yourself."

And with that, they headed to the rear of the bar.

# SHE'S HIS DRUG, HE'S HER THUG 4

## Chapter 34

The back room of the bar was obviously a place meant for entertainment, as it was home to a couple of pool tables as well as a dart board.

In addition to Bear, Kane and Raven, two of the Canaries came with them. One was Trout; the other was a muscular shithead in his thirties with long blond hair and a handlebar mustache. Bear identified him as Luthor, the motorcycle club's Enforcer. Both men gave Kane evil looks – like they'd love to beat him down with rubber hoses.

Once in the rear area, Bear led them to a booth against the back wall, saying, "Welcome to my office."

With that, he slid into one side of the booth. Placing her clothes on the tabletop, Raven sat down across from him. She was about to slide over to make room for Kane when Bear spoke up.

Tilting his head towards Kane, he stated, "We don't huddle with his kind."

Suddenly the atmosphere became tense. All eyes were now on Kane, with both Trout and Luthor looking as though they wanted him to try something – to give them an excuse to go apeshit.

"No problem," Kane announced to no one in particular. He then stepped to the side, leaning against a nearby wall next to a billiards wall rack that held a bunch of pool sticks.

"Now you can finally tell me what the fuck's so important," Bear said.

"Yeah," Raven agreed, "although I'm a little surprised that the President of the Canaries needs his Enforcer *and* Sergeant-at-Arms on hand for a meeting with a woman and a Black guy." As she finished speaking, she hooked a thumb at Trout and Luthor, who were standing close to the booth.

Bear gave her a hard look. He obviously didn't like what Raven was implying – that he was intimidated by his visitors.

Turning to his fellow bikers, Bear said, "Why don't you two just relax."

Luthor warily shot his gaze back and forth between Raven and Kane for a moment, then asked, "You sure?"

"Yeah," Bear affirmed. "Go shoot a lil' pool while me and the lady chat. And if she or her boy get outta line, just shoot 'em."

Trout and Luthor smiled at that, then the latter walked to the wall rack by Kane and grabbed a couple of pool sticks. He tossed one to Trout, after which the two of them headed to one of the pool tables.

"Okay, enough fuckin' around," Bear grumbled. "Why you here?"

"We got hit today," Raven answered. "Some assholes tried to rip us off."

"That's fucked up," Bear commiserated. "But why you tellin' *me*?"

"One of the motherfuckers involved was a shitbird called Remo with a canary tattoo."

"Never heard of 'im," Bear declared, shaking his head.

Raven's eyes narrowed. "You want to take a minute to think about it?"

"Don't need to. Plus, I know what you tryin' to say, but it wasn't us."

"Oh, so this asshole just happened to have your club's symbol emblazoned on his neck," Raven stated skeptically.

"We the Canaries. Lots of motherfuckers wanna ride with us. How's it our fault if some wannabe tattoos a bird on hisself so he can pretend like he in the club?"

Raven gave him an intense stare for a moment. "That's you're going to go with?"

Bear shrugged. "It's the truth."

"Hmmm," Raven droned. "You know, the average motherfucker wouldn't dare to put on the name, symbols or patches of some club they weren't affiliated with, 'cause they know most biker gangs will put your ass in the ground for that shit. So if this is some wannabe, like you said, he obviously ain't scared of the Canaries."

"Ha!" Bear barked. "Everybody scared of us."

"Obviously this guy ain't. Makes me think y'all reputation ain't all it's cracked up to be."

"You let me worry 'bout our reputation," Bear told her. "And if that's all you wanted, you can get the fuck out."

"Fine – we'll go," Raven said, pulling her clothes towards her. "But let me ask you something: why you protecting this guy? You in love with him or something?"

Bear blinked a few times, seemingly caught so flatfooted by Raven's question that all he could do was mutter, "What?" in response.

Raven continued as if he hadn't spoken, saying, "I mean, is he cornholing you at night? Maybe rubbing that big, fat fish-white belly you got while slipping you the dick from behind?"

"Bitch," Bear growled, "I'm gonna fuckin' kill you."

## SHE'S HIS DRUG, HE'S HER THUG 4

He extended his hand like he was trying to reach across the table, but all of a sudden there was loud popping sound, like a firecracker being set off indoors. At the same time, Bear's shoulder jerked backwards, like something to his rear had tried to yank him in that direction.

Bear looked at the shoulder in question like he had never seen it before.

"What the fuck...?" he muttered.

It was then that Kane noticed two things: first, Raven was holding a mouse gun in her hand. In addition, he saw Bear's shirt near his shoulder starting to turn red. Trout and Luthor, who had frozen upon hearing the popping noise, apparently didn't realize that it had been caused by a gun or that their boss had been shot.

At that juncture several things seem to happen all at once, starting with Bear suddenly reaching for the gun tucked down the front of his pants. At the same time, Trout and Luthor went for theirs.

Kane was already in motion by then; grabbing a pool stick from the wall rack, he charged the two bikers who had been playing billiards. Trout was in front, and as he brought his weapon up Kane gave him a solid whack on his gun hand with the pool cue.

Trout yelped in pain as the gun went flying off to the side. Kane, still charging, rammed into Trout, forcing him backwards towards Luthor.

With his friend in between them, Luthor couldn't get a shot off at Kane without possibly hitting Trout. Before there was time to do anything else, Trout was forcefully shoved into him, and they both went down in a tangle of arms and legs.

Having Trout fall down on top of him clearly knocked the wind out of Luthor, leaving him a little discombobulated. Kane took the opportunity to stomp on the wrist holding his gun. He both heard and felt bones crack under his heel as Luthor howled in pain. Meanwhile, Trout rolled off his buddy and attempted to rise, only to have Kane smack him on the head with the pool stick.

"Stay down," Kane ordered as the pool cue struck so hard that it broke, causing Trout to collapse to the floor, clearly dazed. Smiling, Kane said, "Good boy."

Luthor let his weapon fall from his loose finger as he cradled his injured wrist. Dropping the remnants of the broken pool stick, Kane picked up Luthor's gun.

In the meantime, as Bear had been trying to pull out his gun, Raven swiftly drew back her leg and then kicked him hard in the nuts. Bear howled in anguish, during which time Raven lithely slipped from her side of the booth and then slid in next to him. She put the mouse gun to his temple, at which point – aside from some painful writhing below the waist – Bear became still and allowed Raven to take the gun from his hand.

Risking a quick glance at Kane, she asked, "We good?"

"Yeah," Kane replied. "It's under control."

At that point, they heard footsteps – lots of them – coming down the hallway in their direction.

"Shit," Raven muttered. Turning to Kane, she shouted, "Catch," and tossed him her mouse gun.

Following this, she grabbed a fistful of Bear's hair and, with his own gun pointed at his head, dragged him – grunting in pain – from the booth. The difference in height meant that Bear had to walk with his head bent over, and the discomfort was clearly compounded by his wounded shoulder. Raven, however, didn't give a shit about that as she spun him to face the hallway leading to the main area of the bar.

As expected from the footsteps, almost every Canary on the premises was headed in their direction. That said, they stopped short when they saw their leader with a gun to his head. Meanwhile, Kane had positioned himself so that he could back up Raven, if necessary, but at the same time keep an eye on Luthor and Trout, both of whom were struggling to their feet.

Boldly standing her ground, Raven leaned towards Bear's ear and hissed, "I believe there's something you want to tell these assholes."

Understanding what was expected of him, Bear nodded and ordered, "Everybody clear out."

The other bikers seemed hesitant to obey, at which point Raven pressed the gun hard against Bear's temple, making him wince.

"I said clear out!" he roared.

At that, the Canaries began heading back the way they had come, but not without evil glances at their visitors.

"That goes for you assholes, too," Kane told Luthor and Trout. He kept Luthor's gun on the two of them as they followed their compadres.

Still holding Bear at gunpoint, Raven went down the hallway behind the bikers, warily keeping a safe distance. Still in the back room, Kane took a moment to scoop up her clothes before following. He debated grabbing Trout's piece, which was still on the floor, but settled for kicking it into a corner.

Back in the main area of the bar, the Canaries were filing out the front door, but at what seemed like a leisurely pace. Kane didn't like it; the longer it took, the more likely it was that one of those shitheads would try something.

Apparently Raven felt the same, because she once again pressed the barrel of the gun forcefully against Bear's head, who got the message.

"Hurry up and get the fuck out!" Bear yelled. At this, the bikers seemed to double-time it, noticeably increasing their pace. "Get on your bikes and don't come back 'til I tell ya."

"That goes for you, too, Johnny Reb," Raven said to the bartender wearing the Confederate flag shirt, who seemingly hadn't moved. "Get the hell out of here."

"I can't leave the bar," the man said defiantly, although he raised his hands as he noticed the gun Kane held suddenly pointed at him.

"If you don't wanna catch one in the dome," Kane told him, "you'll get to steppin'."

"No can do," the guy said, coming from behind the bar. "I gotta stay in here – it's part of my work release."

"What?" Kane demanded, raising his voice slightly as the sound of numerous motorcycles starting up and taking off reverberated loudly from outside. It reflected one of the few things Kane knew about biker gangs: they all tended to modify their exhausts to make them loud as fuck.

Rather than reply to Kane's query, the bartender slowly reached down with one hand and pulled up the right leg of his pants, revealing an ankle monitor.

"If I leave the bar during work hours, I go back to the joint," the bartender explained.

Brow creased, Raven glanced at Kane, plainly soliciting his opinion. Kane gave an indifferent shrug.

"Alright get on the floor, spread-eagle," Raven ordered. "And if you so much as twitch, going back to the joint will be the least of your problems."

# SHE'S HIS DRUG, HE'S HER THUG 4

The bartender nodded, then lay down on the floor as instructed, arms and legs outstretched.

Still gripping Bear's hair, Raven dragged him to a nearby chair and shoved him towards it. Bear flopped into the seat with an audible grunt, grimacing in pain and reaching for his wounded shoulder. At that moment, the sound of motorcycles outside seemed to dwindle and finally dissipate altogether.

Handing Raven her clothes, Kane hustled to the door and carefully peeked out. From what he could tell, almost all of the bikes were gone, which suggested that the Canaries had left as ordered. The only motorcycle left was a sleek hog that he assumed belong to Bear. Satisfied, he closed the door and locked it, then turned and gave Raven a nod as he walked back in her direction.

With Kane keeping watch on the bartender and Bear, Raven placed the latter's gun on the bartop.

"Now," Raven droned, as she began putting her clothes on, "let's try this again: what do you know about this shitbird Remo?"

# SHE'S HIS DRUG, HE'S HER THUG 4

## Chapter 35

No longer having a gun to his head apparently allowed Bear to grow some balls, because rather than answer Raven's question he began talking shit.

"You're dead, bitch," he growled at Raven. "You done fucked with the Canaries, so you can kiss your ass goodbye. We gone be comin' for you. Augustus, too, since he sent you."

"Really?" Raven remarked skeptically as she finished getting dress and retrieved Bear's gun from the bartop. "And what the fuck do you think you're going to do?"

"We gone bury y'all."

"Oh, yeah?" Raven snickered. "You and what army?"

"The Canaries, bitch!" Bear shouted. "*That* army! We got over a thousand soldiers – enough muscle to take out Augustus and anybody else on this fuckin' green Earth."

"Including Bush?" Raven asked nonchalantly.

Bear was silent for a moment as his brow furrowed, and he blinked a couple of times, as if he couldn't quite comprehend what Raven was talking about.

"What?" he uttered after a few seconds.

"I said, is Bush one of the people y'all got the muscle to take out," Raven responded.

Bear gave her a confused look. "What does Bush have to do with this?"

"Oh, didn't I mention it? His people were there to make a buy, and your boy Remo tried to rip them off as well."

Bear's eyes went wide in surprise, and a second later he blurted out, "Hold up. Just hold up a fuckin' minute." He seemed to take a moment to get his bearings, then said, "You tellin' me that Remo tried to steal from *Bush*?"

"Oh, so you *do* know him," Raven commented.

"I'm just tryin' to figure out what the fuck happened," Bear countered.

"I already told you what happened," Raven shot back.

"And you sure Bush is involved?"

"Yes, I'm fucking sure, but you can always ask my pet monkey, as you called him" – she tilted her head towards Kane – "since he works for Bush."

Bear jerked his head towards Kane, looking like he wanted to shit his pants.

"Look, man," Bear began, "sorry 'bout what I said before. No offense meant."

"None taken," Kane replied in a tone that sounded insincere, even to him.

Bear looked as if he had more to say to Kane, but Raven interrupted saying, "Save the apologies for later. Right now, just tell us about Remo."

Bear nodded, licking his lips nervously. "He *was* a Canary, but not anymore. He went rogue – started doin' some unsanctioned shit on his own – so officially, he's been booted from the club."

Kane raised an eyebrow inquisitively. "And *un*officially?"

"Unoffically, he's still allowed to come around," Bear confessed. "But he's treated like a guest. He can hang out and drink with us, but we don't talk club business in front of him. He's not included in anything *we* do, and we don't get mixed up in any shit he's involved in."

"So you've seen him?" Raven asked.

Bear nodded. "He checked in when he got to town, even though it wasn't required."

Seeing a curious look on Kane's face, Raven explained. "When a biker visits a new city, he's supposed to check in if his motorcycle club has a chapter there. It's a good way to get the lay of the land if there's some shit going on – like a feud with a rival gang. It's also a way to recruit if you're planning a big job."

She looked at Bear as she finished speaking, who immediately shot back, "No fuckin' way. Like I said, he was basically a guest, but the word went out that absolutely *nobody* was supposed to get involved in any of the shit he was stirrin' up."

"And we s'posed to believe that," Kane remarked.

"It's the truth, I swear," Bear responded.

"Well, we'll figure out if you tellin' the truth from one last question," Raven commented. "Where's he staying?"

Bear frowned, the question clearly causing him some consternation.

"Come on, motherfucker," Raven continued. "If Remo checked in, he probably asked where he could hole up or left word where he was crashing, so where the fuck is he?"

"A'ight, I'll tell you," Bear said. "But you gotta make sure Bush knows the Canaries ain't have shit to do with Remo or this fucking job he tried to pull."

"Just give us the fucking address," Raven ordered.

# SHE'S HIS DRUG, HE'S HER THUG 4

## Chapter 36

Kane and Raven retrieved their weapons, and left almost immediately after getting the address for Remo. Plainly aware that someone might be waiting for them outside, they had made Bear walk out of the bar first. Surprisingly, the coast was clear, suggesting that – despite being racist muhfuckas – the Canaries were apparently well-disciplined. (Or else they simply figured they could get payback later when Bear was out of danger.)

Bear himself seemed to harbor no ill will towards them. His main concern seemed to be to be that they stress to Bush that the Canaries had no connection to what Remo had done. Although they let Bear go, Kane and Raven made no promises in that regard. All that he got from them was his and Luthor's guns – wiped down and *sans* ammo – as Kane and Raven got into the minivan and drove off.

*******************************************

The address they'd been given for Remo was in the city. Kane wasn't wild about the notion of going further away from Mika, but he tried to stay focused on the task at hand. It would take them about twenty minutes to get to their destination, but it gave him a chance to ask a few questions.

"So," he mused to Raven, "you had a second mouse gun on you. Pretty slick. I never even saw you pack it."

"You weren't supposed to," she said with a smile. "Anyway, I figured that, if given a chance, those horny fucks would rather see me *strip* down than do a *pat* down."

# SHE'S HIS DRUG, HE'S HER THUG 4

"So that whole, indignant *you-not-gone-search-me* thang was just an act."

Raven smiled. "Hey, a girl's gotta do what a girl's gotta do."

"You played it up well, then damn near drove Bear apeshit when you talked 'bout him takin' it up the ass."

"Yeah," Raven snickered. "I needed to distract him while I slipped the mouse gun out of my pants pocket. As you can probably guess, bikers are uber-macho, so about the worst thing you can do is call them a fag. I knew that once I did that, Bear would be so fucking pissed he wouldn't be able to see straight."

"Obviously it worked, so good job."

"You, too. That shit would have gone differently if you hadn't taken care of those other two fuckheads."

Kane merely nodded at this, suddenly realizing that Raven had taken a huge gamble on him. Basically, she had trusted him to handle Luthor and Trout. If he had fucked it up, the odds were slim that either of them would have lived to see another day.

Changing the subject slightly, he said, "I noticed that Luthor's attitude did a full one-eighty after you mentioned Bush. What's the story there?"

"I don't know all the details," Raven replied, "but apparently a few years back, some motorcycle club stole some shit that belonged to Bush – either money or product, it was never clear which. One of Bush's people showed up at their chapter headquarters, saying Bush wanted his shit back, and if they gave it up Bush would forget it ever happened."

"Let me guess," Kane chimed in. "They told him to fuck off."

"More than that. They broke his arms and legs."

"Fuck..." Kane muttered.

"Apparently they were trying to send a message," she explained. "See, they were supposed to be some bad-ass biker gang, and clearly believed their own press. They allegedly had two thousand members and chapters all over the place – even overseas – so they felt nobody could touch them. Or maybe they just thought Bush's rep on the streets was overrated."

"So what happened?"

"Hard to say exactly, because none of the stories are consistent on how it occurred, but about a week later the top five ranking members of the club all suffered broken arms and legs."

"If that ain't fuckin' karma..." Kane noted. "I take it they gave Bush his shit back then?"

"Actually, they didn't," Raven told him. "Despite what had happened to them, the club leaders decided that giving Bush his shit was a bitch move, so they thumbed their noses at him again."

"I'm guessin' Bush reacted."

"You could say that. Basically, the national president of the club just disappeared shortly thereafter – went home one day after a doctor's appointment and was never seen again. But a few days later, a box containing his jacket was delivered to the club headquarters. The obvious message was that the club prez didn't need it any more."

"Kind of a *sleeps-with-fishes* move," Kane remarked.

Raven looked at him in surprise. "Good reference."

"What?" he uttered, noting her expression. "You surprised I know that?"

"A little," she admitted. "Most guys who want to look all hard can only cite *Scarface* if you ask them about gangsta movies. Not many seem to know *The Godfather*."

"Well, I saw the movie *and* read the book," Kane declared. "Plus, that *sleeps-with-the-fishes* thang is famous."

"True," she noted.

"And as to *Scarface*," Kane continued, "were you talkin' about the one from the eighties or the original from the thirties?"

"Now you just trying to impress me," Raven noted with a smile. "Anyway, back to the Bush story… After the club president vanished, the club didn't know what to do. Half of them wanted to go to war, the other half wanted to give back what they stole and cut their losses. And while they were debating, the vice-president – who was acting prez at the time – went missing."

"Don't tell me: his jacket got delivered later."

"Yep," Raven confirmed with a nod. "At that point, the writing was on the wall: motherfuckers at the top of the club hierarchy were going to keep fading from view as long as shit with Bush was unresolved. So they finally broke down and tried to give back what they took – even offered to pay it back with interest."

"What did Bush say?"

"His people said it was too late. According to them, Bush never really cared about the shit the club took – it didn't affect his bottom line at all. It was really about respect. And since they hadn't shown him any, he now had to send a message by making an example out of them."

"So what happened next?"

"The remaining club bigwigs resigned, like immediately. That left the rest of the gang in complete disarray, until a couple of members tried to step up by becoming the new national officers. But that didn't last long."

"Why not?"

"Because the new club leaders started vanishing just like the old ones, starting with the just-sworn-in prez. When his jacket got delivered, all of the other officers stepped down. After that, nobody was ambitious enough to try heading the club – at least not officially."

"Meaning what?" Kane asked.

"Meaning that a couple of dumb fucks tried taking over without benefit of a formal title," Raven explained. "But the end result was the same."

"They disappeared."

"Bingo," Raven said. "Allegedly, it reached a point where if anybody tried to step up in any way – if they so much as proposed a meet-up between chapters or just suggested a conference call – you never saw or heard from them again, aside from their jacket getting delivered."

"So they lost all form of leadership," Kane concluded.

"And without leaders, the club fell apart. Basically, they don't exist anymore – except as a cautionary tale for other biker gangs."

"I'm beginning to understand Luthor's about-face now," Kane said.

Raven nodded. "He knows that if Bush is involved, this shit is beyond being serious. It could be the end of the road for his motorcycle club."

# SHE'S HIS DRUG, HE'S HER THUG 4

## Chapter 37

It took them about another fifteen minutes to reach the place where Remo was purportedly holed up: an aging, twelve-story apartment building in a fast-declining neighborhood. (More specifically, according to Bear, the ex-Canary was staying in room Five-Thirteen.) Kane circled the block once as a matter of course, trying to get the lay of the land.

"What do you think?" Raven asked as they completed their circuit.

"I don't like it," Kane said as he continued driving. "It's the middle of the day, for one thang. If I'm gone confront some muhfuckas who packin', I prefer to do it at night, when they less likely to see me comin'. There's also less chance that any witnesses will see anythang, or have a firm recollection of what they saw. On top of that, even though it looks like a mixed neighborhood with all kinds of races, a Black man and a White girl hanging tight are gonna stick out around here."

"Girl?" Raven repeated, smiling. "Now you trying to make me blush." At that, Kane grinned as well.

"Anyway," she continued, "we can always wait and come back when it's dark."

Kane shook his head. "Naw – there's no guarantee that Remo will be here then."

"We don't even know that he's here *now*."

"True," Kane admitted. "But I'd rather check it out than sit on my ass doin' nuthin' for the rest of the day." He didn't add that, per Regis, he had a limited window to get this shit resolved, and the clock was ticking.

Raven simply stared at him for a moment. "You do know he's got, like, four guys with him, right?"

"I did the math. What's ya point?"

"I can always reach out to Augustus – ask him to send backup."

Kane looked at her, eyes narrowed. "If you wanted backup, you wudda called him soon as we found out where Remo was stayin'."

An amused expression settled on Raven's face. "You got me. I prefer doing shit like this on my own. Other motherfuckers usually just get in the way."

"Includin' me?"

"No," she declared, shaking her head. "You're actually competent – an asset. Plus, you're a special case."

"Right," he noted, remembering. "I'm Bush's rep, so you required to let me tag along."

"Yeah, but like I said, there's actually a benefit to being paired with *you*. Most motherfuckers don't understand, but there's a lot more to this shit than just being able to squeeze a trigger. You don't just magically transform into a badass just because someone puts a gun in your hand."

Kane couldn't help but be impressed, and it showed on his face.

"Okay, Ms. Badass," he said after a few seconds. "Whachu thank we should do here?"

"Well," Raven mused, "if we have to do this now and we're too conspicuous together, then the solution is obvious: we split up."

# SHE'S HIS DRUG, HE'S HER THUG 4

## Chapter 38

Raven's idea was pretty simple. The apartment building had what appeared to be a basement entrance at the back, identified by a set of stairs leading down to a door below street level. The plan was for Raven to get out, go inside, and find her way to that entrance while Kane parked the minivan. He would then make his way to the basement door, at which point Raven would let him in. That way, the odds that they would be seen together – and stick out in anyone's mind – were diminished.

Fortunately, everything went pretty much as anticipated. When Raven got out, Kane watched her for a moment as she headed to the front of the building, noting that she had the hood of her jacket pulled up to obscure her appearance. (She also had it zipped up to conceal the fact that she was carrying the sawed-off shotgun.) Confident that she'd make it inside without any issues, he drove off.

Ultimately, he ended up parking a few blocks away. Before getting out, he took a moment to adjust his new gloves, making sure they were snug. (As with the SUV, he had worn them while driving the minivan.) He then hustled back to the apartment building as quickly as he could without drawing attention, slowing down only to answer a call on his phone.

It was from Mr. Fix, stating that he was at Annabelle's and would be moving his "patients" to a spot in the city. Kane felt relief after Fix confirmed that both would be fine (although Castor would need time to fully recover). After getting the address and hanging up, Kane put his game face back on and continued to the apartment building. However, when he reached the basement area, Raven wasn't there waiting and the door was locked.

Feeling utterly exposed, Kane knocked gently on the door, which was made of metal, and heard the sound echo inside. After about thirty seconds, he knocked again, wondering where the hell Raven was. She should have had plenty of time to get to the basement entrance, even if she wasn't completely familiar with the layout. More importantly, Kane didn't like waiting outside like this. To anyone passing by, he would look suspicious as a muhfucka.

Now starting to feel a little anxious, he was about to rap on the door a third time when he heard motion inside. A moment later, Raven opened the door and Kane slipped inside. She immediately closed it behind him, and then began leading him down a dimly-lit corridor filled with an assortment of items that included everything from boxes and luggage to appliances and bicycles.

"Da fuck happened to you?" he demanded as they walked. "You got tired and decided to take a nap?"

"Quit bitchin'," Raven shot back. "This place is a fucking rat maze. Plus, do you know how much shit I had to move to get to that door? Fucking crates, refrigerators and everything else. They're not supposed to have an exit blocked like that. The Fire Marshall would have a damn field day in here."

"Fine – yo tardiness is excused."

"Thanks, but you'll be happy to know that I also did a little recon before coming down here."

Kane frowned. "On what?"

"When I got inside the building," Raven replied, "I decided to roam around the lobby and check the mailboxes."

"Why?"

Raven contemplated for a moment. "You remember the apartment that Bear told us Remo was staying in?"

"Five-Thirteen," Kane answered.

"Right. Well, I figured checking the apartment's mailbox might give us an idea how many other assholes – besides the five we looking for – might be in there. Also, if any residents here saw us and got suspicious, we could spit out a legit name of somebody who lives in this shithole and say we were visiting."

"Smart," Kane acknowledged. "So whachu find out?"

"I was planning to poke around in the basement for a minute or two before you got here and try to find something to pry the box open with: a screwdriver, a butter knife, a crowbar… Anything that would let me get to their mail and see who might be living in that apartment. Luckily, I went to check the box first to see how tough it might be to get into, and I saw that it was marked 'Vacant'."

"Vacant?" Kane echoed.

"Yeah," Raven said. "They do that sometimes when an apartment's empty. Otherwise the mailman will keep stuffing the box with junk mail until shit's falling out all over the place every time he opens it and the super has to clean it up. It's easier to just stick a vacant label on the box so the postman knows he can just toss any junk mail in the garbage."

"Hmmm," Kane droned. "So Remo and his crew are crashin' in an apartment that's s'posed to be empty. What are the odds that there's five or ten muhfuckas livin' in a vacant unit here, and the super of this buildin' don't know shit about it?"

"Sound like we need a chat with the super," Raven concluded.

# SHE'S HIS DRUG, HE'S HER THUG 4

## Chapter 39

The building super lived in a first-floor unit that conveniently had a placard reading "Superintendent" on the door. He presumably had people regularly coming by, because he opened the door without seeming to use the peephole or asking who was knocking. What he probably wasn't used to, however, was having a gun shoved in his face, which is what Kane did before the guy could utter a word.

Kane motioned with the gun for the super to back up, which he did, arms raised. Kane and Raven immediately stepped inside and closed the door.

The super was a guy in late middle age with a medium build and thinning gray hair. He also had rheumy eyes, a five-o'clock shadow, and was dressed in a wife beater T-shirt. Finally, he smelled strongly of alcohol, but didn't look like he was drunk…yet.

Glancing around, Kane saw that they were in a living room that was full of outdated furniture, including an old-school tube television and a battered coffee table covered with liquor bottles. There was also a bunch of random shit littered about, such as a music stand, a super-soaker, and a small fire extinguisher.

"What's yo name?" Kane asked the super.

"Glen," the man replied.

"Okay, Glen," Kane said. "Who else here?"

"Nobody," the super declared.

"Well, I hope you not insulted if we don't just take yo word for it."

With that, Kane went to check the rest of the apartment, leaving Raven covering Glen with the sawed-off shotgun.

## SHE'S HIS DRUG, HE'S HER THUG 4

The place turned out to be a two-bedroom, one-bath. Thankfully, it only took Kane a few minutes to search it, including checking under beds and in closets. From what he could see, Glen was telling the truth: no one else was there. Also, judging from how unkempt and cluttered the apartment was, Glen lived alone, although from all appearances his home could definitely use a woman's touch.

As he went back towards the living room, Kane suddenly heard sounds of a struggle. Racing back to the area, he found Raven and Glen both fighting for control of the shotgun. However, before Kane could interfere, Raven lashed out with a foot, viciously kicking the inside of Glen's right knee. The leg suddenly wrenched to the side, causing Glen to yelp in pain and drop down to one knee. He also seemingly lost his hold on the shotgun, because Raven suddenly yanked it free of his grip and then brought the stock down hard on the top of his head. Glen let out a howl and dropped to the floor, his hand going to the spot where Raven had whacked him on the noggin.

"You alright?" Kane asked Raven.

"Oh, yeah," Raven assured him. "My boyfriend here just thought he might get lucky with you out of the room."

Kane looked at the super. "Stupid move, Glen. This is one lady you don't wanna fuck with."

"Well, whachu expect?" Glen retorted. "You come in here, waving guns in my face, don't tell me what you want... I'm just s'pose to wait 'til you decide to blow my head off?"

Kane ruminated on that for a moment. "A'ight, Glen, that's a fair point. So let's just clear the air: we not here for you. You got some people staying here in a vacant apartment that we need to talk to. That's it."

"Okay," Glen said, coming to his feet. "Which one?"

Kane and Raven shared a surprised glance, then Raven asked, "Just how many people you illegally renting rooms to in here?"

"Uh, just a handful," Glen told them, sounding completely disingenuous.

"Okay," Kane said, "but we only interested in the assholes in Five-Thirteen."

Glen drew in a sharp breath. "I don't know… Those not the kind of people you wanna fuck with."

"Neither are *we*," Raven said, leveling the shotgun at his head.

"A'ight, a'ight," Glen muttered, putting up his hands defensively. "I getcha point."

"So what kinda kickback you get for lettin' muhfuckas stay here off the books?" Kane asked.

"For the crew you talkin' 'bout, they give me a thousand for a week."

"That's a lot for this dump," Raven noted. "They tell you what they up to?"

"Fuck naw," Glen admitted. "And I didn't ask."

"Well, I'm sure they gettin' sommin' for they money besides a roof," Kane stated. "What is it?"

"I fiddled with the meter and the water main," Glan confessed, "to give they room electricity and runnin' water."

"Hmmm," Kane mused. "So if you told 'em you need to get in the room to fix sommin', they'd open the doe' to let you in without bein' suspicious."

"I could call 'em and try," Glen opined, "but I don't think it would work."

"Wait a minute," Kane blurted out. "You got a numba for 'em?"

Glen nodded. "Just to a pre-paid phone that they boss-man carry, but the only reason I got the numba is 'cause of Caller ID when *he* calls *me*."

"What kind of shit does he call you for?" Raven asked.

"Liquor, usually," Glen answered. "He knows I almost always have some on hand."

Looking around at all the liquor bottles (not to mention the way the super smelled), Kane could understand how Remo probably got that notion. Obviously Glen had a little drinking problem.

"They ask 'bout where to get food sometimes, too," Glen continued. Seeing odd looks on his visitors' faces, he added, "They all from outta town, so they don't know where shit is."

"Anyway," Raven said, "you were telling us that you didn't think you could get into the apartment these shitheads are living in – even to fix something. Why not?"

"'Cause they made it real clear that they don't want nobody in there," Glen informed them. "Said they'll call if they need me, but otherwise mind my own fuckin' business and keep out."

"So much for getting them to maybe open the door for us," Raven observed.

"Well, maybe we don't need to worry 'bout gettin' *in*," Kane offered as a thought occurred to him. "Maybe we need to focus on gettin' them to come *out*."

## Chapter 40

Glen wasn't wild about the idea that Kane had come up, but it wasn't like he had a choice. Thus, after a few dry runs concerning what he was to say, the super called Remo, who answered on the second ring.

"You seen 'em?" Remo asked anxiously, plainly unaware he was on speakerphone so that Raven and Kane could listen in.

"Huh?" Glen asked in confusion.

"That salt-and-pepper combo you s'posed to be keepin' an eye out for," Remo told him. "I'm guessin' they finally showed up."

"Uh, naw," Glen responded, his eyes darting back and forth between his guests, who shared a knowing glance. "I ain't seen 'em."

"Then why da fuck you callin' 'me?" Remo demanded irritably.

"Just needed to let you know sommin'," Glen stated. "The owner's here."

"Who?"

"The owner of the buildin'," Glen explained. "Some snot-nosed kid barely out of diapers. His granddaddy's some real estate tycoon who gave him this place as a gift when he finished college."

"So what's that gotta do with us?" Remo inquired.

"Well, there's a reason a lotta the units in here are vacant: they not up to code," Glen said. "And if they not up to code they can't be rented – not legally, anyway. And if they can't be rented, then Snotnose Shithead the Third ain't makin' no money from 'em, and that's a no-no."

"So," Glen continued, "he been showing up 'bout once a month with a team of architects and shit, plannin' to scope out all the vacant units and see what they need to do to comply with the regs. They started at the bottom and workin' they way up. Guess what flo' they startin' on today?"

"The fifth," Remo concluded.

"You got it."

"So he'll be comin' up in here."

"At some point – either him or one of his architect lackeys. The main thing is, you and yo people gotta get outta there."

"Ha!" Remo snorted in derision. "We can handle a bunch of pencil-necks and some rich college boy."

"Not this one," Glen warned. "He don't like the neighborhood, so he always got a security detail with 'im when he come here – some ex-Navy Seal types. They gone sweep every vacant unit before they let the owner set foot in one, makin' sure ain't no squatters or crackheads in there waitin' to bash 'im in the head. So unless you wanna have a shootout with some mercs who was prolly military snipers, you should leave."

"Shit. We still need to lay low and stay off the street. You got another place you can put us up?"

"Oh, so now you wanna rent a *second* unit, where you can hunker down 'til you get yo shit resolved. Well, you in luck – I got a place. It's a unit in the building, but the owner ain't gonna go up in that one 'cause it's got mold and shit on the walls. It ain't a fuckin' resort, but you can use it 'til this other shit's taken care of."

Remo seemed to deliberate for a moment. "A'ight, we can make that work."

"Okay, just sit tight," Glen said. "I'll come get you in a few minutes and take you to it."

## SHE'S HIS DRUG, HE'S HER THUG 4

"Make it happen," Remo uttered flatly, then hung up.

Glen turned his phone off, then looked from Raven to Kane. "How'd I do?"

"Great," Raven responded. "We practically friends now."

Glen looked at her hopefully. "Really?"

"Oh, yeah. But just answer me this, 'friend'," Raven said, leveling the shotgun at the super. "When the fuck were you gonna say something about being on the lookout for us?"

"Huh?" Glen muttered nervously.

"Remo's comment about you keeping an eye out for a 'salt-and-pepper combo'," she said. "That's slang for a Black-and-White couple, meaning *us*."

"You been playin' us?" Kane said angrily. "Plannin' to let them know we here soon as you get a chance?"

"No, no, no," Glen blurted out anxiously. "I wasn't."

"So they *didn't* tell you to keep an eye out for us?" Raven queried.

"No," Glen insisted. "I mean, yeah – they did – but I wasn't gonna do it. Truth is, I didn't even remember being asked about it. That's why I was here in my apartment when you knocked instead of keepin' lookout in the lobby. Shit like that don't stick in my head 'cause I'm drunk most of the time. I'm half-drunk *now*."

Raven and Kane exchanged a glance, but neither said anything. Kane knew that she was thinking the same thing he was: Remo was expecting them. He'd known they were coming, which meant that muhfucka Bear had presumably given him a heads-up.

"Doesn't sound like he knows we're here yet," Raven finally said.

"A'ight, let's see it through," Kane said. He then grabbed Glen by the scruff of the neck and began dragging him towards the door, saying, "Brang yo ass on…"

# SHE'S HIS DRUG, HE'S HER THUG 4

## Chapter 41

They took the stairs up to the fifth floor. However, they had to pause for a few seconds after every set of stairs because Glen was completely out of shape – even for someone his age. Of course, he begged them to take the elevator, but neither Kane nor Raven was much interested in getting stuck inside of it if anything went wrong.

They passed a few people in the stairwell on their way up, but other than someone occasionally saying a few words to the super, no one paid them much attention. Raven walked next to Glen, with the sawed-off shotgun once again zipped up in her jacket. She kept one of her arms looped into his, with the other hand holding one of her handguns surreptitiously pressed to his side. Kane brought up the rear, his hand on his piece and tucked into one of the outer pockets on his own jacket.

Upon finally reaching the fifth floor, they left the stairwell and stepped out into a corridor near the intersection of two hallways. They paused for a moment so that Glen, who was practically wheezing, could catch his breath.

"Which way?" asked Kane, glancing around warily.

Still breathing heavily, Glen pointed towards the far end of the hallway that they were in.

"Okay, let's go," Raven insisted, practically dragging the super forward via their still-looped arms.

As they walked, Kane studied the apartment numbers on the doors that they passed. Noting that the units were all directly across from each other with even numbers on the right, he assumed that apartment Five-Thirteen would be on the other side. But just to confirm, he asked Glen.

"Last one on the left," the super stated in a hushed tone, which jibed with Kane's thinking.

"How many other tenants down that way?" queried Kane.

The super shook his head. "None. That's part of the reason I put Remo and his people down there – he didn't want a bunch of other folks around them."

Kane simply nodded at that, understanding. With a crew that was up to some serious criminal mischief, Remo hadn't wanted a lot of prying eyes around.

When they were about ten feet from the apartment door, Raven suddenly came to a halt.

"Hang on for a second," she whispered as she unlooped her arm from Glen.

She then tucked her handgun into the rear of her waistband before unzipping her jacket and taking out the shotgun. A moment later she broke it open, revealing two empty chambers.

"Wait a minute," Glen whispered incredulously as Raven pulled a couple of shotgun shells from her pocket. "That thing's not loaded?"

"It is *now*," Raven announced softly as she put the shells in the chambers and closed the gun. Noticing Glen's stupefied look, she said, "Did you really think I was running around with a loaded shotgun in my jacket? Then all I'd need to do was get jostled or trip, then I'd blow my own fuckin' head off."

Still looking stunned, Glen looked at Kane, who raised his own gun up and said, "Oh, *my* shit's loaded. Believe dat."

Glen simply nodded, plainly understanding that at least one loaded gun had been on him the entire time, so the fact that the shotgun didn't have any shells earlier was immaterial.

"We ready?" Raven asked. "This shit's about to get real."

"Wait, lemme make sure I unnastand what's gone happen," Glen said. "I'm just gonna knock and tell them to come with me. You two gone be waitin' 'round the corner where the hallways come together and get the drop on 'em, and that's it, right?"

"That's puttin' a lotta trust in *yo* ass," Kane said.

"Yeah," Raven agreed. "I think we'll do this a little different."

Glen suddenly looked nervous. "Different how?"

"We're going to march down to the door with you, and stand to the side while you knock," Raven said. "Then, when they come out, they'll be looking down the barrel of a shotgun."

"What if they don't wanna come out?" asked Glen.

"What the hell are you talking about?" demanded Raven. "The whole reason you're coming up here is to take them to another room."

Glen licked his lips nervously. "I mean, what if they invite me in for a second – like they not quite ready to walk out the doe'?"

"Well, you better hope they don't," Raven advised. "'Cause otherwise we go in blasting."

"Just a second," Kane said as an idea suddenly occurred to him. "Maybe there's an easier way to get them to come out."

As he finished speaking, he pointed to the wall next to them – specifically, at a bright red fire alarm with a pull-down lever that was situated there.

# SHE'S HIS DRUG, HE'S HER THUG 4

Apparently understanding what he was thinking, Raven simply said, "Do it."

Kane nodded, then reached out and set off the fire alarm.

# SHE'S HIS DRUG, HE'S HER THUG 4

## Chapter 42

Klaxons immediately began blaring at a deafening level, accompanied by flashing lights. Seconds later, residents began pouring from their apartments, anxiously hurrying towards the stairs.

All of this was happening to the rear of Kane's little trio. As Glen had stated, this part of the floor appeared to be void of tenants – official tenants, anyway – so there was no one crowding their area of the hallway. Bearing that in mind, Kane and Raven generally stayed facing the end of the corridor where Remo and his crew were residing, their bodies positioned so that their weapons were not visible by anyone behind them.

Like the other tenants, they were expecting Remo's team to step out into the hallway after the fire alarm started going off. Simply put, almost no one wants to get barbecued. Much to their surprise, however, the door to apartment Five-Thirteen remained stubbornly closed.

After about thirty seconds, it became clear that their quarry was in no particular rush to come out. Raven gave Kane an inquisitive look. He knew what she was asking: whether he was down with being proactive in this situation. Kane looked around quickly to make sure no one was paying attention to them. Plainly convinced that everyone was focused on getting to the stairwell and getting the fuck out, he replied to Raven with a subtle nod. At that point, she nudged Glen with the shotgun, effectively telling him to walk forward, with her behind him and Kane bringing up the rear.

In essence, it looked like they were going with the option of having Glen knock on the door and try to lure Remo's team out. Unsurprisingly, Glen himself seemed jittery; as they approached the end of the hallway, Kane noticed tremors set in with respect to the super's right hand. He also appeared to nervously glance from side to side, like the walls were going to open up and swallow him.

They came to a halt almost directly in front of apartment Five-Thirteen, with Kane still a few feet behind Raven and Glen. Kane was about to hug the left wall by placing his back flush against it. Presumably Raven would do the same, so that they would both be out of the apartment peephole's line of sight when the super knocked on the door.

Before Kane could move, however, Raven suddenly swung towards the door of the apartment opposite Five-Thirteen and fired.

The boom of the shotgun going off would ordinarily have been thunderous, but with the fire alarm roaring Kane didn't think anyone positioned more than a few feet away would notice. In addition, although he wasn't certain, but he thought he also detected a howl of pain.

The buckshot shredded the wooden door of the apartment, and the force of the blast apparently disengaged the lock because the door swung open. Grabbing a terrified Glen by the neck, Raven yanked him in front of her and forcibly marched him towards the open doorway. Just as they crossed the threshold, Kane saw Glen's body twitch spasmodically a couple of times, as if he was having convulsions. At the same time, with the shotgun resting on Glen's shoulder, Raven fired again.

By that time, Kane was in motion. He raced to the doorway, and as he stepped inside his mind took in numerous details all at once.

First of all, he noted that the apartment entrance opened up into a living room and appeared to have the same floorplan as the unit the super lived in. Not far from the door, he saw a guy on the floor with multiple bullet wounds – an obvious victim of the shotgun. He also saw Glen cowering on the floor and bleeding from at least two gunshot wounds. Finally, he saw Raven hunkered down in the living room behind an incredibly filthy couch that looked like it belonged on a trash heap. She was in the process of dropping the shotgun while simultaneously reaching for the gun in her waistband.

All of this registered with Kane in less than a second. Recalling the layout from Glen's place, he knew that the rest of the apartment opened up to the left, around a corner from where he currently stood. There would first be a kitchen, and an adjoining hallway that led to a couple of bedrooms.

Stepping forward with his gun raised, Kane turned the corner. There were two guys in the kitchen and two others at the hallway entrance – one of whom was Remo (He recognized the other three as well, but didn't know their names.) They were apparently so focused on Raven that they had seemingly forgotten that she wasn't supposed to be alone. Kane's sudden appearance obviously caught them off-guard, because every one of them seemed to go bug-eyed when he came into view and began firing.

Unfortunately, it had taken Kane a moment to mentally map the scene and decide on a target. Naturally, he selected Remo – not just because he was the main guy, but also due to the fact that being in the hallway made him easy prey. Remo's reaction time, however, was fucking uncanny; in the split-second it took Kane to decide on who to shoot, Remo dropped low, reached to the side, and slid an accordion door into place.

## SHE'S HIS DRUG, HE'S HER THUG 4

The door in question was obviously designed for privacy – intended to keep visitors from being able to see the rest of the apartment (namely, the bedroom and bathroom areas). At the moment, it did an excellent job of blocking Kane's view of the hallway.

Kane fired anyway, his shots blasting the cheap wood of the door and sending splinters flying everywhere. Also, despite not being able to see his quarry, the hallway was so narrow that he was more likely than not to hit one of them – preferably Remo.

That said, he had only fired four or five shots when the two in the kitchen began shooting at him. Kane returned fire, but didn't think it likely that he was hitting anything. The two in the kitchen had ducked down, and were essentially putting their gun hands over a nearby countertop and firing blindly in his direction.

Their shots didn't really come near him, but instead slammed into the living room wall a few feet away, striking an area that was covered with mold. To Kane, the entire thing had a surreal quality, as the fire alarm essentially drowned out the sound of any gunplay, although the damage being done to the apartment was visibly notable.

Kane's reverie was suddenly interrupted by a shot from the kitchen that struck the plaster of the wall near the corner where he stood. The men in the kitchen were still firing aimlessly, but – as the old saying goes – even a blind squirrel occasionally finds a nut. In this instance, the plaster hit by the bullet was just above Kane's head, and it partially collapsed into a cloud of dust that immediately came down onto his head and face.

The dust caused Kane to begin coughing. Even worse, some of it got into his eyes, and he instinctively closed them. He fought panic, as he suddenly realized that – without sight – he was at an incredible disadvantage.

Slipping back around the corner, he quickly began rubbing his eyes, hard and vigorously, trying to clear them. A moment later, he almost panicked when he heard a soft popping noise nearby over the sound of the alarm. He immediately recognized it as gunfire, then relaxed when he realized that it was Raven exchanging gunfire with the two assholes in the kitchen. Forcing his eyes open, Kane saw her moving towards him as she continued shooting at their adversaries.

"You good?" she asked when she reached him, yelling to heard over the alarm as she brushed dust from his face.

Kane nodded. "Let's get these muhfuckas."

At that point, there didn't seem to be any more shots coming from the kitchen. That suggested that the two in there might be out. However, considering how they'd been armed at the farm, Kane thought it unlikely. Therefore, he and Raven crept towards the kitchen, rounding the corner that the gunmen were crouched behind from opposite directions. Ultimately, however, it turned out that they were wasting their time: the guys they'd been shooting at were gone. It was then that Kane noticed that the remaining portion of the accordion door had been pushed open.

"Shit," he muttered before going swiftly but carefully down the hall, with Raven next to him. They came to the master bedroom first, which Kane peeked into, then entered with his gun at the ready. A second later, he lowered it, as he looked at what was in front of him: an open window that led out to a fire escape.

# SHE'S HIS DRUG, HE'S HER THUG 4

## Chapter 43

It wasn't difficult to figure out what had happened: Remo and his team and gotten out via the fire escape, with the last two apparently slipping away while Kane was rubbing his eyes and Raven was wiping his face. In fact, there were a ton of people on it now, racing down to the ground. Of course, that's what you'd expect in a fire; it was the entire reason the fire escape existed. That said, the people on it were lucky that no stray bullets had come their way; had they known a firefight was taking place right next to them, full-blown panic might have set it.

Kane fought the temptation to give chase using the same route. For one thing, Remo and his crew had a head start. As crowded as the fire escape seemed to be, even ten or fifteen seconds probably provided enough separation for them to get away.

In addition, the fire escape looked rickety. Knowing that Glen was superintendent – which presumably meant he was the guy running point on building maintenance – Kane wasn't confident that everything in this bitch was up to code. Needless to say, that included the fire escape, and Kane kept envisioning it breaking away from the building or simply collapsing from the weight of so many people.

Finally, it would be pretty fucking obvious that some shit had gone down in this unit, and he didn't want anyone remembering later that they'd seen some random nigga coming out the window of the place. Thankfully, Remo's apparent need for privacy had included putting newspaper on the windows. In addition, the bottom of the window was flush with the fire escape walkway, so all Kane could actually see were the legs and feet of those going by.

That also meant that – unless somebody went crawling down the fire escape on their hands and knees – nobody could see him inside.

Although certain everyone was gone, Kane and Raven still did a quick check of the rest of the apartment. It took less than a minute and they didn't find anyone else. (Kane also didn't find any evidence of the missing money, but he honestly hadn't expected to. It was way too much cash for anyone to leave behind.) Aside from a beer bottle that had been used as an ashtray and was full of cigarette butts, the only thing Kane took serious note of was some blood on the floor of the master bedroom and the window sill. It suggested that he had probably winged Remo or that other fool who had been in the hallway with him.

"They're gone," he told Raven when they were finished, stating the obvious.

"We need to toss this place," she said. "See if we can find a clue as to where they headed."

"No time," Kane told her. "Cops will be here in a few, along with firemen, ambulances… damn near everybody on the city payroll who wears a uniform."

Raven frowned, not liking it, but then nodded. A moment later, they were hustling to the front door. However, Kane paused for a moment as they passed the mold-covered wall, staring at it as something started stirring in the back of his mind. A moment later, it came to him, and he turned angrily towards Glen, who was still on the floor and in obvious pain from bullet wounds to his shoulder, side and leg.

"You muhfucka," Kane growled, reaching down and hauling Glen to his feet before putting his gun to the super's head. "You fuckin' set us up."

"No!" Glen screamed. "I promise I–"

"Yes, you fuckin' did," Kane interjected forcefully. "All that shit you said to Remo about a second apartment with mold in it and shit. You basically told him to come over here and wait for us."

"No!" the super insisted, shaking his head. "That's not—"

"Don't fuckin' lie!" Kane roared, pressing his piece hard against Glen's forehead. "'Cause if you gone lie, we can end this conversation right *now*."

"A'ight, a'ight!" Glen said nervously. "There was like ten of 'em that I had to put up – too many to stick into one unit, so they actually got *two* places, across the hall from each other."

"So," Raven chimed in after retrieving her shotgun, "what was supposed to happen when we came up here? The two of us were going to be keyed in on the other apartment, making us easy pickings?"

"I don't know that they was gonna do anything," Glen argued. "I thought they just might hide over here until y'all left."

"Bullshit," Raven shot back. "They tell you to be on the lookout for a salt-and-pepper combo, but their plan is to hide when we show up? That make sense to you – that a bunch of motherfuckers armed to the teeth plan to slink off with their tails between their legs when we put in an appearance?"

Glen didn't immediately respond. Instead, he just stared at them, his lower lip trembling.

""Kill this drunk fuck and let's roll," Raven said after a few seconds.

"No, please!" Glen begged. "I can help you!"

"Help us how?" Kane demanded.

"If you ever need a place, I can hook you up," the super replied. "No charge, I promise, and on the dee-ell."

Kane looked at Raven, who shrugged indifferently as she put the sawed-off shotgun in her jacket and zipped it up.

"A'ight," Kane said. "We'll take that offer, but you gone have to stick to the story 'bout what happened up in here."

"Whatever you want," the super declared, nodding, "I'll tell 'em whatever you want."

"Keep it simple," Kane advised. "Just tell 'em that you was trying to make sure everybody was gettin' out after the fire alarm got pulled. You thought you saw somebody comin' out of a unit that was s'posed to be vacant, and when you investigated you found a bunch of squatters. They shot you, but also killed one of their buddies by accident befoe' runnin' off." Kane paused for a moment, then added, "You got that?"

"I got it," Glen assured them. "'Specially since it's pretty close to the truth."

"Good," Kane stated. "Now gimme yo fuckin' phone."

"Wh-what?" Glen stammered.

"Yo phone, muhfucka," Kane repeated. "You got a numba for Remo on that bitch, so I want it."

Glen nodded nervously, then reached a hand into his front pants pocket, wincing as he did so. Presumably his wounds were bothering him, but from what Kane could tell, the super would probably make it. That said, he found himself losing patience after just a few seconds, as Glen seemed to have trouble getting the phone out of his pocket. Kane briefly wondered if the muhfucka might be intentionally trying to delay giving him the phone, but a moment later Glen pulled it free and handed it over. At that juncture, Kane saw what the problem was: there was a bullet lodged in the phone.

In essence, one of the bullets that had been flying in Glen's direction had actually struck his cell. More than likely, it was the wedged bullet that had given the super trouble in terms of pulling the phone from his pocket.

Grunting in annoyance, Kane fiddled with the phone for a few seconds, but couldn't get it to work.

Turning to Raven, he simply said, "It's shot."

"In more ways than one," she added.

Kane simply nodded, then tossed the phone back to Glen, who bobbled it for a moment before actually catching it. Kane and Raven then headed for the door, but she stopped for a moment by the guy who she'd first shot. The buckshot had done a serious number on him, but surprisingly, he was still alive (although probably not for long). In fact, he seemed to be reaching ever-so-slowly for a gun that was on the floor near him – probably the weapon he'd been holding when Raven had opened up on him.

"We got time to search him?" Raven asked.

Kane's gut reaction was to say "No." However, every word he'd spoken since pulling the fire alarm had practically been a shout – including the discussion with Glen – and he was tired of yelling. In addition, they didn't have any other leads at the moment, and this guy might have something on him. With that in mind, Kane nodded at Raven then kicked the man's gun away.

Raven dropped to her haunches, then began searching the guy's pockets. As she did so, Kane saw the guy mouth something to her, which seemed to be "You shot me."

"Yeah, I feel bad about that" Raven commented snidely as she continued searching him. "Especially since you were about to jump out with a bouquet of flowers for me."

"Bitch…" the guy appeared to mutter.

Raven laughed as she finished and stood up.

"He didn't have shit," she told Kane. "Let's get the fuck out of here."

## Chapter 44

They managed to exit the apartment building without drawing attention to themselves. Of course, with throngs of people around – including folks from the neighborhood as well as tenants from the building – it was fairly easy to blend in. As they left, they heard sirens approaching; truth be told, they sounded damn close, which meant that Kane's decision to leave rather than search the apartment had been the right call. Making it back to the minivan without incident, they drove off, confident that they wouldn't be tied to any untoward events at the apartment building.

Almost immediately, Raven unzipped her jacket and took out the sawed-off shotgun.

"Hey," she said as she put the shotgun back into the gun range bag. "Kudos on that fire alarm thing. That was good thinking."

"Except it didn't get 'em to come out," Kane noted.

"Only 'cause they knew we were coming. Otherwise, that trick works any day of the week. So again, kudos."

"Thanks," Kane said. "You were on the ball, too. How'd you know Remo and his crew were in that apartment across the hall?"

"Glen kept glancing towards that door," she replied. "The, when we got close, I saw the peephole go dark like somebody was looking out. On top of that, I remembered that the mailbox for that apartment was marked vacant. Altogether, it just felt off, and in those situations I tend to go with my gut, so I guess I just reacted."

"Good thing for us you did."

"I suppose," Raven concurred. "So what now?"

Kane shrugged. "We all out of leads, so I thank we're done for the moment. I'll take you back to the farm, then I've got some stuff to do in the city. After that, I'll put on my thinkin' cap and see what I can come up with as a next move."

"Sounds good, but you don't need to take me all the way back out to the farm. I got a place here in the city. You can just drop me off there."

"Works for me," Kane said.

Raven smiled. "Cool."

She then proceeded to put her address into the minivan's GPS, which estimated that it would take twenty minutes to get there. Then, after making sure Kane was okay with it, Raven kicked off her shoes and placed her feet up on the dash. (Kane, of course, didn't give a fuck – it wasn't *his* ride.)

With her feet together and legs straight, Raven then leaned forward, continuing to bend at the waist until her head touched her legs. Staying in that position, she slowly ran her hands from her thighs all the way up to her toes, which she gripped for a few seconds.

Although he still paid attention to the road, Kane watched her in fascination. He himself was nowhere near that limber, so he had an earnest appreciation for people who get that kind of physical performance from their bodies.

With her head still on her legs, Raven turned in his direction. Noting his attention, she gave him a bright smile.

"Sorry," she murmured as she sat up straight. "Shit like today tends to get me wound up. Stretching eases the tension."

"You seemed fine to me today," Kane said. "I couldn't tell you were stressed at all."

"When I'm in the moment – the middle of a gunfight or some shit like that – it's not an issue. It's only afterwards that I start feeling restless. I guess you can think of it as a less-disturbing form of PTSD."

"I thank I unnastand," Kane stated. Then, seeing Raven pull her left foot up to her right shoulder, he asked, "So, you take yoga or sommin' to stay that flexible?"

Raven laughed. "Actually, I'm double-jointed."

To show what she meant, Raven gripped her left thumb with the opposite hand, then bent it all the way back until it touched her left forearm.

"Damn!" Kane blurted out in awe, making Raven laugh again.

\*\*\*\*\*\*\*\*\*\*\*\*\*\*\*\*\*\*\*\*\*\*\*\*\*\*\*\*\*\*\*\*\*\*\*\*\*\*\*\*\*\*\*\*

Raven's home turned out to be a three-story townhouse in a middle-class neighborhood.

"This is you?" Kane asked, eyeing the place as he put the minivan in Park. "It's nice."

"Thanks," Raven said. "There's room at the farmhouse for people to stay if they like and there's always a crew on duty there, but almost everybody has their own place. Basically, it's good to occasionally get away from the office, so to speak."

Kane nodded. "Makes sense to me."

"Anyway," Raven droned, "I have to report in to Augustus and bring him up to speed. But if you can hang tight for a few, I'll throw a fuck your way."

Kane simply stared at her, not sure he'd heard her right, then muttered, "Huh?"

"I said I'd fuck you," Raven repeated with a prurient grin. "Give you some pussy. Trim. Punani. Break you off a piece."

Kane blinked, his mind failing to come up with an immediate response, as her comment had caught completely him flatfooted.

"What, too forward?" she asked.

"Uh, no," Kane assured her, shaking his head. "I love a woman who ain't afraid to speak her mind and say what she want – especially in the bedroom."

"Well, is it the Black-White thing?"

"Fuck naw," Kane shot back truthfully. He'd never been discriminatory when it came to fuckin'.

"I didn't think so," Raven noted with a wink. "So it's the age difference then."

"Uh-uh," Kane told her, and had to consciously keep from adding, *I done fucked bitches with more years than you*.

"Good," Raven said, "because I'm not that fucking old."

Kane laughed. "Naw, you not old at all as far as I'm concerned. Plus you gorgeous, and fine as a muhfucka."

Raven smiled. "I was wondering if you noticed."

"Yeah, and normally I'd be takin' you up on that offer," he admitted. "It's just that…"

He trailed off, sighing, but Raven knew where he was going.

"You have somebody," she concluded.

"Yeah," Kane answered. "And I'm trying to be good."

"Well, just to be clear I'm not trying to blow up your spot," she explained. "I'm not looking for a relationship, so your girl don't have to be in the know. I could just use a deep dicking right now, and I just got a feeling that you know how to slang that shit."

Kane chuckled. "You right on the money, but seems to me that if you need that particular itch scratched, you could call just about any of those muhfuckas at the farm and they'd come runnin'."

"Yeah, but I already fucked all of them," she stated. "Well, not *all* of them. Not Augustus, 'cause he's my dad. And not Otto, because he's my kid. But pretty much all the rest."

Noting an odd look on Kane's face, she added, "I have a high sex drive. I make no apologies for it."

"I wasn't judgin'," Kane insisted. "I was just surprised that Augustus would send his daughter out on an errand like we handled today."

"He raised me to take over the business some day, which means I have to be able to personally deal with shit. Otto's being brought up the same way. On top of that, I'm actually the most competent person on the payroll, so who else would he send?"

Kane nodded. "I feel you."

"But as I was saying, I like to fuck, plain and simple. Plus, I smoke this special strain of cannabis that, like, quadruples your libido and makes the sex super intense."

"Wait," Kane blurted out, suddenly concerned. "You was high this whole time?"

"Hell, no," Raven clarified. "I like a clear head when I'm handling business. I was just trying to explain how, if you down, I could give you the ride of your life."

"I don't doubt it," Kane stated.

"And you do remember that I'm double-jointed, right? Trust me, you haven't lived 'til you've fucked a girl who can lock her ankles behind her head. You get crazy deep penetration."

Kane fought hard to keep the imagery out of his head. He was a hundred percent focused on being true to Mika – what they had was special – so he really didn't need Raven tempting him like this.

"Look," he said, "You got it going on – you know that. But what I got with this girl right now... It's amazing, and I don't wanna fuck it up."

Raven seemed to consider that for a moment, then held out her hand. "Hand me your phone."

Kane complied, and Raven hastily tapped on the screen for a few seconds before handing it back.

"I'm giving you my number," she said. "The offer's open indefinitely, so if you change your mind..."

She trailed off, winking, then reached into the rear of the minivan and grabbed the gun range bag. As she opened the door and stepped out, Kane noticed something on the passenger side floor. Leaning over, he reached out and grabbed the item: one of Raven's mouse guns, which had probably fallen out of her pocket when she was stretching.

"Hey," Kane called out, holding up the diminutive firearm. "I think you dropped this."

Raven, who had been on the verge of closing the door, looked at the gun for a second, then smiled.

"Keep it," she told him. "Now you have an excuse to come see me."

With that, she closed the door, waved goodbye, and walked off. Kane watched her, telling himself he was only hanging around to make sure she got in okay (even though it was still daytime), then drove off after she unlocked the door and went into the townhouse.

# SHE'S HIS DRUG, HE'S HER THUG 4

## Chapter 45

After dropping off Raven, it took Kane about another half-hour to get to the place that Fix had directed him to. It turned out to be a secluded manor house situated on a couple of acres in a stately subdivision. As Kane pulled up and parked in a circular driveway, he pegged the house as being at least seven thousand square feet in size. Surprisingly, the vet – Annabelle – was there, opening up the door for him as he got out of the car.

"Didn't expect to see you here," Kane said as he approached.

"I don't operate on people often," she remarked as Kane stepped inside. "I was curious as to what the professional opinion of my work would be."

"She did fine," declared a nearby masculine voice.

Kane recognized it as belonging to Fix, and turned to find the former doctor behind him.

Fix was a tall, good-looking guy with black hair and blue eyes. At the moment, he was wearing a white lab coat with a stethoscope around his neck, which made him the stereotypical image of a doctor.

"Good to see you again," Fix stated as he extended a hand, which Kane shook.

"You, too," Kane said sincerely. Glancing around, he added, "Nice place. Bet yo patients love convalescin' *here*."

"Like hell," Fix muttered. "I see most of my 'patients' in a converted warehouse space in another part of town. That's where your friends were headed when I got a call from Buggy telling me that I needed to give them white glove service. So I brought them here."

Kane simply nodded at this, going on the assumption that Buggy had merely been passing along a message from Regis. He didn't even try to guess how Regis might have known about Fix. Again, that nigga had eyes everywhere, and probably had a list of everybody Buggy had introduced Kane to – including the good ex-doctor.

"So, how they doin'?" Kane asked.

"The girl – Mika? She'll be fine," Fix told him. "Just needs to take it easy for the next few days."

"And Castor?"

"He'll live, but I can't promise a swift recovery," Fix admitted.

"Can I see them?"

"Sure," Fix told him. "But I'd recommend going to see the gunshot victim first. He was awake a few minutes ago, but I don't know how long that will last."

"Sounds good," Kane said. "Lead the way."

# SHE'S HIS DRUG, HE'S HER THUG 4

## Chapter 46

Castor was set up in a room that Fix described as the "second master" – an oversized bedroom on the first floor that had a nice view of a large backyard pool. He was lying in a king-sized bed, looking pale but awake, when Kane and the others came in. Much to Kane's surprise, he was also hooked up to an IV and a bunch of medical equipment, just like a real hospital. (And just like a real doctor, Fix went to one side of the bed and immediately began checking out his patient while Kane went to the other.)

"Hey, man," Kane said. "How you feelin'?"

"Like I got shot," Castor deadpanned in a wheezy voice as Fix appeared to check his pulse. "Fucked up my high…"

"I bet," Kane muttered. "Slugs have a tendency to do that."

"So they tell me," Castor muttered. "Where you been?"

"Had some things to take care of," Kane replied cryptically. He liked Fix and felt the man could be trusted, but being circumspect was simply part of Kane's nature.

"Well," Castor mused, "I hope you brought back some weed."

Kane chuckled at that, as did Fix and Annabelle, who had come in as well. In fact, she was watching Fix with almost spellbound fascination – like a kid seeing Santa put presents under the Christmas tree. Fix didn't seem to notice, but it was blatantly obvious to Kane that Annabelle was crushing on him.

"Anyway," Castor continued, "thanks for not leaving me earlier."

"No problem. You wudda done the same for me."

"Don't bet on it. I'm kind of a chicken-shit."

Kane laughed again, as did everyone else. Castor obviously wasn't a gangsta, but Kane had a feeling that he wasn't the type to run out on his friends.

"Well, I'm gonna leave you to rest now," Kane said. "Besides, I need to check on Mika."

Suddenly, Castor looked concerned. "She okay?"

"Just a mild concussion," Kane replied. "She gonna be fine."

"Oh, okay," Castor said as eyes fluttered slightly.

He looked like he wanted to say more, but a few seconds later, Kane realized that Castor had fallen asleep. At that point, Fix quietly ushered everyone from the room.

\*\*\*\*\*\*\*\*\*\*\*\*\*\*\*\*\*\*\*\*\*\*\*\*\*\*\*\*\*\*\*\*\*\*\*\*\*\*\*\*

The room Mika was in was just down the hall from Castor. It wasn't as big and didn't have the same view, but was still rather nice. Also, rather than a bunch of medical equipment, it was outfitted more like a traditional bedroom with a dresser, mirror, and so on. Finally, instead of accompanying Kane as they had with Castor, Fix and Annabelle let him go in alone.

Mika was asleep when he came in, looking like an angel. There was an easy chair nearby, and he quietly moved it closer to the bed before sitting down. Reaching out, he gently took her hand and kissed it before pressing it to his cheek, then simply looked at her.

She seemed comfortable, so he assumed Fix and Annabelle had taken good care of her. Thankfully, the bump on her head hadn't gotten any bigger. Other than that, Mika looked the same as always, but that was the thing about concussions: they fucked you up *mentally*, so that physically you might look okay, but you'd forget simple shit like your own name.

He found himself wondering if Mika might have any issues like that, but his thoughts were interrupted when she unexpectedly started stirring. Moments later, she opened her eyes, looked at him, and smiled.

"Hey, babe," he said in a hushed tone, kissing her hand again. "How you doin'?"

"Okay," she answered, then winced as she began to sit up.

Kane found himself suddenly concerned. "What's wrong?"

"Headache," she replied, tapping her temple with her forefinger. "Massive."

"Okay, well let me get Fix. He can give you sommin'."

"No," she insisted, shaking her head and tightening her grip as he tried to release her hand. "Stay…"

"Okay," he said. "I'm not goin' anywhere."

Mika smiled at that, then frowned. Kane realized after a moment that she seemingly had something on her mind but was having trouble concentrating. He was about to tell her not to worry about it – that whatever it was could wait – when she spoke.

"Where…been?" she asked.

"Out. Had to deal with some shit related to this morning."

Mika gave a gentle nod to indicate she understand exactly what he was referring to. "By…yourself?"

Kane shook his head. "No. I had a sidekick – that chick who was at the farm."

Rather than respond verbally, Mika made a twirling motion with her free hand, basically asking, *What else?*

"We had a meet-up with the opposition. Intense negotiations, but we didn't get the outcome we wanted."

Mika took a moment to process what she'd heard, then asked, "What now?"

"Don't know," Kane admitted, shrugging. "I'm outta leads at the moment. All I got is one name, but can't go any further with it. There's other muhfuckas involved, but ain't no signpost tellin' me who they are."

"Buggy?" Mika suggested.

Kane nodded, understanding what she was trying to say. "Buggy could prolly help, like he did with that Sway situation. But I need to be able to give him sommin' to work with: a name, a pic, or some shit like. We ain't got jack, so it would be like sayin' we saw some random nigga on the street and then askin' Buggy to find 'im."

Mika frowned, concentrating, then the fingers of her free hand started to flutter, almost like she was playing an invisible piano. Obviously she was trying to work up to something, but had trouble getting it out.

Finally, she blurted out a single word. "Tablet."

"Tablet?" Kane echoed in confusion, then his eyes went wide as he suddenly understood what Mika was getting at. "Oh, you want your computer tablet."

Kane had to think back for a moment, then remembered that he had left it in the room with her at Annabelle's clinic. He stood, preparing to go ask the vet about it when he suddenly saw the tablet on the dresser. (Apparently Fix and Annabelle had been thorough when moving their two patients.) He quickly retrieved it and brought it back to the bed, handing it to Mika.

## SHE'S HIS DRUG, HE'S HER THUG 4

Kane watched for a moment as Mika appeared to bring up videos of some sort. His immediate assumption was that it was the usual footage of cats doing random shit – like maybe Mika thought he needed to see something humorous to take his mind off the day's events. Suddenly she spun the tablet so that it was facing Kane right-side up, then pushed it towards him.

"Look," she said, tapping the screen.

"It's okay," he assured her without glancing at the tablet. "I don't need to be cheered up."

"Look," she insisted, pointing at the tablet.

"I'm fine, babe," he said. "Really."

"Look!" she practically demanded, brow furrowed.

Seeing that she was getting worked up, Kane acquiesced and looked at the screen – and his mouth almost dropped open.

"Oh shit!" he blurted out, then looked at Mika in amazement. "Damn, girl…this is why I love you."

As he finished, Kane practically froze. The sentiment he'd just expressed was genuine, but he'd never said the words out loud before – hadn't even really said them just now in the way a woman wants to hear them spoken. But apparently he'd come close enough to saying those three little words for Mika.

Smiling, she simply said, "'Bout fuckin' time…"

Chuckling, Kane leaned over and gave her a quick but tender kiss on the lips, then left with the tablet under his arm, staring at the image on the screen.

Apparently Mika had videoed Remo and his crew at the farm.

# SHE'S HIS DRUG, HE'S HER THUG 4

## Chapter 47

As he left Mika's room, Kane still found himself in awe of what Mika had done. Somehow, while hunkered down in the SUV, she'd had the presence of mind to turn a camera on those muhfuckas who had tried to rob them that morning. In short, although he didn't have anyone's name other than Remo, he did have pics now.

Now in the hallway again, he noticed Fix and Annabelle chatting a few feet away. Although they had let him go in alone, they had apparently chosen to stay close by in case they were needed.

Plainly seeing an unusual expression on Kane's face, Fix asked. "Everything okay? We need to check on her?"

"No, no," Kane stressed. "She good. But I need to make a phone call, so I'm gonna step outside for a minute."

"Sure," Fix told him. "You can go out back, if you like."

"Thanks," Kane said, then followed as Fix led the way through the house. Moments later, they were at a pair of glass double doors that opened onto a beautiful veranda, as well as the pool Kane had seen earlier.

Kane stepped out and took a second to admire the scenery as Fix closed the doors behind him. The veranda was expertly designed with a gorgeous hardwood deck. There was also an outdoor kitchen and bar, and – just a bit beyond the pool – a large gazebo. Fix might not be a licensed physician anymore, but he obviously still knew how to live the good life.

Remembering why he was there, Kane took a seat on a couch that was part of a swank outdoor living room set. Next, he pulled out his phone and called Buggy, who answered on the first ring.

"Been expectin' to hear from you," Buggy stated without preamble. "Heard you had some shit go down today."

"That's puttin' it mildly," Kane said.

"So whachu need?"

"I got pics of some guys that I need ID's for."

"Shoot 'em to me. I'll hit you right back."

"Okay, give me a minute."

"Alright. Send 'em when you ready."

Kane hung up and then spent a few minutes going through Mika's video. Counting Remo, there were four of the muhfuckas left who had tried to jack them, and he was pretty sure he could identify the other three. Thus, he simply had to isolate those images on the footage, which he then sent to Buggy. His phone rang less than two minutes later.

"Sorry man," Buggy began, "but I don't know any of those muhfuckas in the pics you sent."

"Shit," Kane muttered. "That puts me back at square one."

"I could reach out to my network if you want, see who else might know 'em based on the pics, but ain't no guarantee anybody gone recognize they face."

Kane didn't immediately respond. Buggy's words triggered something in his brain, but it didn't rise to the surface right away. And then it came to him.

"Kane?" Buggy asked. "You still there?"

"Yeah, I'm here," Kane answered.

"So whachu wanna do?"

"That depends: you got any contacts in the police department?"

"A few. Whachu thankin'?"

"Nuthin' too complicated," Kane promised. He then gave a brief overview of what he wanted.

"Fuck, man," Buggy griped when he was done. "I thought you said it wasn't complicated."

Ignoring the comment, Kane asked, "You thank you got a contact that can do it?"

"Maybe, but I might have to peck around. I'll call you back. Stay glued to your phone."

Buggy then hung up.

# SHE'S HIS DRUG, HE'S HER THUG 4

## Chapter 48

Kane didn't go back inside right away. Instead, he simply sat outside for a moment, enjoying a few minutes of calm solitude. It felt as though he'd been running all day (and that wasn't far from the truth), so having a little time to himself was practically bliss. (He also spent a moment contemplating whether to update Regis, but decided against it, as he really didn't have anything new to report.)

He'd been out there maybe five minutes when he heard the door open. Glancing around, he saw Fix coming out.

"Mind if I join you?" Fix asked.

"It's yo house, man," Kane answered. "I should be askin' *you*."

"Well, you're a guest at the moment," Fix noted, "so your preferences get priority."

"In that case, please have a seat."

"Thanks," Fix said, then flopped down on a loveseat diagonal to Kane.

Fix didn't say anything initially. Like Kane, he simply sat there for a minute, seeming to enjoy the day. That said, he obviously had something on his mind, so when he cleared his throat a few moments later, it was obvious he was ready to talk.

"Look," he began, "as part of my business model, I typically don't ask my patients a lot of questions. They come to me, I fix them up, then send them on their way. End of story." At that point, he leaned forward, looking Kane in the eye. "But this is my *home*, and one of the people in there has gunshot wounds, so I have to ask: should I be worried?"

Kane shook his head. "Naw. This wasn't some vendetta thang, where there's somebody out for blood. We was victims of an attempted robbery. The would-be thieves didn't get what they was after at first, but they was able to snatch it from some colleagues later. Long story short, they got what they wanted, so they wouldn't waste time puttin' in an appearance – even if they knew where we was. And again, it wasn't personal, so they got no reason to come after us."

"Alright," Fix murmured with a nod. "Sounds plausible. But if that's the case and you guys didn't do anything wrong, why didn't you just take your friend a hospital?"

Kane thought for a moment. "I like Castor, but I met 'im for the first time today. He don't strike me as the hardcore gangsta type with a damn rap sheet long as my arm, but I don't know for sho'. And if I take 'im to a hospital, the doctors gone be callin' the cops inside of two minutes."

"Yeah," Fix concurred. "They're required to report all gunshot wounds to the police."

"Exactly. And even though he prolly ain't done nuthin' worse than get a speedin' ticket, I didn't want 'im to wake up cuffed to a hospital bed."

"Understood," Fix remarked. "And I hope you understand that I had to ask."

Kane nodded. "It's a fair question. You got a right to know what you might be gettin' into."

"Well, I'm glad to know that I don't have to worry about some asshole showing up with an uzi. When we got here I didn't know what the fuck to expect, so I sent my assistant home."

Kane raised an eyebrow. "You have an assistant?"

"Hell, yeah. Otherwise I have to do shit like empty bedpans and give sponge baths myself."

Kane chuckled at that, and Fix joined in.

"Anyway," Fix continued, "I tried to get Annabelle to leave as well, but she wasn't having it."

"I cudda told you that. That one ain't goin' nowhere, even if a fuckin' suicide bomber run up in here with a warhead strapped to his chest. She's got a mad crush on you."

"I know, and it's my fault," Fix confessed. "Back when I was using, she was my regular booty call – meaning that if I couldn't pick up some young coed in a bar, I'd give her a call."

"And she never let you down, right?"

Fix smiled. "If they don't come running after you dial up, it ain't a booty call." They both chortled at that, but then Fix went on, saying, "Anyway, I've apologized for the way I was back then and she forgave me."

"I think she wants to give you more than forgiveness," Kane suggested slyly.

"Maybe, but she deserves better. She's a good woman at heart. And me? I'm not as fucked up as I was when I was constantly shoving white powder up my nose, but I'm still chasing coeds."

"Hell, that don't make you fucked up," Kane advised. "That just makes you a regular man."

"Maybe, but Annabelle should get more than a 'regular' guy," Fix commented.

"Well, maybe that ain't what she want. Instead of Mr. Right, maybe she just lookin' for Mr. Right *Now*."

Fix shook his head. "Annabelle's not built that way."

"Oh, so you sayin' she down to *be* somebody's booty call, but not have somebody be *hers*."

Fix contemplated for a moment. "Good point."

"Look, she obviously pinin' for you, and it sound like you might owe her more than just an apology – especially considerin' how she was there for you when you needed her."

"Hmmm," Fix mused. "We did have some good times. You wouldn't know it to look at her, but she's absolutely ferocious in the bedroom."

Kane laughed. "It's always the quiet ones."

"And Annabelle's pretty damn quiet – at least *out* of the bedroom," Fix noted. "By the way, she's actually the person who brought Mika here."

"Huh?" muttered Kane. "Whachu mean?"

"I have a commercial van that's basically outfitted on the inside like an ambulance. It's in the garage right now, but it's what I used to bring Castor here. But there's really only room for one patient inside, so Annabelle put Mika in her car and drove her over."

"That was nice of her," Kane said.

"Yeah, but that's the way she is," Fix said. "Nice."

"Sure, but let's be honest: even if Mika hadn't been there, she wudda found a way to tag along."

"Probably," Fix agreed, coming to his feet. "Anyway, I need get back inside and see to some stuff."

"Understood," Kane said. "And thanks for everythang today."

"No problem, but don't forget to thank Annabelle as well."

"You got it."

"Lastly – and please don't take this the wrong way," Fix said, "but there's fried chicken in the fridge if you get hungry."

Kane laughed. "The only way I'm gonna take that is with gratitude, 'cause I fuckin' *love* fried chicken."

# SHE'S HIS DRUG, HE'S HER THUG 4

## Chapter 49

After Fix went back inside, Kane stayed outside a few more minutes. He might have stayed there indefinitely, but his phone rang. It was Buggy.

Kane answered with a curt, "Talk to me."

"Okay," Buggy began, "I got a friend on the force who can get what you want, but he got to brang someone else in 'cause this ain't his area of expertise. Basically, there's a tech muhfucka who's gotta be part of this."

"I get that. It's fine."

"Good, now here's the other piece. There's risk involved in this shit, so it ain't gone come cheap."

"How much?"

"They want ten grand. A piece. In advance."

*Fuck!* Kane thought to himself. He figured the shit would expensive, but these muhfuckas were gouging him. But it's not like he had a choice at the moment.

Taking a deep breath, he said, "That's cool. Can you cover it for me 'til I get you the money?"

"Not a problem," Buggy assured him. "I'll let everybody know it's on, but it might take a minute to handle up on this. I'll reach out when it's done."

"Sounds good," Kane told him before getting off the phone.

Satisfied that he was making progress of a sort, Kane stood, preparing to go back inside. Just then his stomach rumbled, reminding him that he hadn't eaten anything since breakfast.

Deciding to take Fix up on his offer of a meal, Kane went back inside and found his way to the kitchen. Once there he checked the fridge and found a large bag of King Pluck chicken. He then checked the cabinets until he found a set of plates and some drinking glasses. A minute later, he was seated at a nearby breakfast table, gobbling up fried bird and washing it down with water from the tap.

When he was done eating, Kane swiftly cleaned up behind himself, washing and drying both the plate and glass he'd used. He put the glass back where he'd found it, but left the plate out. After placing a couple of pieces of chicken on it, he put the bag of King Pluck back in the refrigerator, then carried the plate of chicken to the room Mika was in.

Much like himself, he assumed that Mika hadn't eaten all day. However, she was asleep when he came in. That being the case, he placed the chicken on the dresser along with Mika's tablet, which he still had with him. He then resumed sitting in the chair next to the bed.

As before, Mika looked incredibly serene while asleep. Being in a peaceful environment probably helped, and Fix's home seemed more tranquil than most – uncannily quiet, in fact. It was at then that Kane realized that he hadn't seen Annabelle or Fix since coming back inside.

That didn't necessarily mean anything. It was a big house, so it made sense that they might not always be in view. At the same time, however, Fix's concern came to mind – that someone might come there looking for Kane and the others. Kane really did think it unlikely, but didn't want to make a slip because of overconfidence. With that he mind, he decided to go in search of his host.

Gun in hand, he started on the first floor, checking Castor's room and a few places he hadn't seen earlier, like Fix's home library and a well-stocked bar that was just off the kitchen. Not finding any sign Fix and Annabelle, he went upstairs.

Here, he hit pay dirt almost immediately. Walking up to a door that he assumed led to a bedroom, he suddenly picked up on an odd noise: an insistent, rhythmic squeaking that appeared to be coming from the room in question. More to the point, it was accompanied by intense moans, forceful gasps, and animalistic grunting.

Needing no more information as to the location of Fix and Annabelle (or what they were doing), he put his gun away before quietly stepping away from the door and creeping back downstairs. He then went straight to Mika's room.

Once there, Kane went to the chair and practically dropped into it. He then sat back, relaxing. He hadn't realized it, but searching the house had made him incredibly tense. Consequently, he closed his eyes, intending to rest them for only a moment, but in no time at all he was fast asleep.

# SHE'S HIS DRUG, HE'S HER THUG 4

## Chapter 50

Kane woke to the sound of his phone ringing. It took him a moment to realize where he was and get his bearings. When he did, he noticed two things: first, according to his watch, he had dozed off for a couple of hours. In addition, he saw that Mika was already awake and moving around. She gave him a sly wink, which made him smile, then he turned his attention to his phone.

It was Buggy, and Kane answered in a matter-of-fact tone saying, "Hey, man. How'd it go?"

"I got what you wanted," Buggy replied.

"Cool. Can you send it to my phone?"

"Naw. You gotta come get the files, or else I can drop 'em off to you."

"Files?" Kane repeated, unable to keep the surprise out of his voice.

"Yeah – *files*, muhfucka," Buggy stressed. "This shit you wanted done is fuckin' serious, and my contacts downtown don't want no damn digital trail leadin' back to them. So I couldn't even send them those pics you gave me; I had to put that shit on a flash drive and physically hand it off. Likewise, with the shit they got for you, they didn't want anythang pointin' to them, so that shit's in some file folders. *Comprende*, muhfucka?"

"Got it," Kane told him. "I'll be by to get it asap."

"Good."

"And Buggy," Kane added. "Thanks."

"No problem," Buggy said. "That's what I'm here for."

Kane hung up, then noticed that Mika – having finished her chicken – was staring at him.

"How you feel?" he asked.

"A lot better," she told him, and Kane agreed that she at least sounded like she had rebounded. She certainly wasn't struggling for words any more.

"So what was that all about?" Mika asked.

"I need to get a lead on those muhfuckas who tried to jack us at the farm," Kane explained. "Buggy's helpin' me out – got some info, but I need to go see 'im to get it."

"Well, let's roll."

Kane gave her a skeptical look. "Ain't you s'posed to be restin'?"

"Fuck that. I ain't lettin' you go out and try to handle this shit on yo lonesome."

Kane felt proud of the way she was willing to ride for him, but felt obligated to talk her out of it, saying, "Shit, babe. I 'preciate what you tryin' to do, but you ain't nowhere near a hundred percent. You need to stay here and rest."

"Well, on my worst day, I'm still twice as good as anybody else you gone find. Plus, you need somebody watchin' yo back."

"Well if I need somebody, I can reach out to Mikey – or maybe even Raven."

"Who?" Mika asked.

"The chick from the farm. I told you 'bout her earlier."

"Oh, yeah…I remember. But she can stand down. I gotchu."

"I hear you, but–"

"No fuckin' 'buts'," Mika suddenly blurted out. "I'm doin' this."

# SHE'S HIS DRUG, HE'S HER THUG 4

## Chapter 51

Kane continued trying, but there was no talking Mika out of tagging along. On the one hand, he was happy to have her back with him, because his girl was true ride-or-die. On the other hand, you don't just magically recover from a concussion, so there was every chance that she'd be more of a liability than anything else.

Fix agreed with Kane. After cleaning up with respect to the chicken Mika had eaten, she and Kane had went to find their host, ultimately locating Fix and Annabelle having a drink in the bar. They were talking animatedly, and Annabelle had such a bright smile on her face that she was practically glowing.

*More like* after*glowing*, Kane thought to himself as he and Mika approached the other two.

After Kane explained that they had to go run some errands, Fix adamantly argued that Mika shouldn't be going anywhere because of her concussion.

"You may look fine for the most part and actually think you are," Fix told her, "but you're not. Concussions are serious, and you need to wait before you try to return to normal activities."

"You wastin' your breath," Kane told him. "Even if the clouds parted and a voice sounded from Heaven ordering her to rest up, she wouldn't listen."

"He ain't lyin'," Mika stated defiantly.

"Alright," Fix said, taking her comment in stride. "Well, if you insist on ignoring medical advice, at least let me give you something to help with the symptoms."

Mika was open to that, so Fix told her to follow him to what he called his "Pharmacy." Moments later, it was just Kane and Annabelle in the bar.

"Hey," she said, "you want something to drink? Dale has everything here."

"Dale?" Kane echoed.

"That's his given name, although he doesn't use it much."

"It kinda fits," Kane said. "This seems like the sorta place that would be owned by someone named Dale."

"Well he can't take credit for that. His great-grandfather built this place, so it's been in the family for generations."

"Must be nice," Kane said.

"Yeah - we should all be so lucky," Annabelle noted. "So, about that drink?"

"No thanks," Kane said. "We got some thangs to attend to, and I need my head on straight. But that reminds me: I don't even think I introduced you to Mika when we came in."

"It's okay. She was knocked out when you got to the clinic, but she woke up a few times while you were gone – both there and while I was driving here – so we're acquainted. You'll be happy to know that all she did was ask about you each time."

Kane felt his cheeks turning red.

"Oh that's cute – you're blushing," Annabelle teased. "Well, there's no need to be shy about being in love. It's a beautiful thing when you have someone who just sets your world on fire like that."

"You speakin' from experience?" Kane asked with a knowing look.

Now it was Annabelle's turn to blush, which made Kane laugh.

"You're right," he told her. "It is a beautiful thing. And it looks good on you."

Annabelle, uttered a soft "Thanks," but before she could say anything more, Fix and Mika came back.

"A'ight," Mika said. "We can roll."

"So you're really leaving?" Annabelle asked, walking towards Mika, who nodded.

While the two women hugged and started chatting, Kane stepped towards Fix.

"I gave her some pills," Fix told him, apparently anticipating Kane's question. "They'll help with any pain. Make sure she takes them."

"I'm on it," Kane told him. "Also, we'll be back to check on Castor. I'll hook you up then."

"No worries on that front," Fix assured him. "Buggy vouched for you, so I know you're good for it."

"Thanks," Kane said. "See you in a few."

Then, after confirming that they had everything (including Mika's tablet), Kane began ushering Mika towards the door, and a minute or so later they were on the road.

# SHE'S HIS DRUG, HE'S HER THUG 4

## Chapter 52

Buggy's preferred hangout spot was a watering hole called *BDE*. Mika had only been there a couple of times, but felt the owners should be sued for false advertising because – aside from Buggy – neither the place nor the clientele actually exuded any "Big Dick Energy."

On the way there, Kane made a quick stop to get more gloves. (He had a feeling they'd need them.) He also gave Mika a more detailed rundown of everything that had happened – including his conversations with Regis and the twenty-four-hour clock he was on.

"Well now I'm glad I demanded to come along," Mika declared when he finished. "You fuckin' need me."

In truth, Kane still hadn't decided if she'd be a liability or not, but didn't want to argue with her about it. Instead, he focused on the task at hand, calling Buggy when they were a few blocks away and thereby prompting him to meet them outside. He was in his wheelchair next to his minivan when they pulled into *BDE*'s back parking lot. It was only early evening so the lot was essentially deserted. They parked next to him and got out.

"Hot damn," Buggy commented as they walked up to him. "I see y'all done upgraded ya ride. Nuthin' like the style and comfort of a minivan."

"Yeah," Kane chuckled as he gave Buggy some dap. "Won't be long before every muhfucka in the hood's drivin' one."

"No doubt," Buggy added. "Anyway, I know you like gettin' straight to business, so…"

He tapped on the side of the van as he trailed off. The side door slid open, and one of Buggy's scantily-clad girls stepped out, holding a cardboard file box that contained a number of manila folders. She walked towards Kane and held the box out to him. As Kane took it and began leafing through the contents, the girl turned to Buggy.

Bending over, she gave him a kiss on the cheek and said, "See you inside." She then headed for the entrance to *BDE*, with Buggy watching her lustily every step of the way.

"What is all this?" Mika asked, looking at the box's contents over Kane's shoulder.

"Exactly what yo boyfriend asked for," Buggy said. "Results of runnin' facial recognition software against some pics he sent me."

Mika looked at him in surprise. "*You* did this?"

"Fuckin' *cops* did this," Buggy clarified. "They the ones got access to the tech. Kane asked me if I knew anyone on the force who could run the software on some images, and luckily I knew some folks."

"What da fuck, Buggy?" Kane suddenly complained. "There's folders on like eight or nine muhfuckas in here."

"Ten," Buggy corrected.

"But I only gave you pics of foe'," Kane argued. "How da fuck that mushroom into all this?"

"Okay, nigga, lemme lay this out for you," Buggy grumbled. "See, there's a reason why Crimestoppers be askin' the public to help identify criminals, even when they got that muhfucka on video muggin' a ole lady or carjackin' some shithead at a gas station. It's 'cause this facial recognition shit ain't all it's cracked up to be."

"If you talkin' 'bout accuracy," he continued, "it ain't nowhere near a hundred percent – not even close. So when you feed a damn pic into that bitch, it come back with a lot of fuckin' matches. Excuse me – *possible* matches. What you got there is the top three matches for each of yo pics."

"The top *three* matches?" Mika repeated. "How many matches does it usually make for a pic?"

"My contacts say between five and fifty," Buggy answered.

Mika snorted in derision. "If it comes back with fifty matches, it's fuckin' useless."

"Not useless," Buggy argued. "Just not that accurate."

"If there s'posed to be three matches per pic, shouldn't it be twelve in here?" Kane asked.

"The tenth is the guy you called Remo," Buggy replied. "Cops said that with a name – even an alias – to work with, they was able to pinpoint that muhfucka in the system."

"A'ight," Kane said. "So what's all in these files?"

"The usual ID shit," Buggy told him. "Name, aliases, address, known associates… Crap like that."

"A'ight," Kane said. "I 'preciate you comin' through like this for a nigga."

"Anythang for my homies," Buggy said.

"I know I owe you," Kane told him, "but I'm workin' with a tight window, so Im'ma have to hook you up next time."

"I ain't worried 'bout that," Buggy insisted. "Just go handle yo business."

"I will," Kane said. "For sho'."

# SHE'S HIS DRUG, HE'S HER THUG 4

## Chapter 53

After leaving Buggy, they drove to a parking garage – a place where Kane felt they could spend a few minutes sorting through the files they'd gotten. After finding a spot away from any other vehicles, Kane parked and then pulled all of the files out of the box.

The cops had seemingly had the presence of mind to put Remo's file first. Kane quickly flipped through it, noting that the inside of the manila folder had the pic he had sent paper-clipped next to what was presumably the image from the facial recognition system.

"Real name – Renardo Mortelli," he read. "Last known address was three years ago in the Midwest. Only known association is the Canaries. Rap sheet a mile long."

There wasn't anything else noteworthy on Remo, so Kane set his file aside. He quickly skimmed the rest and – based on the matching pics from the facial recognition system – nailed down the other three guys in short order.

However, he had only gotten a good look at them during the shootout in the apartment, and even then it had only been for a few seconds. More to the point, witnesses misidentified culprits all the time, and – although Kane considered himself better-than-average in that department – this was important enough to get it right. With that in mind, he decided to check the info in each of the other files to make sure he wasn't making a mistake. In doing so, he found three right off the bat that were obvious misses.

"None of these are our guys," he said, tossing the files back into the box.

"How you know?" Mika asked.

"'Cause two of 'em are military, and one's servin' a three-year bid for larceny."

"Oh," Mika muttered. "Okay."

"Not this muhfucka, either," Kane announced, removing another from the pile. "He missin' a hand."

Continuing, he added, "This one live in the city."

"So what?" Mika inquired. "How that get 'im off the hook?"

"The super of that apartment buildin' I was in earlier said all these muhfuckas were from outta town," Kane explained. "So anybody local is excluded."

"So how many left?"

"Five, and I can eliminate one more because the file says he's in his fuckin' sixties."

"He don't look that old," Mika noted as Kane showed her the facial rec photo.

"Like bitches on datin' apps, it's probably not a current pic," Kane offered.

With a sixth potential cast aside, that left Kane with Remo's file and three others. Fortunately, the last trio were the same files he had initially identified as Remo's compatriots. Quickly diving into their files, he saw that two — a couple of ex-cons with the surnames of Baskett and Rommel — had no local connections. He got lucky with the third, named Fosse.

"Bingo," Kane announced as he finished eyeing Fosse's file. "This muhfucka has a sista in the city."

# SHE'S HIS DRUG, HE'S HER THUG 4

## Chapter 54

It took about half an hour for Kane and Mika to reach the home of Fosse's sister – a modest one-story house with an orange brick exterior in a lower-middle-class neighborhood. Going there was a little bit of a gamble, since Remo and his cohorts could actually be anywhere in the city. But seeing as how none of them were local (and their prior abode in the apartment building was compromised), it represented the best chance of finding those muhfuckas.

They ended up parking a few houses down on the opposite side of the street, choosing a spot that would let them keep an eye on the front door of the home. They assumed that someone was there, as there were two vehicles parked in the driveway: an aging station wagon, and some kind of off-road vehicle that looked like a cross between a dune buggy and a truck.

Kane didn't recognize either vehicle from the farm, but that was to be expected. Basically, he had assumed that a couple of the cars that were present when they first arrived to make the buy that morning had belonged to Remo's crew. Naturally, they hadn't seen which cars those muhfuckas had left in, but it was a sure bet that at some point they had switched vehicles. The question was, had they switched into one of the cars currently in the driveway?

The only other place Kane had seen Remo and the others was at the apartment building. But just like at the farm, he had no clue what type of car they were in when they drove off. However, he and Raven had circled the block – including the building's parking lot – and he had eyeballed the vehicles there. In his mind, the off-road

# SHE'S HIS DRUG, HE'S HER THUG 4

vehicle looked like something he had seen then, but he couldn't swear to it.

In short, Kane didn't really have a plan of action at this point. That being the case, they simply staked out the house while he pondered their next move.

"So what now?" Mika asked, intruding on his thoughts. "We go in?"

"No," Kane told her, shaking his head. "We don't know who's in there for one thing. For another, we basically got this address from the cops. If something goes down here, they prolly won't be happy 'cause it'll look like they aided and abetted us."

"Fuck them," Mika spat out. "They hooked you up with the info and prolly took reams of cash from you to do it. They had to know what was up, and that it might lead to some muthafuckas gettin' capped."

"They may not care if it's a bunch of dipshits who prolly just between prison stints right now. It's a different story if some nigga and his ride-or-die bitch break in and shoot Nana Josephine while she slurpin' Jell-O and watchin' her favorite game show."

"So we need to know moe' befoe' we make a move," Mika surmised. "Well, let's see what we can find out."

Before Kane could stop her, she opened up the door and stepped out. Closing the door behind her, she swiftly crossed the street and went marching down the sidewalk towards the house they were staking out. Fortunately, it was dark at this point, so she was somewhat inconspicuous.

Once she reached the driveway, Mika turned and approached the station wagon. The house had a porch light on, and anyone looking out probably had enough illumination to see her. From his vantage point, it didn't appear to Kane that the drapes in the house moved, so he felt Mika was safe. But whatever she thought she was doing, she needed to do it quick.

On her part, Mika put a hand up to her eyes and leaned forward, peeking first into the driver's side window, then the rear window on that side. Seemingly satisfied, she then hurried back to the minivan.

"What da fuck?" Kane hissed when she got in. "We need to be more subtle than that."

"We ain't got time to be subtle," Mika told him. "We gotta grab the bull by the fuckin' horns."

"Is that were you were doin' just now?"

"Damn straight."

"And did you find out anythang?"

"As a matter of fact I did," she stated, causing Kane to look at her in surprise. "There's a car seat in the back of the station wagon."

Kane frowned. The file on Fosse hadn't provided much info on his sister other than name and address. It didn't go into details like whether she was married, had kids, and so on. However, a car seat in the back of the station wagon suggested that it was probably a family car and that there was a small child in the house.

"Alright, I guess we wait this out," Kane finally said, "and hope sommin' breaks."

"Okay," Mika said, then crinkled her nose. "Tell me again, who was the bitch you had up in here?"

Kane sighed. "I done already told you like three times that it was Raven, who was at the farm this mornin'."

"Did you fuck her?"

Kane laughed. As always, he found Mika's jealousy amusing.

# SHE'S HIS DRUG, HE'S HER THUG 4

"No babe, I didn't fuck her. I only fuck you these days."

"Then why does it smell like pussy in here?"

"Because it don't. That's just the concussion – it can fuck up your sense of smell."

"So that's not pussy I'm smelling?"

"No," Kane assured her.

"Or estrogen – like some bitch was in here in heat?"

Kane simply stared at her for a moment. "You sure you up to this?"

"Damn straight," Mika insisted. "Are you?"

"Yeah," Kane said. "Why you ask?"

"'Cause you seem tense. Like maybe you need some kind of release."

As she finished, she waggled her eyebrows at him suggestively.

Kane stared at her in disbelief. "You fuckin' kiddin', right?"

Rather than answer directly, Mika turned towards the rear of the minivan. "Sure is a lot of room back there. You can practically stretch out in this bitch."

"No way," Kane declared, shaking his head. "I ain't about to make yo toes curl in the back of this van."

"Like you ain't never fucked in a car before," Mika admonished.

"Yeah, but this ain't the time or the place," he declared. "For one thang, we on a stakeout. For another, you got a concussion, which mean yo head's all screwed up and you not yo'self. It would be like fuckin' a retard."

"Oh, so it'll be like when *I* fuck *you*," she quipped.

Ignoring her barb, Kane said, "And lastly, with a concussion, you shouldn't be doin' the nasty 'til all your symptoms go away."

"Not true," she argued. "I asked Fix about it when he gave me those pills, and he gave me the green light for gettin' laid."

"Bullshit," Kane shot back. "I done had a concussion befoe', so I know for a fact that you not supposed to be bonin' when you recoverin' from one. No strenuous activity – including sex – is what they told me."

"Fine, I lied," Mika confessed. "Fix didn't give me the green light, but that don't mean we can't throw down."

"Actually," Kane countered, "that's *exactly* what…"

He trailed off as a car pulled into the driveway of the house they were watching. It was an older model – a charcoal gray sedan with at least ten years on it in Kane's estimation – and not in great shape. The driver parked behind the station wagon.

The windows on the car were tinted, so Kane couldn't really make out what the driver looked like. It might be one of the guys in Remo's crew or someone else entirely, but he only had a few seconds to make a decision.

"Wait here," he told Mika, then swiftly got out of the minivan and closed the door.

Staying on their side of the street, he swiftly jogged down the sidewalk, staying in the shadow of the trees for the most part. He stopped when he was directly to the rear of the sedan. At that juncture, the driver's door opened; Kane swiftly crossed the street just as the person behind the wheel started getting out.

The driver turned out to be a perky little bleached blonde, average in height and maybe sixteen years old. Stepping out, she swung a purse over her shoulder and then leaned back inside to retrieve something from the vehicle. She didn't even see Kane until she straightened up – now holding a couple of pizza boxes in her arms – and prepared to close the door. At that point, Kane was right next to her.

Inconspicuously pointing his gun at her (but making sure she could see the weapon), Kane said, "Don't scream."

The girl, who looked like she was about to do just that, instantly closed her mouth, trembling.

"Get back in the car," Kane ordered.

As the girl moved to obey, Kane opened the rear passenger door. As the girl got inside and closed her door, he slid into back seat behind her and closed his.

"Now don't anything stupid like blow the horn or set off the alarm," he warned. The girl vigorously nodded to let him know she understood, to which Kane replied, "Good. Now just keep facing forward."

"Please, mister," the girl said despondently, "I ain't got much money, but you can have it." As she finished speaking, she held her purse up over her shoulder, attempting to hand it to him.

"You can have the car, too," she added. "Just don't hurt me – please."

"I don't want your money or your car," Kane told her.

The girl drew in a sharp breath at that and let out a soft whimpering noise.

"Oh please, no!" she begged. "Please don't...not that."

"Just be quiet," Kane told her. "I'm not gonna hurt you."

"Please, please, please!" she pleaded, apparently not hearing him. "Please, just take the car and the money. I won't even report it. Just please don't–."

"Listen," Kane hissed, putting the gun to her head, at which point she stopped speaking, but was visibly trembling.

"I'm not gonna hurt you," he continued. "I'm not gonna lay a finger on you, unnastand?" The girl nodded. "Okay, now what's your name?"

The girl swallowed, then muttered. "Sh-Sh-Shar."

"Shar?" Kane repeated.

Shar nodded, saying, "It's sh-short for Ch-Charlotte."

"Okay, I get that," kane said. "How old are you?"

"S-Sixteen."

"You in school?"

Shar nodded. "Tenth grade."

"And this where you live?"

"Yes, sir," Shar answered, sounding reasonably calm.

"A'ight, Shar, here's what's gone happen. Im'ma take my gun off you. I only pulled it in the first place 'cause I needed you to listen to me, and you wasn't listenin'. But you listenin' now, right?"

"Yes, sir."

"Cool," Kane said. He lowered the gun, and Shar seemed to visibly relax. "Now as I said, I ain't got no interest in you. What I *am* interested in, is who's in that house."

Shar seemed to freeze for a moment, then she unexpectedly turned to the back seat, looking Kane in the eye.

"You here 'bout Uncle Bobby," she blurted out.

For a second, Kane wasn't sure who she meant, then he recalled from the file that Fosse's first name was Robert.

"Uh, yeah," he said after a few seconds. "But just like you, I ain't gonna hurt 'im. I just need to talk to 'im."

"Bullshit," Shar declared, showing more spunk than Kane would have given her credit for a few minutes earlier. "Nobody like you just wants to *talk* to Uncle Bobby."

Rather than answer directly, Kane said, "Turn back around."

Remembering that she was supposed to be facing forward, Shar complied.

"You here to kill 'im?" she asked, looking at Kane in the rearview mirror. When Kane didn't immediately answer, she said, "It's okay if you are. I hate that asshole."

Kane found that surprising. "You okay with somebody showin' up to kill yo uncle?"

"He's a piece-a-shit. Him *and* his asshole friends. The only time he come here is when he in trouble, and my mom always let him stay 'cause he's her older brutha and she scared of him."

"So him and his friends are in there now?"

"Should be," Shar replied. "They sent me out for pizza, 'cause they don't wanna go out." Her eyes narrowed as she eyed Kane via the mirror. "Or maybe they *can't* go out – 'cause of *you*."

Ignoring her comment, Kane asked, "How many in there besides yo uncle?"

"Three. There's Remo, who I guess is the leader – everybody do what he say. There's another one they call 'Basket-case,' I guess 'cause he seem a lil' crazy. And then there's one they call Romeo – a fuckin' pedophile who always leerin' at my lil' sista, tryin' to get her to sit in his lap or some shit like that."

Kane thought about that for a moment. He assumed "Basket-case" was Baskett, and "Romeo" was Rommel.

"How old yo sista?" he asked.

"She eight."

Kane frowned. "Seem kinda big for a car seat."

"She don't ride in a car seat," Shar declared, looking confused.

"There's a car seat in the station wagon," Kane said. A moment later he remembered that Mika had a concussion. With her brain muddled, she could have been seen almost anything and thought it was a car seat – a suitcase, a hamper, whatever... But he had just blindly taken her word for it.

With that view of the facts, he was about to say "Nevermind" with regard to the car seat when Shar spoke up.

"Oh, that's for the baby," she explained. "I also got a two-year-old sista named Juno – a lil' going-away present from my mom's supposedly-sterile ex-fiancé."

Kane didn't comment on her statement but felt a slight bit of relief as it related to the car seat. It meant Mika wasn't as fucked up in the head as he had feared.

"So," Shar continued, "You here to kill 'em?"

Kane considered for a moment, then just decided to be blunt.

"Look," he began, "your uncle and his friends stole a lot of money from some important people. I'm here to get it back."

"How much?"

"Over a mill."

"Ha!" Shar snorted in derision. "A million bucks? That's a joke. Those assholes just made me go spend *my* money on these fuckin' pizzas." As she finished speaking, she tapped the pizzas, which were sitting in the passenger seat next to her.

"Maybe they keepin' it on the down low."

Shar shook her head. "No way my uncle scored a million bucks. If he knocked over a liquor store and made off with a hundred, he'd be waving it under my mom's nose, like he some criminal mastermind and she a braindead idiot for working a straight nine-to-five. But a million? Trust me, ain't no way it happened."

Kane found it curious that she was so adamant about the money, but he wasn't about to argue about it with some Pixie who didn't even have her wisdom teeth yet.

"So what's yo plan?" Shar asked. A second later, her eyes went wide. "Wait a minute! You not 'bout to go in there shootin', are you? My mom and sistas in there!"

"Calm down," Kane ordered. "I promise you, I got no intention of doin' that, but that's why we talkin'. I need some way to get yo uncle and the rest of 'em to come out."

"Like I said, they talk like they need to keep a low profile. They only been here a few hours, but they actin' like they might be here for a while – coupla days, at least"

"Why you say that?"

"'Cause they made a list earlier and made my mom got get a bunch of food and shit from the store for 'em. She don't want 'em here, but she too scared to kick 'em out or say 'No' when they tell her to do sommin'."

"So yo uncle just popped up out the blue, sayin' him and his friends need a place to stay?"

"Naw, him and that asshole Romeo came by a few days back. They only stayed 'bout an hour, but Uncle Bobby told my mom that he was just checkin' in 'cause he might need a place to crash. We was hopin' he had left town by now, but next thang you know him and his friends ringin' our doorbell."

"So they not plannin' to go anywhere," Kane surmised. "If they need sommin', they just gonna make you or yo mom run they errands."

"That's what it look like."

Kane pondered for a moment. "So what do they do in there?"

"Drank beer," Shar said. "Talk shit. Play cards."

"What kinda cards, like poker?"

Shar shrugged. "I guess. They also play some stupid game where you draw cards, and whoever gets a spade has to tell a Black joke." Noting a somber expression on Kane's face, she added, "They're racist assholes."

Kane became pensive. Shar's statement reminded him of something Raven had said about the Canaries – and presumably Remo – being bigots. That gave him an idea.

"Hey," he droned. "That place you went to for pizza - how far is it from here?"

"Five or ten minutes," Shar said without hesitation.

"Okay, that's good," he noted. "Now the big question: you wanna help me get those muhfuckas outta yo' house?"

"Hell yeah."

"Okay, then do this: go in and tell 'em that you didn't get the pizzas. Tell 'em there was a bunch of niggas outside the pizza shop, and one of 'em grabbed yo ass. They scared you so bad that you came back without the food, and you scared to go back 'cause you thank they still there."

If Kane was hoping that Shar would quickly jump on board, he was dead wrong. After he finished, she didn't say anything, and a moment later he noticed that she looked horrified.

"It'll work," he assured her. "I know you scared, but don't worry. Those racist muhfuckas will go runnin' out the door to defend yo honor, and we'll be able to catch 'em off guard. Your mom and sistas won't get hurt."

"It's not that," she finally said. "I'm not scared, or worried 'bout my family."

"Then what is it?"

Shar let out a deep breath. "I can't say that word."

"Huh?" Kane muttered, perplexed. "What word?"

"*That* word," she insisted. "The 'N' word."

Kane frowned. "You mean 'niggas'?"

Shar nodded. "Yes! I can't say that word. My boyfriend's Black."

"But it's not *real*," Kane argued. "You just actin' a part."

"I unnastand, but still…"

Kane wiped his face with his hand, frustrated. "Just my luck to pick one of the few White people in America who don't secretly wanna say the word 'nigga'."

Shar giggled. "Actually, lots of people, White *and* Black, don't wanna say that word."

"Well, if you got a Black boyfriend, at some point you gone get mad enough to call him that – even if it's just in yo head."

Shar laughed again. "You know, that's exactly what *he* said."

# SHE'S HIS DRUG, HE'S HER THUG 4

"Anyway, let's stick to the business at hand," Kane suggested. "You've been in there with 'em. If you don't like my idea, then whadda you thank will make them come out?"

"Honestly, I don't know," Shar confessed.

"Well *think*. They must step out for sommin'. Do they take out the trash? Take your dog for a walk? Have a beer on the back porch? Maybe off–"

Shar had been shaking her head methodically at everything Kane suggested. However, she suddenly perked up when he mentioned the back porch. Kane abruptly stopped speaking, as it was obvious that something had occurred to her.

"What is it?" he finally asked.

"The patio," she said. "Romeo's a chain smoker and has to have a cigarette, like, every few minutes. Mom won't let him smoke in the house 'cause of Juno - it's the one area where she stands up for herself – so he goes out on the patio. Sometimes my uncle or one of the others will join 'im, but most times he out there by hisself."

"Well, next time he go out, he gone get a surprise," Kane promised.

# SHE'S HIS DRUG, HE'S HER THUG 4

## Chapter 55

The conversation with Shar essentially ended at that juncture. Shar then grabbed the pizzas and hurried inside. Kane's instructions to her had been very simple: just go inside and act normally. Shit would go down when Rommel – the one Shar called Romeo – stepped out for a smoke. At that point, no matter what (if anything) she heard, Shar was supposed to stay inside and keep her family there as well.

On his part, Kane slipped out the sedan and headed back to the minivan. Once there, he got inside and gave Mika a brief overview of his chat with Shar. He then gave her the key to the vehicle, which was the real reason he'd come back. If anything happened to him, he didn't want to leave Mika stranded.

Naturally, Mika wanted to come with him, But Kane nixed the idea.

"Just stay in here and be ready to roll," he told her.

"But what if this girl is settin' you up?" Mika asked.

"She's not," Kane said matter-of-factly. It was obviously something that had occurred to him, but he had dealt with devious muhfuckas his entire life, and he hadn't gotten the sense that Shar fell into that category. He had garnered the impression that she was being sincere; he stressed that fact to Mika, who didn't like it but reluctantly agreed to stay back.

With that settled, Kane then left and crept back down the street, keeping as much to the shadows as possible and trying to stay out of the light from streetlamps. Seeing a middle-aged couple that appeared to be out for a walk across the street, he bent down and pretended to tie his shoe while furtively watching them.

Thankfully, they didn't seem to notice him (or if they did, nothing about him seemed to arouse their suspicions). Once they were past, he stealthily dashed towards Shar's house, making a beeline for the side of the structure.

Shar's backyard was fenced, but fortunately the gate was unlocked. Kane tried to open it silently, but the hinge squeaked loud as a muhfucka. Or rather, it sounded that way to Kane, but the good news was that it didn't seem to draw any attention – not from the neighbors on that side, or more importantly, from anyone inside Shar's house. Rather than risk it creaking again when he departed, Kane left the gate slightly open. Someone passing by might see that it was agape, but considering how gloomy it was and the fact that Kane was in the shadow of the house, it was unlikely that any passersby would see *him*.

Sticking close to the side of the house, Kane stepped swiftly to the rear and peeked around the corner. There was a porch light on at the back of the house, next to a sliding glass door that was currently closed. The door opened onto a modest concrete patio that was maybe six-by-ten feet in size. The yard itself was maybe thirty-by-sixty feet, and contained a small children's playhouse as well as a plastic kiddie pool. Sitting on the patio was a set of plastic outdoor furniture consisting of four chairs and a table with an oversized umbrella sticking up from a slot in the center. All in all, it looked like a typical backyard.

There wasn't anyone outside at the moment, but Kane did see something that drew his attention: near his side of the patio was a bunch of stomped-out cigarette butts. It gave credence to Shar's story about Rommel being a chain smoker. (It also brought to mind the bottle of cigarette butts he'd seen at the apartment building.) That meant that all Kane had to do now was wait.

As luck would have it, he didn't have to wait long. He'd been standing at the rear corner of the house for less than two minutes when he heard the door slide open and Rommel stepped out.

He was a stocky guy in his forties with a bald head and a thick-ass, red handlebar mustache. He was dressed in jeans and a long-sleeved hickory stripe logger shirt – the same ensemble Kane recalled him wearing at the apartment complex earlier.

Someone inside yelled something about closing the door, and Rommel complied. Next, he reached into one of his shirt pockets and pulled out an open pack of cigarettes. He tapped the open end of the pack and a cigarette slid halfway out. Pulling the cigarette completely from the pack, he flicked it towards his mouth and caught it expertly between his lips. He then put the pack away before reaching into his jeans pocket and pulling out a lighter. He brought the lighter towards his face and, using his free hand to protect the flame, flicked it on and lit his cigarette.

It was then, with both of Rommel's hands in view, that Kane quietly took a step forward from the shadows with his gun raised. Rommel, catching the motion out the corner of his eye, jerked his head in that direction. His eyes narrowed in recognition when he saw Kane, but he clearly took note of the gun pointed at him as well.

Kane raised a forefinger to his lips, indicating silence. Rommel seemed to understand because he kept quiet and started to raise his hands. However, Kane made a lowering motion indicating that the man should drop his hands, which he did. Kane then made a come-hither gesture, and Rommel began walking towards him, stopping a few feet away when Kane held his hand up, palm out.

"Where's the money?" Kane whispered.

# SHE'S HIS DRUG, HE'S HER THUG 4

Rommel gave him a blank look. "What money?"

"The money you muhfuckas stole earlier today."

"You barkin' up the wrong tree, son. We ain't get shit. Maybe you wasn't payin' attention, but you and yo friend got away."

"Somebody followed us and ended up takin' the cash."

"Well, it wasn't us. You thank we'd be hangin' out in this dump if we'd made any kind of score?"

Kane's brow crinkled in thought. What Rommel was saying squared up with what Shar had told him earlier, but left Kane with more questions than answers. However, before he could ask anything else, the gate to the backyard squeaked unexpectedly.

The sound momentarily drew Kane's attention and he glanced in that direction to make sure no one was trying to get the drop on him. He immediately realized it was just the wind, but the split-second distraction was all the opening Rommel needed.

Faster than Kane would have thought him capable of moving, the man stepped forward and grabbed the wrist of Kane's gun hand, yanking it to the side.

"They're here!" Rommel bellowed as he and Kane began struggling for control of the gun.

Kane was immediately furious with himself. First, he had let Rommel to get close enough to him to make a move; second, he had allowed himself to become distracted. However, he realized that any mental self-immolation would have to wait as the patio door slid open and Remo stepped out, accompanied by Fosse and Baskett. And they were armed.

Tussling with Rommel over the gun had caused Kane to turn so that now he was sideways to the patio.

## SHE'S HIS DRUG, HE'S HER THUG 4

Even worse, the trio who had just come outside had a direct line of sight to him. Knowing what was coming, Kane swiftly shifted his weight and spun, just as Remo, Fosse and Baskett raised their guns and fired.

The sudden and unexpected movement by Kane caused Rommel to shift position, effectively putting him between Kane and his friends. In fact, it put him in almost the exact spot Kane had been standing as Remo and the others started shooting, their guns booming like cannons.

Kane hunkered down as best he could behind Rommel's stocky frame as the man was pelted with friendly fire. Rommel's body jerked wildly for a few seconds, and then he dropped to his knees. Kane dropped down with him, still intent on using the man as a human shield.

By that time, however, his companions had realized their error and had stopped firing. They simply stood there, apparently confused about what to do next. Kane, however, decided to take advantage of the lull in the action.

At that point, Rommel's grip on Kane's gun hand had naturally loosened. Kane raised it towards Remo and the others and fired.

Normally, his aim was pretty good, and at such close range it should have been a turkey shoot. However, he was still using a hand to prop Rommel up and use him for cover. It wasn't clear whether Rommel was still alive, but his body was swaying and it threw Kane's aim off. As a result, instead of hitting, one of the three men facing him, his first shot hit the back porch light, which was to the rear of the trio.

Unfortunately, his first shot turned out to be his only shot, because immediately thereafter, the gun jammed.

# SHE'S HIS DRUG, HE'S HER THUG 4

## Chapter 56

The porch light exploded in a shower of sparks, with a sound like a thunderclap. A split-second later, the backyard went almost completely dark, with the only light coming through the glass doors from the interior of the house. However, it provided almost no illumination as far as Kane was concerned.

Remo and his companions were plainly confused about what had happened, because at least one of them – apparently thinking the exploding porch light was gunfire – turned to their rear and started shooting.

"Ambush!" one of them cried out, making it clear that he believed there was an armed adversary behind them. A moment later, they were all randomly firing both towards Kane and in the opposite direction.

Kane stayed where he was behind Rommel's body. With a jammed gun, there really wasn't much more he could do, although he had a pretty good idea of what the problem was with his weapon. That said, he couldn't do much about it at the moment. His more pressing problem was going to be getting out of this without getting capped.

Unexpectedly, the gunfire ended. Peeking around Rommel's body, Kane caught a glimpse of Remo and the others rushing through the glass door, without even bothering to close it behind them. Moments later, he heard commotion from inside the house – basically shouting. Letting Rommel's body fall, he was about to creep towards the glass door and risk a glance inside when he heard an engine rev from the area of the driveway.

Realizing what was happening, Kane dashed towards the gate and to the front yard. He arrived just in time to see Remo, Fosse and Baskett speeding off in the off-roader, driving so haphazardly that they almost T-boned another car as they flew through a stop sign.

Kane's gut reaction was to go after them…to jump in the minivan and give chase. Realistically, however, he knew that – without some idea of where they were going – he was unlikely to catch them. Thus, he went with the next best option: searching Rommel's body to see if he could turn up a clue as to where their quarry might be headed.

Mind made up, Kane swiftly returned to the backyard, this time closing the gate behind him. Next, he turned on the flashlight on his cell and shined it on Rommel. From all appearances, the muhfucka was definitely dead. Thankfully, it didn't take long to pat him down (despite having to do it with one hand), but all Kane turned up – aside from cigarettes – was a wallet and cell phone.

The wallet he put back, along with the twenty bucks in cash that it contained. (Occasionally it made sense to make a homicide look like a robbery, but he didn't think this was one of those occasions.) He spent a moment fiddling with the cell phone only to realize that it required facial identification. Bearing that in mind, he shined his light on Rommel and put the cell about an inch from the man's nose. Rommel's face was contorted in death, and Kane wasn't sure it would work. Luckily, after a few seconds, the phone unlocked. Kane hastily disabled the facial ID program, then pocketed the phone before switching off the light and putting his own cell away.

At that point, he was ready to leave. But, in a bout of inspiration, he put his gun in Rommel's hand, making sure to get the man's prints on the trigger.

Now satisfied that he'd done all he could for now, he went back to the gate, preparing to leave. Gunfights had a tendency to distort a person's sense of time, but Kane estimated that no more than three minutes had passed since Remo, Fosse and Baskett had started shooting. As loud as the shooting was, someone had surely called the cops by now, but he probably had adequate time to get the fuck away from there. However, when he opened the gate, three things happened.

First, Kane had forgotten how much noise the gate made, and it squealed loud as fuck when he opened it. Second, he noticed three people – a man and two women – all on the sidewalk directly in front of him. Lastly, all three turned in his direction as the gate creaked.

"Who's there?" asked the man, who was White and in his early forties (as were the women with him).

The question made it clear to Kane that the three on the sidewalk couldn't see him. His first inclination was to run – just do an about-face and start hopping backyard fences. But that would make him look guilty as fuck, which he didn't need with a body nearby. Deciding to be bold, he tried a different tack.

"I need some help here," he called out. "Somebody's been shot."

The man and his companions barely hesitated, suddenly dashing up the yard to the fence.

"He's over there," Kane said as they reached the gate, although it was unlikely they could see where he was gesturing in the dark. "Anybody got a light?"

"Hold on," said one of the women. A moment later, she had a cell phone out with a light shining on Rommel's body.

"Holy shit," murmured the man. "What happened?"

"I don't know," Kane lied. "I was passing by and I heard someone calling for help. I ran up here and found him like this. It was right after somebody set off some firecrackers or something."

"Not firecrackers," the man said authoritatively. "Gunshots."

"I wouldn't know," Kane stressed. "I don't like guns."

The man turned towards Kane, his body language indicating skepticism at what he'd just heard. However, there wasn't enough illumination to make out anyone's features, so neither man could see the expression on the other's face; the woman with the light kept it firmly trained on Rommel. Kane guessed she'd never seen a dead body before – or a dead body that was this fresh.

Kane felt certain the man was going to say something, but before he could, the other woman – the one *not* holding the light – spoke, asking, "You call 9-1-1?"

"I tried," Kane insisted. "It was busy."

The woman he'd replied to simply nodded at that. "That happens sometimes when a bunch of people call about the same incident. I guess that was everybody around here calling about the gunshots." She paused for a moment, then added, "I suppose somebody should probably check on Naomi and the kids."

"Who?" asked the man.

"Naomi," said the first woman holding the light. "The woman who lives here. You must have seen her... Three girls? Big boobs? Doesn't seem to care for bras?"

The man appeared to shake his head. "I don't think I know her."

"Sure, Frank," muttered the second woman sarcastically. "Like you're not eyeing her every time she steps outside in one of those skimpy outfits. Not to mention the fact that we only live three doors down…"

"Now Ginnie," the man – Frank – began, "Dr. Granville said couples therapy won't work unless you accept the fact that other women occasionally cross my line of sight."

"Fuck off," Ginnie growled. "I'm going to check on Naomi and the girls."

With that she began heading back out the gate. However, Ginnie had barely left before Kane heard someone at the front of the house call her name and mumble something that he couldn't quite catch.

"Someone's been shot in Naomi's backyard," he heard Ginnie announce. "I'm gonna check to see if she and the girls are okay."

There must have been more than one person out front, because Ginnie's statement seemed to cause a stampede. Less than a minute later, there were probably a dozen people crowding around Rommel's body.

As folks poured into the backyard, Kane drifted nonchalantly towards the gate. Having a crowd back here, trampling the crime scene and fucking up any evidence, actually worked in his favor. He hadn't exactly planned it, but he wasn't going to look a gift horse in the mouth. That said, it was well past time for him to leave – a fact punctuated by the sound of sirens suddenly reaching his ears.

"Uh, I think I have a first aid kit in my car," he said to no one in particular.

"Good idea," someone blurted out in his direction, although anyone with half a brain should have known first aid was useless to Rommel at this point.

# SHE'S HIS DRUG, HE'S HER THUG 4

With unofficial approval, Kane departed, moving as swiftly as he could while remaining as inconspicuous as possible. Fortunately, everyone out on this part of the street was probably massed in Shar's backyard. As a result, he made it to the minivan essentially unseen. A moment later, he and Mika were driving away.

# SHE'S HIS DRUG, HE'S HER THUG 4

## Chapter 57

Kane drove without any real direction in mind, just intent on putting some distance between them and the shit that had just gone down. However, he took the time to give Mika a brief overview of his recent backyard escapades. Needless to say, she had heard the gunshots and then seen Remo and his buddies come flying out the house and take off. She had also seen people heading towards the same backyard area where Kane had gone. However, she had managed to avoid getting too anxious about what was happening or whether Kane was in trouble. Still, she was overtly relieved when he finally came back.

Upon hearing how things had gone, she smugly remarked, "So it sounds like you *did* need me back there."

"No," he insisted, "I needed you to stay with the van and be ready to roll."

"Muthafucka, yo gun jammed. You needed all the help you could get."

"Not from a chick suffering from a concussion. You might have passed out in the middle of a gun battle."

"Like hell I would," Mika shot back. "Anyway, how the hell yo gun jam?"

"Prolly limp-wristing," Kane admitted, "although I didn't get a chance to check it."

Mika simply nodded at this. Most people didn't realize it, but not gripping a gun correctly could cause it to get jammed. It was a phenomenon known as "limp-wristing," and it usually occurred when a shooter didn't have a proper grip on his firearm *and* didn't have his wrist locked.

"That's not like you," Mika noted. "You typically rock solid when it come to handlin' a heater."

"Well, don't forget that, at the time, I was tryin' to prop up this muhfucka and use 'im as a human shield. That kinda shit will keep you from hittin' on all cylinders."

"You ain't have to leave the gun, though. A jam is usually easy to fix."

"I needed to dump that piece anyway. I used it to shoot up an apartment earlier today, and just fired it in somebody's backyard. Last thang I need is for the cops to find a gun on me that they can tie to bodies at two crime scenes."

"But now they got a weapon and another muthafucka they can link to both places."

"Right," Kane confirmed with a nod. "And that reminds me…"

As he trailed off, he leaned over and opened the glove compartment. Inside was Mika's gun, where he had placed it earlier.

"Hey," Mika droned as Kane took the gun out and closed the glove box. "I was lookin' for that."

Kane gave her a dubious glance. "So how the fuck was you gonna help me earlier if you ain't even know where yo piece was at?"

Mika seemed to reflect for a moment, then reached into a pocket and pulled out her switchblade. A moment later, the blade popped open.

"Me and Pierce had yo back," she declared, using the nickname – Pierce – that she had given the weapon.

Kane shook his head in derision. This was further proof that Mika wasn't quite herself yet.

"Unless that knife can stop bullets," he remarked, "leaving yo ass in the car was the best thang I could do."

"Fine," she huffed as she folded and put the blade away. "But if that's how you feel, then gimme my gun back."

"I thank Im'ma hang on to it – especially since my own piece is gone now."

"Oh, so you pullin' rank?" Mika grumbled.

"Damn straight," Kane stated. "But not because I'm a man or any shit like that, but 'cause that concussion still got you fucked in the head."

Mika crossed her arms, plainly piqued. "So what the fuck am I supposed to use?"

Reaching into his pocket, Kane pulled out the mouse gun that Raven had left with him.

Mika stared at the weapon in disdain. "Nigga, you *must* be jokin'."

"Uh-uh," Kane stressed, shaking his head. "It's this or nuthin'."

Letting out an exasperated breath, Mika practically snatched the diminutive gun from him, muttering "Asshole."

Kane simply chuckled.

"So what's next?" Mika asked.

"Don't know," Kane confessed. "Sommin' 'bout this ain't sittin' right."

"Whachu mean?"

"I asked that muhfucka back there 'bout the money. That fool ain't have a clue what I was talkin' 'bout."

"You sho' he wasn't just playin' dumb?"

Kane shrugged. "He cudda been, but I ain't get that impression."

"So if they ain't got the money, who does?" Mika asked.

"Probably whoever they partner is."

## SHE'S HIS DRUG, HE'S HER THUG 4

Mika gave him a confused look. "Partner? What da hell you talkin' 'bout?"

Kane spent a moment contemplating. "You remember two or three years ago back home, this armored car got robbed?"

"Yeah," Mika stated with a nod. "They made off with like five, six million. It was all over the news."

'Right," Kane said. "Cops thought they'd get a hint as to who did it pretty quick, 'cause that's a lot of cash. When niggas come into that kinda money, it's fuckin' impossible for them to keep they mouth shut about it. They gotta brag."

"Or else they go do some stupid shit, like try to buy a brand new car with cash when they been unemployed for a year."

"Exactly," Kane concurred. "Anyway, the cops expected there to be all kinds of chatter on the street, but they never heard shit – not in *our* city, anyway. Nobody in town knew a damn thang. But some shiftless muhfucka like three states away suddenly got cash to burn; he flashin' a thick wad and orderin' custom-made grillz for his teeth that cost, like, fifty large. Local cops picked his ass up and got a warrant to search his house, where they found like half a mill. They was able to trace some of it to the armored car robbery."

"I remember – that nigga they picked up was one of the robbers."

"Yep. After that, it was just a matter of time before they tied him to the rest of the crew and got all those muhfuckas. Turned out the robbers was all from out-of-town. They got recruited for that job by a muhfucka who worked for the armored car company."

"So it was an inside job."

"Happens mo' often than you thank," Kane remarked. "But the guy was smart in recruitin' niggas who wasn't local. They didn't have no reason to stick around after the job, so there was less chance of them sayin' the wrong thang to the wrong people, and nobody missed 'em when they was gone."

Mika frowned. "So you thankin' the shit that happened at the farm was an inside job?"

"Raven didn't thank so, but it's damn sho' possible. Regardless, I'm fuckin' convinced that somebody recruited Remo and those other muhfuckas. Basically, you don't try to pull off a lick like that in a town you where you don't live – where you don't know what the cops are like, or patrol patterns or response times. Where you don't have resources. Where you don't have a network or contacts. Think about where me and you would be if we hadn't got an intro to people like Buggy, Fix, and Mikey."

"I hear you. But don't Remo have people here like that biker gang you mentioned – the Canaries?"

"Yeah, and those racist muhfuckas sold us out...told Remo we was comin'. But I don't thank they involved in the shit that happened at the farm. Why recruit a bunch of hittas from outta state when you got a crew of dumbasses hangin' around that can do whachu need? Naw, there's somebody else behind this."

"Who you thank it might be?"

"No fuckin' clue," Kane admitted. "But I'm bettin' Remo does. I just need to find his *ass*...again."

Mika seemed to think for a second. "Maybe the phone from that muthafucka you left in the dirt can tell us sommin'."

"I ain't had time to look at it, but I'm guessin' it's got numbers and shit. If he had half a brain, he ain't got the names of Remo or their crew on there – at least not under their *real* name. But even if he do, I doubt if Remo will pick up if we call, or tell us where he is."

"But can't we try to track 'im?"

Kane frowned. "You mean by tracin' signals from cell phone towers and shit? Naw, that's cop work. Even if we got Buggy to reach out to Five-Oh again, we'd need some basic info to give 'em – like Remo's number – and we ain't got it. Plus, all a tower signal can tell you is the area where a muhfucka was when he made or got a call, not the exact spot where he is right now."

"Naw," Mika insisted, shaking her head. "I'm not talkin' 'bout crap like cell towers and antennas. I'm talkin' 'bout…"

She trailed off, with her brow crinkled in thought. She was clearly trying to latch onto a thought but was having trouble articulating it. It was obviously the fucking concussion again, making Kane acutely aware of the fact that Mika really didn't need to be riding shotgun.

"Gimme the phone," she finally said, holding out her hand.

Kane wasn't sure what she was thinking, but – against his better judgment – he pulled out Rommel's phone and gave it to her.

"I'm givin' away one of the secrets of the Girl Club here," she said as she began tapping the phone screen, "but most niggas are ignorant about all the shit phones do automatically. But one of the things that cells keep track of is the locations you visit on the regular. So if you wanna see if yo man tappin' some side-chick ass, you can check his phone to see if that nigga been droppin' by her place. Now, in the case of this Rommel muthafucka, I'm just lookin' at his most-visited locations recently and…*voilà*."

As she finished she held up the cell phone, smiling triumphantly as she showed the screen to Kane.

"Oh shit," he muttered, plainly impressed by what he was seeing.

## Chapter 58

Kane pulled into the lot of a big box store and parked into the first available spot, well away from the store entrance. He then took Rommel's phone from Mika and studied it for a moment.

As Mika had indicated, the cell – like most smartphones – was designed to track the movements of whoever had it. Truth be told, it was a little scary when you thought about it, and reminded Kane of an article he'd read a while back which opined that cell phones were little more than government-sanctioned tracking devices. However, he put that out of his mind as he focused on Rommel's phone, which had mapped out three locations as being the places he had visited the most in the past few days.

"Damn, this is great, babe," he told Mika. "This tell us exactly where that muhfucka been spendin' all of his time."

"And where was that?" Mika asked.

"Looks like one of the top three spots was the apartment buildin' where those muhfuckas was stayin'," Kane stated as he manipulated the map.

"No surprise there," Mika noted.

"Hmmm. Looks like he also spent some time in the area 'round Augustus' farm. I'm guessin' he and the rest of Remo's crew spent a coupla days scopin' the place out before they tried to jack us this mornin'. That way they'd have a feel for everybody's routine."

"Makes sense."

"Now this last place..." Kane droned. "I got no idea where this is. Let's blow it up and see what we got."

With that, he began expanding the map on the phone, increasing the available detail until it not only showed street names but also businesses in the area. Moments later, he was able to pinpoint the place where Rommel had spent a bunch of time.

"Shit," Kane muttered. "I shudda figured sommin' like this."

"Like what?" inquired Mika.

"The third location Rommel hung out at – Outlaw Motor Garage. Accordin' to the info on the map, it's a fuckin' custom motorcycle and car shop," Kane remarked. Still getting a perplexed look from Mika, he added, "That muhfucka Remo was in a biker gang. So, naturally that asshole has a bike, and he got to be keepin' it somewhere 'cause he ain't been ridin' 'round on it."

"Okay, that might explain why Remo would be spendin' time there, but why Rommel?"

"Fuck if I know. Maybe he a biker, too. Or maybe he just went there to pick Remo up a coupla times. Or maybe prison mentally conditioned that muhfucka so that he don't feel at home unless he around a bunch of license plates."

"So I take it we goin' there next?"

"Good fuckin' guess, since it's the only lead we got."

Mika appeared to reflect for a moment. "How long it gone takes us to get there?"

"I dunno… Twenty or twenty-five minutes, I s'pose."

"You in a particular rush?"

"Considerin' that some vicious muhfuckas want some alone time with me in a basement, I'd prolly argue that time is of the essence," Kane answered. "Or did you forget about that?"

"No," Mika told him. "It's just that – like I said befoe' – this van is spacious as a muhfucka."

Kane gave her an incredulous stare. "Are you out cho' fuckin' mind? We on the clock."

"I know, but just hear me out," she insisted. "We 'bout to run up into another situation where there's a good chance we get our asses shot off. Now I'm already keyed up about this shit, so I really need sommin' to take the edge off."

"I ain't disagreein' wichu. But we ain't got the time, plus you still got a head injury and not s'posed to do anythang strenuous."

"I know," Mika told him, "but I'm horny as a muthafucka."

"It's the concussion," Kane said. "About half the niggas who get concussed lose some of they sex drive. But for some people it actually increases."

"Guess I won *that* lottery. But even if it is the concussion, we still might end up gettin' our heads blasted off, and ain't nuthin' worse than dyin' horny."

"I can thank of a couple of thangs that are worse," Kane shot back "Like gettin' yo dick shot off and livin'."

"Damn, nigga – if you ain't fuckin' morbid. But if you really worried about some shit like that happenin', then you should be beggin' *me* to fuck – not the other way around."

Kane laughed. "How 'bout I make it up to you by beggin' for the pussy later?"

Mika crossed her arms and shook her head. "Not good enough. You might be dead then…or have yo dick shot off."

Kane grinned. "Look, babe, you know I'm always down to fuck. But if you my runnin' mate on this shit tonight, I need yo head on as straight as possible, so that mean I can't be bouncin' you up and down on my dick while you got a damn brain injury."

"Okay fine, let's forget fuckin'," Mika said. "How about a blowjob?"

"If it'll shut you up so we handle business," Kane snickered, "I'm down."

*******************************************

The minivan actually had three rows of seats: two in the front, another two in the center, and a third row that could seat three. However, despite being able to carry seven, the van was constructed so that the second and third rows of seats could fold down into the floor to allow for extra cargo space. Thus, after removing his jacket and slipping into the back, it only took a few seconds for Kane to fold down the two center seats, thereby creating quite a bit of space in the center of the vehicle.

Mika joined him in the middle of the van. She glanced around as if approving of the available space, then gave Kane a frank look.

"Lay down," she ordered, and Kane obeyed.

She then leaned over and gave him a big kiss while stroking his dick through his pants. Knowing what was coming, he was already rock-hard. Slipping a hand under her shirt, he fondled her tits for a moment, flicking her nipples in a way that Mika always found delectable.

She moaned in delight as he squeezed her girls. At the same time, she frantically unbuttoned his pants, unzipped them, then whipped his dick out. Thick and heavy, she stroked it a couple of times, running her thumb over the head in a teasing fashion.

# SHE'S HIS DRUG, HE'S HER THUG 4

Reluctantly, Kane removed his hand from her shirt as she moved her head down towards his groin. Eyes closed, he was bursting with anticipation at the thought of what was coming. Then he gasped as she took him in her mouth.

As always, the way she worked his dick with her tongue and lips was amazing, and he found himself clawing the floor of the van with his hands. Mika was a perennial All-Pro when it came to giving head, and she knew it. Whether licking the shaft, toying with his balls, or just plain deep-throating his shit, Mika was fucking adept at blowjobs. And she also had this little trick where she'd twirl her tongue in a circular motion around the head while sucking – it was enough to make a nigga want to scream in ecstasy. (Likewise when she put one of his balls in her mouth and gently sucked on it.)

It didn't take long for Kane to lose track of time as Mika worked her magic. At some point, though, she took her mouth off his dick and let her hand work his pole. Eyes still closed in delight, Kane sensed her moving back up his body. A moment later, her lips were at his ear.

She nibbled his ear lobe gently then sucked on it for a second in a way that was always a turn-on for him. Then she pursed her lips and spoke in a breathy whisper.

"Dumbass," she said.

Kane's eyes sprang open to find Mika's face directly over his. But he suddenly realized that she wasn't just *over* him; she had *straddled* him. Before he could do anything else, she lowered her hips, letting her pussy slide down over his dick. It felt so deliciously amazing that Kane drew in a harsh breath and arched his back. Then Mika proceeded to fuck the shit out of him.

# SHE'S HIS DRUG, HE'S HER THUG 4

Mika rode his dick mercilessly, like she wanted to break that shit off and take it with her. Putting his hands under her shirt, Kane gripped her tits with wild abandon, loving the way her erect nipples pressed firmly into his palms. On some level, he realized that this had been Mika's plan all along: while giving him a mind-bending blowjob, she had slipped out of her pants and gotten in position. And his dumb ass (as she correctly labeled him) was so wrapped up in the way she was sucking his dick that he didn't even realize she had practically mounted him until it was too late.

And of course, now that he was inside her, with that tight-ass pussy making him feel like he was on cloud nine, he wondered what the hell he had been resisting for. Concussion or not, if his girl wanted the dick, who the fuck was he to deny her? If she wanted to fuck, he was gone tear that pussy up, down, sideways and across the middle…

And it was with that thought in mind that he came ferociously, yelling without restraint. Mika came at the same time screaming like banshee and banging her hands so hard on the roof of the minivan that Kane thought she was going to punch on a hole in that bitch.

# SHE'S HIS DRUG, HE'S HER THUG 4

## Chapter 59

After getting dressed and slipping his jacket back on, Kane once again found himself behind the wheel of the minivan. Likewise, Mika had gotten dressed and resumed her position in the front passenger seat.

"Satisfied?" Kane asked her.

"Very," she replied with a smug grin. "So what now?"

"Well, makin' sure you don't die horny cost us about ten minutes. Let's get over to this garage and see what's what. Im'ma be pissed, though, if it turn out that we missed Remo and them other muhfuckas by, like, five minutes."

"And what if we do? You gone be too mad to ever fuck me again?" she teased. "Good luck with that."

Rather than answer directly, Kane simply said, "Let's just focus on the task at hand."

\*\*\*\*\*\*\*\*\*\*\*\*\*\*\*\*\*\*\*\*\*\*\*\*\*\*\*\*\*\*\*\*\*\*\*\*\*\*\*

The drive to the garage went by pretty fast, even with Kane and Mika not speaking very much. For Kane, much of the trip was taken up with thoughts of whether he should call for backup – maybe Mikey or even Raven. The problem was that they were trying to retrieve a lot of fucking cash. So, while he trusted those two, he hadn't known them long (in Raven's case, he barely knew her at all), and didn't know how they'd react with seven figures within reach. That being the case, he decided to only have Mika by his side for this, concussion and all.

When they reached the garage, Kane noted that it was situated on a fairly sizeable corner lot in a commercial area. The business was fenced, with a rolling chain-link gate at the entrance that was currently closed. This was in conjunction with a nearby sign which indicated the garage's business hours, and it was currently well past closing time. There was also a sign which read "We Rent Cars!" As if to prove up this statement, numerous automobiles were parked around the lot.

The business itself appeared to be housed in an elongated one-story structure that contained a half-dozen service bays and some additional workspace. There were a couple of wall sconces outside the building, and the modest illumination they provided showed that all the bay doors were currently closed. However, lots of lights seemed to be on in the interior, giving the impression that there was a fair amount of activity taking place inside.

Mika and Kane noted all this from the lot of a strip mall across the street, where they were presently parked. It was a spot that gave them a good view of the garage while still remaining somewhat inconspicuous.

"So what now?" asked Mika.

"I'm thinkin'," Kane answered. "Best guess is that this is where Remo and his people got the vehicles they been usin'."

"You also said you thank he keepin' his bike here."

"That would let him kill two birds with one stone: store his motorcycle and get another ride all at the same place."

"Well, I don't see that car they was drivin', so they prolly still in it – assumin' it ain't inside."

"That's a good point," Kane told her. "And–"

He stopped midsentence as a car suddenly pulled into the entrance to the garage, stopping at the gate. It was a late-model sports car that probably cost somewhere in the high five-figure range. A moment later, a guy that Kane hadn't noticed before was suddenly at the gate, rolling it open. The sports car went inside and headed for one of the bay doors while the fellow at the gate rolled it shut again.

Clearly impatient, the driver of the sports car gave a short honk, and seconds later the bay door slid up. As the car drove inside, Kane glimpsed several guys in the garage holding various automotive tools, as well as a couple of vehicles in various stages of disassembly. The bay door then slid back down.

"I'll be damned," Kane muttered. "It's a chop shop."

"Really?" Mika intoned.

"Well, I ain't see nobody get carjacked or notice any money change hands," Kane admitted. "But I see a bunch of shifty-lookin' muhfuckas in there taking expensive cars apart after hours. If that don't spell 'chop shop', I dunno what does."

Mika looked as though she had a comment to add, but at that moment a door to the garage opened and a guy in a baseball cap walked out. Kane wasn't sure, but he thought it was the dude who had been driving the sports car.

Kane was about to jump out the van, then hesitated, glancing at Mika. She still wasn't a hundred percent, and in all truth her ass should be in bed instead of riding shotgun with him. That said, even if she wasn't hittin' on all cylinders, there really wasn't anyone that he trusted more, or who was better at having his back.

Mind made up, he said, "Come on."

A moment later, they were out the minivan and walking hurriedly across the street.

## SHE'S HIS DRUG, HE'S HER THUG 4

The dude at the gate rolled it open for the guy in the baseball cap, who quickly stepped out. Kane was hoping he'd head the other way, but instead he turned and walked towards him and Mika, casually saying, "Whazzup?" as they passed him. Kane simply muttered something unintelligible in reply as he and Mika made a beeline for the gate, slipping inside just before it shut.

The guy at the gate merely stared at them for a moment, like they were a couple of ghosts who had materialized out of thin air. "Uh, we closed," he finally managed to mumble.

"That's fine," Kane told him. "We don't need no work done. We just need to ask a few questions."

"You gonna have to come back tomorrow and talk to the boss," the man insisted. "We closed."

Pulling out Mika's gun, Kane asked, "Would it help if I said 'Please'?"

# SHE'S HIS DRUG, HE'S HER THUG 4

## Chapter 60

It turned out that the fellow manning the gate went by the name of Cisco. It was obvious right off the bat that he wasn't the sharpest knife in the drawer, but he knew enough not to offer any resistance when Kane pulled a gun on him. Thus, covered by the weapon, he led Mika and Kane through a door and into the auto shop.

As Kane had suspected, the place was a chop shop. At a glance, he saw maybe eight or ten guys at work taking apart several cars. From what he knew, a good crew could disassemble a car in one or two hours, and the constituent parts were usually worth way more than the resale value of the car itself.

Only one or two of the fellows in the shop looked their way. (Apparently they got enough visitors that an unknown man and woman didn't merit much attention.) At that point, Kane had the gun in his pocket but still pointed at Cisco, who was leading them to what looked like an office at the back of the shop. Once there, Cisco opened the door and went in, with Mika and Kane on his heels.

The office was maybe a hundred square feet in size, and rather Spartan. The furnishings consisted of a desk and office chair, some bookcases filled with more pictures and bric-a-brac than tomes, and a couple of beat-up chairs for guests. Seated behind the desk was a portly, middle-aged man with an iron-gray mustache and thinning hair. He was wearing reading glasses and looking at a laptop, but glanced up after noticing that he had visitors, just as Kane closed the door behind them.

"Cisco, why the fuck ain't you at the gate?" demanded the guy sitting at the desk. Then, gesturing towards Kane and Mika, he added, "And who the hell is this?"

"I'm Miss Smith," Mika informed him, pulling out the mouse gun. Next, she tilted her head towards Kane, saying, "And that's Mr. Wesson."

"Careful, sweetheart," said the man, grinning as he eyed Mika's firearm. "You might scratch my glasses with that thing."

"I'm sure this one will do more than just scratch," Kane announced, pulling the gun from his pocket.

At that point, the man behind the desk stopped grinning and raised his hands. Scowling at Cisco, he hissed, "You dumb lump of shit..."

"Sorry, Jake," Cisco muttered, looking cowed.

"So, Jake," Kane said. "This yo place?"

"My name's on the deed," Jake answered, "but it ain't mine. And befoe' this go any further, I'm gonna give you some free advice: turn around, walk away, and we'll forget this ever happened. Trust me, this is the last place you wanna rob."

"Really?" Kane stated in surprise. "I would thank you'd be high on the places-to-rob list. You ain't got no cameras inside or out, you got a lot of parts that can be sold quick and easy, and finally, chop shops are usually all-cash businesses, so you gotta have money around. I'm surprised you ain't got a line of muhfuckas outside waitin' to hit this place."

"Well, there's a reason nobody does shit like that," Jake shot back. "It's because the owner — the *real* owner — ain't somebody you wanna cross."

Kane raised an eyebrow. "Is that a fact?"

"You bet your ass," Jake responded, nodding. "He's a Russian mobster — goes by the name Romanov and claims he's descended from the last Czar or some shit like that. But that's not important. All you need to know is that he's a stone-cold psycho, and gettin' on his bad side is just about the worst fuckin' thang you can do."

"Well, we ain't here to fuck with yo boss," Kane noted, "or get cross-wise with 'im."

"Don't matter," Jake insisted. "Just doin' whachu doin' right now – walkin' in here and wavin' a gun around – is enough to make him cut yo balls off and shove 'em down yo throat. And I mean that literally."

"Oh my," Mika deadpanned. "I'm terrified. Guess it's a good thang I ain't got no balls."

"Joke now, smart-ass," Jake grumbled, "but you'll be singin' a different tune when yo boyfriend's nuts are bein' stuffed in yo mouth."

Mika laughed. "I had his nuts in my mouth like an hour ago, and I loved it. I'm pretty sure he did, too."

Jake just stared at her for a moment, plainly unsure of how to respond.

"Look," Kane said, getting Jake's attention. "Let's get a few thangs straight. We ain't here to rob you, steal any of yo shit, or fuck up yo business in any way. As for yo boss, we got people who can smooth shit over if we ruffle his feathers."

"I doubt that," Jake declared. "But if you ain't here for a payday, what da fuck you want?"

"We after this muhfucka called Remo and a coupla his runnin' mates. We got reason to believe he been by here lately."

"Okay," Jake droned with a nod. "I know who you talkin' 'bout. But you mind if I put my hands down while we palaver?"

# SHE'S HIS DRUG, HE'S HER THUG 4

"Sure," Kane told him. "But before you do that, lemme ask: you got any guns in here?"

Jake nodded. "I got a revolver I keep in the middle right drawer here."

"Babe?" Kane said, looking at Mika.

Knowing what was expected, Mika went to the desk and looked in the drawer indicated. Sure enough, there was a fully-loaded revolver in there, which she took. She also methodically checked the other drawers, but found nothing noteworthy except a box of ammo for the gun. She also checked the kneehole; in the movies, that's where a sly nigga might have a gun taped to the underside of the desk, but Jake didn't have anything like that.

Satisfied that she had turned up everything noteworthy, she gave Kane a nod. "We clear."

"Great," Kane noted, then turned to Jake, who lowered his hands but kept them in sight on top of the desk. "Now, as I was saying, we not here to fuck up yo day. All we want is Remo."

Jake nodded. "Like I said, I know 'im. Not personal – just as a customer. He showed up maybe foe' or five days ago. He had a sweet ride that he wanted to store for a few days. Also, he wanted to rent some cars without going through the hassle of showing ID, credit cards, and all that shit."

"So you helped him out," Mika surmised.

Jake shrugged. "The man's money was green and he was willin' to pay the goin' rate. That's all that mattered far as I was concerned."

"One thang I don't get," Kane observed. "Why da fuck would he store his bike at a chop shop?"

"I know," Jake chuckled. "Seem like he giftwrappin' it for us. But we keep our word around here."

"Honor among thieves?" Mika said skeptically.

"Believe it or not, it happens," Jake stressed. "Plus, your buddy Remo didn't have many options. See, he had some ink on 'im that showed he was part of a motorcycle club."

"The Canaries," Kane chimed in.

"Right," Jake confirmed. "But he on the outs with 'em or sommin'. But the thing is, when you join a club like that, you gotta sign over yo bike. The *club* owns it, not you."

"I thank I get it now," Kane said. "If Remo ain't in the club, he not s'posed to have the bike. So if the Canaries wet a whiff of him anywhere around, they'll probably snatch his wheels."

"Officially, that's what can happen," Jake retorted. "But if you a biker that was respected by the club or badass enough, maybe you get to keep it. Or maybe they turn a blind eye to you bein' around. But they can change they mind at any time, so you might wanna guard against that."

"But if he take it somewhere legit," Mika reasoned, "even a regular ole storage unit, he gotta give name, address, and a bunch of other identifying info that Remo don't seem partial to."

"Correct," Jake noted. "That leaves somebody like me as the only game in town. So with me he gets to keep his bike safe and off the street, and also gets some vehicles for daily use."

"So how do we find 'im?" Kane inquired.

"Well, the easiest method is to just wait on 'im," Jake replied. "See, he love that bike – calls her 'Elise' – and come by to check on her almost every day. So sooner or later, he'll turn up."

"What if we ain't got the patience for that?" asked Mika. "How we locate his ass if we in a rush?"

"That's a good question," Jaked said, leaning back in his chair. "Let me think…"

As he trailed off, he lifted his right hand and began running his thumb back and forth across his fingertips – a universal gesture for money.

Kane sighed. "How much?"

Jake seemed to contemplate for a moment. "How bad do you want this guy?"

"Don't dick us around, asshole," Mika hissed angrily. "Just give us a number."

Jake hesitated a moment, then said, "Ten."

"Fuck that," Mika huffed. "We'll find 'im ourself."

Jake shrugged. "Maybe, maybe not. But I'm offerin' you a guarantee."

"I don't know that you can guarantee anythang," Kane told him. "But my girl's right about one thang: ten grand is overreachin'."

"Okay," Jake said. "Eight."

Kane shook his head. "Nope. Try again."

"Alright, five," Jake offered. "But that's as low as I can go."

Kane looked at Mika, who gave a subtle nod.

"A'ight, five it is," Kane said. "But we doin' this shit in installments. A thousand now, the rest later."

Jake looked at Kane with a dubious expression. "And I'm just s'posed to take yo word that you'll be back with the cash?"

"That's our insurance policy to make sure yo don't try to set us up," Kane retorted.

"Like maybe tellin' us Remo's in some warehouse," Mika added, "but you really just lurin' us into an ambush."

Jake let out an exasperated sigh. "Fine, a thousand now, four later." He then shook his head in derision. "Where's the fuckin' trust?"

# SHE'S HIS DRUG, HE'S HER THUG 4

## Chapter 61

As soon as Kane handed over the money, Jake went to work on the laptop, with his two visitors looking over his shoulder. Meanwhile Cisco, who hadn't said a word since they'd come into the office, sat silently in one of the guest chairs.

"I keep trackers on all the cars I rent," Jake explained. "Makes 'em easy to find if somebody try to run off with 'em."

"There's that honor-among-thieves again," Mika quipped.

Ignoring her, Jake said, "Alright, it looks like one is parked in the lot of some apartment complex across town. And the other one... Now that's interestin'."

"What?" Kane asked, plainly interested.

"According to the tracker," Jake continued, "the other car is right outside."

Mika and Kane suddenly looked at each other, both somewhat stunned by Jake's statement. At the same time, a thunderous roar boomed from outside the garage, a sound that Kane recognized as the modified exhaust of a motorcycle.

"Shit," Kane spat out, then went racing from Jake's office, followed by Mika and Jake himself (who was more spry than he appeared at first blush).

Out on the shop floor, Jake's guys were still busy taking apart cars. However, a couple of them were glancing out of an open bay door, where the deafening sound of the motorcycle exhaust was still reverberating through the air. Mika and Kane made a beeline for the exit and a moment later were outside.

## SHE'S HIS DRUG, HE'S HER THUG 4

As before, there wasn't a great deal of illumination from the light sconces, but Mika and Kane could discern the general outline of someone – presumably Remo – on a motorcycle at the gate. Behind the bike was the off-road vehicle that had been at Shar's house earlier. Both seemed to be waiting as the gate rolled open.

Kane fought his initial impulse to just start blasting. He needed at least one of these muhfuckas alive in order to ask about the missing money. Mika, on the other hand, showed no hesitation whatsoever; she simply raised Jake's revolver, which she was still holding, and started firing. At the same time, someone near the gate yelled out, "Behind you!"

The shout was an obvious warning to Remo and his cohorts, and it was accompanied with a flash of light from somewhere near the gate. It made Kane keenly aware that – just as he hadn't initially seen Cisco – the darkness had caused him to miss whoever was currently rolling the gate open. And the light at the gate – plainly a muzzle flash – brought to mind the fact that he and Mika, standing as they were under the light sconces, were easy targets. (As if in evidence of this, the fired slug struck the wall of the auto shop about a foot from Kane's head.

Kane returned fire, at the same time dashing towards a nearby parked car. Approaching the vehicle from the driver's side, he leaped in the air towards it, feet first. In his mind's eye, he saw himself sliding deftly across the hood of the car like some movie star in an action flick, and then landing adroitly on the other side. The reality was somewhat different.

First of all, he came down heavily on the hood, leaving a dent that would have to be knocked out later. Next, as he slid across, his hip struck one of the window washer nozzles; it was hard as a muhfucka and made him grunt in pain. In addition, he had completely failed to account for the car's antenna, which whacked him in the face near the end of his slide. Finally, he hadn't even considered what might be on the other side of the car, and as a result he banged his knee tortuously on a cinderblock and some other shit that was on the passenger side of the vehicle when he came off the hood.

All in all, it was a fucking comedy of errors that would have been hilarious if the situation wasn't so serious.

Ignoring the pain in his leg, Kane used the car as cover and continued firing. At that point, however, bullets were flying everywhere as Remo and the driver of the off-road vehicle joined in the gunplay. Counting whoever was at the gate, that made it a three-on-two gunfight.

Sparing a glance towards Mika, Kane was amazed to see her boldly standing her ground. In short, when he had dashed for the car, she had simply stood there, still firing Jake's gun. (Jake himself – or someone on his payroll – had closed the bay door and was now waiting in the relative safety of the auto shop.)

With his exhaust still blaring, Remo suddenly zipped through the gate, shooting to his rear as he rode away. The off-road vehicle was right behind him, but slowed to allow the muhfucka at the gate a moment to get in. Unfortunately, he didn't make it, as a bullet from the revolver appeared to strike him in the neck. He immediately dropped and the driver of the off-road vehicle, apparently knowing what had happened, hastily drove off, following in Remo's wake.

Limping, Kane swiftly made his way to Mika.

"You okay?" he asked anxiously, visually checking her for injuries.

"I'm fine," she insisted. "Why wouldn't I be?"

"Because you just stood there like you had fuckin' rivets in yo feet while muhfuckas was tryin' to blow yo head off."

"Did I?" Mika mused. "I didn't notice."

Kane rolled his eyes in frustration. Obviously, the concussion she suffered was still affecting her judgment.

"Come on," he said, then began limping towards the gate.

Noting that he seemed hobbled, Mika asked, "What happened to you?"

"The same damn thang that shudda happened to *you*," Kane noted curtly, "if you had any sense."

Mika pondered that for a second as they approached the body at the gate.

"Baskett," Kane muttered, putting a name to the corpse on the ground. "He must have jumped out that off-roader to open the gate."

"That mean they down to two now," Mika noted.

"Yeah – Remo and Fosse," Kane stated as he began searching Baskett's body.

"So, you thank we should get Jake to track that car again?"

Kane pulled out Baskett's cell phone. "We can, but at best it'll only give us Fosse. Remember, Remo's on his bike now."

"Won't they be together?"

"If they are, it won't be for long," Kane surmised as he produced Baskett's wallet. "Remo came here specifically to get his bike. I don't think he wudda done that unless he was plannin' to leave town."

"Oh fuck," Mika blurted out, as all the implications of that statement hit her. "We still don't know 'bout the money, or who recruited these muthafuckas to jack us."

At that moment, Kane finished searching Baskett's last pocket. Pulling the contents out, he noted that it was only a small scrap of paper. He was about to discard it, then found himself staring at it, his eyes going wide.

"Shit," he muttered. "I know who behind all this."

# SHE'S HIS DRUG, HE'S HER THUG 4

## Chapter 62

The nightclub where Kane had previously had his run-in with Sway was much the same as he remembered it. In fact, the same overweight muhfucka as before did another half-assed job of scanning him with the metal detector wand. The aftermath, however, was a little different this time in that two big, burly niggas patted Kane down pretty thoroughly. They went through the pockets of his jacket then moved on to his person – checking him front to back, feeling his arms from shoulder to wrist, then running their hand over his legs from hip to ankle. Satisfied that he was unarmed, they escorted him to an office at the rear of the club.

Unlike Jake's office at the chop shop, this one was pretty swank. It was outfitted with an ornate desk made of mahogany, high-back executive chairs, a wet bar, and more. And seated at the desk was Mako, Sway;s older brother.

"Kane," he said with a magnanimous smile. "Nice to see ya. Have a seat."

The two niggas who had escorted him to the room remained by the door, with two others on guard outside. Accepting the proffered invitation, Kane limped over and took a seat in a chair across from Mako.

"Damn, you looked fucked up," Mako observed. "Walkin' like an old man with his dick cut off."

"It's been one of those days," Kane said.

"You want a drank?"

"I'm good," Kane stressed, shaking his head. "But you know, you cudda mentioned when we met that you owned this place."

"Well, I don't like to brag, but…" As he trailed off, Mako spread his arms in a luxuriant fashion.

"At least now I unnastand why Sway had the run of the place – why he could go into the VIP area without a wristband and all that shit."

"Family perk," Mako admitted. "But I'm sho' you ain't here to talk about shit like that."

"No, but you prolly already got a pretty good idea of why I'm here."

Mako didn't say anything at first, then a big smile spread across his face. "You know, I like you, nigga. You got balls of steel, rollin' up in here – unarmed – to confront a muhfucka."

Wincing slightly, Kane stretched out his injured leg as he spoke. "So it *was* you who set up on us this mornin'."

"How you figure that?"

Kane gave him a curious look. "You denyin' it?"

"Naw," Mako confessed, shaking his head. "I was involved. I'm just curious how you figured it out."

Kane reached for his pocket, a movement that sent the two niggas by the door quickstepping in his direction. Kane froze as they flanked him, guns drawn.

He looked from one to the other. "Didn't you muhfuckas already search me?"

The two guards looked at Mako, who made a dismissive gesture. Scowling at Kane, they returned to their posts by the door. On his part, Kane finished reaching into his pocket and pulled out a scrap of paper.

"Got this off one of the dumbasses who tried to jack us this mornin'," he explained as he slid the piece of paper across the desk to Mako.

Barely glancing at the paper, Mako said, "What da fuck is this?"

"It's a currency band," Kane replied as he began massaging his injured leg. "It's what people use to wrap up stacks of cash. If you take a good look at that one, you'll see it has '$5,000' handwritten on it. Just like the one you gave me when we met."

Mako took the scrap of paper and examined it, then leaned back in his chair, chuckling.

"I'll be damned," he muttered. "That's pretty good detective work."

"Thanks," Kane said.

Mako's sentiment was essentially the same as Mika's had been after Kane pulled the currency band from Baskett's pocket and explained what it meant. A quick call to Buggy had revealed that Mako usually hung out at the club where they had bumped heads with Sway. (It had also come out that he owned the place.) After that, the question had been how to come at that nigga. Mika had wanted to show up blasting, but Kane — wanting to try a different approach — had won out.

"Anyway," Kane droned, "I'm really curious as to why. I mean, I thought we squashed whatever conflict we had."

"Come on, man," uttered Mako. "You been in the game, so you know how it is. A muhfucka come at you, you can't show weakness. Even if they do some shit on the periphery, like fuck with yo family, you gotta handle up."

"I get it. A nigga slap yo momma and you don't put 'im in his place, he gone wonder what else he can get away with."

"Not just the nigga doin' that shit. Every muhfucka on the street gone be wonderin' how weak you is and start testin' you."

"So yo brother…"

"He was in the wrong far as you and yo girl was concerned, but still, I can't have niggas thankin' it's okay to slap him around. Basically, I was gonna have to address that shit."

"So you came up with this heist plan."

"Not exactly. I didn't really have a plan other than maybe having a coupla my boys jump yo ass. Then, out the blue, this envelope get delivered to me. Inside is fifty large and a burner phone." As he spoke, Mako pulled a prepaid cell from a drawer of the desk and held it up. "I don't know where any of it come from, but the message is clear: somebody want to have a conversation with me and they willin' to pay for the privilege."

"Who?"

Mako shrugged. "No fuckin' clue. But the cash was enough to get my attention so I turn on the cell. There's a number already in the contacts, so I dial it. It's answered right off the bat by some muhfucka speakin' through this voice changer app."

"How you know it was an app?"

"'Cause this chick I used to kick it with had the same one on her phone and would call me up all the time using it. She thought it was funny as hell to tell me she wanted the dick in a deep-ass voice like Barry White."

"Anyway," Mako went on, "This nigga on the phone mention he got a job he thank I'd be interested in. He'll get me all the info, I get together a crew, and we split the take – over a mill in cash and 'bout the same or more in weed."

"And you went for it," Kane concluded.

"Not immediately," Mako said. "Shit sounded too good to be true. Then he told me you was involved." Mako leaned forward conspiratorially. "See, he knew 'bout the shit between you and Sway, and figured I was lookin' for a way to settle accounts."

"Well, if that's how you really felt, why give me the five kay?"

"Five thou ain't shit – especially if it get a muhfucka to let his guard down. If you the kinda nigga I thank you are, you prolly carry that around on you on the regular, and maybe a nice watch, a piece, and some other shit worth some ka-ching."

"In other words, whenever your boys jumped me, you'd get the cash back."

Mako tapped his temple with his forefinger. "That's called seein' the big picture. And you obviously missed it."

"Meanin' what?" Kane asked, bringing his injured leg up and crossing it over his other knee.

"Meanin' that it was an inside job. This nigga I talked to had all kinda info on you, the money, the fuckin' weed farm...everythang. Basically, somebody in yo own organization set this up."

"I already figured that much. They just recruited you to put another layer between them and the job."

"Yeah, they was paranoid about that shit. I guess they wanted as few direct links as possible, 'cause on top of that they told me not to use any of my boys for the work."

"So you recruited that muhfucka Remo and the others from outta town."

"I brought in Remo – I didn't know 'im, but he came highly recommended – and he enlisted those other muhfuckas. That currency band you found is from an advance that I gave 'em to take care of incidentals. They was all s'posed to be professionals, but somehow they fucked it up...couldn't even rob a farm full of dopeheads."

Kane didn't say anything, but in his opinion Mako had the wrong idea about the folks at the farm. They probably did get high, but Mako had made an extremely poor assumption if he thought they were incompetent.

"I gotta do a better job of vetting outside crews from now on," Mako continued. "And from what I hear, you been houndin' they ass all day."

"Well, you try to jack a muhfucka, you gotta expect that they gone come at you," Kane informed him.

"And I'm guessin' that's why you here – to come at me?"

"Actually, I just wanted to have a conversation."

"That's funny," Mako said. "'Cause I been wantin' to chat wicho ass all day."

"Well, you got cho' wish, although I'm a lil' surprised you was willin' to lay out for me everthang that's been goin' on."

"Hell, nigga... You know how this shit gonna end. You ain't gone be sharin' the deets of what we talked about with nobody. But I respect yo ass, which is why I was willin' to explain what went down and answer yo questions."

"And I 'preciate that."

"Good. Now I need you to answer one of *my* questions: where's the money?"

"Money?" Kane repeated in surprise. "Da fuck you talkin' 'bout?"

"Come on, man," Mako muttered. "Don't go that route. We been straight with each other this whole conversation, now you wanna play dumb."

"I ain't playin' dumb. I'm fuckin' clueless. In fact, I was gonna ask *you* where the money at that y'all jacked from us."

"Now I know you bullshittin'. Remo said they didn't get the cash this mornin'. Said the shit went completely sideways, and you didn't deny it when I mentioned how they fucked up a few minutes ago."

"Well, part of that shit is right," Kane explained. "They didn't get the money when all hell broke loose at the farm. Later, I sent the money back to my boss because the deal was obviously off, but somebody hit the courier I used and made off with the cash."

Mako just stared at him for a moment, then said, "No fuckin' way."

"Yes fuckin' way," Kane shot back. "I assume Remo or one of his crew followed us and waited for the right moment to make a move."

Mako look confused. "But Remo was just in here maybe an hour ago sayin' he needed some cash to leave town."

Kane found that interesting, but didn't say anything. It certainly explained where Remo had gone after Rommel got shot (and before he got to the chop shop).

"Remo might have just said that to throw you off," Kane finally offered. "And there's still the other nigga – the one who brought you in on this."

"Maybe…" Mako droned, then blinked as he seemed to realize that he was fraternizing with the enemy. Suddenly he gave Kane a harsh look. "I thank you lyin'. I thank you still got the money."

"Right," Kane uttered sarcastically. "And I just walked up in here to ask you about it 'cause I ain't got nuthin' better to do. I been chasin' Remo weaselly ass all over town 'cause it's been a slow day at the office and I thought it'd be fun."

Mako frowned. "But if you ain't got the money…"

There was silence for a second, then Kane unexpectedly burst out laughing. "Shit nigga, don't you get it? One of yo partners is rippin' you off. Either that muhfucka Remo, or the nigga who brought you into this shit. One of 'em followed us, got the cash, and don't wanna share it now."

"Well, we gone find out soon enough," Mako declared. "Remo on his way here – I called 'im soon as they told me you was outside wantin' to talk to me. When he get here, we'll call Mr. Deep Voice" – he held up the prepaid cell again – "and find out what's what."

"Sounds like a plan," Kane said as he continued massaging his sore leg.

"I don't thank you unnastand how this shit gonna go down," Mako shot back. "First order of business will be to find out what *you* know 'bout the cash, and we ain't gone just take yo word that some courier got jacked. We gone have to do some shit that might be considered a war crime in most countries, so I'm gonna have my boys come over and tie you–"

Mako's words were cut off and his body went completely tense for a moment as something like a firecracker sounded in the office. Looking at Kane, Mako saw his visitor holding a diminutive gun. It was then that he realized he'd been shot. But before he could say or do anything, Kane turned and shot both guards by the door.

"Son of a bitch…" Mako muttered, then closed his eyes and slumped over.

# SHE'S HIS DRUG, HE'S HER THUG 4

## Chapter 63

By any account, it would have been considered an idiotic plan. At the time, though, it had been all Kane and Mika could come up with.

Basically, after finding the telltale currency band, they had needed to have a conversation with Mako. However, knowing he was on the side of the muhfuckas who had tried to rob them, it wasn't the kind of sit-down that you walked into unarmed. That said, there was no way they were going to get close to that nigga without getting searched. Thankfully, a solution came to them in the aftermath of the shootout at the garage.

Basically, after searching Baskett's body, Kane had wiped down Jake's gun and returned it to the man, who was actually surprised to get it back. Kane had considered warning him against calling the police, but there was little chance of that. After all, Jake ran a chop shop; the last thing he wanted was cops coming around – especially with a dead body on the premises. Moreover, as loud as Remo's motorcycle exhaust had been, it was unlikely anyone nearby had heard or reported shots being fired.

Afterwards, Mika had insisted on having her weapon returned. This time Kane had complied, and it was when she swapped him the mouse gun for her own that the idea had come to him.

Long story short, he had hidden the mouse gun in his shoe when he went to see Mako. It had been uncomfortable as a muhfucka, but he had been limping anyway so it didn't alter his gait too much. More to the point, bearing in mind all the times he himself had been searched or when he'd seen pat downs in movies or on television, he'd never seen or heard of someone checking a person's shoes.

Surprisingly, it had worked. Following the shitty scan with the metal detector wand, Mako's bodyguards had completely missed the firearm in his footwear. Later, continually massaging his injured leg – specifically, when he had it crossed atop the opposite knee – had allowed him to access the mouse gun without arousing suspicion. And then he had gone on a shooting spree, plugging Mako and the two niggas at the door.

He hadn't really wanted to shoot Mako (at least not at that juncture), but once the nigga started talking about tying muhfuckas up and torturing them, Kane felt the conversation was over. However, he had barely finished putting down the two guards in the room before the door opened and the duo who had been posted outside entered.

It wasn't clear what they were expecting, but they didn't have their guns drawn. In fact, they strode into the room rather casually. That gave Kane the advantage.

"Don't do anything stupid," Kane told them, pointing the gun in their direction. "You don't wanna end up like these other fools."

It was at the point that the two seemed to understand that something was amiss. For one thing, their boss was slumped over; for another, two of their colleagues were down. Finally seeing the gun pointed in their direction, they raised their hands.

"On the floor," Kane ordered. "Spread-eagle."

The two men obeyed without question. Frankly speaking, Kane was a little surprised that they had come into the room so completely unprepared, as they had obviously heard the shots. Then it occurred to him that this probably wasn't the first time they had heard gunfire coming from Mako's office. However, on those other occasions, it had most likely been some other fool slumped over and bleeding from a bullet wound, not their boss. That would explain why they had sauntered in, plainly not expecting trouble.

In a perfect world, Kane probably would have taken the time to search the office. However, it was clear that Mako didn't have the missing money, and the longer he stayed there the more likely it was that something untoward would happen. Glancing around in frustration, he saw only one thing of potential value: the prepaid cell that Mako had shown him earlier.

It was lying on the desk, so Kane swiftly scooped it up and put it in his pocket. He then headed towards the door, warning the two laying spread-eagle on the floor to slowly count to twenty before coming out. As he left, he closed the door. However, he chose to back away – still facing the office with his gun pointed in that direction – just in case those last two guards decided to come after him.

Ergo, he was caught totally by surprise when the cold metal of a gun was pressed firmly to the back of his head.

# SHE'S HIS DRUG, HE'S HER THUG 4

## Chapter 64

Kane could have kicked himself. He had completely forgotten Mako's statement about Remo being on his way. That oversight had allowed the biker to catch him flatfooted.

"Well, well," intoned a voice from behind him that he assumed belonged to Remo. "Lookie what we got here."

Kane didn't say anything. He simply stood still as the mouse gun was taken out of his hand. At the same time, Fosse stepped from Kane's rear and walked to the office door. He cracked it open and peeked inside.

"Anything?" Remo asked as Fosse closed the door and turned back around. Fosse shook his head and made a slashing motion across his neck. (Apparently he assumed that everyone in the office was dead.)

"Too bad," Remo continued. "I guess that's one less person we gotta split the money with."

At that moment, rough hands spun Kane around so that he now was basically eye-to-eye with Remo.

"Now, you *are* gonna tell us where that money is, right?" Remo asked.

Kane still didn't say anything, prompting Fosse to suggest, "Seem like he that strong, silent type."

"Naw, he gone talk," Remo declared. "Befoe' it's all over, this nigger gone be beggin' to tell us everythang he know 'bout that money."

With that, they marched Kane out a nearby side door and out into the night.

\*\*\*\*\*\*\*\*\*\*\*\*\*\*\*\*\*\*\*\*\*\*\*\*\*\*\*\*\*\*\*\*\*\*\*\*\*\*\*

# SHE'S HIS DRUG, HE'S HER THUG 4

Mika had been bored shitless. It might have been because of the concussion, but in her opinion it was because Kane kept leaving her out of the action. Aside from the garage, his general admonition to her had been to wait in the minivan.

To a certain extent, she understood his position. She had taken a solid hit to the noggin when they were racing away from the farm, and there was a time earlier in the day when she could barely string together two thoughts. And even after she reached a point where her thoughts were coming together again, she had trouble articulating them. It wasn't until after that last nap – when she awoke to find Kane sleeping in the room with her – that she had felt "normal" again. But in all honesty, she'd had a couple of spotty moments since then (although tricking Kane into slipping her the dick had been one she could put in the "Win" column).

When they came up with the plan for how to approach Mako, she had wanted to go in as well. Kane, however, wasn't having it. Thus, she'd been left in the minivan (again!), parked a few blocks from the club entrance. Watching the front door of the place, she noticed that there wasn't a line like the first time they had shown up. Then again, it was still early by club standards – early enough that bitches were probably still getting in for free, and for a moment she reminiscence about a time when clubbing was a regular part of her life.

At that point, however, her thoughts were cut off by the sound of a brutishly loud motorcycle. Looking around, her suspicions were confirmed when she saw Remo riding in her direction, followed by Fosse in the off-roader.

## SHE'S HIS DRUG, HE'S HER THUG 4

Mika slumped down in her seat. She wasn't sure if Remo had gotten a good look at her at the chop shop, if he could see her through the van's tinted windows, or if he even knew what their ride looked like, but she wasn't taking any chances. Luckily, Remo and Fosse rolled by without even glancing in her direction. Then, watching them through the rear window, she saw them turn at the next corner.

At that point, she knew where they were headed. There was a parking garage down that way – she had seen it the night she'd come to the club with Kane. Based on where they were, it was a sure bet that Remo and Fosse were going to see Mako, and her guess was that Remo didn't want to park his bike on the street if he could help it.

Mika spent a moment thinking. Kane was a resourceful nigga and they had a plan, but she already didn't like his odds on Mako's turf, surrounded by a bunch of that nigga's flunkies. She was even less enthused about the notion of Remo and Fosse tagging in with respect to whatever was going on in there, especially when it felt like Kane had already been inside for a while.

Her first impulse had been to text Kane and let him know what was up; then she remembered that he had left his phone – pretty much everything, in fact – in the minivan. That reduced the options, but she really saw only one that was viable. Mind made up, she decided to wait for Remo and Fosse to show up and enter the club, then follow them inside.

However, when they didn't round the corner a minute or two later, she started to get the feeling that something was off. Fortunately, it only took her a second to figure it, and when she did she almost smacked herself upside the head.

In essence, she hadn't been to the nightclub yet that only had one entrance or exit. More to the point, Fosse and Remo were plugged in with Mako. That being the case, they didn't have to get in line and go in through the front like the rest of the masses. They could be let in through a back door, side entrance, or some shit like that. Now angry with herself, Mika swiftly got out of the minivan and headed towards the corner that led to the garage.

Upon reaching the corner and going down the street, she did indeed see an alley that ran behind the club, as well as a door that presumably served as some point of ingress and egress. She spent a moment debating on what to do. She could pound on the door and – assuming someone opened it – use her piece to force her way in. But she'd lose the element of surprise to some extent. On the flip side, she didn't relish the idea of simply hanging around outside waiting for a bouncer to maybe step out into the alley for a smoke or some shit like that.

In the end, the decision was taken from her when the door suddenly swung open. Hustling to the side of the alley before she could be seen, Mika stealthily peeked around the corner and saw Kane walking in her direction, followed by Remo and Fosse. His hands weren't in the air, but it was evident to Mika that her boyfriend was essentially a prisoner.

Noting that the pace of the three men seemed steady, Mika got the impression that they weren't going to be hanging around. Assuming they were leaving, they'd probably be heading to the parking garage. Without another thought, Mika went dashing in that direction.

# SHE'S HIS DRUG, HE'S HER THUG 4

As luck would have it, she made it to the garage without being seen by Kane or his captors. Going in through a pedestrian entrance, she found herself facing a ramp that rose up, with parking spots on either side. Sprinting up the ramp, she scanned the vehicles on either side, looking for the off-roader or Remo's bike.

Neither was on the first level of the garage, so she continued going up. As luck would have it, she found what she was looking for on the second level: Remo's bike, with the off-road vehicle parked right next to it.

There was a two-door hybrid parked next to the off-roader. With her gun in hand, Mika went to the far side of it and ducked down. Now it was just a waiting game.

It turned out, however, that she didn't have to wait long. She'd been hiding for no more than a minute or two when Kane came walking around the corner of the ramp, with Remo and Fosse behind him. Needless to say, they were headed in her direction.

"That's far enough," she heard Remo say when they got close.

Slyly glancing from her hiding spot, Mika saw the three men standing near the front of the off-roader. She couldn't see a weapon, but from the way Remo was holding his arm up behind Kane, it was a sure bet the man had a gun to her boyfriend's head.

"We got sommin' to tie this nigger up with?" Remo continued.

"There's some twine in the back," Fosse replied. "I'll get it."

With that, Fosse headed towards the side of the off-roader nearest Mika. Deciding that it was now or never, Mika took a deep breath and stepped out, with her gun raised and pointed at Fosse.

## SHE'S HIS DRUG, HE'S HER THUG 4

The movement naturally drew Fosse's attention, and when he saw Mika – or more specifically, her gun – he froze.

"Turn around," Mika ordered, making sure to keep Fosse between her and Remo.

Fosse complied, turning to face Remo and Kane, both of whom were now aware of Mika's presence. However, just as Mika had done with her captive, Remo had strategically positioned himself behind Kane. In short, any shots Mika fired at him would hit Kane first.

"So what now?" Remo called out smugly.

"Let 'im go, and you get yo friend back," Mika declared.

"No can do," Remo told her. "But I can tell that this Black buck mean sommin' to you, so I tell you what. You let Fosse there go, and I won't blow his nappy head off."

"Fuck you!" Kane suddenly roared.

"Holy shit," Remo muttered. "The monkey speaks."

"Take aim and shoot this piece of shit," Kane said to Mika. "Put both these muhfuckas in the dirt."

"I wouldn't try it," Remo warned. "You mo' likely to hit yo boyfriend here than me."

"Fuck what he sayin'," Kane remarked. "Just shoot."

"If you want to bury this nigger, you go right ahead and listen to 'im," Remo said.

"If he gets buried, you can fuckin' bet that you next," Mika retorted.

"Maybe, but I don't thank you seriously wanna see yo man in a pine box," Remo told her. "So if you lay yo gun down, I won't blow his brains out if fronta you."

"If you do, he won't be the only one with a closed-casket funeral," Mika stressed.

Remo snorted in derision. "Well, let's see how well you gone stick by that. I'm gone count to five, and if you ain't put that gun down by the time I finish, yo boyfriend skull gonna become a jigsaw puzzle, with pieces spread all over the fuckin' place."

Mika's only reply was to press her gun to the back of Fosse's head.

"One…" said Remo.

Mika still didn't move or say anything.

"Two…"

Mika looked at Kane, who gave a subtle shake of his head, clearly saying, *Don't do it*.

"Three…"

Mika's brow crinkled, as she suddenly found herself contemplating a life without Kane. The mere thought was unbearable.

"Four…"

Mika licked her lips nervously. She looked at Kane again, who had steeled himself for what he knew was coming.

Just as Remo opened his mouth to finish the count, Mika cried out, "Okay, okay!" At the same time she moved the gun away from Fosse's head, pointing it straight up. "You win, okay?"

Giving her a self-satisfied smile, Remo said, "See, that wasn't so hard." He then told Fosse, "Get her piece."

Fosse, plainly relieved to no longer have a gun pointed at him, turned towards Mika. Reaching out, he practically snatched the gun from her with one hand while giving her a hard push with the other. The shove sent Mika staggering backwards, causing her to bumb against the hybrid and then go sprawling on the ground.

"You muhfucka!" Kane screamed. "I'll kill you!"

Heedless of the gun on him, Kane went to charge at Fosse. However, he never got a chance as agonizing pain suddenly exploded at the back of his head and he dropped to the ground, unconscious.

# SHE'S HIS DRUG, HE'S HER THUG 4

## Chapter 65

Kane came to with the muhfuckin' granddaddy of all headaches. His head was throbbing like crazy. He attempted to rub his temples, but was shocked to discover that he couldn't move his arms. Looking around, he couldn't quite place where he was, but after a second, he realized that he was in the passenger seat of a car. Looking beside him, he saw that Mika was driving.

He heard a chuckle from the back seat of the car. "Welcome back, Sleeping Beauty."

Looking behind him, Kane saw a white guy whose name eluded him for a second, then he remembered it: Fosse. And just like that everything came back to him – all of the day's events, from the aborted buy at the farm to his escapades with Raven to Remo getting the drop on him at Mako's club (at which point they had taken the mouse gun and the prepaid cell Kane had gotten from Mako's desk).

As to the fucking migraine he was experiencing, it was pretty easy to figure out what had happened. When he was getting ready to charge Fosse, Remo had clubbed him from behind with his gun. They had then tied his ass up and tossed him into the passenger seat of the off-road vehicle before forcing Mika to drive. Knowing what he would see, Kane glanced behind and gave Fosse another once-over. As expected, he saw the man holding a gun on them.

The sound of a thundering exhaust drew his attention. Looking out the front windshield, he saw Remo on his motorcycle riding ahead of them. Taking everything together, it was clear that they were following the racist biker.

Kane was on the verge of asking where they were headed, then realized that several landmarks around them looked familiar. As a result, he suddenly had a very good idea of where they were headed, and didn't like it at all. In confirmation of this, he looked out the windshield and saw their destination up ahead: *The She-Devil's Bush*.

At that juncture Remo began to slow, as did Mika. She followed the biker into the lot of the bar and then parked, as dictated by Fosse.

"Get out," Fosse ordered as he exited the vehicle.

Mika obeyed, but Kane – with his hands tied – stayed seated. Fosse, then grabbed Mika roughly by the elbow and essentially dragged her to the passenger side of the car.

Shoving Mika towards the front fender, Fosse told her, "Stay there." He then opened the front passenger door and essentially yanked Kane out, letting him flop to the ground.

"Leave 'im alone," Mika hissed, running to Kane and dropping down beside him.

Fosse didn't try to stop her. Instead, he just chuckled at Mika and Kane on the ground as Remo approached.

"Get up," Remo commanded.

Unable to use his arms for leverage, Kane found rising difficult, but Mika helped him. At the same time, she slipped something into his bound hands. From the heft and shape of the item, Kane immediately knew what it was: Mika's switchblade, Pierce.

Kane fought to keep his expression passive, especially after Mika made eye contact and gave him a subtle wink. Apparently, after taking her gun and knocking Kane unconscious, Remo and Fosse had failed to search

Mika. It reflected a chauvinistic mindset that a lot of men had, and it was a characteristic that Mika and Kane had been able to exploit in the past. With any luck, it just might save their lives today.

"What's this place?" Mika asked.

"Home of the best motorcycle club on the planet," Remo replied. "The Canaries."

"So what we doin' here?" Mika inquired. "From what I hear, you ain't a Canary anymoe'."

"True," Remo admitted, "but I will be. See, that nigger you all in love with did some fucked up shit today. Came through here and shot the Club Prez, whacked the Sergeant-at-Arms, and got into it with the club's Enforcer. We'll fuck up a White dude for doin' any of that shit, but a *nigger*? He'd be better off gettin' castrated."

"So lemme guess," Mika mused. "Bringin' him here earns you enough Brownie points to get back in the club."

"Not by itself," Remo confessed. "But that and the money yo boyfriend's got should punch my ticket."

"Ha!" Mika laughed. "He ain't got the money, asshole. The courier who had it got hit."

There was silence for a moment as Fosse and Remo exchanged a look.

"Bullshit," Fosse chimed in.

"Naw, it's the truth," Mika insisted. "You thank we'd be out here ridin' herd on you shitheads from dawn to dusk if we had the cash? Hell, naw. So that mean one of you muthafuckas that planned this shit got the cash already, and everybody else is just chasin' they fuckin' tail."

"Well, forgive us if we don't take the word of some nigger-bitch on that," Remo spat out. "We still gone need to figure out what *he* knows." As he finished speaking, he tilted his head towards Kane.

Mika crossed her arms. "So whachu need *me* for?"

"You here to make sure this nigger gives up the goods," Remo answered. "See, considerin' the way he's put me through the wringer all day, I get the feelin' yo man's a tough character. Gettin' 'im to hand over the money probably won't be easy, no matter what we do to him. But if we start doin' shit to *you* – maybe hook a car battery to yo nipples, or do some Chinese water-torture shit – it's possible that might make this motherfucker crack."

Mika, looking stunned, didn't say anything. Meanwhile, Kane kept silent so as not to draw attention to himself – particularly the fact that he was trying to cut his bonds with Mika's switchblade.

"Anyway," Remo continued, "after we get the money, this coon gets to answer for his earlier transgressions. And at the end of the day, everybody's happy."

"I'm tired of all this fuckin' talk," Kane said. "When we gone get this show on the road?"

"Damn," muttered Remo. "Don't often see a motherfucker anxious for his own funeral."

"If that's what it take to stop hearin' you talk," Kane stated, "I'm down."

Remo pulled out his gun and pointed it at Kane's head, saying, "Believe me, I'd be happy to oblige. There's nuthin' I'd like more than blowin' yo head off right now. But the club wants you alive and whole for whatever atrocious shit they got planned. And since you in such a hurry, you'll be happy to know I called ahead while we was en route and let 'em know the second we pulled into the lot. So they know we here."

"Well, go tell 'em to get they ass out here," Kane said matter-of-factly. "I ain't got all night."

Remo and Fosse just stared at him. Kane's attitude had obviously taken them by surprise. However, before they could say or do anything, the door to the bar flew open and Bear came out.

His injured arm was in a sling, and he was scowling. In his other hand, he held a semi-automatic pistol. He was flanked by Trout and Luthor, who looked better than the last time Kane had seen them. Like Bear, the two of them seemed angry as well.

"Good to see you Bear," Remo said as the trio came close, halting about five feet away. "As promised, here's the nigger who disrespected the club."

"Thanks," muttered Bear. "We'll take it from here."

With that, Bear raised his gun. Kane, with nothing left to lose, suddenly brought his hands from behind his back. Holding Pierce in his right hand, he prepared to charge. But he never got the chance as Bear, at point blank range fired twice…at Remo and Fosse.

The two men immediately dropped, both shot in the head. Kane and Mika both simply stood there, trying to figure out what the fuck was going on.

Looking them both over, Bear unexpectedly asked, "You two alright?"

# SHE'S HIS DRUG, HE'S HER THUG 4

## Chapter 66

Mika and Kane stood off to the side while Bear talked to, of all people, Regis. Much to Kane's surprise, his muhfucking boss had come walking out of *The She-Devil's Bush* right after Bear shot Fosse and Remo. Apparently he had been there the entire time that Mika and Kane had been outside. And although they weren't exactly eavesdropping, they were close enough to hear what the two men were talking about.

"So," Bear was saying, "you'll explain to Bush that the shit that happened today wasn't the Canaries. We had nuthin' to do with it, but we took care of the problem."

"Just so you unnastand," Regis replied, "I don't talk to Bush. I'm not that high on the food chain. But I'll pass it along that the Canaries are in the clear."

"Fair enough," Bear stated with a nod. "Also, is yo organization gonna have a problem if we bury Remo as a Canary? I mean, he wasn't in the club at the end, but the way he died…"

"I get it," Regis said with a nod. "He died so the club could survive – that canary-in-the-coal-mine shit. So naw, that shouldn't be a problem."

"Thanks," Bear remarked sincerely, "Now…"

Kane sort of tuned out the conversation at that point, mostly because Mika turned to him with a question.

"So," she began, "exactly when did you slice through that cord tyin' yo hands?"

"While you was talkin' to Remo," Kane replied.

"Then why didn't you make a fuckin' move?"

"'Cause I literally brought a damn knife to a gunfight. I figured I could take one – catch a muhfucka off-guard – but two was risky. That's why I kept eggin'

Remo on, tellin' him to go get those muhfuckas from the bar."

"I see. You wanted him to leave so you could take Fosse."

"Him or Fosse, didn't matter. I just needed one of those muhfuckas to step away for a sec."

"Well, I'm glad to know you was ready to do *sommin'*, even if it turned out that you didn't have to."

Kane was about to make a smart-ass reply when he Regis unexpectedly called his name. Curious as to what he wanted, Kane sauntered towards him, followed by Mika.

"Kane," Regis began, "I believe you already acquainted with Bear."

"We've met," Kane said.

"Now, as you saw firsthand," Regis continued, "Bear and the Canaries came through for a brutha. I know y'all had a rough intro, but he willin' to let bygones be bygones if you are."

Kane gave Bear a steely look. "Really?"

"Absolutely," Bear declared with a nod. "Shit between us got off on the wrong foot, but far as I'm concerned, it's water under the bridge."

"And what about you settin' me and Raven up?" Kane demanded. "Tellin' that muhfucka Remo we was on our way to his place?"

"Wasn't me," Bear swore. "I ain't tell 'im shit about y'all."

"Then how the fuck he know we was comin'?" argued Kane. "It had to be you…you the only other person who was there."

"Naw, I wasn't," Bear insisted.

Kane felt himself getting angry. Maybe it was to impress Regis, but this asshole was flat-out lying about what had happened. Playing out the scene in his mind, Kane thought back to who was present when Bear told them where Remo was holed up: there was Kane himself, Raven, Bear... His thoughts trailed off as the memory suddenly crystallized in his brain.

"Shit," Kane uttered in disgust. "The bartender..."

"Yep," Bear said. "He heard everythang, and gave Remo a heads-up."

"That muhfucka..." Kane grumbled, balling his fist.

"Well," Bear droned, "if it's any consolation, that shithead ain't ever got to worry 'bout goin' back to the joint."

Kane considered what that meant, then said, "Glad to hear it."

"And this thang between us?" Bear asked.

Kane seemed to contemplate for a moment, then said, "Consider it squashed."

"Squashed it is," Bear said, grinning. He then extended a hand which Kane instinctively reached out and shook. (Later, he would berate himself for shaking hands with an avowed racist.)

"A'ight," Regis chimed in, "since we one big happy now, I thank me and my peeps gone take off."

"Understood," Bear told him. "We appreciate Bush bein' understandin' about this situation, and if there's anything the Canaries can ever do for you, just call."

"Yeah, we'll do that," Regis said dismissively. Turning to Kane and Mika, he said, "Y'all ready?"

Mika answered "Yeah," but Kane just stood there for a moment, frowning. Bear's statement about a call had triggered something in his brain. He struggled with it for a moment, and then the clouds in his mind parted.

# SHE'S HIS DRUG, HE'S HER THUG 4

Stepping quickly to Remo's body, Kane bent down and started searching his pockets.

Seeing this, Bear seemed to take offense and turned to Regis. "Hey, I thought you said we could—"

Bear stopped speaking as Regis, watching Kane, cut him off with a sharp wave of his hand.

"Nobody gone desecrate this muhfucka body," Regis assured Bear. "Just let my man finish what he doin'."

By that time, Kane had what he was after: the mouse gun and prepaid cell that Remo had taken from him at Mako's club.

"Okay, I'm ready," Kane announced.

# SHE'S HIS DRUG, HE'S HER THUG 4

## Chapter 67

They ended up leaving *The She-Devil's Bush* in a chauffeured limousine. Apparently that was the mode of travel that Regis preferred, and it had been parked at the rear of the bar. (There had been a concern that parking it out front might have made Remo skittish.)

Sitting in the back of the limo with Regis, Kane and Mika felt like it was the first time they'd been able to relax in forever. It was incredibly spacious on the inside, with two rows of seats facing each other. Regis was in the forward-facing seat while Kane and Mika sat on the rear-facing row.

"Make yo'self at home," Regis told them. "There's a minibar, snacks… Knock yo'self out."

"I'd rather get some questions answered," Kane said. "Like when the fuck did you get here?"

Regis chuckled. "I was pretty much en route soon as I heard shit had hit the fan at the farm this morning. The situation seemed like it needed a master's touch."

"Funny," Kane noted, "I didn't see the 'master' out there almost gettin' his ass shot off today."

"Any muhfucka can point a gun and pull the trigger," Regis replied. "That shit don't require any special skill. I'm talkin' about damage control and managin' the situation as a whole."

"You mean damage control like the Canaries was doin' back there?" Kane asked.

"Not exactly," Regis told him. "Those muhfuckas was fightin' for they very existence. Our shit wasn't that bad."

"How you get hooked up with them anyway?" Mika inquired.

A slight grin settled on Regis' face. "Those racist muhfuckas reached out – said there was some circumstances that might be misconstrued with respect to they connection to certain events, and they wanted to clear the air."

"I'm assumin' they told you that they wasn't involved in what happened at the farm and that Remo was actin' solo," Kane commented.

Regis nodded. "Pretty much. They asked what they needed to do to make it right, and I told 'em that if you got a mad dog 'round the house, you put that muhfucka down befoe' he hurt somebody."

"I'm guessin' they was cool with that," Mika said.

"They ain't have much choice," Regis clarified. "The alternative was havin' Bush obliterate they ass, so they agreed. But I told 'em there was two conditions."

Kane raised an eyebrow. "Which were?"

"Nuthin' too complicated," Regis stated. "One, I had to see the shit get done. I wasn't gone take they word for it. And two, I needed all my people safe and sound at the end of the day."

"So then what?" Mika queried. "They just reached out to Remo and tricked 'im by sayin' he could come home?"

"Well, I don't know firsthand, but here's how they relayed it to me," Regis remarked. "See, when Remo got tipped off about Kane comin' after him, he thought that was from the Canary leadership – that maybe the top brass wasn't pissed at him anymoe'. So he reached out askin' if there was a way back into the Canaries' good graces. They told him there was this particular nigga who did a bunch disrespectful shit to the club and they wanted his ass – bad. In fact, it was the same nigga who was comin' after *him*. So they told Remo if he brought that nigga to 'em, it would go a long way towards settling accounts. But they stressed that they wanted that nigga alive and whole, 'cause the club had sommin' special prepared for his ass."

"Wait… Remo been shootin' at my ass all day. Now I'm supposed to believe they told him to bring me in whole so *they* could fuck me up?"

"I don't know when he got the message, but it wasn't right off the bat. You thank that fuckin' biker gang got a direct line to me? You thank they just picked up a phone, called my personal number and said, 'Regis, my brutha, how we fix this?' Fuck naw. It took time for them muhfuckas to get me on the line. And after they made the ask, I let them racist bastards stew in they own juices for a while before I got back to 'em with our demands."

"So that asshole Remo may not have gotten the word to bring me in alive 'til an hour ago," Kane reasoned.

"Or even if he got the message earlier in the day, he might have misunderstood at first and just thought they wanted you dead," Regis added. "Muhfuckas screw up shit like that all the time. I had a pardnah, took this chick home from the club one time. Next day when he leavin' she still sleep in his bedroom, so he tell his flunkies, 'Take care of that bitch in the house.' He meant to get her home safe, but those muhfuckas thought he wanted one in her dome."

Intrigued, Mika asked, "So what happened?"

"Lucky for that bitch, he forgot sommin' and came back, just as those dumbasses was gettin' ready to cap that hoe," Regis said. "But back to our shit, Remo eventually got the message about brangin' you in shipshape, and the rest is history."

"He said sommin' 'bout the money, too," Kane offered. "He thought *I* had it and figured if they could make me give it up…that it would help get him back in with the gang. But I ain't got it." He reflected for a moment, then added, "*Yet*."

"So you wanna get back out on the street and keep lookin'," Regis concluded.

Kane nodded. "I still got time on the clock, and my dick's still on the choppin' block."

"Let's circle back to that," Regis suggested. "For now, tell me how shit's gone down, from yo point of view, since we conferred this mornin'."

Kane rubbed his chin for a second. "You want the long or short version?"

"Long is fine," Regis said, reaching for a glass and bottle from the minibar. "I got time…"

## Chapter 68

Kane gave Regis a blow-by-blow recap of almost everything that had happened since he was tasked with finding the missing cash. The only thing that he glossed over was Raven's offer (and open invitation) to fuck his brains out.

Although she was already privy to the bulk of what was said, Mika seemed engrossed. On his part, Regis listened intently, occasionally interrupting to ask a few pointed questions that Kane gave concise answers to. He did, however, ask for the prepaid cell that Kane had taken from Mako's office. Kane had handed it over without question; with the resources at his disposal, it was entirely possible that Regis could use the phone to figure out who the inside man was.

"A'ight, let's put a pin in this shit for now and resume this conversation later," Regis suggested at that juncture. "We here."

Confused, Mika looked around, saying, "Here *where*?" She had been so focused on Kane's summary of the day's events that she hadn't even noticed that the car had come to a halt.

Rather than answer her, Regis merely opened the limo door and got out. Mika and Kane followed suit, and found themselves in the expansive, circular drive of a picturesque mansion.

"What *is* this place?" inquired Mika.

"Short-term rental," Regis stated as they began walking towards the entrance. "Usually used for celebrity parties, A-List wedding receptions, rap videos and shit like that."

"How much it go for?" Kane asked.

# SHE'S HIS DRUG, HE'S HER THUG 4

"Ten thou a night," Regis stated without hesitation.

Mika blinked in shock. "And you payin' that?"

'Fuck naw," Regis shot back. "Bush organization own this muhfucka, so I'm gettin' it for free. I'm currently usin' it as a sorta corporate retreat."

At that moment, they stepped inside and Mika found it impossible to contain her reaction.

Eyes wide in awe, she looked around and blurted out, "Holy shit!"

They were currently in a magnificent foyer with regal white columns on either side. Ahead of them two luxurious, winding staircases rose up to the second floor. To their left was some type of alcove that was home to an elegant grand piano. To their right was a scopious solarium which, even at this time of night, appeared stunning. Further down, in the space between the staircases, they saw what appeared to be a lavish great room with several sitting areas and a two-sided fireplace. All in all, the place was amazing, and as impressive as Fix's place had been, their current environs made it seem modest.

"Come on," Regis said as he began walking through the palatial house. Mika and Kane followed him, with Mika looking around in open wonder at the splendor of the mansion, including a breathtaking, two-story library, a capacious dining hall, and more. Kane tried to appear impassive, but Mika could tell that he, too, was impressed.

Eventually, they reached a set of ornate, eight-foot double doors leading to a dazzling indoor pool, complete with Jacuzzi. The pool area had a Romanesque feel, with stately stone columns geometrically spaced throughout and exquisite tile flooring. Nearby was a living room area populated by high-end furniture. There was also a well-stocked bar, and all around the second floor was an eye-

# SHE'S HIS DRUG, HE'S HER THUG 4

catching balustrade that would allow anyone on that level to look down on someone swimming in the pool.

All in all, the indoor pool area was spectacular, and this time Kane was unable to conceal his admiration. Counting the farm and Fix's place, this was the third mansion he'd visited in the last twenty-four hours. He was starting to think that everybody in this damn town lived like a king except him and Mika.

His thoughts were cut off at that point as Regis suddenly called out, "I see you muhfuckas done already made yo'selves at home."

As he spoke, he began walking towards the living room area, and that's when can realized that there were actually people sitting over there – three men and a woman. They appeared to be casually drinking and hanging out, but they all rose as Regis approached, giving Kane and Mika a chance to look them all over.

Two of the men were average height: one was a brother maybe thirty years old who was bald and sported a soul patch; the other was a White guy in his late twenties with a nose ring, pierced eyebrow, and reddish hair braided into cornrows. Mika didn't think there many White guys who could pull off the cornrows look, but this one did it with casual ease.

The third man was a tall nigga, about six-three, who had his hir cut into a flattop fade that was just high enough to garner attention, but not tall enough to be considered a fashion statement. He also wore sunglasses, despite the fact that it was nighttime and he was inside.

Finally, there was the woman – a statuesque sister with a honey-colored complexion, big almond eyes and hair done in a curly afro style. In addition, she had the quintessential hourglass figure with a large bosom, slim waist and wide hips. Looking at ther, the word that immediately came to mind for Kane was "ravishing.'

The four all gave Regis some dap when he reached them. Following this, Regis said, "I guess I need to make some intros. This Mika and Kane." He gestured towards them as he spoke, then continued. "Y'all done prolly heard me mention them. They been kickin' ass out here for us – gettin' shit done in record time. Mika, Kane...these my lieutenants."

Regis gestured towards the nigga in the shades. "This Coaster. We call 'im that 'cause he always holdin' a drank."

This was followed by general laughter, as – true to his name – Coaster currently held a bottle of beer in one hand.

"Next is Coda," said Regis, introducing the woman.

"Befoe' you ask," Coda announced, "my name means 'end.' 'Cause if you fuck with me, it's the end for you."

Continuing, Regis went on to the White guy, saying, "This is Chet – affectionately known as 'White-Boy Chet'."

"Yeah," Chet intoned acerbically. "Keeps folks from gettin' me confused with all the bruthas in the crew named 'Chet'."

More laughter followed this, after which Regis introduced the bald man, stating, "And this here is Baller."

As they were introduced, Mika and Kane had shaken hands with each of the four in turn. From Mika's perspective, they were all cool, although she felt that Coda seemed to make eyes at Kane, and held on just a little too long when to the two shook hands. From Kane's point of view, the only thing that made him bristle slightly was when Coaster – before shaking hands with Mika – tilted his sunglasses down as if to get a better look at her, then graced her with a dazzling smile.

"Now, as I was saying," Regis continued after the intros, "these foe' my lieutenants. I can't do everythang myself, so they help keep the ship on an even keel. Every now and then, though, I like to brang everybody together – kind of a corporate retreat – so we can discuss problems, resolve issues, etcetera. And right now, we got major issues."

"A few months back," he continued, "we started gettin' ripped off. Not small-time shit either. It was when we was doin' big deals, with lots of cash at stake. I'm talkin' seven figures."

By now everyone was fairly somber. The conversation had quickly turned serious, and it was evident that Regis was driving towards a point of some kind.

"Now everybody know how I thank when it come to shit like this," Regis went on. "Gettin' hit once could be coincidence. Twice make a muhfucka suspicious. Three times, and it's a fuckin' pattern – especially when it's never penny ante shit that we lose…it's always big cash. That tell me that somebody on the inside is doin' this shit. Somebody in this fuckin' room with us right now."

At that point, everyone began glancing around somewhat warily. Even Mika and Kane (who weren't even part of the organization during the relevant time frame) began to feel leery.

"Come on, Regis," Chet finally chimed in. "You know everybody in this bitch loyal to you." Then, looking at Mika and Kane, he gestured towards himself and his fellow lieutenants, adding, "The four of us, anyway."

"Yeah," agreed Baller. "We done all proved ourselves a million times."

"True, but that don't mean a muhfucka can't get ambitious," Regis retorted. "That a nigga ain't thankin' how nice it would be to move up the ladder, and how much easier it'll be if he make me look like an incompetent fuck-up to the people upstairs."

"Nobody here would do that," Coda stressed. "We only got this far 'cause of *you*."

"And some might interpret that to mean I'm now in the way," Regis shot back, a comment to which no one dared respond. "Anyway, I figured the best way to catch the fool doin' this was to give 'em enough rope to hang theyself. So I started sharin' a bunch of false info and watched to see who'd act on it."

"Did you figure it out?" Coaster inquired.

Regis shook his head. "Naw. Just couldn't get enough solid info."

At that, everyone seemed to relax for a moment, and a tension that had quietly built up as Regis spoke suddenly seemed to evaporate.

"Or rather, I didn't get enough info until *today*," Regis clarified, and almost immediately the air became strained again. "See, Kane and Mika went to make a buy for us this morning. Knowing it was the type of payday our inside man would go for, I put out some bogus info about it. Basically, I baited some traps for his – or *her* – ass." He glanced at Coda as he finished his sentence.

There was silence as everyone waited for Regis to continue speaking, but he stayed quiet until Coda prompted him by saying, "And...?"

"And I got lucky," Regis explained. "See, our inside man was smart. He contacted a local thug – anonymously

— and got that muhfucka to recruit an out-of-town crew to try to pull off this lick today. All of that put some layers between him and the niggas doin' the grunt work, and I'm guessin' he did that every time we got hit."

"Don't sound smart to me," Chet remarked. "The muhfuckas that are boots on the ground might decide they took all the risk and try to make off with the loot."

"Not if they thank that's the tip of the iceberg," Baller offered. "If they make off with a mill on the first job, the inside man could just say, 'Good work. I got a lick worth *three* million we can pull off next month. Soon as I get my cut, I'll send the deets.' Then, once the inside dude, or girl" – he looked at Coda – "gets they share, the grunts never hear from 'im again."

There was general agreement with this from the other lieutenants.

"There's also other ways a smart nigga could make sho' they get they cut," Regis added. "But that don't matter at the moment. The main thing right now is that we found out who the local muhfucka was that the inside man recruited – a hustler called Mako. Moe' importantly, he had a cell he used to call the inside man. And I got the muhfucka right here…"

As he trailed off, Regis held up the prepaid cell Kane had given him. As he did so, he looked around at all his lieutenants, all of whom looked sober and stonefaced.

"Now," Regis continued. "I can just dial the number on this bitch and see who cell rang, but I'm gone be magnanimous. Whoever it is, just step up now, confess what you did, and I'll be as charitable as possible in terms of punishment."

There was no response to this. The four lieutenants just continued looking anxious and on edge.

"A'ight," Regis said after about thirty seconds. "We gone do this shit the hard way."

With that, he began tapping the screen of the cell phone.

"Shit," Regis muttered after a few seconds. "Fucked it up – man, I hate technology. Now I gotta go back…find the damn phone app…"

"Boss, if you need some help," Coda offered, "I can–"

"I got this shit," Regis interjected, cutting her off. "Okay, here we go."

As he finished speaking, he seemed to tap the screen a final time. There was a tense silence for a moment as the prepaid cell rang – and then a responsive ring sounded. It came from Baller, who looked stunned.

That said, Baller got over his shock in record time. Almost faster than seemed possible, he reached towards his hip and drew a gun from a small holster there. At the same time, he stepped deftly away from the living room area so as to be out of anyone's reach.

"Nobody fuckin' move," he muttered, keeping the gun aimed in the general direction of everyone else. As ordered, almost everyone froze. (The only exception was Kane, who stealthily tried to place himself protectively in front of Mika.) There was dead silence, except for the phone ringing.

"How the fuck you call me?" Baller demanded, looking at Regis. "That damn phone was only s'posed to call another burner, not my personal phone."

"So it *was* you," said Chet. "You the inside man."

"Damn straight," Baller replied, "and I'm 'bout to be the *only* man. The only one left standin', that is."

## SHE'S HIS DRUG, HE'S HER THUG 4

"So you gone gun us all down," Regis surmised as he turned the phone off, "then tell some bullshit story 'bout how it happened – like maybe some rival organization gunned us all down, but you came through without a scratch."

"Sound good to me," Baller stated. "And I could always dress it up so that I get winged."

"That shit won't fly," Regis said. "Nigga, did you forget? We laugh at those muhfuckas who get arrested for shit like this on TV – everybody else in the house got shot in the back of the head execution-style, but they get nothing but a flesh-wound. Nobody ever believe that crap, and the rest of Bush people definitely won't."

"Well, I ain't gotta stay with Bush," Baller declared. "I got enough money now to buy my own fuckin' island. I'll cap you muhfuckas and then disappear forever."

"Ain't nowhere you can hide from Bush," Regis insisted. "And this kinda shit – this kinda *betrayal* – is the type of thang that lead him to make an example out a muhfucka."

"Betrayal?!" Baller belted out incredulously. "Betrayal? Nigga, you don't know shit 'bout betrayal *or* loyalty, 'cause if you did–"

Baller's words were cut off as a nearby gun boomed. His head suddenly jerked to the side and his body went sailing through the air, landing on the tile maybe five feet away. His eyes were still open but he was obviously dead, having been shot in the head. Kane and Mika turned to where the shot had come from and saw Coda calmly putting a gun into a side holster of her own.

Stepping to Regis, she asked, "You okay, Boss?"

"I'm fine," he replied. "You took yo fuckin' time."

"I had to wait 'til he was distracted," Coda told him. "You know how Baller is... *was*. He'd get so wrapped up in an argument that he'd be blind to anything else. Remember, his momma fell and broke her hip in the kitchen one time? That nigga was ten feet away in the livin' room and didn't even notice 'cause he was on the phone arguin' with some muhfucka 'bout who the best player in the NBA."

"I remember," Regis said. "Wasn't that you, Chet?"

Chet nodded. "Yeah. He finally noticed when I started askin' him who the fuck that was screamin' in the background."

Regis and the others chuckled at this. It seemed a lil' callous to both Mika and Kane, but they both stayed silent.

"Too bad," Regis muttered a few seconds later, looking at Baller's body. "What a fuckin' waste of potential." He let out a deep sigh then added, "A'ight, somebody get this fuckin' mess cleaned up."

"We on it," Coaster assured him.

Regis simply nodded, then turned to Kane and Mika. "You two, come with me."

# SHE'S HIS DRUG, HE'S HER THUG 4

## Chapter 69

Kane and Mika had a million things they wanted to ask, but Regis told them to hold their questions for a minute. They acquiesced, staying quiet as Regis once again led them through the mansion; he ultimately ended up taking them to a room designed as an expansive home office. He instructed them to take a seat in the visitors' chairs on one side of an executive desk while he went to a nearby wetbar. A minute later, he was back with drinks in a trio of tumblers for the three of them.

After setting two of the glasses, respectively, in front of Mika and Kane, Regis took a seat opposite them, then took a long sip from his own drink.

"Ah," he muttered in relaxation. "That's better. It's been a long fuckin' day." He then looked at Kane. "You obviously chompin' at the bit to say sommin' and we finally got time, so go ahead."

"Yeah, I got some shit on my mind," Kane told him. "For starters, what the fuck was that back there?" He hooked a thumb over his shoulder as he spoke, aiming it towards the pool area.

"That was exactly what it looked like," Regis informed him. "Me rootin' out a muhfucka who been operatin' against us from the inside."

"Yeah, but you just fucked me without the grease," Kane shot back. "With Remo and Mako dead, he was the last muhfucka we could ask about the money."

"Money?" Regis repeated, frowning.

"Yeah – the money, nigga," Kane grumbled. "The cash that got stole. My ass is still on the line regardin' that shit, and you just literally killed my last lead."

"Well, to be exact, *I* didn't kill that muhfucka," Regis insisted. "That was Coda. But in all honesty, that muhfucka put a noose 'round his own neck the second he figured he could bite the hand that fed 'im."

"I can appreciate yo moral stance," Kane retorted. "But it don't do shit for me if muhfuckas workin' for Bush still thank I might have they money."

Regis took another drink from his glass. "I wouldn't worry about the money."

"Easy for you to say," Kane told him. "You not the one they gone…"

He trailed off as he noticed a sly look on Regis' face. Mika noticed it, too, and actually figured out what it meant a split second before Kane.

"You muthafucka," she muttered. "The money was never missin'. You had it this whole fuckin' time."

"Guilty as charged," Regis stated.

Kane just stared at him for a minute, then simply "Why?"

Regis leaned back, reflecting for a moment. "I pretty much knew before you even went out to the farm that Baller was behind all this shit."

"You knew, and you still sent us into a trap?" Mika demanded.

"I didn't thank he'd do anythang," Regis insisted. "I had dropped enough hints lettin' the nigga know that I was on to him that I figured he'd cool his jets – not do anythang else until he thought he was off my suspect list."

"Obviously, you misjudged that nigga," Kane noted.

"Agreed," Regis said. "But after the shit went down I saw a way to put pressure on that muhfucka: say that the cash got ripped off, then hope he and the crew he workin' with turn on each other. In essence, have all them assholes thankin' one of the others got the money, and ultimately they'll all be at each other throat."

"So why brang me into that shit?" Kane inquired. "You didn't need to lie to *me* to have those muhfuckas tryin' to shank each other."

"Yeah," Regis concurred with a nod, "but how the fuck it look if some crew hit us for over a mill and I don't send nobody after 'em?"

"Well, you shudda come up with sommin' else, cause yo shit plan didn't work out," Kane informed him. "Mako and Remo both thought *I* still had the cash. That mean Baller never told 'em 'bout yo bogus theft, so he prolly knew you was lyin' 'bout the money bein' stole."

"That's possible," Regis admitted. "Or else he figured one of those muhfuckas had it, but didn't wanna accuse anybody because that would make 'em put they guard up. So the better plan would be to just stay quiet and act all buddy-buddy for now – let whoever did it thank they got over…then snatch they ass and torture 'em later to find out what they know."

Mika and Kane shared a glance. Regis' logic actually made sense to an extent.

"You still didn't need to lie," Mika chimed in. "You cudda just told us to go find these assholes."

"Right," Kane agreed. "I mean, we do all the other shit you ask."

"That you do," Regis said. "But I needed you motivated to keep the pressure on the muhfuckas who did this."

"So you turn me into a fuckin' stalkin' horse?" Kane spat out.

Regis gave him a hard stare. "How much risk would you have taken if you didn't thank yo dick was in the wringer? How hard would you have gone after these muhfuckas? How much time and effort would you two have put into this shit?"

"The max – same as always," Mika shot back. "We don't fuckin' half-step on the job, and if you thank that's us – that we some shiftless dumbasses you gotta manipulate and pull strings on like some fuckin' puppetmaster – then you got the wrong niggas on the payroll."

Regis seemed to consider that for a moment, then nodded. "A'ight, you made ya point. Maybe I misjudged you, but I ain't apologizin' for that shit. I'm paid to make those kinda calls, and if you ever get to my position, you'll see that manipulatin' muhfuckas is a mandatory skill set."

"Whatever," Mika uttered dismissively.

Kane took a drink from his tumbler, then asked, "Can we at least assume you won't *deliberately* send us into the lion's den?"

"Can't promise that," Regis confessed. "But I can commit to lettin' you *know* when it's a lion's den, and send you in armed."

Kane looked at Mika, who shrugged, saying, "Better than nuthin', I s'pose."

Hearing that, Regis smiled. "So I guess that mean you still on the payroll."

"For now," Mika stressed. "Although we should be askin' for a raise if we gotta watch out for people like Baller on our own team."

"Speakin' of Baller," Kane said, "I gotta say I'm surprised that nigga put his personal number on that burner he gave to Mako."

"Oh, he didn't," Regis said. "I just used it to *dial* his personal number, which I know by heart."

"That's right," Mika recalled. "He was sayin' some shit 'bout how that prepaid wasn't s'posed to be able to ring him on his personal cell."

Kane gave Regis an appraising stare. "You really are a devious muhfucka."

"Of course," Regis said. "That's why I'm sitting on this side of the desk." He took another drink from his glass. "Now, switchin' gears, how y'all like the house?"

As he finished speaking, he spread his arms in an expansive gesture.

"What, this place?" asked Mika. "It's off the fuckin' hook."

"For ten large a night, it should be,' Kane added.

"Great," Regis said, opening up a drawer on the desk. "'Cause you gettin' it."

As he finished his statement, he tossed a keyring to Kane, who deftly caught it. On it were what appeared to be a number of house keys, as well as a little tag with an address.

"What a minute," Kane stated, frowning. "You givin' us this place?"

"Nope," Regis replied. "But you get to use it for a week. Well, actually, not *this* place. The architect who designed it also built a crib that's almost a twin to it in another ritzy part of town. You get to use *that* one for a week. I'm sure you'll like it better since it doesn't presently contain a corpse."

"That's a definite plus," Mika noted. "I'm almost scared to ask, but why?"

"It's a present for the job you did today," Regis stated. "Apparently Castor put in a call to Bush, told 'im how you saved his ass."

Kane's eyebrows went up in surprise. "Hold the fuck up. Castor has a direct line to Bush?"

"Yep," Regis confirmed. "So now you one of the few muhfuckas in the company at this level that Bush know by name. And just so you know, that's a fuckin' big deal. It's like a corporate CEO knowin' the name of a textile worker in one of they sweatshops overseas."

Kane still found himself somewhat stunned by what he'd heard. "Why the fuck does Castor have direct contact info for someone like Bush? I mean, I like Castor, but that's kinda along the lines of an ant bein' able to call up the President."

Regis chuckled. "Believe it or not, he used to be Employee Number Two 'round this bitch…Bush's second-in-command"

"Who? Castor?" Mika blurted out, clearly as surprised as Kane.

"Yeah," Regis affirmed. "Bush love that muhfucka like a brutha, so you picked the right person to stick yo neck out for."

"Well, it's not like we knew any of that," Kane said. "I just don't like leavin' my peeps behind when shit hits the fan."

"Apparently it's the right attitude," Regis told him, "because it got you a one-week vacation in a mansion, and…" He trailed off as he reached into the drawer again, this time pulling out a large envelope that he slid across the desk. "…it's all-expenses-paid."

Kane opened the envelope, holding it so that both he and Mika could see inside.

"Damn!" Mika blurted out upon seeing the contents. The envelop was full of cash — at least a hundred large.

Kane let out a sharp breath as an odd expression settled on his face.

"What?" asked Regis in surprise. "Not enough?"

"Don't get me wrong, we appreciate the cash," Kane clarified. "But I was just thinkin' that, with all the people I need to settle up with, this cash is practically gone already. I mean, there's Fix, Buggy, that vet Annabelle..."

"I see what you mean," Regis commented as Kane trailed off. "Get me a list and we'll take care of 'em."

"Seriously?" Mika asked.

"Absolutlely," Regis answered. "All that shit was done on the clock — for the organization and not you personally. And gettin' hurt counts as an on-the-job injury. Sound good?"

"Sounds *great*," Mika told him.

"There is one other thang," Kane said. "That chop shop where we had a shootout with Remo's crew — I didn't look the place over afterwards, but I'm pretty sure it took a lotta slugs. The guy runnin' the place said it's owned by some Russian mafia type named Romanov who'll probably be pissed about what happened."

"I know who you talkin' 'bout," Regis remarked. "And for the record, that muhfucka ain't Russian. He from Yugoslavia."

Mika frowned in confusion. "Hugo-what?"

"Yugoslavia," Kane repeated. "It's a country that don't exist anymoe'. It broke up into, like, a half-dozen other countries years ago."

"Right," Regis affirmed. "And that's where this Romanov suckah hail from. But nobody afraid of a nigga who say he with the Yugo mob — sound like some shitheads who own a bunch of clown cars. So this muhfucka Romanov say he with the Russian mob instead."

"I guess that make sense," Mika offered.

"Anyway," Regis went on, "we'll smooth shit over with that muhfucka. Anythang else?"

Kane shook his head. "Naw, except yo minivan still down by the club."

"I'll get somebody to pick it up," Regis assured him. "And if that's it, y'all can step."

"Works for us," Kane said as he and Mika came to their feet. "But I guess we need a ride."

"Oh, didn't I mention?" Regis asked. "The limo we came in — it's yours for the week."

Kane gave him a surprised look. "You for real?"

Regis nodded. "Like I said, it's all expenses paid. So I don't wanna see or hear from you muhfuckas for a week. Now get the fuck out."

Now grinning broadly, Mika and Kane swiftly headed for the door.

"One more thang," Regis added before they departed. "In exactly one week, you muhfuckas better be ready to put in some serious fuckin' work."

Mika laughed. "Ain't we always?"

With that, she grabbed Kane's hand and pulled him from the room.

# SHE'S HIS DRUG, HE'S HER THUG 4

## Chapter 70

"This is nice," Mika remarked.

"Yeah," Kane agreed. "This shit is off the chain."

They were currently in the back of the limo Regis was letting them use, having just pulled away from the mansion. Deciding to take full advantage, Mika was munching on some snacks while Kane mixed himself a drink.

"Say whachu want 'bout that muhfucka Regis," Kane continued, "but that nigga know how to live."

"Maybe," Mika suggested, "but I doubt he livin' life to the fullest."

"Meanin' what?"

"As many times as he done rode in a limo, he probably ain't never fucked a fine-ass bitch in here."

"I doubt that a nigga with Regis' influence has any trouble gettin' pussy."

"I ain't talkin' 'bout just fuckin' some chick. I'm talkin' slippin' her the dick in *here* – in this car. Regis seem like the type of muhfucka who'd say 'No' to that…bitch about it bein' too uncomfortable to do it on these seats, in this space and so on."

Kane chuckled. "I wouldn't know."

"But you'd do it, right?" Mika asked.

"Huh?" Kane asked, not sure he understood her question.

"You wouldn't have any problem fuckin' some bitch's brains out back here, would you?" Mika asked. Then stroking his thigh, she added, "Can't you see yo'self just railin' some bitch back here, tearing that pussy up – goin' balls-deep with every stroke – while she screamin' yo name?"

Kane blinked, suddenly feeling his dick starting to throb. "Whachu thank you doin'?"

"Nuthin'," Mika said with a grin. "We just talkin'."

"We *not* just talkin'," Kane insisted. "You tryin' to get me all worked so I'll fuck you. But you know we ain't supposed to be doin' that shit when you got a concussion."

Mika laughed. "Nigga, you ain't been able to go a day without boning me since we hooked up – even when we was practically livin' out a car. Are you seriously tellin' me you gone be able to last a week without stickin' dick to me when we stayin' in a fuckin mansion, with king-sized beds in every room?"

"That's exactly what I'm tellin' you, 'cause when you fuckin' permanently brain-damaged and in some assisted-livin' facility, constantly droolin' on yo'self, you gone be lookin' for somebody to blame."

"Muthafucka, if I ain't got brain-damage at this point from bangin' my skull on the headboard a zillion times, that shit ain't liable to happen."

"Still, the answer's no," Kane declared.

He tried to sound firm. When they had gone at it in the back of the van, he was so into it that he told himself he'd fuck Mika whenever she wanted it, regardless of her concussion status. Now though, with a clear head (and a dry dick), common sense seemed to prevail. As much as he wanted to give in, sex would only delay her recovery. Ergo, coitus was off the table for now, and he hoped she'd agree.

"Fine then," Mika pouted. "How about a blowjob instead?"

Kane laughed. "Fool me once, shame on you. Fool me twice, shame on *me*."

Mika found herself chuckling with him at the old adage.

"A'ight, I admit I didn't play fair last time," she said, "but I wanna do *sommin'*. Come on, babe. Do you really wanna say that we had a mansion and a limo for a week, and didn't do jack, sexually?"

"It's not safe for you," Kane insisted. "And considerin' what happened last time, I can't rely on you to exercise good judgment."

Mika threw up her hands in exasperation. "Okay, you win. No sex and no blowjob."

"Great."

"So how about a *hand*job?"

Kane burst out laughing.

"Come on," Mika continued. "You know you gone need some kinda release, and that's the last item on the menu." Suddenly, she leaned forward and began stroking his dick through his pants. "You know you want to. Just one lil' handjob."

Kane had been prepared to say "No," but her hand unexpectedly on his dick caught him by surprise...and pretty much shredded his inhibitions.

"Okay, a handjob," Kane said after a few seconds. "But that's it. You keep yo clothes on, and keep yo mouth and any other orifice away from my dick."

"Just shut up and pull yo pants down," Mika ordered. Then she smiled to herself and mentally added, *Dumbass...*

## THE END

## SHE'S HIS DRUG, HE'S HER THUG 4

Thank you for purchasing this book! If you enjoyed it, please feel free to leave a review on the site from which it was purchased.

Also, if you would like to be notified when I release new books, please subscribe to my mailing list via the following link: http://eepurl.com/gShzML

Finally, for those who may be interested, I have included my blog and social media info:

Blog: https://nirvanablaque.blogspot.com/

Facebook: https://www.facebook.com/nirvana.black.3597

Twitter: https://twitter.com/BlaqueNirvana